A SECRET LIFE

LORD HAWKESBURY'S PLAYERS, BOOK 1

C.J. ARCHER

WWW.CJARCHER.COM

Visit C.J. at www.cjarcher.com

Previously published as HER SECRET DESIRE by Amazon Publishing.

CHAPTER 1

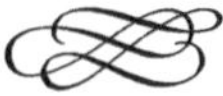

London: Autumn 1589

Min had become accustomed to rejection. She even expected it. After all, she'd been rejected by every theatre company manager in London, sometimes more than once. Every time her play was rejected it felt like a little piece of her heart was stripped off and cast to the City's rats.

Now she stood face to face with the man capable of cutting it out completely. It was enough to make her stomach heave.

"Not you again." Roger Style stopped mid-stride and thrust both hands on hips exaggerated by his fashionably short trunk-hose. He glanced up and down the street and must have realized he had nowhere else to go except past Min. Disgruntled theatre-goers, leaving the White Swan Inn after suffering through his latest play, surged down the narrow thoroughfare, buffeting him like an island in the middle of a rapidly flowing stream. The irony was, they wouldn't have been aware that he was the man responsible for the farce they'd paid good money to see.

However, the crowd wasn't so large that the buffeting would last long. Min had to take her chance—her one final grasp at her dream—while Style could not escape.

Drawing in a solid dose of courage along with a deep breath, she planted her booted feet on the muddy ground and held up her manuscript. The pages flapped in the chilly afternoon breeze. "Mr. Style, I'm simply asking that you read it. Just one little, quick read—."

"No." Style took a step closer. He was short, only a little taller than Min herself, but he had presence borne from years of acting in leading roles. It was an advantage he knew how to use.

Min refused to be intimidated. Again. She'd backed down from Style once already. She'd been very close to throwing her manuscript in the fireplace afterwards but sense had thankfully returned in time to save it from oblivion. She'd decided to have one last attempt with Style, the only manager desperate enough to look at a play written by a woman. Or so she hoped. She felt sure if he just read it, he would fall in love with it. Folly? Perhaps. Vanity? Certainly. Blind faith? Most definitely.

But she wouldn't give up. Not until she was sure he was rejecting it for the *right* reasons. It didn't look promising.

"Women don't write plays," Style said. He linked his hands behind his back, squared his shoulders and thrust out his chin. Or he would have if he had one. "In fact, due to the smallness of their brains, they *cannot* write plays. Alas, it is not of my doing, but God's." He indeed seemed quite apologetic on the Lord's behalf. "It is His will that the gentler sex be given the gifts of beauty and..." He waved his gloved hands as if conjuring a word out of the air. He looked like the wise old wizard he'd played on stage the month before in a rather forgettable play. "...other things. I would be doing you an injustice, my dear, to read the play you thrust beneath my nose. It would simply encourage you to write more. In that endeavor, your poor brain would not be able to cope with so much activity and, in short, it might expire. Nay! It *would* expire. I cannot have that on my conscience." He smiled down at her the way a master smiles down at his favorite puppy after it has pissed on the rushes—with strained patience as he knows it's not the puppy's fault.

Min almost bit her tongue off to refrain from saying something that would completely destroy her last chance. She might be desperate but she liked to think she wasn't a complete fool.

"Now, if you'll be so good as to step aside." He lifted thick, woolly brows, expectant.

Min gave him her best smile. The one she used on her father after telling him she'd failed to finish copying his notes because she'd been writing her play instead. The one that always worked. Almost always.

"Please, Mr. Style, I shall be indebted to you. I'm not asking for money." She put her right arm behind her back to hide the threadbare patch on the cloak sleeve. "Not much anyway. I simply want—."

"No." He sighed and rolled his eyes. "Would you like me to explain it to you again?" He tossed his head and nearly poked the eye out of a passerby with the long white plume decorating his hat. "Women cannot possibly write the sort of plays my company performs. The nuances, the rhythms, are simply too intricate for the poor female mind to comprehend."

"Many women attend your plays, Sir, and enjoy them." *Used to enjoy them,* she might have added. After the most recent outbreak of the plague, Lord Hawkesbury's Men—Style's company—could no longer be relied upon to entertain. With their chief playwright succumbing to the vile disease that had emptied the City and ravaged those who'd remained behind, the new plays had been awful. Not a single one had lasted more than two performances. Most not even that many.

As a consequence, audiences had dwindled. The one that turned out for this afternoon's performance had already turned into a trickle leaving the inn. That alone gave Min hope. A theatre company with a diminishing audience equated to a desperate manager. And desperate people took risks.

Style lifted a hand and caressed the air. "Watching them is one thing," he said, "writing them entirely another."

What remained of Min's heart sank into her stomach. It was hopeless. He wouldn't look at her play if his life depended upon it, or his livelihood as it were. She wasn't surprised. He wasn't the only manager who'd turned her down. He was simply the last. The very last.

The crowd had dispersed entirely, the gray clouds encouraging them to find shelter before the rain broke and made the roads slippery and their ruffs droop. Style moved to step around her.

That's when Min saw Him. Her Savior.

He leaned against the wall of a haberdasher's shop, arms and ankles crossed lazily. He was tall with dark hair and skin that spoke of warmer climes or an intriguing parentage. Unlike the gentlemanly fops she was familiar with, he wore simple black with no outrageously large buttons or elaborate embroidery and not a hint of jewelry, not even an earring. Even his ruff was small. She couldn't determine the material of his doublet and hose, but they fit him well. Not a sag in sight. A talented tailor had made them precisely for this man's body.

And what a body. Wide shoulders and a fine leg. Even from where she stood on the other side of Gracechurch Street she could see his calf was muscled and shapely.

All of these things made him stand out from the people around him, but it was his eyes that sent a shimmer of heat up her spine. Even at a distance she could see they were bright blue, the color of a summer sky. Amidst all that darkness, they were an oasis—vivid and glorious.

And they were staring straight at her.

"Wait!" She caught Style's arm, jerking him to a halt.

"My girl," he said with exaggerated effort, "I am *very* busy." He glanced back at the inn. Looking for assistance from his players? It was unlikely they would come to his aid—they were probably still downing their professional sorrows in the taproom. "Please remove yourself from my presence or I shall have to—."

"There's been a misunderstanding. I didn't write this play."

"Very well." He pried one of her fingers off his arm, using only his thumb and forefinger as if he might catch something from her.

"No, listen." As soon as he let go of her finger, she clamped it down on his arm again. "What I mean to say is, a *woman* didn't write this play, a man did."

Style frowned. "Then why didn't you tell me so before?"

She shrugged. She didn't have an answer for that. Not yet.

"Well, if you didn't," he said, "who did?"

"Him." The man's eyes had bewitched her. It was the only explanation as to why she was doing something so impulsive and foolish. That and an over-active imagination, as her father called it.

"Him?" Style's eyes narrowed as he studied the man.

The figure in question shifted, a barely noticeable stiffening of his back and shoulders. Min noticed it, however. She felt strangely in tune with him—like the fiddler off stage and dancer on it, they were separate and yet together. That must be how it is when one met one's Savior.

"Then why didn't he approach me himself instead of sending you?" Style cocked his head to the side without taking his gaze off the stranger.

"He's, er, shy." Min cringed. She might have an over-active imagination but it wasn't a particularly quick one.

"He doesn't look shy. He looks...interesting."

He most certainly did. Min had never seen a man quite like him. He exuded a self-contained power, and despite his lazy stance, she could see he was alert to his surroundings—a cat lazing in the sun but with a hungry eye on the mouse.

Or in this case, Min.

"Well, he is shy," she said. "Very."

"Let's meet him, shall we?"

"No!" She leaped in front of Style.

He peered over her head and frowned. "Oh. He's gone."

Thank you Lord. Min breathed out and managed a smile. "As I said. Shy."

"He shouldn't be. Men who look like that don't need to be shy. I wonder if he's ever thought of acting. He'd make quite a striking figure on stage."

"I'll ask him next time I see him." She held out her manuscript. "Will you read his play?"

Style took it and Min felt her heart rebuild itself in that instant. She didn't squeal in delight, but it was an effort not to.

"I'll read it tonight," he said.

"Wonderful. I'll meet you back here tomorrow, same time. You won't be disappointed, Sir."

Style cast his eye over the front page. "Bring the playwright."

"The...er, yes, of course. He'll be here." Her face heated at the lie.

"Good day, Mistress... What was your name?"

"Peabody. Minerva Peabody."

Style nodded and left, glancing left and right as he hurried the short distance to Gracechurch Street.

Min watched him go with a growing sense of exhilaration. He was going to read it! The battle was half won. She might finally, *finally* see her dream come to fruition. Her heart was whole again and tears welled in her eyes. It was almost too much. Two years of writing in moments snatched out of her day only to have her hopes ground under both feet of every theatre manager in London, and now she'd won this victory. It was minor really—he still had to read it *and* like it—but the victory felt like a giant leap forward. And it was all hers to savor and cherish.

She felt like she would burst if she didn't tell someone. But who? Her father would be angry that she'd wasted so much time on her play instead of helping him, and her friends didn't quite understand how much it meant to her. Those that knew she harbored the dream of being a playwright thought her mad, and they were few. Not even Ned would appreciate this moment. Especially Ned. He might be courting her but he understood her most precious dream least of all.

Min sighed. Her earlier enthusiasm faded like the setting sun. If only her mother was alive...

She turned to go. And bumped into a brick of a man. A big man, with strong hands that gripped her shoulders to steady her.

"I'm sorry," she said, peering up at him. "I—. Oh! It's you."

"Why were you watching me?" No preamble, no 'Are you all right?' or 'Hello, my name is Percy Percival, what's yours?'

Min swallowed and blinked up at the stranger with the too-blue eyes. He was quite overwhelming up close. From afar he'd been like an exotic delicacy—a delicious morsel that was, alas, out of her reach—but now she received the full force of his presence. Power rippled through his touch into her body, making the tiny hairs on the back of her neck stand to attention. His blue glare bored into her as if he were trying to extract the answer directly from her head. There was a jaded languor about those eyes, as if they'd seen too much but no longer cared.

She swallowed again. She really hoped his name wasn't Percy. That would be such a disappointment to her writer's sensibilities. Lucifer would be far more appropriate.

"I wasn't watching you," she said, her voice small. She cleared her throat. "Anyway, it was *you* who was watching *me*."

His gaze slid to her shoulders. As if he'd just realized he was still holding her, he let them go. "You are mistaken."

"I am not. You were looking directly at me for quite some time."

"No."

"No?"

"As I said, you're mistaken. I was merely looking in your general direction."

"At what precisely?"

A pulse throbbed in his cheek. "You ask a lot of questions."

"I'm merely curious. As a playwright, it helps to be curious about people. Besides, one question does not 'a lot' make. So, what or whom were you looking at if not at me?" She wasn't sure why she persisted. Perhaps it was to learn more about him. He might prove useful as the basis for one of her characters.

But, more truthfully, it was because she'd never met someone so formidable and yet so utterly compelling after such a brief encounter. She was a moth and he was much too bright a flame for her own good. It was futile to even resist. She *had* to know everything about him.

"That," he said in a tone that could have frozen the Thames, "is none of your business."

She sighed. Flame or no, he was harder to talk to than her father in the midst of his research.

"Are you going to tell me why you were looking at me or will I have to force it out of you?" he persisted.

She gasped. "Force? What kind of force?" She glanced around and wondered if any of the lingering youths or hawkers would come to her aid if she screamed. The street had become oddly quiet now that the performance was long over and the sky had turned sinister. Everyone must have gone home or into one of the nearby shops in anticipation of a downpour.

"You could always not answer the question to find out," he said. "If you're curious enough, that is."

He was toying with her. She was almost certain of it. He wasn't smiling and his eyes didn't sparkle, and yet there was a hint of mischief in his tone.

She crossed her arms. She didn't like to be teased. "My reason is not important."

"I'll be the judge of that." He crossed his arms too and suddenly he seemed even taller and far more intimidating than before. How did he do that with only a few small movements of muscle? "Who was that man with you?"

She saw no reason *not* to tell him. "Roger Style, manager and lead actor for Lord Hawkesbury's Men."

"The players?"

"Yes."

She thought she saw him smile but she must have been mistaken. He didn't look like a man who knew how to smile.

He glanced back at the White Swan Inn. "And that parcel you gave him was your play?"

"Yes."

"Ah. I see." He bent down to her level and pinned her to the spot with an unwavering glare. She tried to appear unfazed when all the while she was shivering on the inside. "So what, madam, does Roger Style and your play have to do with me?" She opened her mouth to utter whatever excuse came out first but he stopped her by pressing a finger to her lips. "No," he said. "I want a direct answer this time."

She let out a small breath that would have warmed his finger. Unlike Style this stranger was not afraid of catching anything from her. She tried to see the finger but only managed to hurt her eyeballs. She looked left, right, then finally into the eyes of the man she'd thought of as her savior only minutes before. Now she wished she'd chosen someone else, someone with blander features and considerably smaller in stature. Someone who didn't turn her insides hot and cold with one glance or look like he could squeeze answers out of her.

Someone with a little less strength of character.

"Are you going to tell me the truth now?" he asked, voice rolling through the small space between them like ominous thunder.

She expected him to remove his finger so she could speak but he didn't. Instead, he traced her top lip in a movement so exquisitely gentle it made everything inside Min stop. Her heart, her breath, her thoughts. Every part of her focused on that finger and the way it caressed her lip. It tickled but there was no way she would pull back, no way she would break the touch. She couldn't. She was in his thrall.

A strange hush surrounded them. She could hear nothing except his light breathing, see nothing except his face, so intent on his task, on her lip. It was as if they were floating inside a bubble; the outside world became irrelevant. It was quite simply magical.

Then the stranger did something quite unexpected. He smiled. Not a full, beaming smile but more a twitch of one corner of his mouth. It was accompanied by a derisive curl of his lip and a soft grunt. He was sneering. He removed his hand and the bubble burst.

She swallowed. "I, I... What was the question?" She pressed her fingertips to her mouth but it didn't feel the same. Didn't have nearly the same effect.

He cleared his throat and lifted an eyebrow. She let her hand fall and tried to concentrate on not looking like a silly female who'd never been touched in quite the way he'd just touched her. Even though she hadn't. Not even by Ned. Nor would she again, a small insidious voice inside her said.

She reigned in her galloping attention. "Oh, yes. I remember. Style wouldn't read a play written by a woman. So I told him a man wrote it." She took a precautious step away from him but it didn't weaken his effect on her. It would require the distance of oceans to achieve that—no, not even then. "In short, I told him you wrote it."

"Me?"

"Yes. You."

"Why me?"

Because you have amazing eyes and broad shoulders. She shrugged. "You were standing about, not doing anything in particular and...because you were watching me."

"I thought we cleared that up. I wasn't watching you." Amusement flared in those blue depths again. Min found it irritating, despite her attraction. "However if it pleases your playwright's fancy to think that I was, then go ahead and indulge in that fantasy."

Heat flared from her throat to her hairline. "Your eyes were pointed at *me,* Sir. And since *my* eyes are in perfect working order, I do not think I was mistaken."

He sighed and looked heaven-ward as if seeking a sign. He muttered something she couldn't hear then returned his gaze to her. "I wasn't watching *you,* I was watching your companion."

The sound of her vanity bursting momentarily filled her ears. Her heart dipped. It really was her own silly fault to have assumed he had been watching *her.* She was hardly the sort of woman to inspire a man like him to spend his afternoon staring at a stranger.

She tucked a stray lock of hair back into her hood. "Style? But why?"

He hesitated, just a little, then said, "I want to join his company."

"Lord Hawkesbury's Men? As what?"

He shrugged. "In any capacity. And it seems, madam, that you have helped my plight."

She didn't believe him. He didn't even know Style was the manager of Lord Hawkesbury's Men until she'd told him and now he wanted to work for Style's company? She wasn't a fool.

But why lie? What did this man have to hide?

And what had she got herself into by using him?

Whatever it was, it seemed only fair that he now use her. That would teach her not to think her schemes through properly before opening her mouth.

The stranger rubbed his stubbly chin, lost in thought. "Are you going to see Style again about your play?"

"Yes."

"When and where?"

"Why?" A sense of foreboding congealed in her stomach.

"Just answer the question."

"What if I don't want to?"

"Then I will follow you and tell your father or husband or whoever is head of your household that you have been consorting with theatrical types."

Her jaw hurt. She forced it to move so she could say: "Consorting?"

"They can put their own interpretation on the word." He blinked lazily.

Min wanted to scratch those too-blue eyes out, wanted to punch him on the chin like an insulted man would. But she wasn't a man and he wasn't like any man she'd encountered. He was much too magnificent a beast to respond to such pettiness. "Is your name Lucifer by any chance?"

His cheek twitched. "No."

She spun round and strode off, hating God, the devil and whatever witchcraft had sent this man to her. *Walk away. Walk far away from him now.* "I'm meeting Style back here tomorrow at this time," she shot back over her shoulder. By then she would be fully recovered from this girlish folly.

Her dramatic exit was ruined when he fell into step alongside her. "To make our ruse seem authentic," he said, "we'd best exchange names. I'm Blake."

A fat drop of rain exploded on her nose and she swiped it with her sleeve. "Is that a first name or last?" she said, flipping up the hood of her cloak.

"It's what you can call me. And you?"

More drops fell. She picked up her pace and headed for shelter. The overhanging upper stories of the houses and shops lining the narrow street provided perfect cover for London's fickle weather. The paved surface quickly became slippery and little rivulets began to trickle between the stones, bringing with it mud, horse dung and refuse from nearby Leadenhall Market. Min kept her gaze down and dodged the worst in her haste to reach dryness.

Suddenly a solid arm circled her waist and jerked her back into an equally solid body. "Watch it," Blake murmured in her ear. A barrel-sized man stumbled past, too intent on his wineskin to notice anyone or anything in his path.

Min looked once again into the eyes of her savior. No, not her savior. She really must stop thinking of him as that.

But he *had* just saved her from being knocked over and landing on her rear in the muck. And he was staring at her again, this time with an odd expression that she couldn't decipher.

She smiled tentatively and placed a hand on the arm that still held her snugly against his body. Beneath the leather doublet, she could feel thick muscle. Or was it padding? It was hard to tell so she squeezed. Definitely not padding.

He suddenly let her go with a grunt and glanced around as if looking for any more hazards. Raindrops splashed off his shoulders and plastered his hair to his face. "You should watch where you're going," he said.

She huddled into her coat but it was too thin and had too many holes to be effective against the damp. "Min."

His gaze shifted to her. Water dripped from the ends of his hair and lashes but he didn't seem to care. "Pardon?"

"You can call me Min."

"Min." She thought he would ask her about her name but he didn't. He bowed slightly. "I'll see you here tomorrow, Min." He turned back the way they'd come, his stride leisurely compared to the few remaining people who scurried like ants to get out of the rain.

Min raced off in the opposite direction, resisting the urge to look back at him. She wouldn't give into temptation. She still had enough self-control to resist the blue-eyed Lucifer.

Her resistance lasted all the way to the corner where she weakened and snuck a peak.

Blake was gone.

CHAPTER 2

Min found her father in his study exactly how she'd left him two hours before—bent over a book, his nose grazing the pages. Granted his nose was considerable in length but it looked as if he was trying to inhale the words rather than read them.

"Father, why don't you move closer to the window where the light's better. You'll hurt your eyes reading like that." She didn't suggest he light a candle—they couldn't afford the expense of wax ones and he refused to have any stinking tallow in the house unless absolutely necessary.

He didn't answer her, didn't even acknowledge her entry. She placed a hand over the book.

Sir George looked up, a frown on his forehead and a chastisement on his lips. Then he saw her and smiled. "Oh, it's you, Minerva."

"Who did you think it was?"

"Jane, telling me dinner is ready. That's how she usually attracts my attention."

"I've just seen Jane in the kitchen. Your dinner is there for you, where it has been for hours. She already told you it was ready, as did I before I went out."

"You've been out?" He removed his spectacles and scrunched up his eyes. "Where did you go?"

She removed a glove, careful not to spray droplets of rain over his papers. "I had a few errands to run."

"I trust you took Jane."

"She has enough work to do here. And anyway, I wasn't at the market so there was nothing for her to carry."

"Minerva. We've spoken about this." He rose and came round his desk to face her. Concern edged his tired eyes. "If you wish to go out, you must take a servant."

"Father, we only have one servant left and she's overworked as it is."

"Her work will be here when she returns." He pinched the bridge of his nose and sighed. "What's got into you lately? You never used to go out alone."

True. She didn't. But so much had changed in the last year and the greatest of those changes had been to Min herself. "I'm older now and I wish to go out without a chaperone on occasion. Besides, we simply cannot spare Jane." Not since they had to let four other servants go. And certainly not since Min started going to the theatre as often as possible.

Her father's income from his one remaining benefactor simply couldn't stretch to five servants plus the large Blackfriars house. Retaining only one maid and moving to a smaller residence near Gracechurch Street had eased the burden, but for how long? What more could be done? Min made economies wherever she could and helped Jane with her duties. The maid was in her mid-forties, advancing years for a domestic servant, and yet she was doing more than ever. It broke Min's heart to see Jane rub her back only to stop and smile at Min whenever she caught her watching.

They needed more money, but with only one patron, her father would never be able to fund the entire household. And Sir George wasn't likely to find any more noblemen willing to endorse him after he lost his own fortune plus the fortunes of several investors when the *Lucinda May* foundered on a reef on its maiden voyage with her father's latest invention on board. An invention that was supposed to determine a ship's position with absolute certainty and thus avoid such reefs. Of course, Sir George claimed his invention was accurate but the location of the reef on the maps was not. His investors weren't quite so eager to disparage the queen's map makers and so all funding came to an abrupt halt. Almost all. Min thanked Heaven for Lord Pilkington every day, even though he was unwilling to give more.

Once favored by the queen and touted by Drake as the man who would save thousands of lives and fortunes from sinking into foreign seas, Min's father was now considered a "high risk". As such, funds for his research dried up. In a world where the New Sciences were the latest fashion, her father was the hat that everyone wanted to wear last year but was now gathering dust in the bottom of a chest beneath newer, fancier hats. If it wasn't for Lord Pilkington, a somewhat stuffy and pompous viscount and her father's only remaining friend from their old life, they would be destitute.

"Have you been to the theatre again?" Sir George pointed his spectacles at her. "I've told you, it's a dangerous place for a lady."

"Many ladies attend the theatre, Father." *Some of them are even respectable.*

He tipped his head to the side. "Alone?"

She sighed. He was right. Why was it that the only thing to draw him away from his calculations and paperwork was something she'd wanted him *not* to notice? Fate was being particularly cruel—first Blake and now her father. What next?

"I do not entirely discourage you from attending the theatre, Minerva. I am an enlightened man and despite what some of the City's aldermen think, I believe the theatre is an innocent enough pastime for people of all ranks and sexes. But need I remind you, you are the daughter of a knight, and as such you should be *accompanied* to places like that?"

She should have known there would be a "but". There usually was when they spoke about the theatre or her writing of plays.

"So if you hadn't been knighted," she said, "I could have gone to the theatre alone?" She crossed her arms. "That is hardly fair."

"That is not what I'm saying. Do not twist my words." He sighed and shook his head. "Child, the theatre is full of vagabonds and disreputable men looking to stir up trouble."

"It is also full of nobles and knights *and* their daughters."

He put his spectacles back on and regarded her down the length of his nose with a stern eye that showed no signs of its former tiredness. Oh dear. She'd overstepped the boundary, the invisible line that once crossed, reminded her father that he was the master of their little family unit, even if an absent-minded one at times.

"I do think your time could be better spent here writing up my notes," he said, "but if you *must* go to the theatre on the odd occasion do not go alone anymore. I forbid it." He suddenly brightened. "Why not go with Ned?"

"*Ned*?" she spluttered. "But I'm not wed and he's neither my relative nor a servant. How is that appropriate?"

"I trust him."

He obviously hadn't seen the way Ned looked at her. Not surprising since her father was usually buried in his study when Ned came to pay his respects.

She shook her head. That wasn't entirely fair. Ned might have a tendency to speak to her breasts and not her face, but Sir George was right in that Ned was harmless enough. Perhaps that was his problem. He simply wasn't...interesting.

Now *Blake* was Interesting with a capital I. Interest throbbed from every inch of his flesh. She would be seeing him again tomorrow, with Roger Style. A little tingle whispered across her skin but she couldn't be sure if it was in anticipation of seeing Blake again or hearing what Style had to say about her play.

"Anyway," she added, "Ned doesn't approve of the theatre."

"That's why I find him a suitable companion for you. He'll be a steady influence."

Meaning she was prone to fancy? She was about to argue the point but, once again, he was right. She could sometimes be a very practical person like her father, but she had a strong poetic streak embedded deep within her. She could happily spend hours dreaming up stories. When once she used to sit by the window, now she helped Jane with the dishes or laying fresh rushes, any repetitive task that didn't require her mind to be present. Instead, it could wander to foreign lands and save kingdoms or meet princes. It certainly made the chores go faster.

All except the chore of writing up her father's notes, the one task she had to think about and the one task he noticed when it wasn't done. The dust could be as thick as her forefinger on the furniture and he'd say nothing, but if she failed to write up his notes from the previous day, he would subject her to a lecture about the duties of an educated daughter.

In the absence of a son, he had seen fit to have his only child tutored in the works of Ovid and Cicero amongst others. She'd been able to read Latin and Greek as well as any boy and had a solid understanding of mathematics by the age of thirteen. By eighteen she knew the works of astronomers Copernicus and Werner backwards. Sir George often reminded her that with an education and brain exceeding that of most men her duty was to use it to assist him in his research. God, and Sir George, would be offended by the waste otherwise.

Sir George returned to his chair, a sign he was finished with the conversation and wished to return to work. He picked up his book, scrunched up his eyes and peered at the pages. With a click of his tongue, he shifted his chair closer to the window but the light had faded considerably since Min's entrance and he tossed the book back onto the desk in disgust.

"Jane!" he bellowed. "Fetch candles. Wax not tallow. Min," he said, softer, "have you finished the paper I asked you to copy?"

The paper! *Oh no.* Min swallowed. "Not quite, Father."

"But you've had it for days." He sighed and leaned back in his chair. "Very well, fetch what you've done and we can go through it together. I'm not entirely happy with it. Perhaps your fresh mind can see problems in the theory where mine can't."

"Ah... Yes. I mean, no, perhaps it'll be best if we go through it all when it's done. I'll have the complete picture then and it'll be easier to—."

Sir George's hand slammed on the desk. Min jumped. A scroll rolled onto the floor and ink sloshed over the side of an inkwell. "You haven't done it, have you?"

Min swallowed her retort about not being his slave. Her father's rare rages didn't frighten her the way they had when she was a child, but it wasn't wise to fan the flames. Best to let it blow over. He was usually as quick to calm as he was to flare, especially these days. He was simply too tired to stay angry for long. Or perhaps he knew that his temper wasn't as effective on her as it once was.

"That's twice now, Minerva."

"Twice? Twice what?"

"Twice that you've failed to deliver your work within a suitable time frame. And this time it appears you've not even started it."

"Father," she said in a placating tone, "I've been busy helping Jane with some of her chores and..." She bit the inside of her lip. It wasn't right to hide behind Jane. This was Min's doing, no one else's. She needed to own up to her passion, especially now that Style had agreed to read her play. "I've been writing."

"Writing! Ha!" He shook his head. "Poetry again I suppose?"

She linked her hands behind her back, twisting her fingers. "A play as it happens."

"Poetry, plays..." He pressed both his palms on the desk and half rose from his seat. Min expected an explosion of temper the likes she had never seen before. It didn't come. Instead he sat down again and sighed. "Minerva, you disappoint me," he said heavily. "I had you educated by the finest tutors in modern thinking so you could understand my work and assist me when I needed it. And now that I need it," he removed his spectacles and rubbed the deep grooves of his face, "you choose to squander your time and intelligence on plays. If your mother had borne me a son, he could have continued my work after I depart this earth."

But a girl could not. And certainly not this girl. She simply didn't have his passion, his drive, for the New Sciences. Min willed her eyes not to moisten. When she knew her voice would be stable, she said, "Father—."

"No! No more excuses." His face flushed a dangerous shade of red. "I have been patient. I have allowed you your freedom, more than other fathers would. I have indulged your flights of fantasy but I will not do so anymore. Not to the detriment of what is important."

"Important?" Min nearly choked on the word. "My poetry is not important?"

"Will it change the course of the world? Will it save the lives of men? Will its benefits echo down the years?" He stabbed a finger on a map of the world spread out on one side of his desk. "My work will." He picked up a handful of notes and shook them at her with more vigor than he'd shown in months. It would have been heartening if it wasn't directed at her. "These pages will make history. Scientists will pore over my work long after I am gone and use them to leverage their own theories. *My* work will change the way future generations think."

Not a word about putting food on the table, paying Jane's wages or keeping a decent roof over their heads. It was about the world, and making his mark in it, and about the future.

But what about me? she wanted to shout. What about the present and the daughter who should have been wed by now? The one who'd been quickly forgotten by dozens of suitors only a year ago when her father lost her dowry and his reputation somewhere in the ocean off Newfoundland. The daughter who could still have been wed to safe, dull Ned Taylor but wasn't because her father wanted to keep her at his side as his assistant.

What about me?

It was selfish and childish but she didn't care. Not anymore. Not now that she was so close to seeing her dream come to fruition. She would *not* give up on it. Even if Style didn't like this play, she would write another and another. Because she couldn't *not* write them. Stories flowed in her blood and they would not stop until every drop had drained from her body.

Her father must have seen the defiance in her face. With a sudden violence so out of character, Sir George threw the pages onto the desk and brought a fist down on top of them. "My work—science—is *vital,* Minerva. You of all people should know that."

The words spewed forth in a torrent, aimed to wound. And wound they did. Min had never seen him so angry. So angry with *her*.

But she was her father's daughter, and her own anger could burn just as brightly. It burst before her eyes, a fierce ball of fire that spread quickly through her, heating her skin, prickling her scalp and burning her insides.

"I do know it," she said above the pounding of her heartbeat. "How can I not, when you remind me daily? But my writing is also important. It is important to *me*."

Sir George opened his mouth but shut it again and blinked at her. Something passed over his face, perhaps shock at his otherwise dutiful daughter's outburst. For she had never spoken her mind to him so vehemently, never disagreed with him before. Never been anything other than the even-tempered child he'd believed he'd raised.

But that child had grown up while he'd been buried in his books. She'd developed her own passions. She had thoughts independent of his and she wasn't afraid to voice them. *That* was the daughter he'd raised.

It seemed he was only just beginning to understand that now. "You will give up this poetical nonsense and do your duty," he said with calm authority. "Your place is here with me, writing out my work. Given time and reflection, you will come to realize this and thank me for directing you towards a more industrious activity than poetry."

Railing at him would not work. His mind was not capable of seeing her point. He believed what he said to the very depths of his being. And so she quelled the surge of anger and bit back her opinions. Voicing them would achieve nothing except more hurt.

"Yes, Father," she said instead. "As you wish."

He approached her, for a kiss perhaps or to speak gentler words, but she lowered her head and curtsied as she would to one of the highest rank.

"Minerva," he said, suddenly sounding old, "let's not quarrel."

"I'm going to my room. Your paper will be complete by the morning. We can discuss it over breakfast if you like."

"But you'll be up all night!" He took her hand in his own and patted it. "Minerva, I'm pleased that you see the error of your ways, but you do not need to prove your earnestness to me."

"I'm not. Good night, Father." She turned and left before they both said something they would regret. Something else.

CHAPTER 3

Robert Blakewell watched her approach along busy Gracechurch Street. Her black woolen cloak flapped in the wind, exposing the light blue of her gown beneath. She was too far away to determine if she wore the same patched-up cloak as yesterday or if the gown was long out of fashion. The tall black silk hat certainly was. His mother had worn that style several years ago.

She pulled the edges of the cloak together and tugged the brim of her hat down, obscuring her face. It was her though. He knew it by the way she walked. Erect, purposeful, prim. A gentlewoman's walk. One fallen on hard times it would seem. She wore no gloves today and he found himself staring at her long, fine fingers.

Min, she said her name was. Unusual. Like her. He'd never met such a pretty and plainspoken woman outside his own family circle. As with his mother and sister, Min had a quick mind to go with the pouting mouth and big eyes. A combination that had got his sister into trouble.

It had almost got Min into trouble too if his reaction to her was anything to go by. He'd got a handful of soft curves when he caught her. And those lips—full and only a twitch away from a smile. When he'd touched them, he'd almost kissed her. The urge had been powerful and immediate.

He'd not succumbed yesterday. Today...well, he would see. A lot depended on what Style said. More than Blake liked to admit. The irony was, he had no alternative plan. If Min hadn't chosen him, he could still be trying to find a way into the company of players that called themselves Lord Hawkesbury's Men. He knew what had to be done once he was inside, it was the introduction that had eluded him.

Until yesterday when Min had chosen *him*. Out of all the men lingering in the vicinity, she'd fixed on Blake for some reason of her own. The hardest part was over. Now all he had to do was find out which of the troupe's swine turds deserved to have their balls removed for what they'd done to Lilly.

Min continued towards him, her head down, not watching where she was going. Again. He shook his head. Hadn't she learned from the last time? Just as she was about to pass him, he stepped in front of her.

She bumped into him and he caught her shoulders, stopping her falling on her arse.

"What—?" She shook herself free then, several moments too late, finally looked up at him. "Oh. Blake." Recognition dissolved the irritation in her gray eyes.

"Hoping to avoid me?" he said.

Her gaze didn't quite meet his. He had his answer.

"It's too late to back out now," he said. "I'm here. And I think I'd like to be a playwright."

She scanned the faces of passersby, perhaps searching for the elaborately feathered hat Style seemed to favor. Or perhaps she was simply avoiding looking at Blake. "Part of me was hoping you wouldn't be here," she admitted.

"Sorry to disappoint you."

"No you're not." She chewed her lower lip and he lifted a hand to stop her destroying the succulent morsel, but dropped it before she noticed. Touching her had shocked his senses awake. He couldn't risk touching her again.

"You see, it's just that...I really don't..."

"Want me to ruin this opportunity for you?"

"That's it!" She smiled at him, leaving her harried lip alone. "Thank you for understanding. So you'll leave?"

"No."

Her face fell. More lip chewing. Reading her emotions was like reading a book, and not a very difficult one. "Perhaps you could hide then," she said. "Just over there." She nodded in the direction of a tavern where several barrels were being unloaded from a cart. A group of men, some swaying, one singing loudly and out of tune, hovered around the barrels like flees on a dog. He grunted. If he was going to hide, he wouldn't choose a place where he'd stand out like a mermaid on a rock.

"No," he said again. "I'm staying here. I want to meet Style."

She stared at him for a long moment. He accepted the challenge and stared back. It gave him a chance to study her. A splash of freckles decorated both cheeks, and one had slipped down to the corner of her mouth, giving the impression she was constantly smiling. Her nose was slightly crooked and a tiny pock scar marked her chin. Her hair was tucked tightly beneath her hat so that not a strand escaped but he could see that it was fair with only a hint of red, not quite as dark as the queen's. It reminded him of sunrise over a Saracen desert.

Ha! Poetry. Any half-wit could do it.

Min clicked her tongue. "Very well, you may stay," she said as if it had been up to her. "But," she pointed a finger at him, "do *not* speak to Style unless he directly asks you a question. I'll do all the talking. And do not, under any circumstances, say anything about the play. I've told him you're shy, so...act shy. You can do that can't you?"

"I can try." He glanced towards the White Swan but Style was still nowhere to be seen. The company's performance for the day had ended a while ago and yet he'd not appeared amongst the audience leaving the inn.

The crowd was thinner today. Word must have spread through the City that it was more interesting watching two ants crawling up a wall than the dung Lord Hawkesbury's Men called a play. He wondered if Min's play was any better. It couldn't be much worse. But what if it wasn't good *enough*?

Blake would need to find another way, that's what. He could just barge in, fists and accusations flying, but Lilly wouldn't speak to him if she ever found out. No, he needed to be more subtle. Damn. He wasn't very good at subtle.

Thank god for Min.

"However," Blake went on, "perhaps you should tell me about your play so I can answer any questions he may ask me directly." Better to be armed and ready than caught unprepared.

"He won't."

"He might."

"Very well," she said and he was surprised that she acquiesced so easily. She'd seemed ready for a battle. He even looked forward to one. "It's set in Ancient Rome and is about a young couple who fall in love but through a series of unfortunate events directed by the Gods, they're kept apart. It's too complicated to go into more detail."

"It's a tragedy?"

"No, a comedy."

"A romance?"

"Yes."

He watched her, trying to determine if she was being serious or making fun of him. By the set of her jaw, she didn't look like she was about to laugh. Bollocks.

"You don't like romantic comedies?" The sun chose that moment to appear from behind a cloud and she narrowed her eyes against it. Or was she narrowing them against him?

"No. It's not that." A few moments ago, he'd thanked Fortune that this opportunity had fallen into his lap. Now he wasn't so sure. A romantic comedy? Min thought *him* a suitable candidate for writing a romantic comedy? She expected Style to believe it too? He was a privateer for God's sake, captain of his own brigantine. He'd made life hell for Spanish galleons from the Levant to the New World. He'd been chained up in jails not fit for a dog. He'd killed pirates, got drunk with brigands and fought for his country, his honor and just because he damn well felt like it. Now this girl expected him to pass for a writer of romantic comedies? His crew would laugh him off his ship if they found out.

He blew out a breath. Perhaps it wasn't as bad as he thought. "Does anyone get murdered?" he asked. "In this play?"

She frowned. "No."

Pity. "Is there a pirate? Or an evil emperor?"

"No, no villains. Although one of the Gods is quite competitive and thinks up some cruel scenarios to keep the lovers apart."

What sort of play doesn't have a villain? He sighed. A romantic comedy apparently. "What about a cannon?"

"Not in ancient Rome." She looked apologetic. "No guns either." She suddenly brightened. "But there is a sword fight."

"Just the one?"

"Yes. Sorry." There was a long pause in which he could see her warring with herself. Eventually her playwright's curiosity, as she had called it, won. "You like violence." She pulled the edges of her cloak together as if fending off the cold, but the day was reasonably mild. Did he frighten her? He spent much of his day trying to frighten people so it wouldn't surprise him. However it did surprise him to realize he didn't want to frighten *her*.

"If I wrote a play," he said, "it would at least have a murder in it. Probably two. And a villain. A really bloodthirsty one."

"You didn't write it," she said irritably. Irritation was better than fear.

"But if people are to think I did, there should be a dead body."

"Oh. I see what you mean." She sounded genuinely concerned. "You do seem like a man who would have no qualms killing a character."

"Thank you," he said then wondered why he'd said it. This woman addled his mind. He'd had two conversations with her and so far she'd managed to make him do things he wouldn't normally do. Like this. He was actually agreeing to act as the writer of her romantic comedy?

He'd done many foolish things in his life, but this was top of the list.

You'd better appreciate what I'm doing for you, Lilly. And you too, Mother.

"If it's a comedy, does it have a clown?" he asked. There'd better be a clown. All good comedies had clowns dancing jigs.

"There's a comedic servant," she said.

He sighed. "That'll have to do."

"Yes, it will." She crossed her arms and lifted her chin. Had he offended her?

He didn't have a chance to ask because Style appeared. When she saw him, Min caught hold of Blake's hand in a grip that could put many men to shame. Her hands weren't as soft as he thought they'd be. Small calluses marred her palm. The sort of calluses that come from continuous hard work, not the lifting of a quill.

It was wrong. Min was an educated woman of gentle birth. She should have smooth hands—perfect palms to match the perfect fingers. He rubbed his thumb along the hardened bumps, annoyed at them, at whatever had put them there, and at whoever was supposed to be taking care of her. Who could allow a daughter or sister such as Min to do a servant's work? Wrong, wrong, wrong.

With a strangled sound, she suddenly dropped her hand and stared at him like a startled cat. He flexed his fingers, still able to feel the weight of her hand, the warmth of her touch against his skin.

He formed a fist and beat back the fire spreading through him. There was no room for those kinds of fires in his world. Not the ones started by innocent, big-eyed gentlewomen.

Roger Style joined them but Min barely registered his presence. Her mind was elsewhere—in Blake's hand. The tender rubbing of her palm had felt good. Until she'd remembered who he was and that she shouldn't be holding hands with him. He was a complete stranger. She'd only ever held hands with Ned twice and one of those was because he had helped her onto a wherry to cross the Thames.

She snuck a sideways glance at Blake. His face could have been hewn from rock. There wasn't even a hint that holding hands with her had been anything other than an everyday, mundane occurrence.

It probably was. No doubt men like Blake did more than hold hands with women on a daily basis. Her face heated as she thought about what else he could do to her.

"Well," said Style, "you're here. Good." He spoke to Blake.

That annoyed Min. It probably would have annoyed her more if she had been concentrating. She forced herself to listen. Roger Style was the reason why she was there after all. It had nothing to do with Blake. Nothing at all.

Style cleared his throat. "It's a, er, comedy," he said, lowering his voice as if he were saying a naughty word.

"Yes," Blake said, crossing his arms and drawing himself up to his full height so that he towered over both Style and Min. "A romantic one. So?"

"So...it's not what I thought *you* would have written." Style's nervous laugh died like an unfunny jest.

"You're not the only one who thinks that." Blake might as well have poked Min with his elbow, his tone was so pointed.

"But did you like it?" Min held her breath. The moment seemed to drag on forever as Style turned to her.

He blinked as if he hadn't noticed she was there. "Oh, good day...what did you say your name was again?"

"Minerva Peabody." Why didn't he just *tell* her what he thought instead of going through these dull pleasantries?

She felt Blake shift beside her and glanced at him. He was staring at her, unblinking, frowning, as if seeing her for the first time.

What? she mouthed.

But he looked away and Style was talking again. "And your name?" the manager and lead player of Hawkesbury's Men asked Blake. "I didn't catch it yesterday.

"It's Blake. Just Blake," he said before Style could question him as Min had done.

"I see." Style cleared his throat.

"Well?" Min prompted. "Did you like the play?"

"You're a Cambridge man," Style said, ignoring her. "I can tell. All the good poets are from Cambridge. Marlowe, Greene, Spenser... I had a rather impertinent country fellow from a village on the Avon try to tell me that a university education meant nothing when writing plays. But I soon put him right. Hired him as an actor instead."

Did he just say she was a good poet? Good was...good. Wasn't it? But did good mean he wanted to buy the play or did it mean he'd prefer to use the parchment on something more useful like a shopping list? She was about to ask when he spoke again.

"Do you know Kit Marlowe?" he asked Blake.

"No," Blake said. "Should I?"

Style shrugged. "No, no, of course not. Your writing is nothing like his really. A much lighter tone."

"Too light?" Min asked. "I know dark and tortuous is very popular after *Tamburlaine* and *Dr. Faustus,* but I can't—" *write tortuous heroes,* she almost said. "But I can't see Blake writing anything but comedies."

Two pairs of eyes turned to her. The brown pair seemed annoyed that she'd interrupted. The bright blue pair brimmed with something she hadn't seen in them yet. Laughter?

She shrugged. "Well, I can't."

"After reading this," Style said, "I tend to agree."

"So do you want it?" Blake asked him.

"I'll give you two pounds."

"Yes!" Min said at the same time Blake said, "Five."

Five! What was he doing? He was going to ruin everything! Why oh why had she been taken in by those impossibly bright eyes and oversized shoulders?

"Three," Style countered.

"Four is my final offer."

"Blake," she hissed. Her dream was slipping through her grasp as she looked on, powerless to make him keep quiet. It was utterly frustrating.

"You're an unknown," Style huffed. "People won't come to a play written by an unknown." He tossed his head, making the blue and green peacock feather in his hat flutter.

"They'll come when they hear how good it is after the first performance."

Min wanted to throw her arms around Blake and show him how grateful she was for his support. Then she remembered he hadn't even read it. She still wanted to hug him but for an entirely different reason that had nothing to do with her play and everything to do with exploring more of the hard body she'd felt the day before.

"I could ask for the second night's takings," Blake said.

"You've got a lot of faith in your play if you think it would last two nights," Style said.

"You're here aren't you? You obviously have faith in it too or you wouldn't have shown up. Four pounds or I walk away now and offer it to..." His gaze shifted sideways to Min.

"The Admiral's Men," she said quickly.

"Lord Howard is patron of a theatre company?"

Where had this man been living that he'd never heard of London's best company of players? Even her father had seen one of their productions. He'd escorted her last winter. It was the first and last time he'd taken her to the newly opened Rose theatre, or to any other theatre for that matter.

Style snorted. "Henslowe wouldn't touch a comedy. Alleyn is not a comic actor. His range is limited to blustering, diabolical villains,"

"Really?" Blake sounded impressed, darn him.

"Henslowe is the Admiral's Men's manager," Min said, "and Alleyn is their lead player." When Style raised both his eyebrows, she added, "Blake's led a sheltered life. He hasn't been to the theatre much lately."

"How odd," Style muttered, staring at Blake as if he were a creature emerging from the sea.

"Henslowe would take on this one," Blake said with all the certainty of ignorance. Min didn't know whether to kiss him or tell him to be quiet. His blind faith in her work was quite intoxicating—and yet she knew it to be false. "I'd probably get more money from him too."

"Then why not try them first?" Style hadn't become a manger because he was a good actor. A solid business brain must be crammed into that fancy hat.

"I saw a performance of yours years ago," Blake said. "You used to be good. Very good. But not anymore." He nodded up the road to the White Swan. The coaching inn was now deserted of theatre-goers but still busy with the arrival of travelers on horseback, coach or on foot. Inside, the rest of Lord Hawkesbury's Men might be having a drink in the taproom, perhaps dissecting the day's performance or even discussing her play if Style had shown it to the other members.

The thought sent a ripple of excitement down her spine. He hadn't said no yet.

"I felt sorry for you," Blake went on. "That's why I'm offering the play to you first. I want to see Lord Hawkesbury's Men doing well once more. It'll bring back fond memories to see you bowing to a full gallery again."

Style puffed out his chest and tilted his head. The feather shivered. "Yes, of course. That's understandable."

Min rolled her eyes. Only Blake saw it. The ghost of a smile played around his lips. As lies went, it was a blunt one. However Style didn't seem to detect it.

"Four pounds it is." He clapped Blake on the arm. "It's a good play."

Four pounds! With that much money she could give Jane what was owed her and there'd still be enough left over for wax candles, paper and ink for herself and her father. And perhaps a new pair of gloves since she'd ruined her only decent pair that morning attempting to reunite the frying pan with its wayward handle.

"Good man," Style said. "Now, come meet the rest of the company. They loved the play."

"Yes," both Min and Blake said together. He raised one brow at her. She shrugged shoulders still tingling with excitement.

"Excellent." Style beamed. "They're waiting." With his hand on Blake's arm, he steered him in the direction of the inn. Min followed. "Er, perhaps you should wait here," Style said over his shoulder. "An inn's taproom isn't an appropriate place for a girl such as yourself."

"I have been to inns before," she said, resisting the urge to stamp her foot.

"Really? Well, your menfolk can't follow your every move I suppose. Anyway, this one will be full of players and a few remaining audience members. That is, mostly men. We wouldn't want you to see or hear something that might frighten you."

"Frighten me?"

"Men's talk can get a little...ribald. It's not for your gentle ears, my girl." With that, he marched Blake up to the inn. At the door, Blake shrugged at her as if to say he could do nothing.

He certainly *could* do something. A man with shoulders like that could get his own way if he wanted to. But he hadn't even bothered putting a word in for her. He might have pretended he was her brother or a cousin to convince Style she was chaperoned, but no, he chose to do nothing.

Min's eyes stung with anger and frustration. *Just wait until you come back out Blake-whoever-you-are. I'll make sure you remember who is responsible for getting you into Lord Hawkesbury's company.*

A thought nibbled away at her until it became a gaping hole. She'd been so caught up in her own hopes for her play that she'd not asked herself a vital question: Why had Blake so readily accepted the role she'd shoved onto him? What was in it for him? She'd offered him no incentive, financial or otherwise, and yet he was going along with the scheme with enthusiasm. It was an oddity. *He* was an oddity.

She wandered over to a milliner's shop opposite the inn where she could watch for his return. When he emerged, she would take back control of this situation and find out his motives.

If she could wait long enough, that is. Her father might notice if she was gone for the entire afternoon. They'd discussed his research paper that morning over breakfast but she'd not confided her concerns over his new theories to him. Some of his mathematics simply didn't add up and at least one of his conclusions was quite wild. She sighed. What had happened to send him down a different scientific path to the one he'd been working on?

Perhaps he would discuss it with her later. Much later. If he went looking for her now and couldn't find her, yesterday's little argument would become as insignificant as a single snowflake in a blizzard.

CHAPTER 4

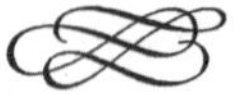

Peabody. Blake knew that name. Every English sea captain did. Sir George Peabody had created a new method of determining a ship's location based on a series of calculations, factoring in the positions of the stars and known landmarks. It was set to revolutionize sea-going adventure. The method and accompanying instrument had the potential to guide a ship around obstacles such as reefs, rocky coasts or treacherous waters. It was the scientific discovery of the century. Peabody had been knighted for it. Noblemen fought over who would be his patron. He was on his way to becoming one of the wealthiest and most lauded scientists in England.

Except his invention didn't work.

Blake, like Drake, Raleigh and other privateers, had been bitterly disappointed when the *Lucinda May*—the ship carrying the instrument—had sunk, taking with it everyone on board as well as the hopes of a fledgling navy. It had been a tragedy beyond measure. The failure of Peabody's Method, as the navigational theory had become known, set English seafaring back several years. All that research come to nothing. All the time and effort of not just Peabody, but every scientist he'd dragged along in his wake, wasted. Gone. The method, the instrument, both useless, worthless.

Many times Blake had thought about the waste of time, effort and most of all the lives of the sailors on that historic voyage. But not once had he spared a thought for the man behind the invention. What had become of Sir George? Was he still alive or had his failure ended him? Had he lost all his friends as well as his life's work or had they rallied around him?

Blake didn't know if Min was any relation to the infamous scientist but hearing her name made him want to find out. If she was, and her patched-up clothes and calloused hands were any indication, then Peabody had not fared well at all.

He entered the White Swan's taproom with Style and his mind shifted away from his real life to this newly fabricated one. It needed his full attention if he was to find out which of the troupe must pay for what he did to Lilly. The room was dimly lit but clean and its few patrons seemed mostly respectable as they huddled together in conversation. Several benches, tables and stools dotted the floor space, leaving little room for maneuvering, which Style did with a kind of grace not usually associated with men.

"And here they are," Style said. "May I present to you Lord Hawkesbury's Men." He swept his arm in an arc, encompassing four men seated at a table in the corner. Or more accurately, three men and one boy barely old enough to grow hair on his chin. Blake struck him off his list of suspects. "Lord Hawkesbury's Men, may I present to you...er, Blake."

As introductions went, it was a grandiose one, said in Style's booming stage voice so that the entire taproom must have heard. All it lacked was the blaring of trumpets and a shower of rose petals.

"Blake who?" the boy said more to his tankard than to anyone in particular.

"The playwright," Style said. Four faces stared blankly at him. "He wrote *Marius and Livia,*" he added.

"Ah," said one of the troupe, nodding. He had gray hair and a long wizard's beard and was the only man Blake didn't recognize from the single performance he'd had the misfortune to see the day before. "The play that will save us from poverty." Blake couldn't tell if he was serious or not. Either way, the man continued nodding as if a puppet-master worked an invisible string attached to his skull.

"It's good," said another man, a younger version of Style. Brothers? "But not that good."

"It's not?" Blake said. He didn't understand—Style had been exuberant in his praise. And he'd paid four pounds for it. It must be good.

"With a little improvement it will shine," Style said quickly, beaming at Blake. "A tweak here, a tweak there and the audience will be begging for more."

"And who's going to do that?" the nodding wizard said. "You? Or the last poet you hired?" He snorted and took a long swill from his tankard.

"Blake will." Style clapped Blake on the back. His smile widened. "All we need to do is tell him where it needs a little more and," he kissed his fingertips the way Sicilians did after a hearty meal, "the play will be perfect. The audience will be eating out of our hands."

"As long as they don't puke all over them afterwards," the boy said.

Style ignored him and patted Blake's back. "And you, my friend, will write us another play to satisfy them."

Blake glared at him. Style's hand dropped to his side but, to give him credit, his smile didn't slip. "What do you mean by 'a little more'? More sword fights? More cannon fire?"

"More..." Style's gaze searched the beams above them, "...suggestion. Yes, that's it. Suggestion."

"Suggestion of what? Violence?"

"No-oo," Style said, pulling at his short beard. "Not quite what I meant."

"He means more rutting," the boy said. Blake mentally put him back on the suspect list. Young or not, the lad wasn't as innocent as his cherubic face implied.

"Just a hint," Style said with a pointed glare at the boy. "A few titillating remarks, some ribald jokes, that sort of thing."

Blake couldn't imagine Min knowing any ribald jokes.

Perhaps he could tell her a few. The thought almost had him smiling. She would blush from her tightly coifed roots to her prissy little toes. And everywhere in between.

It was the everywhere in between that sobered him quickly. Best not to think about her in-between bits. She, and women like her, were to be avoided. He was home for one reason only—to find out who'd got his sister with child and force him to marry her, or kill the prick if he refused. There was no room for distractions of the Minverva Peabody kind.

As to suggestive remarks... Not from Min's quill. She wouldn't know a suggestive remark if it lifted her skirts and bit her on the arse.

"Maybe a stolen kiss," the fourth member of the troupe said, speaking up for the first time. "You could add in a lover's caress here and there."

Min definitely wouldn't know anything about kisses, stolen or otherwise. Even though her mouth was made for them with those soft, full lips the color of ripe strawberries. Did her other, nether lips blush the same shade when she was just about to—?

"My name is Henry Wells," the man said, rising and offering his hand to Blake. With the other, he signaled the serving girl for more ale. "Welcome to Lord Hawkesbury's Men."

Grateful for the distraction, Blake shook his hand and sat on the vacant stool next to Wells. Out of all the company, Wells seemed the likeliest candidate for Blake's list of suspects. Fair-haired and sturdily built—two qualities all Englishwomen seemed to admire—he was also the friendliest of the troupe. Apart from Roger Style himself who didn't stop smiling as he introduced everyone.

The youth was an apprentice, Freddie Putney, who played the lead female roles. He lifted a finger off his tankard in salute to Blake before downing the contents, some of which managed to spill into his mouth. The man who looked like Style did turn out to be his younger brother, Edward, and the nodding wizard was John Croft.

"He's our tiring house manager," the elder Style said. Blake must have had a blank look on his face because Style added,

"He's responsible for all the costumes. Cleaning them, mending them, keeping them safe. It's a very important role. Our costumes are our most valuable assets."

Blake could well believe it. He'd seen some of those valuable assets worn during that one God-awful performance. They might be a few years out of fashion, but the costumes could have graced a nobleman or woman. They probably had. Even his mother had donated a gown once to a troupe because it amused her to see a boy dressed in something she'd worn to court.

"Is this it?" Blake looked at the faces around the table. "Five men make up the entire company?"

"The core of it. We hire out the minor roles and some of the backstage work," Style said.

"There is a vacancy for a bookkeeper though," Edward said. "That usually goes to the writer since he knows the play inside out."

They all stared at Blake. "Bookkeeper?" he said.

"You'll have the only whole copy of the play," Wells explained.

"Protect it with your life," Edward said. "Along with the costumes, the play is our fortune."

"Unless it turns out to be a pile of shit," Freddie mumbled. "Then you can use the pages to wipe the stage clean." He laughed at his own joke which earned him another glare from Style. The boy didn't seem to notice.

"The bookkeeper also has to write a summary of the plot for everyone to refer to before and during the performance," Edward went on. "And you'll need to make sure every actor and any necessary props are on stage when they're supposed to be."

"No," Blake said.

"No?" Edward tugged on his beard in a mirror image of his brother, right down to using his left hand instead of his right.

"I only write plays. I don't do anything else."

"But you have to be bookkeeper," Roger Style said with none of the powerful stage voice of earlier.

"There's no one else," Croft added.

"You have to do it," Style said again. "It was part of the deal we made. Four pounds for the play and your services as bookkeeper."

"That wasn't the deal." Blake rubbed his temple. He really didn't want to have to settle this with swords. A duel with the company's manager might ruin his plans.

Freddie broke the tension by slamming his tankard down on the table then belching. Style jumped then tried to laugh it off.

"It's not that hard," Edward said.

"It is a little bit difficult," Wells countered. "I tried it once and sent Freddie on when it was Roger's turn." He scratched his head and shrugged.

"Don't worry," Edward said to Blake, "I'll show you what you have to do."

"I can't be your bookkeeper," Blake said. "I won't be around for the performances." Five pairs of eyes stared at him blankly, as if he was speaking a foreign tongue. "Straight after I've finished the alterations to the play, I'm leaving London."

In and out, that was the plan. Find out who was responsible for Lilly's predicament, make him pay one way or another, and then leave. Get out of London and get back on board the *Silver Star* where the men were hard but at least they had integrity. Of sorts. He'd forgotten what London was like, with its courtly manners hiding a viciousness that could put the most bloodthirsty pirates to shame.

"B, but," Style spluttered, "who'll do it?"

"I will."

The now familiar voice brought a chuckle to Blake's throat. It seemed Min wasn't going to be left out of this experience—*her* experience—no matter what. She was turning into a most surprising woman.

He turned round and was struck by how small she looked in the roomful of mostly men. But even in her faded cloak and old hat, she was a bright light in the grimy taproom. He smiled at her. He couldn't help it.

Surprise fluttered across her pretty features before she smiled back.

"You can't," Style said to her.

"Who's she?" Wells asked, tossing his head. *Peacock.*

"Her name's Min," Blake said. "She's my friend. And your new bookkeeper."

"But she can't!" Style said, more vehement this time. "She's a woman."

"Thank you for noticing," Min said, standing between Blake and Style. "But I happen to think I'd make an excellent book-keeper. I've read the play so I know it well and I've an eye for detail."

"But you've never done this sort of thing before," Style protested. "You won't know what to do."

"You offered the job to Blake a moment ago and he's never done it before either."

A heavy silence weighed down the air, already thick with the stink of ale and sweat. Min raised her eyebrows. Style clicked his tongue.

"Welcome aboard," Wells said, standing and offering his seat to Min. He smiled at her as she sat and she grinned back.

Wells was definitely going to the top of the list.

"But you'll be backstage!" Style said. He pressed a be-ringed hand palm-down on the table and leaned forward, closer to her. Blake shifted forward too, just in case. "You'll see things that a lady of your...bearing shouldn't see." He shook his head, sending the plume into a frenzy. "No. I can't in all conscience allow you to subject yourself."

"I'll avert my eyes," Min offered with a shrug.

"But...what would your menfolk think?"

"Let me worry about my menfolk."

If the Peabody of Peabody's Method infamy was indeed her father and he'd sunk so low as to allow calluses on his daughter's hands, he probably wouldn't care if she spent most afternoons backstage with a troupe of players. Why in hell didn't someone, anyone, speak to the old fool!

"But backstage can be dangerous for a woman," Style said.

"What could possibly happen to her in the middle of a performance?" Croft said. "Apart from trip over something and break her neck, and we all face that danger, including my own daughter who works in the tiring house. Not that your conscience has ever spared a thought for her," he said bitterly.

"I think what Style is really concerned about," said a dark-haired newcomer Blake hadn't seen arrive, "is your reputation, my lady." The low-pitched voice didn't need to be louder for the group of players to come to full attention. The man—a gentleman, if the black cloak embroidered with silver detail was anything to go by—was obviously used to commanding. And getting his own way.

"M, my lord!" Style spluttered, rising. "What a surprise!"

Min swallowed. Lord? Not Lord Hawkesbury, surely? Just when her courage had completely returned too. The sense of triumph she'd felt once she actually entered the inn had replaced the trepidation gnawing at her insides while she waited outside. But now it too was slowly seeping away thanks to the presence of a very powerful man. Another one.

The gentleman acknowledged each of the five players with a nod. When he got to Min, he bowed low. "The reputation of a lady," he said, clarifying his earlier point, "is very precious indeed." His eyes, as black as two ponds at midnight, gleamed and the faint lines at the corner of his mouth deepened with a smile.

Min felt Blake shift beside her. His fingers toyed with the cuff of his sleeve, a seemingly idle movement if there hadn't been a knife handle poking out of it. She swallowed again. Hard. What could he possibly be going to do with the blade? Surely not... No. Oh no. Not a peer of the realm!

Why oh why hadn't she questioned Blake more before taking this ruse further? She knew nothing about him, not even his name. Foolish, foolish girl. If Blake was to stab Lord Hawkesbury here in the White Swan in front of witnesses what would it mean for her, an apparent accomplice?

The gallows, that's what.

She chewed her lip and considered how to stop the horrible event. But then Blake covered the knife again and both his hands returned to his tankard. Her long-held breath came out in a whoosh and she felt a little weak. Blake seemed the same, passively moody but not like a man who wanted to assassinate Lord Hawkesbury.

"Yes," Style said. "Ladies reputations are very precious. That is what I meant. Wouldn't want her menfolk descending on us with rapiers now would we?" He coughed when no one laughed.

Min, with one eye on Blake's cuff, decided to put him out of his misery. "I come from a family that's neither important enough nor rich enough for anyone to think my reputation is worth something. And my menfolk aren't the rapier-wielding type." Picturing her father storming into the inn brandishing a sword made her laugh.

But then she stopped. Sir George would use words not a sword. Words to make her feel like the worst daughter to a poor father in need of her help. And he'd save them for Min's ears only.

An awkward silence shrouded the little group. No doubt everyone had noticed her threadbare clothes and wondered about her family circumstances. Her speech about the lack of concern over her reputation would only make them wonder more. Well, her circumstances were nobody's business but her own. Let them wonder.

She lowered her gaze to her hands folded in her lap and bit the inside of her lip. She had *made* it their business by her simple statement of fact. She needed to learn to think more *before* she spoke or suffer the consequences and heavy silences.

"Lord Hawkesbury," Blake said, nodding a greeting. Min felt her breath return in a rush. He was acting the part of her savior once again by filling the void. She could hug him. And kiss him. And if it wasn't for her renewed fear of him, she'd—.

"Ah yes," said Style, breaking into her thoughts, "let me introduce you to our new poet, Blake. He wrote a wonderful play for us. It'll improve our fortunes, I'm sure."

Wonderful? Min suddenly felt giddy.

"It only requires a few changes," Style went on.

The giddiness stopped as abruptly as a child's spinning top kicked mid-spin. Changes? What kind of changes? But before she could ask, Lord Hawkesbury said, "A pleasure, Blake, and a hearty welcome. Style, a word if you please."

"Yes, yes of course." Style scurried after his lordship to a dim corner on the other side of the inn.

The throng of patrons in the taproom made it difficult to see them clearly but that didn't stop Blake from staring after them. His finger tapped the cuff concealing his hidden dagger before his hand dropped to his side. His gaze, however, remained on the two men in the corner.

"His lordship doesn't look happy," said the young boy, slouching over the table and coddling his tankard. "No doubt he saw the muck we put on today and wants to withdraw his patronage. We're fucked."

"Freddie," warned another man who looked a lot like Style. "There's a lady present." He turned to Min. "I'm so very sorry. He's a little drunk."

"How remiss of us," said one of the others, handsome of face and fair of hair with a gentle smile and open countenance. "We haven't introduced ourselves."

By the time he'd finished telling her who was who and did what within the company, Style rejoined them. Lord Hawkesbury was nowhere to be seen.

"Well?" said Edward to his older brother.

Four people drew in breath at the same time Style let one out. He sat heavily on the stool and picked up his tankard but didn't drink. "His lordship's patience is wearing thin." He paused to let that piece of information sink in then said, "It's all up to *Marius and Livia* now. And how well Blake's changes turn out."

Everyone looked at Blake. He saluted them with his tankard. "Everything will be fine."

"You sound very sure of yourself," Croft grumbled.

"Do you think you can fix it by tomorrow?" Style asked. "We can put on our first performance in the afternoon."

"Tomorrow?" Min said as Blake said, "Of course."

She shot him a warning look but he didn't seem to notice. Good Lord, she couldn't do the changes overnight! It required careful thought, writing and rewriting to make every word perfect. And besides, she didn't know what they wanted yet. The changes could be too numerous, too difficult, too—.

"We're depending on you," Edward said. Croft and Henry Wells nodded. Style looked like he wanted to get down on his knees and kiss Blake's boots while Freddie appeared more interested in his ale.

Min felt like she was floating above the gathering, not quite present and yet seeing everything with startling clarity. They depended on *her*, on her play and her writing. It was the most thrilling thing.

She'd give them whatever changes they wanted.

"Like I said," Blake said, "it'll be ready. I'll make the changes on my own copy and bring the revisions around first thing in the morning."

Min said nothing. She couldn't have formed a coherent sentence if she'd tried. Fortunately she'd kept a copy of the play at home. Style had the only other one.

"Good man," Style said, clapping him on the shoulder but quickly removing his hand when Blake glared at him.

"We'll need to get the Master of the Revels' approval tonight," Edward said. "Have you still got your contact in his office, Brother?"

"Aye and he owes me a favor. He'll rush it through, never fear."

"It seems like I'll be here for the performances after all," Blake said. "So I can be your bookkeeper."

Min glared at him. What was he up to now? More importantly, why?

"I have to go," said Croft, rising. "The wife's expecting me."

"Me too," said Henry Wells. Then he shook his head and laughed. "Not the wife part, I'm not married. Not that I don't want to be, I've just not finished being a single man yet." He laughed again and shrugged.

"Come on, Freddie," said Style to the boy. "You've got lines to learn and some sobering up to do." When the boy answered with a grunt, Style clipped his ear. "Up! Now! Or I'll find another apprentice to eat me out of house and home."

Freddie rose with effort and a lot of grumbling about cruel masters.

"I'd best go too," Blake said, turning to Min. "Since I've got some writing to do."

But before the writing, they needed to do some talking. She hoped he knew exactly what changes were needed. Perchance they were only minor otherwise she was in for a long night.

Especially if her father wanted his notes written up too.

CHAPTER 5

"So what do they want changed?" Min asked before she'd even sat down. Blake had led her to another inn nearby, a quieter one where most of the patrons were gentlemen and even a few ladies sat amongst them. They could have been travelers or simply dining out with their husbands at the popular establishment.

Min felt conspicuous sitting with someone she knew nothing about. Someone who made her heart thump wildly in an odd combination of excitement, fear and something baser, something she assumed must be desire for it made her feel hot and achy all over. Did anyone notice? Did they all look at her and just *know* the path her thoughts had taken?

Did Blake?

Oh dear. She shouldn't be here with him. And yet she wasn't going anywhere. Didn't want to be anywhere else, with anyone else.

Did that make her a wanton?

Aunt Maud had once called her that after Min had run through the orchard at the aunt's country estate wearing nothing but her shift. She'd only been nine and was pretending to be Boadicea the warrior queen, who Min was sure wore far less than an ankle-length linen shift. But Aunt Maud didn't think that was a reasonable explanation for her niece's unconventional behavior and immediately informed Sir George. Min's father told Aunt Maud his daughter tended to flights of fancy which he was attempting to expel with an intensive education program. It was the only time the word wanton had been linked with her name as far as Min knew.

"A few lines here and there," Blake said, signaling the serving girl for two cups of wine. "Nothing more than that."

"Can you be more specific? Which lines?"

"They want new ones."

"Where? What do they want to achieve?"

He crossed his arms and leaned them on the table so that his bulk filled the space between them. The force of his presence pulled her in so that she too leaned forward. Their noses were only inches apart. She could feel the warmth of him and smell subtle scents of maleness. If she leaned over just a little more she would be able to taste him.

She licked her top lip, remembering how he'd caressed it the day before. As if he'd had the same thought, his gaze slipped to her mouth. His eyes became hooded, his face closed, and the room grew hotter. Much, much hotter. He was going to touch her lip again. She knew it, sensed it. Or perhaps he might even...kiss her.

A gasp caught in her throat.

But the serving woman arrived with the wine and the tension suddenly dissolved. She handed one cup to Min and toyed with the other without putting it in front of Blake.

Turning her back on Min, she said to him, "Staying in the country long this time, Handsome?" She leaned one hand on the table and perched her rear on the edge.

Blake sat back and regarded her. "Not if I can help it."

"We've missed you."

Min couldn't see the woman's face but she could hear the smile in her voice. The sort of smile a woman gave to a man she wanted to kiss. Min had caught herself smiling at Blake that way earlier when she arrived at the White Swan. He'd taken her by surprise with his own genuinely welcoming smile that she couldn't help but return it.

"I didn't realize my charms were so appreciated here, Beth," he said with a lop-sided grin. A grin. An actual grin. He'd never cast one of those in Min's direction.

"We most certainly appreciate your...charms," Beth purred. "Every inch of them."

Blake shot Min a glance. She took a sip of wine to hide her blush behind the cup. She might not have experience with carnal relations but she knew what Beth was really referring to because as far as she had seen, Blake was not a charming sort of man. Too embarrassed to reveal her flushed face, Min slowly drained the entire cup.

"If you don't mind," he said to Beth, "I'm in the middle of conducting some business."

Beth looked at Min over her shoulder. "Business?" She studied Min with one raised eyebrow. "I'd never have known. She doesn't look the type."

"Not that kind of business." Blake chuckled low in his throat. "Now go, wench, before I call your father over."

Beth hopped off the table with a *humph*. She finally handed Blake his cup then left but not before giving him a wink.

"A friend of yours?" Min asked. "Or do you just come here often?"

"Often enough," he said, expression blank.

"When you're in London?" she probed. It seemed like the perfect opportunity to get to know him better. After all, if they were to continue with this ruse, she needed to at least know his full name.

He lifted one shoulder.

Min decided to take a more direct approach. "Are you a merchant adventurer?"

"Something like that."

She rolled her eyes. "You're being very evasive. Care to tell me your real name since you know mine? If we're to be business partners of sorts, it would help."

"So you can find me if I run off with your four pounds?"

"I trust you."

"You shouldn't."

"Why? Are you going to leave the country with my money?"

"I don't need your money, Min." The corners of his mouth

lifted with the hint of a smile. *Not* a grin. Not even close. "But you still shouldn't trust me. You know nothing about me."

She threw up her hands. "That's because you won't tell me anything!"

He stared long and hard at her then eventually said, "Robert Blakewell. I travel a lot but my home is here in London."

"Oh." She hadn't expected him to tell her anything let alone give her a name. But, in essence, he'd still managed to tell her nothing about himself.

She wasn't sure how much more she wanted to know. When Pandora opened the box, she'd unleashed all sorts of trouble. But curiosity ate at Min's insides. There was so much she suddenly felt desperate to know. Who were his family? Why did he travel? Was he married or betrothed? Too many questions, so she decided to start with the most important.

"Does your reason for agreeing so easily to help me have anything to do with your wanting to harm Lord Hawkesbury?"

He sat very still. Not even his chest rose or fell with his breathing. After a long, agonizing moment in which she thought he would produce his hidden blade and use it on her, he finally said, "Rest assured, I do not wish Lord Hawkesbury ill. If I did, I wouldn't have bothered to join his company, I would have simply accosted him in the street."

That made a certain amount of sense. But it still didn't explain why he so readily agreed to help her. "Why are you so eager to be a part of the company? What's in it for you?"

His hand flattened on the table, his fingers spread apart. Long, strong fingers. "The secret is not mine to tell," he said.

That was it? How was she supposed to get an answer out of him when he showed such loyalty to an unknown person or persons?

"Now that you know my name," he said before she could find an appropriate response or formulate another question, "tell me about yours. It's unusual."

"Minerva was the Roman goddess of wisdom, medicine and science among other things. According to ancient myth, she invented numbers and musical instruments." She shrugged. "It was my father's choice. He's a scientist."

His head inclined sharply. "Interesting."

She shrugged again. "Not really."

"You don't find science interesting? But we live in a fascinating time with so many discoveries being made and theories developed. And you're the daughter of a scientist..." He leaned forward again and Min's breath momentarily lodged in her throat. Was he trying to get closer to her?

"Perhaps that's why I don't find it interesting," she said. "It's like hearing a piece of music played on a harpsichord. It sounds beautiful and yet if you take the instrument apart, you're left with nothing but pieces of wood and string. I can appreciate the harpsichord as a whole but I don't really care to see how it works."

"You prefer poetry and plays to science."

"There is passion in poetry. A skilled poet can take an audience to new places, heighten their emotions and make them wonder. Poetry is powerful, especially in the form of a play that everyone from a laborer to a nobleman can enjoy."

"Passion," he repeated flatly. There was nothing flat in his eyes however. They grew deeper and darker as they watched her. "I see what you mean. But you are suggesting your father has no passion for his work."

That wasn't fair. He didn't know her father. He didn't know that passion was all Sir George had and that it had become an all-consuming monster since his failure. It was even blinding him to the errors in his own work lately. "There is such a thing as too much passion."

He arched an eyebrow. "But not in poetry?"

She didn't understand him. Not at all. Was he teasing her? "We were supposed to be talking about the changes to my play. You seem to be avoiding telling me what they are." She picked up her cup to take a sip but found it empty. She put it down again without calling that serving woman. There were worse things than empty wine cups.

"I don't avoid," he said.

"Well then?"

He smiled that smile again, the one that barely lifted the

corner of his mouth and certainly didn't reach his eyes. Slow, lazy. Wicked. "Style wants more carnality."

Min choked on air. "Carnality?" she managed to squeak out.

"Kissing. Ribald jests. Innuendo. That sort of thing."

Innuendo. Ribaldry. *Kissing*. "But it's not that kind of play! It's a love story, not a...a bawdy house show."

"I thought you might have trouble with it."

That took her by surprise more than the mention of kissing, and for some reason it rankled. "You did? But...how?"

He tipped his head to the side. "From your trusting nature for one thing, and your view of the world." His gaze searched hers with something akin to...wonder? No, that couldn't possibly be right. Blake didn't seem like the sort of man who *wondered* about things, he simply *knew*. "You see it through fresh eyes brimming with possibility," he said, soft and distant.

She blinked. Was this his way of charming her?

Or was he trying to tell her he thought her an innocent? Someone who'd not experienced real life but had been sheltered and coddled and kept far away from the world's ills.

"I'm not a child." The petulance in her response destroyed her argument. She sighed. Perhaps Blake was right and she was being petty to deny it—she *was* an innocent when it came to matters between men and woman. Carnal matters.

That truth made her want to hide far away from this man. He saw too much. Knew too much. Thrilled her too much. She might not remain an innocent if she stayed in his presence for too long.

But she couldn't hide, not from him and not from the way he made her feel. Her heart wanted to leap out of her chest even as her head wanted to bury itself in the ground.

"You're right," she moaned into her hands. "How am I going to write about kissing when, when..."

"When you've never kissed anyone?"

Lord, it was so *humiliating*. She was twenty-two and had not even teased a peck from the stable boy before her father had let him go. Her female cousins had all experimented with the servant lads before they met their husbands. It was how things were done. But Min had always been too busy studying and the experience had passed her by.

She said nothing. She couldn't admit he was right or ask him to show her what a kiss felt like, even though it was all in the name of research for her play.

His eyes darkened to the color of a stormy sky as his gaze locked on her mouth. "Do you think if someone kissed you that you could write about it?"

"Well...yes." Perhaps she could ask Ned—.

All thoughts of Ned were sucked from her mind when Blake leaned across the table and cupped her face in both his hands.

"For the betterment of the play, you understand." His low rumbling voice sent vibrations chasing across her skin.

And then he kissed her.

Blake knew it was one of the most foolish ideas he'd ever had. She went as rigid as a pole. Her lips were tight beneath his, still shaped in the perfect 'Oh' of her shock. She didn't reach for him, didn't sigh against him, didn't even close her eyes. It was like kissing a rock.

Then, slowly, the rock began to crumble. She closed her eyes and murmured something he didn't quite hear. Her lips softened and opened to him and he took that as a sign to deepen the kiss. She tasted of wine, smelled like lavender, felt like a Goddess.

He knew he should stop, should consider her reputation. They were in a public place for God's sake. He hadn't meant to take it this far. It was supposed to be a simple kiss, a peck on her lips to loosen her, shake up the prudish little miss.

But there was nothing simple about it. Not for him. Heat curled through his body, licking and teasing him until it threatened to swallow him whole. The familiar ache in his groin didn't surprise him either but the other ache, low in his belly and higher up beneath his ribs, did.

He'd worry about that later. He didn't want the kiss to end. Not ever. Right now, in this moment, everything felt right with the world.

That was something to cherish.

Somewhere, someone moaned. He pressed a hand to the back of her head, and—

She pulled away.

He silently swore, not just because she'd broken the kiss but because cold, hard realization began to sink in. He'd just done a very foolish thing. He was going to pay for that kiss. He was certain of it.

"What was that?" she mumbled.

"A kiss." He spoke low, to keep as much control over his voice as he could.

"But...your tongue, it...was, er..."

"Inside your mouth?" He smiled. He couldn't help it. She was so sweet and—.

Sweet! Christ. Too much bloody poetry.

"Well, yes," she said, turning scarlet.

"That's how men and women kiss." He snorted. "Don't worry, it means nothing."

Her big gray eyes blinked slowly. It hadn't meant nothing to her. He could see her digesting her feelings, thinking over what that kiss *did* mean. Could she see from his face what it meant to him? That it had affected him more than any simple kiss should?

Bloody hell he hoped not.

"No one saw," he said, forcing himself to look away from those big eyes and swollen lips. "Your reputation is safe."

"Oh. My reputation. Yes. Good."

He stood up. "I have to go." Somewhere. Anywhere.

"Wait!" She stood too, reached for him, but he pulled away before she could touch him. She looked down at her outstretched hand then pulled it in to her chest as if he'd bitten it. "There was something I wanted to ask you. If only I could remember what." She frowned. "Oh, yes, that's it! Why are you helping me? And I want an answer this time."

Of all the questions she could have asked, *that* was the last one he expected. She was as tenacious as one of his brother's hounds on the scent of a hare. "I had nothing better to do this week," he said.

She crossed her arms. "You are *not* the sort of man who does things without a reason. And I don't want to hear excuses about other people's secrets this time."

He was wrong. She was much too perceptive to be an innocent. "Let's just say I have my own reasons for wanting to be a part of Lord Hawkesbury's Men. Reasons I'd rather keep to myself."

Her eyes narrowed as if she would challenge him. "Whatever it is," she said, "I want nothing to do with it."

"Good, because you will have nothing to do with it."

"And it better not jeopardize my play."

"It won't." Hopefully she didn't hear the heartbeat of hesitation before he spoke.

"Good." She tossed her head. "Now, I have to go home. I can't sit around kissing you all day no matter how much you enjoyed it."

Amused, he watched her leave, her skirts swishing from side to side with the sway of her hips. Definitely too perceptive to be an innocent.

And far too tempting.

CHAPTER 6

Min wasn't sure how she got home but somehow she managed it despite leaving her senses back at the inn. And a great deal more.

Blake had kissed her! Not just a friendly peck but really kissed her. Deeply, and so very thoroughly.

He'd wanted that kiss just as much as she had. She might never have experienced a kiss before, but she knew what desire felt like and could see it in his smoldering eyes and feel it in the urgency of his mouth. He'd wanted the kiss and he'd wanted her.

It was enough to make a girl swoon. Fortunately Min wasn't the swooning type and made it to the doorstep of her Knightridge Street house without doing anything more foolish than stumble over a sleeping dog in her absent-mindedness. She did, however, slump against the door once it was closed behind her and draw as much air into her body as she could. She seemed to need a great deal more of it after Blake had stolen her breath.

Jane found her like that. At her quizzical frown, Min made up an excuse about needing to lie down. It wasn't far from the truth. But what she really wanted to do was lock herself away and write while her emotions were still raw. Words and phrases jostled each other for space inside her head. If she didn't write them down soon something inside her might burst and she'd really need to lie down after all.

"But yer supper is waitin'," Jane protested.

"Is it that time already?"

"Aye. Yer father doesn't know yet." Jane gave Min a wink. "Shall I tell him his supper and his daughter are here?"

"No. Give him his supper by all means, but I have a headache. I think I'll retire early." She couldn't eat. Couldn't even face food. She had more important things to think about, like what would have happened if that kiss had been performed somewhere more private. Would Blake have taken it further, shown her other pleasures? Would he have endeavored to teach her what happens between a man and a woman who desire each other? For the betterment of the play of course.

The play. Yes, the play! All thoughts of Blake were swept aside. She had some writing to do. Now, thanks to that kiss, she knew where the tension could be heightened between the amorous lovers and how her heroine would feel afterwards. She even had a ribald jest for the clown. Blake's teaching methods had proved rather enlightening.

She sat at her desk in the small chamber adjoining her bedroom and pulled out the smudged and creased pages of her play. She read from the beginning, keeping Blake's kiss and her own reaction to it in mind. Not a difficult thing to do at all.

* * *

MIN SAT up with a start and squinted into the sunshine streaming through her study window. She was still at her desk wearing the previous day's clothes. Jane knelt by the fireplace, humming a tune as she added kindling.

"Is it morning?" Min asked. She stretched her neck from side to side and flexed her achy, ink-stained fingers. They weren't the only body parts suffering from sitting at her desk all night. Her legs tingled with numbness and she couldn't even feel her rear despite all the padding of her underskirt and cushioned chair.

"Aye," the maid said, adding more wood. "Thought it was time you rose. Yer father's been askin' for you." She turned to her mistress and smiled. "You might want to wash yer face first. You've got ink all over one cheek."

Min yawned and shuffled the pages. The revisions were done and they were quite good. They certainly made the play stronger. That kiss had proved useful.

Warmth spread through her, thawing her extremities and easing the aches. She smiled. Useful didn't adequately describe Blake's kiss at all.

Jane frowned at her. "You all right, Mistress?"

"Most certainly. Why?"

"It's just that you look...distracted."

Min quickly sobered. "My play is finished. That's all."

"I thought you finished a few days ago."

"I did. But there were some changes I had to make at the behest of the manager of Lord Hawkesbury's Men."

Jane's eyes widened. "He read yer play? M'lady, that's wonderful! But..." the frown returned, "does he know *you* wrote it?"

"That," Min said, rising and stretching her back, "is not your business."

"I know, I know," Jane grumbled. "I'm just a servant." She stood and ran her dust cloth across the top of the mantelpiece. Min braced herself for a lecture but none came. "When you're ready to tell me the truth," Jane said, "you know where I am."

Jane had worked for the Peabodys since the death of her husband nearly twenty years earlier. Ever since Min's mother died, she'd taken it upon herself to care for Min, and had kept the household in better shape than could be expected of a single servant. She knew everything there was to know about Min. Knew when she went out, came home, who she had been with, what she ate and what play she was currently working on. Although illiterate, she enjoyed listening to Min read her sonnets and plays aloud and had even acted out the parts on occasion.

Min adored her. But there came a time when a girl had to have secrets. And Blake was her secret. She wouldn't share him with anyone.

"Have a lad run this down to the White Swan on Gracechurch Street for me," Min said, gathering up the play. She tied a ribbon around the pages to secure them and gave the package to Jane. She then dug into in her leather pouch, the one item she owned that wasn't wearing thin because she hardly used it, and produced two coins. "Give him a penny now and promise him another when he returns." As she handed Jane the coins, she caught sight of the sun out her window. It was well above the rooftops. "It's very important that he go quickly."

She watched the maid leave and a solid lump of mixed emotions settled into her stomach. That was her original copy of the play. Her heart was in those pages, and a large slice of her soul. If the new lines didn't work...

But they would. She was certain of it.

Almost.

Soon Style and the other players would add the new lines to their own copies which would have been written overnight. Each copy would be rolled up into a small scroll to be kept in the player's palm during the performance so he could refer to it as needed. Usually a scrivener prepared them but with the time constraints, it would be every man for himself.

Jane returned when Min had finished freshening up and helped her to dress. She chose a black velvet bodice with green vine leaves embroidered across it, a plain black skirt and matching gown to wear over the top. The outfit was usually kept for special occasions but Min felt like wearing it today. After all, seeing her play performed for the first time *was* special.

"If you insist on wearin' yer best," Jane said as she helped Min into the gown, "then I insist on doin' yer hair all nice. Curls, I think." She sounded annoyed.

Min sat at her table and held up her small looking glass. "But it'll be hidden beneath a hat," she said, glowering at the dark circles under her eyes.

"Well then you'll have to wear a caul. Yer black one will go nicely with the clothes and shows a good lot of hair. You'll look quite fetchin' for—." She broke off and clamped her lips shut.

"For whom? I'm not meeting anyone, Jane. Certainly not a gentleman if that's what you're thinking."

An image of Blake came to mind, his simmering dark looks contrasting with his bright blue eyes. The wide shoulders, the capable hands and kissable mouth. No, not a gentleman in the chivalric sense of the word. No gentleman would avoid questions about himself the way Blake did. And no gentleman would have kissed a young maiden in full view of the patrons at a busy inn. Nor had any gentleman Min ever met made her stomach flip or her mind scatter every time she thought about him.

"That's a shame," Jane said around a mouthful of hairpins.

"As a matter of fact, I'm going to see the first performance of my play at the White Swan today."

Jane gasped and the pins fell onto the rushes. "Today! So soon! Oh, dear child," she kissed the top of Min's head, "to see *Marius and Livia* on the stage! I wonder who'll play Marius. Not Roger Style, he's too old." She bent and picked up the pins. "Ooh, that lovely new man would be perfect. What's his name?"

"Henry Wells?"

"Yes, him. He's got such nice shoulders. Such stage presence. He'd make a glorious Marius." Her gaze locked with Min's reflection. "Are you goin' to the inn alone?"

"Yes."

"Yer father won't approve."

"If he finds out."

Jane thrust a pin hard into Min's hair. "It's likely he won't notice." That was the maid's way of saying she wouldn't tell him.

Min smiled and Jane smiled back at her in the looking glass. "There's always Ned," the maid said.

"Yes." Min sighed. "There's always Ned." That was Ned—always there.

Jane worked silently on Min's hair until the final pin slid into place. "Lovely. Now, off with you downstairs. Yer father's waitin'."

"I thought you said he wouldn't notice."

"Don't fret. Go on, off. I've got work to do up here." She began to stab spare pins into the pincushion but Min put a hand over hers.

"I'll do it later. I'm sure you've more pressing work to do."

The maid sucked in her top lip. "Well, there is dinner to prepare..."

"Go then. I'll be with you soon to help."

"You'll do no such thing. Not in that dress. I don't want either of us to be up all night cleanin' it." She chuckled at her mistress when Min put her hands on her hips and attempted a glare. Jane never did take her very seriously.

Sir George met Min at the bottom of the stairs. He held his arms out and she stepped into them, reluctantly at first. Then she drew in his familiar inky smell and hugged him tighter. She hated arguing with him.

"I've been waiting for you to come down," he said, holding her by her upper arms and smiling.

"I'm sorry I slept late."

"Never mind that. Are you well?"

"Quite well, thank you. I did have a headache last night," she said, remembering her lie to Jane the night before, "but it's gone now."

"Good, good. Jane tells me you missed supper. Come, it's warmer in the kitchen. We can sit and talk while she prepares dinner."

"Talk? About your work?" Perhaps now was the time to tell him his latest theory needed more thought or to be entirely discarded altogether if he didn't want to become a laughing stock. Any more than he already was, that is.

"Whatever you want to talk about," he said. "I must say, my dear, you look pretty today." He held her at arm's length and studied her. Pride filled his eyes and tears filled Min's. She hated arguing with him. She would try harder in future to be more considerate. "That gown does suit your coloring."

Her father noticed what she wore? Either the moon had turned blue or he was still feeling guilty about their little argument the day before last. It had been a long time since he'd admired her. Certainly not in the past year.

They shared some bread and cheese in the kitchen while Jane bustled around them preparing the midday dinner. They spoke about a new idea he was pursuing—one that Min encouraged because it had to be better than his last one—and a copy of a map he wanted to acquire if only he had the funds. It was mostly a one-sided discussion, but Min didn't mind.

She was reminded of how they used to be, talking comfortably about ideas and worldly matters. She might not know as much as her father about the sciences of geography, mathematics and astrology but she knew enough to join in the discussion. In some ways, it was her lesser knowledge that pushed him further. By asking pertinent questions, he had to explain his work which often led to his own deeper understanding or the generation of more ideas. She wasn't sure how their partnership worked, but it seemed important to his process to discuss his theories with her.

It was important for her as well. They'd talked like this for many years, since her mother died. It was familiar, and if she was being honest with herself, interesting, despite what she'd said to Blake the day before. Not exhilarating like her poetry, with its blinding need to write down the precise word and get the story onto the page before it vanished, but thought-provoking.

A knock at the front door interrupted their discussion and Jane went to answer it. "Mr. Taylor is here, Sir," she said on her return. "To see the mistress. He's waitin' in the parlor."

Sir George peered down his long nose at Min. "That's the second time this week the Taylor lad has stopped by."

Actually it was the third but Min had told Jane to tell Ned she was out the last time. As she moved past her father, he stopped her with a hand on her arm.

"Do you think he...he has intentions towards you?" he whispered so Jane couldn't hear. It was pointless because Min knew Jane's hearing was superb. She could eavesdrop on conversations going on at the other end of the house.

Min shrugged. "I don't know. He's not said anything to make me believe he has marriage on his mind."

"What about... has he tried... something..." Her father stretched his neck as if his ruff itched.

"Like kissing me?"

"Yes!" he blurted out along with a breath. "Well, has he?" His face darkened. "Because I'll need to have a word with him if he has."

"No, he hasn't," she said, also blushing. The discussion was a little embarrassing, especially coming on the heels of her kiss with Blake. Even worse, her father noticed her reddening face.

"Ah," he said, with a fatherly nod and a grim set to his mouth. "I see. Well, I think it's time I find out what his intentions are."

"No! Not yet. Please. Don't pressure him. Perhaps he's not ready to reveal his intentions."

"But if they're dishonorable..."

"They're not. I'm sure of it. You know Ned. He'd never do anything to hurt me or my reputation." Not like Blake. The rogue hadn't given her reputation a second thought when he kissed her.

Min smiled her sweet-daughter smile and Sir George's expression softened. "Very well. But if this goes on for much longer, I *will* be talking to him. I need to know what he wishes to do with you." Min had thought that part was obvious. "Because I'll still need you here after you are wed," he went on. "There's no one else I trust to write up my notes."

Min squeezed his hand, feeling like an imposter—she lived with her father now and yet she hadn't written out his latest notes. She couldn't imagine the situation changing once she was wed. "I'm sure Ned wouldn't mind if I visited every day."

The clunk of a pot thumping down on the table made Min jump. She turned to see Jane glaring at her.

"What is it?" Min asked her.

"Nothin'," the maid said without looking away. But her unspoken words were written clear across her face—*It sounded like you're thinking about marrying Ned*. Min didn't need to hear it said aloud.

"I might," Min said as if Jane had spoken. "I haven't made up my mind."

"About what, my dear?" her father asked.

"About...my old hat. I haven't decided if I like it enough to keep wearing it or not."

"Very well," Jane said. She stacked a smaller pot inside the first without taking any care and the sound of copper banging copper reverberated around the kitchen. "But the hat isn't really *you* is it, m'lady? It lacks...fun."

"Fun?" Sir George said, looking from one to the other. "A hat's a hat isn't it?" Both women shook their heads. He shrugged. "I suppose I'm not really qualified to talk about these things."

"But my old hat is reliable," Min said to Jane. "And nice. There'll never be any surprises with that hat. It'll never fall off, for example, and disappear."

"It's dull," Jane said. She heaved both pots into her arms and cradled them like a fat child against her chest. "And you, my girl, require a hat that matches you in wit. Somethin' suited to yer spirited nature. If you can find that kind of hat, it'll never fall off and disappear." She dropped both pots onto a shelf.

Min winced at the noise. Sir George shook his head. "I think Jane's in one of her moods," he said under his breath to Min. "Although the Lord only knows why talk of your old hat would set her off. Come, let's see what the Taylor lad wants."

Min was only too happy to oblige. She wasn't sure what had set Jane off either but it certainly wasn't anything to do with a hat. Didn't she like Ned? How could she not? Everyone liked Ned. He was a personable man with an easy, polite manner. He was also quite handsome, if a little portly. And rich—his father was one of the premier merchants in the City. His business was doing exceedingly well by all accounts. Most women would be happy at the attention he paid them. Min was.

Was. In the past. She had once thought about marrying Ned. It would be a good match on both sides. He would acquire a knighted father-in-law, a step towards becoming a gentleman himself, and she would gain financial security.

But that mercenary attitude had fallen by the wayside some time ago. She simply couldn't marry for money. Well, in all honesty she probably *could,* just not to a man who thought the theatre was a breeding ground for the devil's minions and therefore a place to avoid at all costs. Jane was right as usual.

Besides, how could she think about Ned in *that* way after Blake had taken her face in his hands and kissed her. The kiss had been intense, fierce and bold.

Passionate.

She'd written the word many times but never known the raw power of it until yesterday. Never known that passion could fill a person's soul with desire so hot it burned. Never known the sheer joy it brought, the heady, drunken pleasure generated by a single heart-stopping kiss.

There was nothing polite or safe about the kiss or about Blake. That in itself should have sent her running to Ned. She should want someone reliable like him, someone gentle and thoughtful, open and honest. But, shockingly, she didn't. She yearned for more of Blake's kisses.

The realization sent a jolt through her. Until recently she'd never have thought she wanted anything other than her old hat, the one she used for every occasion because it went with almost every outfit. But the hat had lost its usefulness. Oh dear, that seemed so utterly vain and selfish. But she couldn't help thinking that way. She wanted, *needed*, a new hat with every ounce of her awakened flesh. She would do almost anything to see how it looked on her, how it *felt*. Just for a few minutes. A few delicious, sinful, glorious minutes.

Min shook off the tingles that washed down her spine. She had to concentrate on Ned for now, not Blake. The sooner he left, the sooner they could dine and she could go see her play.

And Blake.

She entered the parlor and smiled a greeting at Ned, standing near the unlit fireplace. The room was cool, made even more so by its lack of furniture and hangings—only two uncushioned chairs occupied the space in front of the hearth and a single embroidered cloth, made by her mother, hung on the largest wall. Everything else had been sold.

Ned bowed, his tall hat slipping a little over his forehead. He pushed it back. "It's good to see you, Sir George, Minerva. The weather has turned a little cool of late, don't you think? I dare say winter will be upon us soon."

After half an hour of banal small talk, Sir George made his excuses and returned to his study, leaving Min with Ned, all polite conversation exhausted. Surely dinner must be ready soon.

She smiled at him but glanced past his shoulder to the open door. Where could Jane be? Couldn't she see she needed assistance? Jane, the one who was vehemently against the dull hat, had deserted her too.

"Are you listening, Minerva?" Ned asked, dipping his head into her line of sight. "I asked what you were going to do this afternoon."

"I'm going to the theatre," she said without thinking.

"The theatre! Minerva, are you sure that's a good idea?" His pinched mouth told her he didn't think so.

She didn't want to get into a discussion on the respectability of theatres with Ned. She would probably lose. Ned, like her father and most City officials, worried about the effect the theatres had on Londoners. Granted, a large congregation of people in one place could lead to scuffles, sometimes violent ones, but they were rare. And being winter, the packed audience hardly ever spread the plague, only a little fever here and there. Besides, Min wouldn't be in the pit where London's poorest stood shoulder to shoulder, breathing down each other's necks. She would be safe in the gallery. Really, the playhouses and inn-yards that sometimes acted as theatres weren't all *that* bad.

"I know you enjoy writing your little plays," Ned went on quickly, "but can you not simply do it for your own amusement? Is it really necessary to see others being performed?" He stood by the fireplace, one hand resting on the bare mantelpiece, the other spread over the belly of his crimson peascod doublet. The stiff-ened pod-shaped garment might be the height of fashion but it only served to make his waist seem disproportionately round.

Min got to her feet but stopped her tongue from saying the first thing that came into her head just in time. Ned was completely without guile in asking his question. He honestly thought she should be satisfied with writing for herself. Poor, silly Ned didn't have any idea what drove her to the theatre so regularly. He didn't know what kept her up at night, feverishly writing until her hand cramped and her eyes went dry.

"What?" he said, frowning. "Why are you looking at me like you feel sorry for me?"

"Because I do." She laughed and kissed his cheek on impulse.

He suddenly took her by the arms and held her close but not hard. "Why?" His breath was hot on her nose. He smelled of cheese.

"Ned," she said, still smiling as she stepped out of his grasp, "a play is *supposed* to be performed. You cannot read it to yourself and think you understand it completely. A play's soul can only be captured by players, with props and costumes and sound effects that reverberate around the uppermost galleries. And most of all, a play needs an audience who respond to it with tears or laughter or a sharp intake of breath. It is not just my own play I would like to see performed. One day," she added because she wasn't prepared to tell him her secret. Not yet. "I wish I could see all the plays. Oh Ned, *do* try and see one put on by a good company. You might find you enjoy it. Lord Hawkewbury's Men are—."

"I have been once." He sniffed and returned to his earlier repose with one hand on the mantelpiece and the other resting on his belly. It looked practiced and rather ridiculous. "Five years ago. It was a comedy but wasn't very funny. Several men in the audience, apprentices I suspect, started a fight before it had even finished. I barely escaped with my purse and my life."

"Well I've never seen any trouble," Min lied.

He made a clucking sound in the back of his throat as if he didn't believe her. "Doesn't your father disapprove?"

"Only if he wishes me to write up his notes instead." It was the truth, but not all of it. She bit the inside of her cheek and hoped he wouldn't ask her who chaperoned her to the theatre. She really didn't want another lie on her conscience.

"My poor Minerva," he said, coming closer. A strange look, intense and yet soft, descended over his features. It was most disconcerting and Min backed away until her legs hit a chair.

With nowhere else to go, she sat down and hoped he wouldn't draw any nearer. "What do you mean?"

"Your father works you too hard. You shouldn't have to be locked away in your room as if you were his apprentice. It's not...normal."

She pushed to her feet. "I am not locked away and I do it voluntarily. Father needs me."

"That may be, but you shouldn't *have* to do it. When we are wed, you won't need to work so hard. You can put away your inkwells—."

"Wed?" She sat down again. This was all happening too

suddenly. She wasn't ready. She hadn't prepared a proper speech. She wasn't even sure what her answer should be. He *was* quite rich. And safe...

He knelt before her and took one of her hands in both of his. They were warm and damp. "Perhaps in the spring..." When she opened her mouth and nothing came out, he went on, "I adore you, Minerva. You're everything I could ever want in a wife. Gentle, honest, loyal and pretty." He wrung her knuckles as if trying to smooth them down. "A humble merchant like myself could go far with a wife like you. Who knows, I might even become lord mayor one day." He laughed, loud and hollow.

She gave a weak smile in return. "But...this is so sudden. I had no idea you harbored such feelings..." Oh dear, another lie. She knew what he wanted from her. She'd always known, she just hadn't expected him to do anything about it. Ned had been around for years, always there, constant and steady, showing no more interest than was acceptable. Until now. Why?

"Dearest Minerva." He shifted his weight and his knee let out a resounding *crack* of protest. He winced.

"Do get up, Ned, I have no wish to hobble you."

He rose, drawing her up with him. "My father is dying Minerva."

Ah, so that was why. "I'm so sorry."

"Don't be. He's been ill for some time, it will be a relief from the pain." He looked away, blinked once, then returned to the conversation with a shake of his head. "On his death I will inherit the shops, part ownership of a ship, the house and two other leased properties. I'll be in need of a capable wife to manage my home. A loving, caring woman from a distinguished family with a reputation as pure as snow. Like you."

Oh dear. Would he revoke his offer if he found out that her reputation had been compromised? She withdrew her hand from his and wiped her palms down her skirt. "Ned—."

"No, don't answer now. Think about it first."

"I will."

"Keep in mind that I shall be incredibly rich upon Father's death. You have no idea how much money he has. You can buy all the beautiful new clothes and hats you want." He cast a discerning mercer's eye over her velvet gown. It might be one of her good ones but it was still showing signs of long use. "There'll be no more old things for you. No more working your poor fingers to the bone writing up your father's work. I'll be able to keep both of you in comfort. He won't have to worry about his silly scientific hocus pocus again." He smiled. She managed a smile too even though something inside her shriveled. "I'll discuss the terms with your father another day. I must return home now." He bent and kissed her dryly on the cheek. "Soon, my sweet. Soon."

Min's jaw dropped as she watched him leave and she stayed like that until Jane entered. "You look like you've seen a ghost," she said, waving a hand in front of Min's eyes to draw her attention away from the door. "What is it?"

Min blinked. "Do you know, Jane, you and Ned have a lot in common?"

The maid screwed up her nose. "Is this yer way of telling me I have bad breath? I know I eat a lot of cheese—."

"No. You both think I need a new hat."

"Ah." Jane smiled knowingly. "And what do you think, m'lady? Do you think you need a new one?"

"I'm not sure. But I think perhaps I'll try one on this afternoon, just to see if it fits."

CHAPTER 7

It was a good play. Very good. It would have been better with a death or maiming but at least it had a sword fight. A somewhat pathetically acted swordfight, all slow thrusts and predictable parries. Limp swordsmanship aside, Blake found himself riveted to the action on stage. He wasn't the only one. The audience hardly breathed as they listened to the players' every word. Min really knew how to write a story that appealed to nobles and laborers alike. She was turning out to be quite a surprise, in more ways than one.

That kiss for instance. How could one woman appear so innocent and yet steal the air from his chest with a single kiss?

Beginners luck. It must be.

"Move it," Freddie said, pushing past Blake as he came off stage. The boy lifted his Roman dress, revealing pale reed-thin legs, and raced to the back of the tiring house behind them where the costumes hung on pegs arranged in the order they'd be worn and props were laid out on a table—Cupid's bow and quiver, Mercury's wings and sundry short swords and shields.

Blake held back from clipping the lad over the ear. He didn't want to cause a scene. He checked the prompt book instead. Freddie was due back on stage soon dressed in a boy's costume. A boy playing a girl pretending to be a boy. Not exactly original but Min had made it unique with clever phrases and intriguing characters.

The scene ended and both the Style brothers came off stage, dressed in patrician togas. "Where to now?" Roger asked Blake. He ran a finger down the plot pinned at the entrance to the tiring house. "Ah, the heavens," he said, answering his own question.

The brothers joined the other players at the back of the now cramped tiring house just as Wells joined Blake. "Getting the hang of bookkeeping?" he asked.

"I'm managing," Blake said.

Wells laughed and clapped him on the shoulder. "Good man. If only all our bookkeepers had been as reliable as you. Some of them couldn't even read," he said, still smiling. Always smiling. It was damned annoying.

"There's a woman back there," Blake said. "A comely one." He looked for her but couldn't see past the throng of players and props cluttering the tiring house.

"Alice Croft, John Croft's daughter," Wells said. "Why? You want her? I warn you, she can be prickly."

Blake ignored him. "You get many women back here?"

Wells shrugged. "Sometimes. Style doesn't like too many people clogging up the heart, as he calls the tiring house. Why? You want one?"

Blake snorted softly. "Do you remember any in particular in the last few months? Any that have caught your attention?"

"Any what? Oh, you mean women." He stopped smiling. "No. Why? What's this got to do with me?" His voice rose at the end of his sentence and his Adam's apple bobbed furiously. "Er, I've got to go, that's my cue." He launched himself through the curtain onto the stage beyond to join one of the hired actors playing the hero's servant.

Freddie emerged from the depths of the tiring house and shoved past Blake. From the way he put his shoulder into Blake's chest, the lad was trying to prove a point.

Blake was in no mood for disrespectful youths. He caught him by the scruff of his costume, bunched the cotton dress in his fist and pulled the lad off his feet to look at him eye to eye.

"Put me down!" Freddie whispered loudly.

"Not until you apologize."

"But that's my cue!" The lad glanced frantically at the curtain. Wells could be heard repeating his line for the second time.

"The sooner you apologize the sooner you can go on."

"What's the hold up?" Croft came up, took one look at Blake and the boy and nodded. "I'm sure he deserved it," he said, "but we wouldn't want the play to suffer now, would we."

Blake squeezed tighter. Freddie's face turned a satisfying shade of red.

"Sorry," the lad squeaked.

Blake dropped him and the lad stumbled before getting to his feet, gasping for air and rubbing his throat.

"Next time," Blake said, "watch where you're going. Now get up there or you'll ruin my play."

The boy scampered onto the stage. Through the gap in the curtain, Blake could see Wells' face brighten with relief.

"He needed that," Croft said. His daughter Alice appeared at his side, a swathe of crimson fabric draped over her shoulder. She was tall for a woman, about Min's age or a little older with fair hair escaping from her loose cap and pins sticking out of the padding where sleeve joined bodice on her other shoulder.

"Style can't keep the lad in order," she said, nodding at the boy on stage.

"Hush, child." Her father held up his hand and glanced around. "You don't want him to hear you."

"He's not here," she said, pulling a pin out of her shoulder and sticking it into the fabric. "And you should tell him how you all feel about Freddie anyway. These mutterings behind his back aren't helping and they're growing tiresome."

"It'll be fine now we have a good play."

"I don't see how," she said, fixing an intent glare on her father. "The play has nothing to do with Freddie's behavior." She turned to Blake. "It is a very good play," she said. "If only I could sit in the audience and watch the whole thing, but I have to do this." She fingered the fabric. "It's been a while since we put on a Roman play and the general's costume needs mending."

"You're in the tiring house a lot then?" Blake asked.

"All the time." It was said with a sigh and a sideways glance at her father, but he was too busy watching Style, dressed as a god, appear from behind the painted material slung above the stage depicting the heavens.

"Then you might remember a woman coming back here about two months ago." Blake asked.

"Two months ago?" She shrugged. "We have a lot of people come backstage after the performance, many of them women. They like to meet the actors." She shook her head and stabbed another pin into the fabric. "Lord knows why, they're a pack of—."

"Alice," her father warned gently. "Enough. This company puts food on our table."

"Not much. Lord Admiral's Men pay—."

"Enough!" He glanced at Blake then back at her. "Not in front of our new bookkeeper."

"This woman's name was Lilly," Blake went on. "She's dark haired, young and..." He had an urge to say *foolish* but instead he said, "pretty."

"Lilly?" Alice's pale blue eyes narrowed. "Yes, I recall her. As I say we get a lot of women back here but she was different. Noble birth with a curious mind. She asked a lot of questions, about everyone and everything." She chuckled and the sharp planes of her face softened. She wasn't as pretty as Min but she was striking in her own way. "She certainly knew how to charm. She had every man eating out of her hand."

That sounded like Lilly. Or the way Lilly used to be. Ever since Blake's return, his sister hardly spoke. She wandered through the house like a mournful ghost, or stayed in her apartments, not letting anyone but her maid near her. Not even their mother. It was most unlike Lilly and if it hadn't been for that change in her, Blake wouldn't be so concerned.

He opened the curtain a fraction to see Wells and Freddie on stage. Could either of them have done that to her? Or was it the indomitable Lord Hawkesbury himself? The man certainly had presence enough to tempt Lilly, and to make Blake want to question him at knifepoint when he first saw him in the White Swan.

The hired actor came into view and Blake's heart skidded to a stop as a new prospect struck him. The culprit might not have been any of the regular company members at all, but someone they'd hired to fill a vacancy.

That meant the scoundrel could be long gone by now.

Blake swore under his breath. "Did she spend time with anyone in particular?" he asked Alice.

She shook her head. "I didn't take that much notice. Why?"

He shrugged. "It's not important."

"It sounds important."

He locked onto her gaze. "No. It's not."

Applause and whistles erupted from the audience and the actors rushed into the tiring house, sweaty and grinning. Wells and Freddie passed Blake without comment but the hired player stopped.

"Wonderful play," he said, pumping Blake's hand. "Simple and honest, yet fresh." He ran his fingers through the hair crowning his dome-shaped forehead. "Yes, that's it. Fresh. I've not seen anything like it. It gives me hope."

"Hope?" Blake asked, but the man simply shrugged and left.

Blake closed the prompt book and placed it in the chest. He shut the lid and locked it, pocketing the key.

Freddie was the first to emerge from the back of the tiring house a few minutes later in his non-acting attire. He gave Blake a wide berth and didn't make eye contact. Next came Edward.

"They loved it," the younger Style said, smiling. "Good job. We're all heading to the taproom to celebrate. Coming?"

"Your hired man going?" Blake jerked his head to where the players were changing behind screens. The sooner he got to questioning everyone the better. Wells was still a suspect but for some reason, he wasn't quite right. Not for Lilly. He was a little too shallow for someone as deep as his sister. And Lord Hawkesbury wasn't present so that left Blake with few options to explore at that moment.

"Shakespeare?" Edward shrugged. "Don't know. Sometimes he drinks with his poet friends instead of us. See you there."

He left. The elder Style, Wells and Shakespeare came up to him then, talking over the top of each other like three crows on a branch.

"...more life," Shakespeare was saying. He paused when he saw Blake and nodded appreciatively. "Ah, the man himself."

"We were just discussing your play," Style said. "This lad likes to think himself a poet but he's not university trained like yourself." He beamed at Blake, seeming not to care that the man he disparaged could hear every word.

"I'm not sure a university education is a requirement for writing a good play," Blake said. Min might be educated but she was either self taught or had tutors. Females didn't go to school at any level.

"Thank you," Shakespeare said, his easy smile widening. "I was just noting how great the play was. But it could do with a little more...something."

"Life experience you said," Wells added. He looked to Blake then back at Shakespeare. "But I don't think he lacks that."

"No," Shakespeare said, studying Blake in a thoughtful and slightly disconcerting way. As if he could smell the lie the way a hound sniffed out a fox. "True."

"Are you going for a drink?" Blake said. "You can tell me more about the play and where it needs work."

"Nothing of great consequence," Shakespeare said, striding alongside Blake as they crossed the inn yard to the taproom. "Just a few tweaks here and there. In fact, I wouldn't bother. Perhaps for the next one, however..."

Blake watched him without really listening. The more the man talked, the lower he slipped down Blake's list of suspects. Lilly didn't like overly conversational men. It interrupted her own flow.

He almost smiled. That wasn't fair. A lifetime of teasing his sister was a hard habit to break, even now when she was at her lowest. The truth was, his sister did talk a lot but it was always interesting, never dull. Not to him anyway.

Besides, there was nothing about Shakespeare to tempt a woman like Lilly. Too high of forehead, too wiry of body, too—

"Blake!"

It was Min. Great. Just what he needed, another complication. Lucky for her she was a damn pretty one or he'd have caught her by the scruff of her neck as he'd done with Freddie and sent her on her way.

"Well?" she said. "What did you think of the play? Did you like it? How did it go backstage? Did you manage with the prompt book?"

Min and Lilly were getting more similar by the minute. "Which of those questions do you want me to answer first?"

Beside him, Shakespeare chuckled.

"Oh, hello," Min said, noticing Blake's companion. "You played Greco, didn't you?"

"And two other parts," Shakespeare said. He bowed. "Will Shakespeare, player and poet, at your service."

Min's face lifted in a bright smile, transforming her from pretty to extraordinary. Blake blinked, slowly, trying to work out what exactly had changed in that moment. A day earlier, he'd never have expected she could look so...amazing. And yet, here she was. She laughed at something Shakespeare said, tilting her head back, exposing a slender white throat above her ruff. Her gray eyes sparkled, no mean feat in the darkening inn yard which only minutes ago had been filled with groundlings. She put a hand up, as if she was about to rest it on Shakespeare's arm, a sign that something akin to friendship had passed between them.

She never looked at Blake like that.

He blinked again and shook the thought out of his head.

"What say you, Blake?" she asked him. When he didn't answer, she added, "Shall I join you for a drink? Mr. Shakespeare here has invited me."

Shakespeare must have some mysterious quality obvious only to the female eye. That knocked Wells off the top of the list with a mighty blow.

"If you like," he said, lifting one shoulder.

She frowned. "What's wrong?"

"Nothing."

"Something's wrong. I can sense it."

Shakespeare coughed discreetly then bid them farewell. He made a hasty retreat in the direction of the taproom, dodging the servants clearing away apple cores, nuts and empty cups scattered around the inn-yard.

"Is it the play?" Min went on. "Because I was in the audience, and although they seemed to enjoy it, there was something missing. Something..." She sighed. "I don't know. I can't put my finger on it."

"Maybe you should ask Shakespeare," Blake said, hearing the sour note in his voice.

She raised one brow and amusement tugged at her lips. "Why?"

He *humphed* and crossed his arms. She thought he was jealous of the hired player. Just like a woman, she'd read too much into that kiss.

That hot, delicious, take-me-now kiss.

"Because he seems to have some ideas about how to fix the play," he said. "God knows it bored me witless listening to him."

The look on Min's face told him he'd made a direct hit. He cringed and wished, not for the first time, that he'd tempered his words. She didn't deserve his bitterness. None of this was her fault.

"I didn't mean the play was boring. It was good," he said, trying to undo some of the damage. "Very good. I liked it. A lot. I don't think it needs fixing."

Her lower lip wobbled. Christ. She was going to cry. He hated tears. Give him a horde of pirates over a crying woman any day.

"It still needs more..." She lowered her head, the rest of her sentence lost in her ruff.

"Here now." He lifted her chin so he could see her properly. Despite the tension in her face as she tried hard not to cry, a single tear slid down her cheek. He wiped it away with the pad of his thumb and found himself caressing the freckle at the corner of her mouth, the one he couldn't stop kissing last night. "It's a great play." His voice sounded far away to his own ears. "Everyone said so backstage. They keep congratulating me. My head's swelling just thinking about it."

She gave him a wobbly smile and he tried to capture it by cupping her cheek in his hand. She leaned ever so slightly into his palm and heaved a sigh. More than anything he wanted to kiss her again. But this time he drew on his self-control and found enough to stop himself doing something foolish.

He dropped his hand to his side and balled it into a fist. He looked away, anywhere but at the hurt he'd caused to swell in her eyes again.

But instead of crying, she straightened and tossed her head. "You were right before. I can write better. I think I'll go to the taproom and find Shakespeare."

He could tell by the way she spun away from him that she was angry. He blew out a breath and watched her cross the now clean inn-yard. The only sign that a play had been performed there was the stage, still erected at one end of the square courtyard.

"Women troubles?" said one of the ostlers leading a saddled horse. The traveler who'd ridden it held the door of the taproom open for Min and she disappeared inside.

"Aye," Blake muttered. "You have no idea."

CHAPTER 8

"Passion," Shakespeare said, triumphant. "That's it! That's what it needs."

Not *that* word again. Min had thought she'd infused the play with as much passion as she could squeeze out of herself, but here was someone else telling her the play didn't have enough.

The door to the inn-yard opened and Blake's bulk filled the space. He surveyed the taproom but the pause allowed everyone to regard him too. Their heads turned as one, like puppets controlled by an invisible hand. Remarkably, he seemed unaware of the attention, or perhaps he was but didn't care. Most men would puff out their chests or prance about—Ned certainly would—but Blake merely took in every face in the taproom before finally settling on Min's.

Under his inscrutable gaze, *she* was the one who swelled. She did, however, refrain from puffing out her chest.

"You'd think he would know a thing or two about passion," Shakespeare murmured in her ear.

Oh, he certainly did know about passion. It had poured out of him during that kiss they shared, as if he contained an excess of it. "Yes, you'd think so." She shrugged, trying to appear nonchalant when her heart was clanging like a blacksmith's hammer. She was still angry with Blake, but in truth, she wasn't sure why. He'd only been honest when he'd said her play still lacked something.

"Perhaps he needs help in...channeling that passion into his plays." Shakespeare watched her intently, his eyes hooded, his mouth curved in a mischievous smile. She liked the hired player. He was friendly. He was also proving to have more insight into the human spirit than anyone she'd ever met.

"Perhaps," she echoed, studying her ale and pretending she wasn't aware of Blake's every move as he sat on the other side of the table from her.

"Love," Shakespeare said.

"Pardon?"

"Love will feed his passion and that in turn will strengthen his plays."

"Oh. I see. Love." She rubbed the ink stains on her fingers even though she knew it wouldn't remove them. "I don't know anything about that."

"You will. And when you do fall in love, it'll fill your heart and soul to bursting. For a poet, that means having quill, ink and parchment ready to catch whatever falls. Not being a poet, you wouldn't have to worry about that." He nodded at her fingers. "It's a devil to remove. I use a paste of sorrel and water."

She folded her hands in her lap under the table. "I write up a lot of my father's notes."

"So I see." His smile gave nothing away.

"What about the next play?" Style's question to Blake cut through the other conversations going on around the table.

Next play? Min tried to catch Blake's attention but he wasn't looking her way.

"You'll get it soon," Blake said.

"Another romantic comedy?" Edward asked.

Blake nodded.

"As good as this one?" Style said, leaning forward.

"Better."

"Better?" Wells also leaned forward. "So it's got more of this passion everyone's talking about?"

"You mean rutting." Freddie snorted into his tankard.

Blake removed it from the lad's hands and put it down on the table with a thud, sending ale sloshing over the sides. Freddie frowned, a protest on his lips, but swallowed it when he caught Blake's loaded gaze.

"Do you want another lesson in keeping your mouth shut?" Blake said.

"No. Thanks." Freddie's nervous laughter filled the taproom. "I think I get it now."

"His next play does have more passion," Min said. Everyone turned to her, but their expressions ranged from annoyed at the interruption (Style) to intrigued (Shakespeare) to amused (Blake). "I've read it," she said.

Blake, the cur, sat back and folded his arms over his chest, a quirk of a smile on his lips. "Somewhere between writing the first one and the second, I got over my shyness," he said. "The next one contains more life experience than a ship full of sailors possess between them."

Min glared at him. "Yes," she said through a tight jaw, "you've certainly overcome your shyness."

"Practice," Shakespeare said. "I find it does wonders for my plays." He grinned at Blake. "And shyness."

"Practice what?" Min asked. "Writing?"

As one, the group stared down at the table, all except Blake who was glaring at Shakespeare, none of his earlier humor showing on his shadowed face.

The hired player's grin didn't falter as he lifted his tankard in salute. "Enjoy the practice," he said. "I'm sure your poet's soul will rejoice in it."

Blake rose, a hand on his sword hilt. Shakespeare put up his spare hand in surrender. "Simply an observation, good sir."

"Practice *what*?" Min asked. What were they talking about? And why did everyone else understand except her? It was as if she was reading a different book to them. It was most infuriating.

The door leading out to the inn-yard opened and Croft and his daughter entered the taproom. Min could just make out the bulky shapes of the galleried buildings surrounding the square yard in the late afternoon shadows beyond.

"It grows late," she said, rising. "I must go." Her father and

Jane would be growing worried, or at least Jane would be. Hopefully Sir George hadn't noticed his daughter's long absence.

Min also had to get home to fix her next play. Even though *Marius and Livia* had been a success in its first performance, Style would want her next one soon to keep the audience coming back. She had another already written but it lacked the passion everyone was so eager to see. She probably only had a day or two to improve it. To do that she needed to practice—.

Oh, *now* she understood. Shakespeare was referring to practicing rutting, as Freddie called it, to pour more emotion and real-life into her plays. Except not a single soul in that room would think Blake needed more experience at *that*. Especially not the observant Shakespeare.

The hired player looked up at her, an impish gleam in his eyes. He *knew*. Somehow he'd guessed she was writing the plays and not Blake. She swallowed and willed him not to shatter the fragile illusion she had Blake had established.

He winked. "You'd best have an escort," Shakespeare said without rising. "It grows late."

Blake stood and said nothing, as if it were accepted by everyone, including her, that he should be the one to escort her through the darkening streets to her house. She tilted her chin, about to say something to defy him, but stopped. It was their best chance to discuss the next play. He would need to know about it if he was to pretend he wrote it.

That's if Shakespeare didn't ruin everything and tell Style that Min was the real author.

"We'd best all be going soon," Alice said, sitting down anyway. "Wouldn't want the Watch to lock us up for breaking curfew."

Edward barked a laugh. "If I can't avoid the half-wit who calls himself the Watch around here then I deserve to be locked up."

Min and Blake left them and headed outside. She drew her cloak tighter about her body in a futile attempt to block out the sharp wind whipping up Gracechurch Street. Blake, she noticed, wore no cloak over his leather jerkin.

"Your four pounds," he said, handing her the coins.

She stared at the gold sovereigns nestled in her palm. She'd not seen that much money in a long time, certainly not all in one place. "Thank you." She dug out her purse through the slit in her skirt and slipped the coins inside. "I do appreciate all you've done for me," she said on a whim.

He shrugged. "I'm benefiting from this arrangement too."

"Ah, yes, the secret that is not yours to divulge. Still holding to that story?"

One corner of his mouth lifted. "Aye."

"I see. But..." She sucked in air and let it out again in a whoosh. She should just say it. Get it out and have it over with. "I was referring also to the kiss. I appreciated it too. Very much."

He began walking, fortunately taking the right direction to her house.

"Well?" she said, running to catch up.

"Well what?" he said, looking straight ahead.

"Aren't you going to say something about the kiss?"

"No."

"Why not?"

"There's nothing to say."

"Yes there is. You could thank me."

His pace quickened. She had to trot to keep astride him. "Thank you?" he said. "For what? It was just a kiss."

He was teasing her. He must be. That kiss hadn't been *just* anything. It had been the most bone-loosening experience of her life. It had turned her world on its head. And he'd enjoyed it too. She knew he had—from the way he'd pulled her closer to the way his mouth had devoured hers. If only he would admit it, they could move onward. To what came next.

"Down here," she said, stopping.

"What?"

"I live down here."

He doubled back and they turned into Knightridge Street together. She wished she'd worn a hooded cloak to lower over her face. They were still a good distance from her house and it was unlikely that anyone she knew would be venturing out at such an hour, but she still didn't want to take the risk of being recognized. Walking with a stranger as dusk fell would certainly have a few tongues wagging and she couldn't be certain that her father wouldn't hear, even though he rarely spoke to the neighbors.

"Anyway..." She cleared her throat. "Anyway, the thing is...I'd like to ask a favor."

"That's not a good idea."

"You don't know what it is yet."

"No but it's never a good idea to be in debt to anyone. Especially someone like me. I might take advantage of it one day."

Her breath quickened. "I was rather wishing you would."

"Would what?"

"Take advantage of it." She exhaled slowly. "Of me."

He stopped mid-stride and stared at her. A muscle high in his cheek pulsed. She thought he would berate her, tell her she was a fool, but he didn't. His expression, as always, was unreadable.

"No," he said and started walking again, his strides so brisk and long he was all but running.

"But—."

"No!"

"Why not?"

He stopped again and when she halted beside him, he bent to her level. In the inky light she could just make out the V of his forked brow, the flat lines around his mouth and eyes. "Respectable maidens like you are not supposed to ask favors like that. There. Is that reason enough for you?" He straightened but she gripped his upper arms before he could walk off.

His muscles flexed beneath her fingers, the tiny ripple sending a responding ache low in her belly. Imagine what those arms looked like without the many layers of fabric. Imagine what they *felt* like.

"Who said I was respectable?"

Blake threw his head back and laughed. Laughed! It was so infuriating and humiliating.

"What's so funny?" She thrust her hands onto her hips and gave him her best how-dare-you glare. It seemed to have very little effect on him. He still grinned like a half-wit.

"You are. Min, only an innocent would ask a potential lover for permission before she seduced him."

"I see. I should have simply kissed you without preamble." The way she'd wanted to. Why oh why hadn't she followed her instincts?

He wouldn't have laughed at her then.

"I just want a little life experience," she muttered. "Something to draw on to enhance my writing, to make my plays more realistic."

"Your plays. Of course." He sighed and gave a half shake of his head. "Is seeing your play performed really that important to you that you would exchange it for your virtue?" There was none of the humor in his voice now, none of the teasing. However there was another emotion simmering below the surface—she could feel it vibrating off him, but couldn't identify it.

"It's nothing to do with seeing it performed," she said. "Not really." How could she explain to someone who'd never *felt* the beauty of poetry in his soul, never known the power of the right word or phrase? "It's for perfection. I want my plays to be the best they can be. I want them to resonate with the audience in a deep and meaningful way. I want them to be remembered months, years, after the last performance. And if I can only gain perfection by exchanging something I don't really value—."

"You should," he said gruffly. "Damn it, Min, you should!" He all but shouted at her. "A woman's virtue is the most valuable commodity she possesses. And I know you say you're not rich, but doesn't that make it all the more important?" He pushed his hand through his hair. "Don't give it up so lightly, Min. Not to anyone. Especially not to me."

Did she risk telling him he was the *only* one she would give it up to?

She shivered, unnerved by the speech, lengthy by his standards. He was angry with her, she understood that, but he wasn't entirely correct. Nor had she been entirely honest with him. It wasn't simply about perfecting her plays, it was about Blake too. About scratching the deep itch that had surfaced the moment she'd seen him. But if he knew that, would he still say no?

He began walking once more. "I'll find someone else," she

said, lifting her skirts and running after him. It was easier to avoid the murky puddles when she wasn't worried about her hem.

"Good."

Her step faltered, but she continued on. "You don't mean that."

"Don't I?"

"No. You don't want me randomly kissing strangers."

He stopped again and she almost bumped into him. "Tell me there's at least one other man of your acquaintance you could turn to."

"Freddie?"

He made a sound, half grunt, half groan.

"No," she admitted, "there isn't. No one who could make me feel the way you did when you kissed me."

His blue eyes flared and his hands fisted at his sides. Apart from that small movement, he was still. Calm. "Min," he said. "Don't." No, not calm at all. There was raw need in his voice, heavy and grating.

Or was she imagining it? Perhaps he really didn't want her. Perhaps she only *thought* she'd tasted desire on his lips during that kiss.

She hated admitting it, but it was entirely possible. For a playwright, imagination was everything. Unfortunately it complicated real life.

"It doesn't have to go as far as you're thinking," she said, backing away. She'd made a big enough fool of herself, it was time to lose gracefully. Or at least grudgingly. "Just another kiss, that's all I ask. There's no need for anything else. You could simply *explain* what happens between a man and a woman after they kiss."

He lifted a brow. "What happens?"

"Well, I know *what* happens, of course." Her laugh sounded like a giddy girl's. She cleared her throat. "What I meant was, how it *feels*."

"Let me see if I understand you. You want me to kiss you then you want me to describe what...lying together feels like?"

"That's it."

"No."

"But—."

"No!" He chopped his hand through the air. "This conversation is ending. Now. Where is your house anyway?"

He sounded flustered. Surely that was a positive sign that his feelings had been thrown into at least a little bit of turmoil by her proposal.

"Blake," she said.

"What do you want now?"

She stood on her toes and reached up to cup his face. Then she kissed him. The first thing she noted was that he didn't resist her. The second thing was how pliant his mouth was considering it was usually set in such a firm line. The third thing...

There was no third thing.

When his tongue gently probed hers, she wouldn't have noticed if the surrounding buildings tumbled down around them. Nor, she was certain, would he.

She moaned against his lips and the small sound seemed to urge him on. He captured her waist, holding her against his body. There was none of the fashionable padding in his clothes. She could feel every supple movement of sinew, muscle and flesh, smell the hint of lavender bath water beneath his unmistakable scent, and feel his protruding—.

She sprang back. He wasn't wearing one of those ridiculous codpieces so that meant... Oh. Oh!

Don't look down, don't look down.

"You shouldn't have done that," he said, voice as rough as a country lane after a storm. He swore and ground the heel of his hand into his brow. Then he swore again. "Min..." He tipped his head back and stared up at the sky, a narrow stripe of gloomy grey separating the overhanging upper stories of the houses on either side of the street. "Christ."

"This is my house." He didn't acknowledge her. Perhaps her whisper hadn't been heard over the torrent of blood rushing between her ears. "Come to me tonight," she said, louder. "Second window from the right on the second floor."

He shook his head once.

"Don't worry if you see a lamp on downstairs," she persisted.

"Father sleeps little these days but if he's still awake and in his study, he's unlikely to notice you unless you jumped out of one of his books."

Again, a single shake of his head. He didn't speak, didn't look at her, didn't say yes.

Nor did he say no.

CHAPTER 9

It was the sort of offer Blake usually accepted. An eager woman, pretty and soft in all the right places, who was happy to alleviate the ache in his balls. He wasn't sure why he refused. Perhaps he'd been bewitched by an over-protective neighbor of Min's or a servant eavesdropping on their conversation. He'd certainly had the uneasy feeling of being watched.

Blake grunted into the darkness. Now *he* was the one making up fanciful stories. The irony tortured a grudging laugh from him—he'd refused the one woman in London capable of turning him into a fool who couldn't separate fantasy from real life.

Except she wasn't the only woman in *London*—he'd never met a woman like her in all the world and he'd been almost everywhere.

Refusing her had been one of the hardest things he'd ever done.

Hardest. Ha! An apt word. He was still hard even after trudging along the damp streets. He'd crossed the City from wall to wall, twice, and still felt as hot and bothered as when he'd left her. Min had a way of inveigling herself into his mind and body, making it impossible to dismiss her lightly. An hour later and he was still thinking about her fine, fragile limbs, her soft curves and pert mouth with its teasing freckle at the corner. The one he still couldn't capture with his lips, despite one hell of an attempt.

He stopped at the Cheapside conduit as the moon peered out from behind a cloud. It reminded him of the conduit at the entrance to Knightridge Street. The wide, clean thoroughfare with its grand shops was nothing like the cramped lane on which Min lived, but it seemed everything this night would remind him of her.

Had he actually refused to go to her?

He couldn't recall. He remembered the kiss. How could he not! He also remembered shaking his head afterwards. But he couldn't recall saying no. Not then. Earlier yes, but not after that kiss.

Did she still hope? Was she waiting for his return? Was she sitting at her desk, writing her play by candlelight, wearing a thin cotton shift that displayed her shapely thighs to perfection and her—.

ENOUGH! Imagination was for poets and fools. He liked to think he was neither.

He strode on. The best way to get Min out of his head was to go home. Nothing like a strong, bitter dose of family to chase away unwanted images of a delicious woman.

He found his mother in her apartments, reclining on the daybed by the fire, her eyes closed, her full skirts billowing about her like a black cloud. His sister sat beside her on a deeply cushioned chair, reading aloud from a book of poems.

"I don't think she's listening," he whispered on entering.

Lilly looked up and smiled, not the bright, full smile of her girlhood but a more whimsical one, fringed with sadness. Blake's insides clenched and not for the first time since his return he wished he knew how to put the old, carefree smile back on her face.

It was that simple desire that had sent him on his quest to infiltrate Lord Hawkesbury's men. And that, he should never forget, had led him to Min.

There he went again, thinking about Min when he had more important things on his mind.

"I can hear every word," Lady Warhurst, said without opening her eyes.

"You could have warned me she was awake," Blake said to Lilly, holding out his hand.

His sister took it and squeezed. "You should know by now that Mother hears everything, asleep or not."

Their mother sighed and sat up, touching her wig to ensure it hadn't slipped. Naturally, it was as stiff and elegant as ever. "How pleasant of you to join us," she said to Blake. "Care to tell us what you've been doing all day?"

"Not really." He sat on a stool near Lilly. "What about you?" he asked his sister. "Have you been out?"

"The afternoon turned a little too cold for my liking," she said, smoothing down her skirt which looked smooth enough to him. She wore the plainest clothing he'd ever seen her wear, with no embellishments on the russet colored skirt whatsoever and only a simple embroidered pattern in the same color covering the black bodice.

"That never bothered you before," he said.

"She wasn't with child before," Lady Warhurst said, stating the bald truth as only she could.

Lilly stiffened but said nothing.

"And that makes a woman feel the cold more?" he asked his mother. "Strange. I've never heard that complaint before."

"That's because you're a man," she said, twisting one of the many emerald rings on her fingers. "I've carried six children, borne three, and I can tell you, an expectant mother feels the chill. Your sister is wise to stay indoors and rest on a day such as this."

"I'm hardly an invalid," Lilly snapped at them both. "Nor am I incapable of speaking for myself." She turned to Blake, a hint of color in her pale cheeks. "I simply wanted to stay indoors today. I had no reason to step out. Happy?"

"No," he said. "Nor will I be until this man is caught."

She stood quickly and the book fell to the floor with a solid thud. "You make it sound like he has committed a crime."

He rose too. "Hasn't he? To get you in this way then abandon you?"

She rounded on him and he was reminded of their mother in

one of her full-blown aristocratic tempers. Her face flushed, her brow forked and her blue eyes flashed. It made a heartening change to the wan outline she'd become.

"You know nothing of it," she snapped, "so do not presume what he is like." She picked up her skirts to leave but he caught her arm, holding her in place. The glare she gave him would have set him on fire if he'd been made of straw.

"Then tell me what he is like," he said softly.

Her eyes narrowed to slits. "Why?"

"I want to know."

"So you can hunt him down like you would a Spanish galleon?" She thrust out her chin, a sure announcement of her defiance to all present. "Brother, there are several thousand men in this City. If you find him, I shall name this child after you."

He crossed his arms and bent to her level. "What if it's a girl?"

"Roberta."

"Then you'd best hope it's a boy because that's an awful name. And I *will* find the man responsible."

She couldn't have known he'd interrogated the servants about her movements during the last two months. Her maid had mentioned the visits to the theatre, in particular productions put on by Lord Hawkesbury's Men. The maid had only mentioned it because she'd been to one of their performances herself and had found it too painful to watch in its entirety. After his own attendance on that first day he'd met Min, he could well believe the maid's skepticism. She, like Blake, suspected Lilly had gone to the White Swan inn for something other than the plays.

It was time his sister learned what he knew. If only to tease out the truth from her.

"Is the father Henry Wells?" he asked.

"Who?" both women asked at once. Then the name must have registered with Lilly because she made a choking sound. "How do you know about him?" Then a gasp. "Have you been spying on me? How dare you!" She flew at him, fists raised, but he caught them before she pummeled him.

"Well?" It was Lady Warhurst, using her I'm-your-mother voice. The one that had always put a halt to their childhood games when they became too boisterous. "*Have* you been spying on her?"

"I didn't want to," he said to Lilly. "But you wouldn't tell me anything."

"Because I knew you would try to confront him. I don't *want* you to confront him!" She pulled out of his grip to swipe at the tears dripping down her cheeks. "Damnation, Robert, this is none of your business."

"Lilly! Language," their mother chided.

Dark, foul anger welled deep within Blake and he all but spewed it over his sister. "It is very much my business. You are my sister and therefore my responsibility whether you like it or not." As soon as the words were said, his anger dried up and he regretted shouting. He'd always been quick to flare up and just as quick to calm again. His brother was the one who brooded for hours, if not days.

He bent to pick up Lilly's book from the rushes and handed it to her. She took it and folded both arms over it against her chest. "The problem is, I care about you," he said. "I came home and found my little sister gone, replaced by this miserable ghost. I want her back. I want to see you smile again, Lil."

Their mother sniffed and dabbed at the corner of her eye with a black lace handkerchief. Blake ignored her. This wasn't about her, it was about Lilly. She, however, appeared unmoved by his words, a marble statue staring into the flames of the fire.

"The sooner you tell me who it is," he went on, "the sooner I can speak to him and you can be wed."

"You cannot force him," she said so softly he had to strain to hear her.

"Why not?" Then a sickening thought struck him. "He's not already married is he?"

Their mother gasped. "Lilly!"

"Mother," Blake warned her. He wished he wasn't having this conversation in her presence. She wasn't helping.

Lilly stood still. Her unmoving figure contrasted starkly with the reflection of the orange flames dancing merrily in her eyes. "No," she said.

Only a deaf man would have failed to notice the hesitation.

"Damn it, Lilly, I thought you would have more sense than to attach yourself to someone already wed."

"I said no!" There was none of the warmth from the dancing flames in her eyes now, they were pure ice. "And you leave Henry Wells alone. He's a kind man and he has nothing to do with this."

"Hawkesbury himself then?"

Her eyes narrowed to slits. "Stop behaving like a fool, brother."

"Then tell me who it is!"

She crossed her arms and turned her back to him.

"Why won't you tell me?" When she didn't answer, he said, "How can I help you if you won't tell me?"

She spun back round and pinned him with a murderous glare that reminded him of their older half-brother. "Did I say I wanted your help?"

"Children!" Their mother's shrill voice took Blake back to all the times he'd tested her patience as a youngster. "Enough bickering. Robert, your sister is in a delicate way, you are not to upset her. And Lilly, it is important to rest. No more excitement. Understand?"

That his mother had taken such an interest in the welfare of a bastard child of an unknown man had surprised Blake on his return to London. That her interest had grown with each day, even more so. But that was Lady Warhurst. Always surprising. Never predictable and certainly never dull.

He sighed. It was his great misfortune to be surrounded by headstrong females. Curse them all.

He stormed out of his mother's parlor without looking back and headed to his own apartments on the next floor. Since his father's death almost a year ago, Blake's older half-brother, Leo, had moved into the master's lodgings adjoining their mother's and Blake stayed in Leo's old ones whenever he returned to London. The rooms were spacious and faced south.

He sat in the window and stared in the direction of the Thames. His home was situated several streets from the river but just knowing it was within easy walking distance soothed him. If he listened really hard, and used a little imagination, he could hear the gentle bumping of the wherries against the waterstairs where they were moored for the night.

Water and a vessel on which to float, that's all he wanted. All he needed.

Then why wasn't he on the water now in the *Silver Star*? She and her crew were ready, waiting like patient mistresses for a lover to return. He could climb aboard tonight and shout the order to sail and it would be done at the first high tide. He would be gone. Free.

But he wouldn't be free, not while Lilly was miserable. If Leo wasn't so far away at his Northumberland estate, Blake would gladly leave it to him to unmask the cur who hurt Lilly. As it stood, Leo wouldn't arrive for another week at least, and only then if the roads were good enough for fast riding, unlikely at this time of year.

As soon as Leo did return, Blake would hand over every scrap of knowledge to his half-brother then leave. Let the self-righteous Baron bloody Warhurst take care of the situation. Leo and Lilly were as block-headed as each other, and just as moody. It would be dangerous living under the same roof as both of them.

At least Blake could be certain Leo wouldn't rest until he'd avenged their sister. He wouldn't allow himself to be distracted by a pair of big gray eyes and a freckle that begged to be kissed.

Blake pressed his forehead to the cool glass and sighed. His warm breath clouded the window and he saw *her* face reflected back at him.

Min. He'd known from the moment he left her that he would return to her tonight. It was pointless trying to battle against it, trying to deny the way she made him feel.

Best to face this complication head on, sail right through the eye of the storm and hope like the devil he came out the other side still afloat. Only then could he shake off the spell she'd cast over him and move on.

He got up and called for his man. Doyle arrived within

seconds. "Supper and fresh water," Blake said. "Scented. I'm going out again."

"Clothing, Master?" Doyle asked.

"If I have to."

Doyle's wrinkles bent into a smile. "I meant what would you like to wear?"

"Something easy to remove."

CHAPTER 10

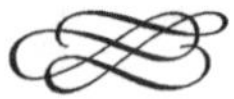

Min had managed to avoid her father when she entered the house but not Jane. The maid emerged from the kitchen as Min tried to creep past.

"Who was that outside?" she asked, holding a candle up to Min's face.

"Were you spying on me?" Min said.

"Spying is such an ugly word, Mistress."

Min blushed. Oh Lord, Jane had seen Blake kiss her! Or more accurately, Min kiss Blake.

She pushed the candle away—her face was hot enough. "He's a gentleman friend," she said. "He escorted me home from the White Swan."

Jane raised both her eyebrows. "Well? How did it go?"

"I, ah, well, I don't know that I want to answer that," she said, putting as much imperialism into her voice as she could muster.

"I meant the play," Jane said. She wasn't smiling but the flame picked out a gleam in her eyes.

"Oh. The play." Min grinned. She couldn't help it. All of a sudden the realization that she'd seen *her* play performed on stage by a real company of players hit her. "It was absolutely wonderful. They did a great job. The acting was superb, the costumes perfect and not a single apple core was thrown."

Jane smiled through shimmering tears. "Ooh, how exciting. I can't wait to see it. Is it on again tomorrow?"

Min nodded. "You should go."

Jane pulled at her lip. "I have so much to do here..."

"When was the last time you had an afternoon off?" Before the maid could answer, Min went on, "I'll help you in the morning to do whatever is needed. Between the two of us, we'll have all the day's chores done by dinner time."

Jane took so long to answer, Min thought she'd refuse. But then she suddenly smiled. "You're a dear, sweet girl."

"We'll start at first light. Tonight I have another play to write."

"I'll bring up yer supper. But you best go see yer father first. He's been askin' for you. Here, take in his supper." She went into the kitchen and returned carrying a tray which she handed to Min, but she failed to let her side of the tray go so they performed a kind of tug-of-war over it. "So," she said, "is he the new hat?"

"Is who the new—? Oh." Min's blush returned with a vengeance.

From Jane's sly smile, Min didn't think the maid required any further answer. She'd certainly witnessed the kiss then.

"Well?" Jane prompted.

"Well what?"

"Does he fit?"

Min refused to be cowed by her embarrassment or her own maid's eavesdropping. She pulled hard on the tray and the maid let it go. Min stormed off in the direction of her father's study. Perhaps it was time to remind Jane of her place within the Peabody household.

By the time she opened her father's study door, she'd dismissed the notion and was simply grateful she had the sort of servant who kept secrets.

Sir George looked up. "Ah, there you are. Have you been home long?"

"A while." She balanced the tray in one hand and pulled a small table closer to his desk because there was no room amongst the papers, maps and books covering it.

"And where did you go, my dear?" The too-light tone suggested there was nothing innocent about the question.

She met his bald gaze. "I visited some friends. The Downers." The lie slipped easily off her tongue but the guilt settled immediately like a brick in her stomach.

"Ah, how are the Widow Downer and her daughters?" He seemed to believe her. The brick grew heavier.

She took the candle Jane had placed on the tray and lit it using the fire in the grate. The room wasn't completely dark yet but her father needed more light if he was to continue working. "They're well," she said. "Although Grace's cough has returned. They send their regards." The lie would probably never go detected. Sir George never visited any of their old friends anymore, and although they visited him on occasion, it was always Min who performed the role of hostess while her father remained in his study. He couldn't face them. None of them, even those who'd remained steadfast and not disappeared as soon as the *Lucinda May* sank without a trace.

He nodded and pushed his spectacles up his nose. "Good, good."

She nudged the tray closer. "Don't let your supper go cold."

He glanced at it. "I suppose I can eat as I work."

She kissed his forehead. "I'll say goodnight now. I have work to do too."

"Ah, yes, good." He smoothed a hand over a map laid out on one side of his desk. "I've been meaning to ask you how my paper is coming along. Have you nearly finished copying it? I've made some corrections, so you'll need to rewrite some of it but I expect it won't take long."

His paper! Oh lord, there was still so much to do! And now with her other play to re-write, there simply wasn't enough time to devote to his work too. She sighed. She would simply have to find the time. There was no other way. "It's coming along nicely." Another lie. Another brick.

"Excellent. When will it be finished? I'm hoping to have it printed for the next Academy lecture."

"You want to present it?"

He blinked owlishly at her. "Yes, of course. It's a good theory. A little complicated but I think most of them will grasp it."

She sat down with a thud on a stool near him. "Are you sure, Father? It's just that, from what I've read, it seems a little..." How to put it so he didn't get upset? "...speculative."

"That's how theories start out, child. As speculation." He stood up and peered down his nose at her. "Are you doubting my work?"

"No-o, it's just that your conclusions seem to be based on a completely different set of calculations than your last theory."

"Have you read the entire paper, Minerva?"

"I...uh..."

"I didn't think so." He stalked to the fireplace and turned his back to the warmth. "Until you finish copying it, we'll not discuss it at all. You need the full picture. Goodnight."

She sighed and stood. At least there was time to change his mind. The Academy of New Sciences met once a month to exchange ideas. Since their last lecture was two weeks ago, there was enough time to write up his paper before the next one. Even if she did manage to change his mind and got him to rethink his more radical conclusions, there would still be time left to rewrite his paper as well as her next play.

She blew out a breath. "Goodnight, Father."

She trudged upstairs to her room and plopped down onto the chair at her desk with a heavy sigh. She should have been the happiest woman in London. She was the first woman in history to see her own play performed on stage by a company of real players. She'd kissed a man desired by women everywhere, and been kissed back. Yet she was miserable. She'd lied to her father again and again. He didn't deserve such an ungrateful, undutiful daughter. He worked so hard, the least she could do was help him now that he needed her.

She found his paper and began to read his scrawl. She could write a page at a time then reward herself by switching to her play. That way both would get done, not quickly, but in good time.

After a paragraph, however, she yawned and put it down. She'd never stay awake long enough to do her own play if she kept reading her father's paper. She put his aside and felt for the key attached to the girdle at her waist. She found it and unlocked the chest near her desk and pulled out a packet bound with blue ribbon. She untied it and brushed a hand over the first page. *The Fantastical Life and Loves of Barnaby Fortune.* A ridiculous title but it suited the play. She'd keep it. The rest of it needed work. A lot of work.

She began to read, and although she didn't yawn, she knew she was stuck by the time she got to the second page. Nothing was *happening*. The characters merely plodded along without anyone or anything troubling them. But what could she add to the story to shake up their lives?

Nothing immediately came to her. Ten minutes later she still couldn't think of anything. Gratefully, she welcomed the arrival of Jane carrying a tray of supper. She took the tray from the maid and placed it on the desk beside the play. "I'm starving." She lifted the cover and screwed up her nose. "Not black bread again. And the cheese has mold on it."

"It's all there is, Mistress."

Min sighed. "Is there no left over meat from dinner?"

"Not a shred. I'm afraid it'll be black bread and moldy cheese for the rest of the week unless we find some money under the rushes."

"That reminds me!" Min dug into her skirts and pulled out her purse. She emptied the contents onto the desk.

Jane gasped. "Is all of that for your play?"

"Four pounds." Min tried not to smile at all the glorious money—she didn't want to appear avaricious after all—but she couldn't help it. It was simply a wonderful sight. She handed a sovereign to Jane. "Buy a big, fat haunch of venison at the market tomorrow. Oh and some cheese without mold on it."

The maid put the coin between her teeth and bit down. Satisfied, she closed her fist around it and grinned at Min.

"Keep anything left over for yourself," Min said.

Jane looked like she was about to protest but instead she nodded. "Thank you, dear girl. I'll send it to my sister. Her husband died and she's got three little ones to care for."

Min gasped. "You never told me! Jane, we must send her

more." She gave her another coin. When Jane pushed it away, Min slipped it down the maid's bodice.

"That was naughty," Jane mumbled into her chin as she sought the coin. "When I find it, I'll give it back to you. You need it."

"Not as much as your sister."

"My sister will be well, never fear. She'll have herself a new husband as soon as her mournin' is over, if I know her. Until then, her husband's livery company will look after her and the children."

The maid helped Min undress to her linen shift and found her favorite housecoat to go over the top. She sighed into its fur lining, letting its warmth and familiarity envelope her. It had been her mother's best day gown once. The elegant garment had faded from black to a greenish-grey over the years and the lining had worn away in places, but it served Min well enough around the house.

Jane braided Min's hair for the night then left, leaving Min to her supper and her problem play. By the time the last piece of cheese was eaten, she'd progressed only half a page.

She sat back in her chair with a heavy sigh and blew on her hands to warm them. It was cold. The fire had shrunk to a few glowing embers but she didn't want to put more wood on. They were trying to save for the winter.

She glanced at the pages of her play then at the fireplace then back at the pages again. It was a hopeless play so why not put it to good use? The paper could keep her warm for, oh, minutes at least.

A tap at the window made her heart jump into her throat. In the darkness, she could just make out the figure of a man standing on her balcony, leaning against her window, his arms crossed. She couldn't quite see his face but she'd know that silhouette anywhere. Blake.

She opened the window before she changed her mind. "You came."

He climbed through and glanced around her room, taking in the untidy desk, the three large chests filled with books and the two chairs covered with cushions embroidered by her mother's hand. He strode to the fire and placed a log in the grate.

"Make yourself at home," she said then inwardly winced. The poor attempt to bolster her confidence only made her sound more nervous, not like the sophisticated woman she wanted him to think her.

He stayed by the fire, one elbow resting on the corner of the mantelpiece, his cheek propped against his fist. He studied the cover of a book she'd forgotten she'd placed there. He'd not spoken a word since his arrival. Not even a greeting.

"Wine?" she offered. Jane had brought up the remains of an entire bottle, perhaps thinking Min would need it during the long night ahead. They would have to share the single cup though.

"No," he said. "Thank you." It was tacked on like an afterthought.

She poured some wine for herself then nearly drank the entire cup in one gulp. He continued to study the leather book cover. The man could probably stand there all night and not say anything, such was the benefit of having nerves of stone. She, on the other hand, had nerves of water.

"What is it you want?" she asked.

That got his attention. He turned to her, slowly, and the wicked flame in his eyes gave her the answer. Oh lord, she'd teased the devil and now he wanted to come out and play. She gripped the cup tighter.

This was what she wanted.

"But you shook your head earlier," she said, managing to keep her voice steady.

"I changed my mind." He closed the gap between them and took the cup from her hands. He placed it on the desk and then, because she was watching the cup and not him, put a finger under her chin and lifted it.

His eyes smoldered beneath half lowered lids. "The important question is," he said, "have you changed yours?"

"No." She didn't hesitate. Didn't want to. This might be her only chance of ever bedding a man like Blake, a man who made her knees weak and her heart strong.

"Good." His finger moved from her chin up to her bottom lip. He tugged on it and she thought he would kiss her but he didn't. Instead, he caressed her lip. She squirmed against the tingles, and against the desire slipping through her. He moved on, up to the corner of her mouth and gently rubbed, as if fixated with something there.

Just when she thought she'd go mad waiting for his kiss, his hand dropped to his side like a sinking pebble. He exhaled. "There's something we need to clarify before we start." His voice rumbled deep in his chest. "If I kiss you now, it's not going to stop there. I'm going to explore every inch of your naked body and then I'm going to show you what happens between a man and a woman who want each other. Understand?"

She nodded until she thought her head would roll off. He did say *every* inch, didn't he? Oh sweet night, if only he would stop talking and start *doing*. The waiting was sheer torture. If he didn't do something soon her body might combust from the excessive heat roaring through it.

"There will be no changing your mind once I begin," he went on. "Are you prepared to lose your maidenhead to me, Minerva Peabody?"

"Yes," she whispered.

"Good." But he didn't undress her, kiss her or do whatever it was that usually started these sorts of proceedings. He picked up the cup. "Think I'll take that wine now." He drained it, filled it up then drank again. Only when he'd finished did he offer it to her.

She shook her head. "Do you want to go into the bedchamber?"

"It'll be more comfortable."

She led the way into the adjoining room, Blake close behind her. So close she could hear him breathing.

She stopped at the foot of the large canopied bed centered in the otherwise bare room and waited while he lit candles and tended to the fire. He moved purposefully and didn't once glance her way. When he finished, he came over to her but did nothing, said nothing. He simply stared.

She played with the laces of her housecoat cuffs and wished her wit hadn't deserted her. Ever since he'd climbed through her window, her mind had ceased to function properly. A little humor would do wonders to break through the tension settling between them like a plague.

"Is there something wrong?" she managed to ask.

"No. Everything's...good. I just wanted to look at you."

"Wouldn't you prefer to do that without clothes on?"

He smiled. "Yes." He gently took one of her wrists and undid the laces. She'd meant for him to be the one to remove *his* clothes but if he wanted to touch her like that it was acceptable too. Very acceptable. Already she decided she liked the slow movement of his agile fingers as they worked.

He unlaced her other cuff and slipped the housecoat off her shoulders. She stood in her linen night shift and woolen nether-hose, held up by nothing more than a strip of ribbon above each knee. From the flare of his hot gaze, she knew the swell of her breasts was clearly visible beneath the fabric. Every inch of her became aware of him, from her tight nipples to her moistening inner thighs.

She expected him to remove her hose or shift next. He did neither. He reached behind her and slipped off the ribbon tying up her hair. His fingers nimbly freed the braid then slid through her tresses, caressing the strands as if he were appraising the most expensive bolt of silk.

Min closed her eyes, breathed. The scent of exotic spices—cinnamon, cloves and others she couldn't identify—filled her nostrils. It would be a smell she would forever associate with him, long after he was gone.

And he would go. She knew it. He'd told her. Tonight might be all she ever had.

Min exhaled but her breath was captured by his mouth before it ever left her lips. The kiss was more tentative than the first two. As if he was waiting to see if she changed her mind.

The moon would fall out of the sky before that ever happened. This was what she wanted. This kiss...and more.

The intelligent, sensible part of her knew what she was doing—and was about to do—was wrong and that it could lead to her downfall. But the wanton side of her didn't want to stop. The wanton won. Her desire to experience passion with Blake was utterly overwhelming and totally debilitating.

She reached up and pressed her hands to the back of his head, just in case *he* changed *his* mind. But he deepened the kiss, and she knew he couldn't stop any more than she could. Not when her breasts were pushed against his chest, only a few layers of material between her aching nipples and his flesh. She'd never been this close to him the other times they'd kissed, never had so little between her body and his.

It was still too much. She pushed his black leather jerkin off. Better, but still too much. She broke the kiss to unfasten the row of buttons down the front of his doublet and the points joining doublet to hose. He removed it and threw it into a corner of the room, closely followed by his hose, boots and netherhose. Not once did his eyes leave hers.

Not once did she glance down. She dared not, even though she knew what a man's penis looked like. She'd heard the maids talking when there'd been more than just Jane. She'd even read a description of one in a book from her father's library she probably wasn't supposed to have been reading.

But her curiosity to see the real thing got the better of her. She lowered her gaze...and was transfixed by the pole jutting out from between Blake's thighs. It wasn't at all like *The Historie of Man* described. And from the maid's giggles she'd expected something odd. There was nothing odd about Blake's member.

"Now I want to see you," he said. He slowly unlaced her shift then scrunched it up to pull it over her head. When the hem had risen to her upper thigh she had a desperate urge to ask him to extinguish the candles, but she didn't. She wanted to experience everything and she could only do that if she allowed him to see her.

The shift gone, he dropped to one knee to remove her netherhose. His eye level was right, well, *there* but she tried not to think about how embarrassed she should feel. She gripped his shoulder for balance as he removed one netherhose then the other.

With the last piece of clothing banished to the floor, she was completely naked. And it didn't feel at all shameful or humiliating. Aunt Maud had been wrong. Having another gaze upon her nakedness was quite liberating. It was as if her skin was *feeling* for the first time. The coolness of the air across her stomach, her nipples, the subtler warmth from the fire against her right buttock, the internal heat generated from her own body as it slowly became aware of Blake's breath on her most secret place. He was still on his knees in front of her.

What was he doing? It's not like there was anything special to look at. A thatch of wiry hair covered all the important parts. He'd have to—

Oh!

He parted her folds and his thumb nudged against her opening. She gasped and reached for the closest thing for balance—his shoulder. Her nails dug into his flesh as his thumb strummed her bud like a lute string. Her resounding wail was anything but tuneful.

It was so much better than she expected. Every piece of her felt sensitive and aware, like a hunter's trap, ready to spring at any moment. Her skin tensed and tightened with every throb of her inner thighs, her toes curled into the floor rushes and she squeezed her eyes shut against the surge of tingles rising, rising.

She was going to explode. Right there on his thumb. With him watching. It was enough to make her body quiver all over.

Then his finger entered her and the quivers became a quake. She threw her head back and gripped his shoulders as a cry burst from her lips.

He pressed his other hand to the small of her back and held her until her shudders eased. When finally she could speak again, he planted a kiss on her stomach and stood. He watched her through heavy-lidded eyes, a mysterious smile teasing his lips.

"You liked that?" he asked.

"Like isn't quite the right word," she said, breathy. "That was..." But her mind couldn't think of the right words so she abandoned the attempt at an explanation. Time for that later when she put pen to paper.

For now there was Blake and his big, powerful body and equally big member. He picked her up and lowered her gently on top of the faded red and gold bed cover then took another moment to graze the length of her body with his hot gaze. She blushed from scalp to toenails and pressed her thighs together.

"No, let me look at you." He parted her legs then gently took her wrists and drew her arms over her head. The position thrust out her breasts, arched her back. "So beautiful," he whispered.

She shook her head. He was humoring her. She was no celebrated beauty.

"Yes you are." He stretched out alongside her, his hard erection pressed against her outer thigh, and kissed the hollow at her throat. "You've the body and face of a Goddess. Minerva. I bet the ancient Romans worshipped her for more than just her mind."

She giggled. He was teasing. But then he kissed her fully on the mouth. Nothing teasing about that, just a hard and hungry kiss that swept her up with its fervor.

"I adore you," he murmured against her lips. "Every inch of you." He nipped a trail of tiny kisses across one breast. "The way you gave yourself to me, the way your body trembled and blushed and the look on your face..." He kissed the other breast. "All mine. My Goddess."

He took her nipple into his mouth and she relinquished all hold on rational thought. There was nothing at all rational about the pleasure swamping her. With every lave of his tongue, her body bucked and writhed like a thing possessed.

Just as she thought she would explode again, he stopped. Horrible man! His weight shifted and his thigh trapped her leg. He let go of her wrists and leveraged himself up onto his elbow, stroking her hip with his free hand. His eyes smoldered as he watched her, reflecting the slow burn of her body beneath his attentions. She touched his cheek. So handsome. And all hers. For tonight.

She felt a tiny shudder ripple across her skin. He breathed deeply as if trying to inhale her. "This may hurt a little." He sounded as if someone had him by the throat and was squeezing.

"I know." It didn't matter. Nothing mattered except having him. All of him.

"Do you have a cloth?" he asked.

She got up and padded across to a cedar chest, the only other piece of furniture in the room, and pulled out a cloth. She returned to the bed and handed it to him.

He laid it on one side of the bed alongside his body. "For my seed," he said.

She nodded. Jane had once told her there were ways a couple could enjoy the act without begetting a child, the easiest being for the man to spill his seed outside the woman's body.

"Have you changed your mind?" he said, watching her.

"No!"

He nodded and his top lip quivered as if he were fighting a smile. "Good. Because I've not changed mine. I want you, Min." He shifted so that he was on top of her. "Tell me if this hurts and I'll ease back if I can."

If I can?

Blake didn't know where that promise had stemmed from. It wouldn't be easy to stop once they got started. He was already harder than a brigantine's bowsprit and he hadn't even dipped into her well yet. Stopping would be torture.

But if it's what she wanted he would do it, even if it made his balls fall off from the effort.

He pressed his tip into her wetness and her tight sheath surrounded him, a snug fit. Ah, but she was moist and ready for him. He pushed against the barrier, felt her tense beneath him, and reached down to rub her swollen nub. She responded by moaning and opening up.

For one brief moment he hesitated. He was doing something he swore he'd never do—take the virginity of a woman. But he was too far gone to let that worry him. He'd been too far gone ever since they'd separated outside her house hours earlier. A troubled conscience was hardly going to stop him now.

Her hands reached around and pressed into his arse. A small moan escaped her lips as he eased himself into her. Her every move told him she wanted to do this and he could almost fool himself into thinking he was simply obliging her. But only a bigger fool would believe him.

He slid all the way in and knew it was exactly where he

wanted to be. He caught her gasp with his mouth, and set a slow rhythm to ease the shock of his entry. He pulled back a little to watch her face, contorted in either pain or pleasure, he wasn't quite sure. But then she dug her nails into his back and moaned and he was in no doubt that pleasure controlled her.

He couldn't remain slow after that. Not when her breath came in short, sharp pants and she pulsed around his thickness. It was more than he could bear. When she opened her eyes and he saw a tumult of emotions swelling within them, he lost the battle against self-discipline.

He drove into her with one, two deep thrusts and ground his teeth to stop himself roaring her name. At the last possible second, he pulled out and spurted his seed into the cloth.

He collapsed next to her, their heavy breathing filling his ears, the heat fusing their bodies together.

They must have fallen asleep because when he opened his eyes, the candle had burned to a stub and the fire had turned to glowing embers in the grate. Min's perfectly round behind pressed against his erection, her warmth folding around him like a blanket. He kissed her shoulder and climbed out of bed, gently so as not to wake her. He dressed in a hurry then picked up the candle and moved the single flame closer to her face. He watched her as she slept, committing every detail to memory so he could recall them on the long, lonely nights ahead—the rise and fall of her breasts with her breathing, the flutter of her eyelids as she dreamed. He stroked a lock of hair off her cheek to reveal the freckle nestled in the corner of her mouth like a secret smile.

Then he woke her with a kiss. She stirred and opened her mouth sleepily to him. "I must go," he said, pulling away. If he didn't leave now, he might not get out before daybreak. He was already hard for her again.

"Why must you?" she said with a pout of her thoroughly kissed lips. "It's early yet."

"No, it's late. I don't want to be caught here." It would be a disaster for her.

"Of course." She rose and covered a yawn. "I have work to do anyway."

That wasn't the sort of response he'd been expecting. "Work? Your play?"

"And father's paper." She sighed and swung her legs off the bed. "Go now before I change my mind and tie you to the bedposts to keep you here."

"Now there's a tempting offer. Maybe I'll just stay—."

"No!" But she laughed as she picked her night shift up off the floor.

She followed him into the study. He helped her into her house coat and passed her the candle. Their hands touched briefly before he let go but the warmth of her skin remained with him.

She looked away and cleared her throat. "Thank you," she said, clutching the candlestick with both hands as if it was too heavy to hold with one.

If she hadn't said it so seriously, he would have laughed. "You don't need to thank me, Min. I enjoyed every bit of it too."

He could see her battling against a smile. The smile won. "So did I." She stood on her toes and kissed him lightly on the lips. "Goodnight."

He opened the window and stepped out onto the small balcony. "Goodnight, Min." He swung down to the balcony on the first floor then it was an easy jump to the ground. He looked up and saw her in the window, the flame from the candle highlighting her mouth and the smile there.

His heart wrenched to see that it was a sad one.

CHAPTER 11

Min didn't eat much of the bread Jane delivered to her room for breakfast only two hours after Blake left. She was too busy writing. Emotions and thoughts spilled onto the pages of her play, words jostled for attention and ink smudged in her haste. When her hand cramped and her fingers had turned black from the ink, she put the pen down and sat back to survey her work.

There. A good start. A very good start. The main character, Barnaby Fortune, had met his true love, Mistress Truly but his second love interest, the duplicitous Widow Fowler, had also been introduced to the audience. There was passion on every page and Min even managed a rather rude jest from one of the minor characters that should have the groundlings laughing.

She set the play aside and pulled out her father's paper. She wrote out an entire paragraph before a yawn escaped her. Jane, bless her good timing, entered with a ewer of fresh water.

"Ah, good, you ate," she said, eyeing Min's empty trencher. "I was worried you'd be too busy when I brought it up. You was writin' like yer life depended on it."

Perhaps not her life but certainly her sanity. She *needed* to write. It fed her soul.

"Thank you, Jane, I was famished. Has father eaten?" she

asked, setting aside his paper to remove her house coat and nightshift.

"Aye, he's in his study. Two peas in a pod you both are this mornin'." She knelt before the fireplace and stoked the ashes with the poker. "Can't get to yer work quick enough. The words a-comin' fast today?"

"Very," Min said. She dipped the sponge into the warm water and washed her face, her throat, wiping away all hint of Blake's kisses.

No, not all hint. They were in her memory, where they would remain forever. As would the way he looked as he thrust into her —his jaw clenched tight, his features skewed as if he were trying very hard not to hurt her or make a sound.

She smiled and circled her breasts with the sponge. Moisture dripped between the valley, down to her navel and thatch of hair. It was wet and warm and felt a little like Blake's tongue when he'd licked her everywhere. A responding pulse between her thighs sealed the similarity.

"You must have had a good night's sleep," Jane said. She suddenly stood, swung around, poker in hand, a frown taxing her brow.

Min dipped the sponge into the water and tried to banish Blake from her mind. Quite an easy task with Jane looking like an avenging angel. "A reasonable night's sleep, I suppose."

"Hmph" Jane nodded and turned back to the fireplace. "I'm glad you weren't kept awake by the same noises as kept me from my slumber."

Min froze. "Noises?"

Jane placed kindling into the grate and blew on the glowing embers. "Aye. Talkin' and moanin' and the like. You didn't hear it?"

"No!" Min finished washing and dried herself. "I slept soundly."

"Then you'll be ready for our chores."

Chores? She'd almost forgotten she'd promised to help Jane so the maid could go to the play in the afternoon. "Yes, of course."

"If you've got work to do, I could go another—."

"No, I'll not hear of it. You never know with plays, it might not be on ever again if the audiences don't improve. Today could be your only chance."

Jane helped Min dress in her plain woolen gown then pinned her hair beneath a white cap. "I'll just rearrange the bed and—."

"No!" Min rushed past her and scooped up the sheets and the cloth in which Blake had spilled his seed. "I'll do it. You...do something else."

Jane frowned again and thrust a hand onto her hip. "Anythin' you want to tell me, Mistress? Because if there is, I'll not breathe a word of it to anyone."

Min shook her head, hardly breathing herself. *She knew.* Jane knew Blake had been there last night. Min could see it in the maid's eyes—they were clear orbs with the power to see everything, especially a guilty conscience. No, not guilty. Min refused to feel guilty over something so thoroughly fulfilling.

"Very well." Jane sighed. "But if you need anythin', anythin' at all, you come to me. Understand? I know a thing or two about...things."

Min swallowed and managed to nod again. She hugged the sheets closer to her chest. They smelled like Blake. "I will. Thank you, Jane. I'll be down shortly."

Dismissed, the maid left but not before she squeezed her mistress's arm and gave Min an odd little smile. Sympathetic? A secret shared?

Jane closed the door behind her and Min groaned, dropping the sheets onto the floor. Perhaps with time the embarrassment would ease, but she doubted it. She only hoped that Jane was the only one wise enough to suspect what had occurred during the night. Even so, it was probably for the best if Min avoided her father for as long as possible.

She gathered up the sheets again and followed Jane down the stairs. Since it was washing day anyway, she filled the large copper pot from the cauldron of water constantly boiling over the kitchen fire and rolled up her sleeves. It took nearly an hour to wash sheets and shirts and another hour to brush down and spot-clean all the finer clothing but she didn't mind. It gave her time to think about her play, and about Blake.

Mostly about Blake. The way his hands had felt on her skin, how his kisses had revealed his hunger, and how he'd swelled inside her in the moment before he'd pulled out and spurted his seed.

She hadn't planned on going to the play that afternoon, but by the time she finished the washing, she'd changed her mind. Jane might enjoy the company. And Min simply had to see Blake again or she'd go mad.

He was all she could think about. All she *wanted* to think about. Not even her next play could nudge aside images of him in her bed, gloriously naked and hard for her. Only her.

But the thrilling thoughts were edged with sadness. He'd made it clear their union wouldn't happen again. She didn't know the reason. A previous betrothal? More likely it was Min's lack of status and money. She wasn't sure who the Blakewells were but he was a gentleman and gentlemen had to marry well. The daughter of a failed scientist, even a knighted one, was hardly a sought-after prospect.

She sighed. She was foolish to be even courting the idea of marrying him. Silly thoughts like that could make a fanciful girl like her sad. And she had no reason for sadness. She was healthy, had a loving father although a sometimes absent-minded and cross one, and her play had been performed by a real company of players for the first time. She'd also lost her maidenhead to a very desirable gentleman. There was much to be proud and thankful for. She shouldn't *want* more.

"Ah, there you are," Jane said on entering the kitchen. She set down two baskets filled with breads, cheese, joints of meat and vegetables.

Min set aside one of her skirts she'd been mending and helped the maid unpack the baskets. "No black bread," she said with satisfaction. "Is that a leg of mutton?"

"Aye. I was able to buy the best of everythin' thanks to you, Mistress." She smiled at Min, none of the suspicion of earlier in her expression at all.

Min smiled back. It *was* all thanks to her. And if she could sell her next play to Style too, she might even be able to afford a new skirt and perhaps even the map her father wanted.

"You'll never guess what the talk is at the Stocks Market today," Jane said, a lettuce balanced on her palm.

"Mistress Flood's latest confrontation with her neighbor?"

Jane laughed. She looked happier than Min had seen her in a long time. "No, yer play!"

Min stared at her. "Really? You're not teasing me?"

"I would never tease you about that, Mistress. It's true, yer play is on everyone's lips. Mistress Harrison the fishmonger's wife wanted to see the play put on by Lord Strange's Men yesterday but she and her husband got to The Theater too late. There was no seatin' left in the gallery and what with Samuel's bad back, they couldn't stand. So bein' in mind to see a play, they set about to find another and someone mentioned there'd be seatin' at The White Swan since Lord Hawkesbury's players aren't even fillin' half the inn-yard. And to their surprise, it was a new play called..." she paused for what could only be effect, "...*Marius and Livia*! And it was a real gem, Jenny Harrison said. She told me herself but you know what she's like. By the time I reached her stall, she'd said to everyone who'd listen that Lord Hawkesbury's Men have a ripper of a play on their hands. She said young Wells turns a fine leg as Marius." Jane put the lettuce down on the table and sighed. "Oh, to think it is *your* play she was talkin' about, my dearest girl."

Her play. Min could hardly believe it herself. Surely she must be asleep and dreaming. People were discussing her play at the market! "You didn't tell her I wrote it did you?"

"Of course not! I'm no ninny. Yer secret is safe with me. Oh, I can't wait to see it. I think I'll pay the extra and get a seat so I'd best get there early. Last time I went, I couldn't see over the lout in front of me."

"I'll join you," Min said.

"Oh? And to what do I owe the pleasure of yer company?"

"I want to see it again of course."

"Really?" Jane cocked her head to the side. "Are you sure it's not because yer new hat will be there?"

Min should have been cross with her maid for being so forward but Jane said it with such a mischievous grin that she couldn't summon anything but a smile herself.

"That is none of your business, Jane. Now, we'd best get dinner ready or we won't be going anywhere."

They worked side by side preparing the mutton in the kitchen until a knock sounded at the front door. Jane went to answer it.

"It's Ned Taylor," she said on her return. "Do you want me to tell him you're not home?"

"If you didn't tell him that straight away then he'll not believe you." Min studied her hands. They were greasy and smelled of raw meat. "I'd better see what he wants, but not like this." If Ned saw her in her stained and roughened work clothes he might bring it upon himself to be her knight in shining armor and save her from her life of drudgery. The image caused a giggle to bubble to the surface. At Jane's raised brow, Min said, "Have Father speak to him while I change."

Jane went to retrieve Sir George from his study while Min went upstairs to throw a nicer gown over her working clothes and freshen up. She lifted her looking glass to check her hair but decided not to push the stray strands back beneath her cap. Ned didn't need any more encouragement.

Oh lord, what if he was here for an answer to his proposal?

She sighed. If he was, she'd simply have to give it to him.

She found her father and Ned in the parlor discussing shipping news. It was the one topic they could both converse on without boring the other. Ned, however, was more interested in the cargo while Sir George wanted to hear about the uncharted coasts. It seemed they'd found one ship that satisfied both their needs.

"The *Silver Star* has been in port for nearly a week now," her father said. "She ventured into the East Indies on her last voyage."

"Brought back cotton by the barrel load and indigo for dyeing," Ned said, nodding. "But I've not managed to get my hands on any yet. The captain proves elusive despite my efforts to petition him and the first mate won't strike any bargains without his captain's orders. Ah, Minerva, there you are." He took her hand and bowed over it, clicking the heels of his shoes together. "You appear quite...over-wrought." He stared pointedly at her unkempt hair. "Are you unwell?"

"You're not are you, Minerva?" her father asked before she could answer. His concern warmed her heart.

"No, I'm quite well," she said.

"Perhaps there's something on your mind," Ned said. "Something you wish to discuss with me." He raised both eyebrows and Min was left in no doubt he *had* come for an answer to his marriage proposal.

She sighed inwardly. It was best to get it over with. She opened her mouth to speak but her father cut across her once again.

"Or is there something you wish to tell *me*, my child? Did you copy out the rest of the paper last night and find something amiss? Is that it?"

She looked from one to the other, trying to decide who to go into battle against first. It was like choosing between entering a burning building or a flooded river. Both looked at her, expectant and—oh dear—hopeful.

She looked to the door. Where was the ever-present Jane now?

"Father," she said, choosing her words carefully, "I had a...an ache in my head so I went to bed early. Your work is not quite finished." Her head was about the only place that hadn't ached last night. Every other piece of her had yearned for Blake—before, during and after his nocturnal visit. And still did. It was like a disease—thinking about him made her go hot and cold all over.

And made her bold and just a little foolish. That could be the only explanation for why Min's lie rolled surprisingly easily off her tongue despite the two men watching her with a mixture of curiosity and concern. Her indiscretion with Blake had proved a disconcerting experience on many levels.

She swallowed and couldn't quite meet their gazes.

Her father snorted in disbelief. "Then why was there a candle burning in your room for half the night? Well, Minerva, answer me that!"

Oh no! Had he heard noises too?

"You were writing your Roman play again, weren't you?" he said, taking her silence for guilt.

Ned's brows rose. "*Roman* play?"

Min ignored him. "I wasn't." Her response was quick and came without her even thinking, proof of just how familiar she'd become at telling falsehoods. "I must have forgotten to extinguish the candle. I'm sorry, Father, I know we're trying to save them. I shall be more careful next time."

He pushed his spectacles up his nose then removed them altogether. His gray eyes stared hawkishly down his beak-like nose at her. "You've never forgotten to blow out a candle in your life, Minerva. The dangers of leaving candles burning has long been drilled into you, and you yourself are always conscious of their cost."

"Are you saying you don't believe me?" If he wanted to argue with her once more then so be it. Sometimes it was better to be up-front than let issues stew beneath the surface.

Beside her, Ned shifted and scratched his temple. He looked to be deep in thought, not really listening to the conversation. Good.

"I am saying you put more emphasis on your plays than on my work," Sir George said. He stood by the window, a rigid, imposing figure dressed in a black gown, his long gray beard twitching as his jaw worked. "Need I remind you of the importance of my—?"

"No, you need not." She would not let him shame her into thinking her dream was any less worthy than his. It wasn't. It was simply a *different* dream.

"Minerva, I am you father! Do not speak to me as if I was anything less."

She stiffened. "Your paper will be finished in time for the Academy's meeting," she ground out. "Isn't that enough?"

Ned coughed. "Ah, I think I'd better go. We can discuss the other matter tomorrow, Minerva. Good day, Sir George. I'll see myself out."

Min gave him a curt nod. Her father didn't even do that. He was completely focused on Min, a fury like she'd never seen before darkening his features and deepening the grooves around his grim mouth. She could practically see steam rising from his nostrils and ears.

"I wish you to do more than copy it, Minerva," he said, "I want you to read it, digest it, then talk to me about it. The way we usually do." His words were almost sentimental except for the righteousness slicing through his tone. "The way you're supposed to do."

"Supposed to?" She barked out a humorless laugh. "As a loving and dutiful daughter, you mean?"

His shoulders hunched and he suddenly seemed less imposing and more like the old man he'd become in recent months. "But of course," he said sadly. "Isn't that how your mother and I raised you? Isn't that why we gave you an education to rival any boy's?"

"You gave me an education to rival any boy's because you had no boys. I am all there is." Her father's anger may have dissipated but she still boiled with it and she couldn't stop it from spilling over. "And I already tried to discuss your theory with you yesterday but you wouldn't listen. As always, you had that oliphantine nose stuck in a book and your head in the clouds."

The nostrils on his offending nose flared. "As I recall, you told me it needed more work and I told you I wanted you to read the entire thing before you jumped to any conclusions. Please Minerva, let's not—."

"I don't think I was the one jumping to conclusions, Father."

His eyes narrowed and the rigidity returned to his body. The crunch of glass filled the taut silence.

He grunted and opened his fist. Shards of glass fell onto the rushes. He'd broken his spectacles.

She gasped. "Are you hurt?" She caught his hand but he pulled it away. Not before she saw the red stripe of blood crossing the palm. "You are hurt." She called for Jane as she told him to close his fist over the wound to stem the flow of blood. He wouldn't. He simply stared at it. "It's not too deep." She tried to smile but it wouldn't come. If her father's hand was damaged beyond use because of their argument, she'd never forgive herself.

"Blood," he said, continuing to stare. Jane rushed in and applied a clean cloth to the wound. "So much blood and death."

"Pardon?" Min said. "Death? Father, you'll not die."

"But they will."

Min exchanged glances with Jane. The maid shrugged. "Father, who will die?"

"Oh. What?" Sir George blinked rapidly and looked up at his daughter. He smiled. "I'm glad we're no longer arguing," he said.

"So am I but...who were you talking about just now?"

He shook his head. "What do you mean? I spoke only of us not arguing. Jane, do you have any of that salve left? It worked wonders that time I cut my finger."

"Aye, Sir," the maid said. "Come with me to the kitchen and we'll clean the blood away first."

Min stared after them then plopped down onto a chair. What had her father been talking about? And why could he not recall saying it? Was her mind playing tricks on her? No, she'd definitely heard him, as had Jane. Which meant *his* mind must be playing tricks on *him*.

Oh Lord. For a man who needed a quick mind as much as he needed air to breathe, losing it would be a disaster. She sighed. For a day that started out so sublimely, it had turned rather awful.

CHAPTER 12

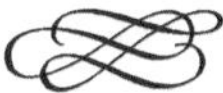

Lord Hawkesbury was an elusive man, Blake found. The steward at Hawkesbury Hall said his master wasn't home and he didn't know where he'd gone. Ha! Of course he knew. Stewards knew everything. It was a requirement of their position.

Blake had waited for an hour on the opposite side of The Strand to the mansion but the master had not returned, at least not that way. On the likely chance that he'd returned home via the river and entered the house using the grander entrance fronting the Thames, Blake once more questioned the steward. Lord Hawkesbury still had not returned.

He glanced to the sky. The sun hung high, brighter than it had for days, untroubled by the few gray clouds drifting past. It was time for Blake to prepare for the day's performance of *Marius and Livia.*

It would have been quicker to take a wherry down river but he chose to walk. The exercise would hopefully soothe his frustration and the ache that had gripped him by the balls ever since he'd left Min's room the night before. So much for assuaging that craving.

He trudged along Fleet Street back to the City. He paused near the Bell Savage Inn to allow a dray packed with children and caged ducks to rumble through Ludgate. A lad nailing a handbill to the inn's door caught his attention. It wasn't until the boy finished that Blake saw that it announced the day's performance of *Marius and Livia* at the White Swan.

It seemed he would be reminded of Min no matter where he went.

A well-dressed couple stopped to read the handbill and Blake caught snatches of their conversation on the breeze.

"... very good," the woman said. "Should we go?"

"Isn't it a love story?" the man said, his derision obvious. Blake smiled to himself.

"If Mr. Dickson liked it..." The woman's sentence was lost beneath the thunderous roll of a coach's wheels over the cobbles.

The man still looked undecided so Blake wandered over. "It's an excellent play," he told the gentleman, "despite the romance. I thoroughly recommend it."

The woman smiled and said, "See."

The gentleman didn't look convinced. He eyed Blake up and down, as if assessing his taste in plays. "You've seen it, Sir?"

"I have. It's an entertaining way to spend an afternoon." He sounded like a peddler, or worse, Roger Style.

"Thank you," the woman said, "we'll go today."

They left. Blake read the handbill again. It really was a good play. Min had great talent. And fortitude—she'd had her play performed despite the odds against her. It was a pity she couldn't take credit for it.

Not that it seemed to concern her. Not yet. It may one day. After the continued success of her plays, she might come to regret not being known as their author.

A disturbing thought struck him. What would she do if he left London? Who would she claim penned her plays then?

An even more disturbing thought needled its way into his head. What would happen to Min if Blake took out the Lord Hawkesbury component of Lord Hawkesbury's Men?

He shook his head. He wasn't even sure if Hawkesbury was the man he sought. It might be Wells, Shakespeare or one of the other hired actors. Making one of them own up to his unborn child wouldn't see the demise of the company. And if the company became successful again on the back of Min's plays, perhaps another patron could be found if Hawkesbury couldn't continue in the role due to an unfortunate injury Blake might be forced to inflict upon him.

A lot of Ifs. He didn't like them.

"Bloody Style," muttered a man frowning at the *Marius and Livia* handbill. With a vicious swipe, he tore it down, ripped the paper into tiny pieces and threw them into the air. The shreds hovered on the breeze for several moments then fluttered to the road where they were trampled by hooves and feet.

"What did you do that for?" Blake asked him.

"This here establishment's puttin' on a play by Lord Carleton's Men this afternoon. Style knows he can't advertise here but the pompous scum always does it." The flat faced man squinted at Blake. "You comin' for the performance, Sir? Care for a drink in the taproom first?"

"No, thank you, I need to be across town."

"Aye, well as long as you're not goin' to that other play. I'm sick of hearin' about it." He limped off, grumbling all the way into the inn.

Blake kept walking. He was surprised to find himself in a good mood. He should have been frustrated by Hawkesbury's elusiveness, angry at whoever had taken his sister's innocence and disturbed by his own fierce reaction to Min.

But he wasn't. All he cared about was when he could see her again. If not at the performance today then perhaps tonight. That's if she let him into her rooms.

What if she'd had her fill of him? What if she'd got the experience she'd needed and decided no more?

But she'd gone off like a cannon last night—she would want him back again, he was sure. Unless she regretted their lovemaking altogether. It *had* been a risky step for her to take. A gentlewoman's maidenhead was a valuable thing and he should have known better than to seize it so thoughtlessly.

He shook off the dark thoughts. He'd had enough of them to last a lifetime. He wanted to enjoy this newfound euphoria, even if it only continued another hour, another minute.

Min *had* wanted him last night, just as much as he'd wanted her. She'd been willing, ready. Hell, she'd even instigated it with that kiss. There was no doubt in his mind.

Sometimes, when the ugly head of guilt threatened to rear, he needed to remind himself of that.

CHAPTER 13

Blake reached the White Swan and forced all thoughts of Min aside. It was time to concentrate on the other task ruling his life. He watched the players practice their lines in the cramped tiring room, most already dressed in the costumes required for the first scene. Alice Croft knelt in front of Shakespeare, fixing the hem of his toga. She still managed to carry on a conversation despite a mouth full of pins. Her father sat on a stool in the corner, brushing down one of Freddie's dresses. The boy was the only one of the troupe missing.

"Where is that ill-bred lout?" Roger Style grumbled. He strode to the curtain and peeked at the stage and inn-yard beyond. "Oh. My lord."

"What is it?" Edward stood on his toes and peered over his brother's shoulder. Then he turned back to the room, eyes alight, mouth twisted into a foolish grin. "Gentlemen and lady," he said with a small bow in Alice's direction, "we have a full house."

"Are you sure?" Henry Wells joined the Style brothers at the curtain. He whistled. "There's not a single seat left in the gallery."

"And the groundlings are packed in too," Edward said. "How many do you think that is, Roger?"

"The inn holds around five hundred." Style let the curtain go but a hand caught it before it completely closed.

Freddie rushed through, breathless. "Have you seen the mob out there!"

"Where have you been?" Style snapped. "Never mind. Get changed. We're about to start."

Freddie began to strip off clothing. "Behind the screen, lad," Croft said, pointing his sponge at a piece of large cloth hung from pegs that acted as a screen when necessary. "There's a lady present."

"Alice? Ha!"

Croft rose and looked ready to squeeze the air out of the lad.

"All right," Freddie grumbled, "I'm going."

Croft sat back down. Alice caught Blake's gaze and rolled her eyes. He smiled at her. She smiled back.

"Everyone ready?" Style said. "They're getting restless. Edward?"

Edward bounded through the curtain and onto the stage beyond. The audience cheered and whistled then went silent as Edward introduced the play. He returned to the tiring house amidst thunderous applause, his face aglow.

"They're a jolly lot today," he said. "Go on Henry, you're up now."

Style handed Blake the prompt book. "You'll be needing this." He nodded at the screen behind which Freddie was still changing into his costume with the help of one of the hired men. So the lad hadn't learned his lines yet? He must be too busy nursing his ale. "How's the new play coming along?"

"Very well," Blake said. He took the book and settled onto a stool near the curtain so he could watch the performance through the gap.

Around him, players came and went on cue. The Crofts were kept busy with costume changes, repairs and handing out the necessary props. Twice Blake had to whisper a line to Freddie but apart from that, he had little to do except watch the action on stage and in the audience. Their faces were enraptured by what they saw. They laughed at all the funny parts and oohed when appropriate.

He could only see the first few rows of groundlings, those men and women standing in the inn's courtyard nearest the stage, but he could see everyone in the two tiers of galleries surrounding the yard on three sides. He found himself searching for Min. Instead he spotted Hawkesbury in prime position to the left of the stage where he could see and be seen.

Peacock.

He was flanked by two women, one middle-aged but immaculately dressed in gold and black with a fashionably wide ruff that gave the appearance her head was floating above a white lake. The other woman, younger and fairer with a serene, slack-jawed expression, was dressed in deep blue taffeta from head to toe. Where several necklaces cascaded over the elder woman's bosom, the younger wore no jewelry that Blake could see. Both women watched the play. Hawkesbury didn't. Although he occasionally spoke to or smiled at one of the women, his gaze wandered around the audience. Searching for someone?

For Lilly?

"Alice," Blake whispered.

"Yes?" she said, hanging up the costume Edward had worn in the first act. "Something wrong?"

He beckoned her to the curtain but the door at the back of the tiring house opened and she paused to see who entered. It was Min. Blake's heart leapt into his throat and he felt his face grow hot. Christ, anyone would think he was a schoolboy. He forced his body to relax.

"What are you doing here?" So much for being relaxed. His words came out harsher than he'd meant them to. Damn it, he was known from the Levant to the New World for his self-control, but it had deserted him after one night of memorable coupling.

Every part of Min went still at his words. All except her big gray eyes. Those windows widened and blinked rapidly at him. "I've seen the play from the gallery," she said tightly, "so I thought I'd come and see it from back here." Her gaze shifted to his left shoulder, avoiding his eyes—she wasn't entirely telling the truth.

Had she come into the tiring house to see him?

Blake ground his back teeth to keep himself from smiling. He couldn't afford to smile, to encourage her to think their relationship meant anything beyond the occasional nocturnal tumbling. During the day, they were merely business partners of sorts, and perhaps even friends.

He swallowed and blocked out the small voice of derision in his head. There wasn't room in is life for that voice, and certainly no room for a woman like Min.

Min hadn't been sure what reaction to expect from Blake. A smile or a wink or some other acknowledgement of their night together perhaps. Anything but the tightly wound man with hooded eyes and a cutting tongue who greeted her. She discarded the wittily flirtatious salutation she'd been practicing during the first half of the play and instead made up an inane excuse about seeing the performance from a different perspective.

She threaded her way through the hanging costumes, swords, shields and other props carefully arranged about the room for efficient and swift changes, nodding at Alice and her father as she passed them. She came up beside Blake, keeping as much space between them as possible, and parted the curtain. All of the players were on stage for the final group scene. She could only see their backs but what she really found interesting was the audience. So many of them! And all transfixed by her play. Up in the gallery sat Lord Hawkesbury, and there was Jane, riveted to the stage, and she even spotted Kit Marlowe lurking in the shadows. What was the renown playwright doing watching her play?

"It's certainly interesting seeing it from back here," she said, closing the curtain. She looked from Blake to Alice. The seamstress was a pretty woman, with a confident air and an odd smile on her lips that Min couldn't decipher. What had she and Blake been discussing before Min entered? A stab pierced her rib cage where it remained like an open wound. She recognized it as jealousy. A curse where Blake was concerned because Min had no right to be jealous. He didn't belong to her. She had no claim to him, not even after their love-making the night before.

But the thought of sharing him made her fingers curl into a fist. "Were you watching the play too just now?" she said to both of them in an attempt to learn more of what precisely *had* occurred between them.

"We were spying on Lord Hawkesbury," Alice said with a twinkle in her eye. A twinkle, not a gleam or a shine but a *twinkle*. Women's eyes only twinkled when they had mischief on their minds.

Min could think of all sorts of mischief a man and woman could get up to in a tiring house while the actors were on stage. Although with old man Croft looking on, perhaps not.

"He's sitting with two women," Min said, ignoring the green-eyed monster lurking on her shoulder. "Do you know who they are?"

Alice poked her head through the curtain. Behind her back, Blake's gaze met Min's. She smiled but couldn't summon a single ounce of happiness into it. Blake had made it clear last night would not happen again, and it seemed he'd already moved on.

"Lady Enderby and her daughter," Alice said, closing the curtain again. "Patience or Temperance or something like that. Hawkesbury's charm doesn't seem to be working on his intended though. See how she leans away from him slightly as if—."

"Intended?" Blake stared at Alice and nearly dropped the prompt book. Min carefully took it out of his hands and placed it on a nearby coffer. A ruined prompt book would be a disaster. "They are to be wed?" he went on.

"Aye. You didn't know?" Alice said. "I thought everyone knew."

"I obviously don't move in the same illustrious circles as you," he said wryly.

"You'd be surprised at the things I hear," Alice said, a somewhat secretive smile on her lips. "Actors have access to courtiers *and* their servants and can move between the two societies seamlessly. Some, like Henry and Edward, are desired by so many who watch the plays and think them to be the heroes they portray..." She shrugged. "Let's just say they are privy to much gossip. And since actors like to talk by nature, they talk to me, the little seamstress no one takes any notice of."

"I find it hard to believe you could ever go unnoticed," Min said. She meant it too. The woman wasn't a beauty but she was intriguingly pretty, added to which she had a certain quality about her—a quick wit and the confidence of a woman capable of befriending anyone.

Alice cast her a sardonic smile. "Oh, you'd be surprised. The actors quite forget I'm here sometimes." She glanced to her father then leaned towards Min. "I see all sorts of things I'm not supposed to. When Father's not here of course. He makes sure everyone behaves themselves when I'm around." She sounded a little disappointed by that.

Min couldn't help laughing. And with that simple exchange, she felt herself relax. Despite her jealousy, she liked Alice.

Blake cocked an eyebrow. "I'm not sure I want to hear any more. What else can you tell me about Lord Hawkesbury and his bride-to-be?"

"Their mothers arranged the betrothal when the girl was a babe in arms," the seamstress said.

"Is the match a favorable one? I know nothing of her family."

"They're rich and she's the daughter of a viscount so I'd say it's definitely favorable on both sides. She'll move up a rung in rank and he'll gain her dowry which is considerable if the rumors are to be believed."

"He doesn't need it," Blake said. "Hawkesbury is a very wealthy man."

"How odd." Min peeked through the curtain once more at the threesome in the gallery. Blake shifted beside her, drawing closer, and the exotic scent of him filled her nostrils, his heat caressed her skin. Thank goodness she wasn't the sort to swoon or she'd have been flat on her back at his feet already. "A love match?" she heard herself ask. She couldn't be entirely sure who she was discussing anymore.

"Who can tell?" Alice said. "She's much younger than him."

"She can't be more than seventeen," Min said, closing the curtain once more. "And he would be at least your age, Blake."

He gave her a thin look. "Thirty is not so old."

"It is when you're seventeen."

He stared at her for longer than decent. Just as she was about to look away, he said, "How old are you?"

"Twenty-two."

"I thought you were older," he said and shook his head. Whatever for?

"Why have they not yet married?" Alice asked, breaking into their conversation.

"Perhaps they're trying to decide if they like each other," Min said, tearing herself away from Blake who was watching her with far too much intensity. "I've seen Lord Hawkesbury here several times but this is the first with her."

"Aye." Alice nodded. "He used to always come with his sister or alone. I've never seen this girl before either. Perhaps it's an indication they will be wed soon."

"He looks a little...disinterested in her," Min added. "He's not looking at her at all."

"That in itself is odd," Alice noted. "It's been my experience that Lord Hawkesbury gives women his full attention no matter who they are."

"She's a remarkably pretty girl," Blake added.

Another one. There were far too many pretty girls in London, and they all seemed to be parading themselves in front of Blake.

"He's not looking at the play either," Alice said. "Who could he be seeking, I wonder?" She suddenly wagged her finger at Blake. "That reminds me. You were asking about a lady the other day. Lilly."

Blake whipped around to face her. "Yes? What about her?"

Who was Lilly? And why was he reacting so strongly at the mere mention of her name? The green-eyed monster's talons clawed at Min's heart. It hurt.

"I remember her speaking to Lord Hawkesbury on more than one occasion," Alice went on. "Not that that's surprising. He's an easy man to talk to and very charming."

"Alice," Croft said, coming up behind them, "we do not gossip about our betters, especially our patron."

"Oh Father, don't be such a puritan. Gossiping about the people who run this country is a legitimate way to pass the time and as far as I know it hasn't been outlawed."

"Yet," he said with a pointed glare.

Blake coughed. "Lord Hawkesbury and Lilly," he prompted.

"Who's Lilly?" Min asked again.

"Oh yes," said Alice over the top of her father's mutterings and Min's question, "they struck up a conversation when they met in the tiring house after one of our performances. A dire play called... Oh, I don't remember but it was awful."

Blake grew pale beneath his sun-kissed skin. This Lilly woman certainly had a profound effect on him. He'd never gone pale because of Min before.

"Blake," Min said, hands on hips, "who is Lilly?" Whoever she was, Min knew with absolute certainty that she was linked to the reason he wanted to join the company. Perhaps the secret he couldn't share with Min was Lilly's secret.

It didn't stop her from wanting to know the truth. All of it. She was beyond caring about other people's secrets, she wanted to know why Blake was so interested in Lord Hawkesbury, why he'd used Min to find a way into the company, and most of all, she burned to know who on God's earth was Lilly. She no longer wanted to be left in a darkened room without so much as a candle for light. Blake had embroiled her in his situation, and she deserved to know.

"Well?" she said.

He rubbed a hand through his hair and down the back of his neck. For an entire heartbeat, Min thought he would tell her.

But then he said, "Not here. And not now. I'll explain later."

"Yes," she said, "you will."

A flicker of surprise at the determination in her voice crossed his face before he controlled his features once more. "Wasn't she chaperoned?" he asked Alice.

The seamstress frowned. "Yes, by her mother." Her face cleared and she laughed. "Now there's an interesting woman."

His eyes widened for a fleeting second. "You have no idea."

"You know her? Now what was her name again?" Alice clicked her tongue in thought. "Ah yes, Lady Warhurst, the widow of a baron from up north. Apparently she married for love the second time around to a merchant adventurer. Now what was *his* name...?" She snapped her fingers then pointed at Blake. "Blakewell!"

"Blakewell!" Min blurt out. Style, coming off stage through the curtain, shushed her. "But you are—."

Blake half shook his head, warning her—*commanding* her?—not to say his full name—Robert *Blakewell*. It irked her, particularly because she didn't know *why* she had to keep his identity a secret. But she shut her mouth anyway. For now, she would keep her own counsel.

"Blake and Blakewell," Alice mused, "are remarkably similar names." The seamstress stared unblinking at him, her jaw set firm. A spare pin fell out of her padded shoulder roll and landed silently on the floorboards.

He picked it up and handed it back to her. "Thank you. You've been most helpful."

"The young lady's name was Lilly Blakewell," Alice said and Min silently cheered her. Alice had no such qualms about questioning Blake right there in the tiring house. "Are you related?"

The stabbing in Min's chest eased. The girl in question must be a relation, not a love interest. She felt her face cool and her hand unclenched at her side, not that she'd realized she'd balled it into a fist until that moment.

"Blakewell?" Croft said, joining them. "As in the pirate?"

Min choked on air.

"Our bookkeeper is a pirate?" Alice said on a gasp.

Blake swore. "*Privateer*." He glanced at Min. She could only stare like a half-wit back at him. For once, there were no words in her head let alone her mouth. "Lilly Blakewell is my sister," he said to them all. "Lady Warhurst is our mother."

"You're a pirate," was all Min could manage. She simply couldn't get past that piece of information. She did register that his mother had a title but it seemed quite insignificant compared to the fact that he stole from people for a living, and probably murdered them to do it.

"*Privateer*. I have a letter of marque from the queen and everything. I'd show it to you but I don't have it on my person at this moment."

She gave him a withering glare. How could he treat his occupation so lightly? No wonder he had a jaded look about him, as if he'd seen too much in his lifetime. He certainly *had* seen too much. And done too much.

"You didn't know?" Alice said to Min.

"No."

"I assumed you were...good friends."

Good friends being code for lovers?

Out of the corner of her eye she saw Blake go very still. "Not at all," Min said. "In fact, I know very little about him."

He expelled his breath in a *whoosh*. What had he expected her to say? That she'd just met him two days before and only then because she'd needed someone to act as the writer of her plays?

"You'll have to tell me the story of your meeting one day," Alice said. "It sounds interesting."

"And what could a *privateer* possibly want with Lord Hawkesbury?" Croft asked, squaring his shoulders and rolling a long needle between his finger and thumb.

Blake eyed the needle. "That is my personal business, and it has nothing to do with this company."

"But it does. You are part of this company now, for good or evil. Just make sure it's not the latter. Remember, whatever befalls our patron befalls every single one of us too."

Min shuddered and crossed her arms against a sudden cool breeze that fluttered the edge of the curtain. She caught Blake watching her and she looked away.

Alice snorted. "Good Lord, Father, you've been associating with actors too long. Your dramatic heart is showing."

"Can I have some assistance here!" Style shouted from the back of the tiring house where he was changing costumes.

Croft stared Blake down for several more seconds before retreating to help Style. Alice followed him. Min peered out towards the stage and the audience again. Lord Hawkesbury had gone.

"You're a pirate," she said without turning back to Blake. No matter how hard she tried not to, she kept returning to that piece of news.

"Privateer," he ground out. "Why can no one see the difference?"

"Because there is no difference." She threw her hands up in

the air. "Tell me, Blake, how many seamen have you killed to retrieve enough gold to satisfy your lust for it?"

He leaned against the wall and crossed his ankles. In that stance, the long lean lines of his body appeared elegant and lackadaisical. A false impression because he was certainly neither. "They were enemies of our country." He shrugged.

"They were still people!"

"You forget that we went to war against the Spanish Armada only last year. I captained my ship in the battle, alongside Raleigh. Without us *privateers*, you would be under Spanish rule by now." The cool, casual tone was at odds with the muscle pulsing in his jaw and the whiteness of his lips. "Is that what you want?"

"That is not the point," she said. But how to make him see that it was all right to defend one's country but to seek out and destroy ships purely for profit was...disturbing to say the least?

The coldness filtering into the tiring house from outside seeped through to her bones and settled there. How had she ever got herself entangled with such a dangerous man? She'd suspected he was no saint but she had at least thought his soul was a good one, a trustworthy one, despite the assurances he gave her to the contrary.

She'd been so wrong.

"Does your...career have anything to do with your presence here and your questions about your sister and Lord Hawkesbury?" she said.

"No. That is a private matter."

"So you've said."

He winced and something akin to pain sliced through his features. "Min, please." He moved to her with lightning speed, not giving her a chance to even flinch. He pressed his thumb to the corner of her mouth and cupped her jaw. The unexpected and gentle touch was like a wave of heat, thawing the ice within her.

She had her answer—she'd become entangled with Blake because she couldn't resist him.

"I'll come to you later," he said. "And tell you all."

Her body lifted and she felt like she was floating about the room. "Later?" In her chambers?

But she didn't get an answer. Applause erupted from the inn-yard and Style came up to them. Blake's hand fell away and Min felt the loss of his touch as keenly as she had last night when he'd left her bed.

"You should be pleased," Style said to Blake. He looked like a fat king after consuming a sumptuous meal—very pleased with himself.

The rest of the players came through the curtain and made their way to the back of the tiring house to change. Several clapped Blake on the back. Shakespeare stopped, a grin from ear to ear.

"A first rate effort," he said. "It seems your newfound passion and life experience have paid off."

The glare Blake gave him could have withered an entire field of wheat. Shakespeare's already high hairline lifted further as he raised both eyebrows at Min. She flushed. Had he guessed that Min and Blake had become lovers?

"The audience seemed to enjoy it too," Shakespeare went on. "Everyone was here today. Hawkesbury himself of course, but did you see Marlowe and Henslowe skulking off to the side?"

"Henslowe!" Style's top lip curled into a sneer. "If I see that whey-faced maggot anywhere near my play I'll run him through with my blade."

"Best learn how to use it first," Freddie said from behind the screen where he and some of the other players were changing.

Style pulled at the hem of his jerkin and tossed his head. He hadn't put his hat on so the gesture didn't have quite the same grandiose effect as when the feathers jiggled about. He pointed at the prompt book, sitting on top of the chest where Min had placed it earlier. "Guard that book with your life," he said to Blake. "Don't let those vermin anywhere near it. If they get their hands on it I've no doubt that unscrupulous cock will put on his own version down at the Rose as soon as he can." He then proceeded to lock it away himself.

Edward joined them, dressed once more in his immaculate day attire. "We haven't had an audience that size in years."

"That's because we haven't had a good play for years," said Freddie from the rear door. Some of his white face paint clung to the edges of his temples and his lips were still pink from the stain he'd applied to play Livia. Alice handed him his cap. He slapped it on his blond head. "Who's for a drink then?"

Two of the hired players followed him out.

"You still haven't told us what you think, Blake," Style said. Wells, Edward, Croft and Alice all stopped what they were doing and waited for their bookkeeper's response. Shakespeare was struggling with his ruff and didn't appear to be listening.

"I've told you what I think," Blake said with a shrug. "It's a good play."

Min chewed her lip. One slip, one small hint that she was the author, and he would ruin everything.

It made her slightly ill to think perhaps he *wanted* to ruin it. He did seem unnaturally interested in Lord Hawkesbury and not in a friendly way. Did he want to bring about the earl's downfall for something he had done to his sister as Croft suggested? There had to be a connection between the two. Blake's interest in both was no coincidence.

Did he realize that bringing down Lord Hawkesbury would also bring about the demise of the troupe? And of Min's own dreams?

Did he care?

She watched him, trying to garner some clues as to his intentions, but his usual blank expression had returned. The one that gave nothing away. The one that made him appear like the cold, unforgiving man she'd assumed him to be at their first meeting.

First impressions are often correct.

She plopped down on a nearby stool and folded her shaking hands in her lap. Foolish, foolish girl. She'd quite possibly made love to the man who could ruin everything she'd ever wanted.

Blake's narrowed gaze slid to her. She looked down at her hands and tried to breathe in deeply to overcome her sudden nausea.

"What did you think of today's performance?" Style said. "Better than yesterday's?"

"Does it matter what I think?" Blake said. He suddenly

looked like he wanted to get away from them all. Not so much a trapped and frightened hare but a caged and angry lion.

"Of course!" Style pouted. "As an educated man, and a talented playwright, I value your opinion."

"Then the performance was fine."

Style almost looked like he would accept Blake's judgment, but then he licked his bottom lip, rocked back on his heels and said, "But...?"

With a loud sigh, Blake picked up a gladius from the prop table. He tossed the shorter, heavier Roman sword from hand to hand, as if getting the feel for it. His own sword remained snugly at his hip.

Style reeled back, eyes wide. The others appeared uncertain as to what Blake intended to do with the blade, except for Shakespeare who merely glanced their way, an odd smile on his lips. As with most of the costumes, the gladius was authentic. A swordsmith had crafted it in the same forge as rapiers and other swords. It could kill or severely injure depending on how the wielder used it. And Min was in no doubt that Blake knew what he was doing.

"The sword fight needs work." He tossed the gladius into the air and caught the blade end, flat side down. He held the handle out to a white-faced Style.

The manager cleared his throat before taking it. "Work?"

"Have you ever been in a real sword fight with real weapons?"

"These are real." Style thrust the point out so Blake could see. Blake had to take a quick step backward into the curtain separating tiring house from stage. Style earned a glare for his stupidity.

"I know," Blake said. "But you don't use them as if they are." He picked up another gladius and beckoned Henry over. "You've got the most moves to do in the sword fight, Wells, the one and only I might add." He shot Min a mischievous smirk which quite unnerved her. One minute he was scowling and looking like he wanted to use the sword on someone, anyone, and the next moment he was playful. Perhaps it was the prospect of violence that had cheered him.

"There's no space in here." He opened the curtain. "Come onto the stage."

"No space for what?" Style said, following him out. Everyone except Shakespeare joined them. The audience had dispersed, only a few inn servants remained, clearing away all evidence of the crowd who'd either gone home or into the taproom. Jane was nowhere to be seen and had probably returned home as Min had suggested she do.

"Practice," Blake said to Style. "You and Wells are going to re-enact the sword fight and I'm going to make suggestions for improvement."

"B, but—."

"Do you want your play to look authentic? Or would you rather have every man in your audience who's ever used a sword snicker at your ineptitude?"

Style's jowls wobbled in indignation. Then he pushed Henry Wells forward. "As you said, Henry here has the most moves. Demonstrate on him."

"Very well. You're Marius," Blake said to the young actor, "and I'm Titus. Come at me as you do in the first scene."

"Second," Style and Min said together.

Blake beckoned Henry to attack him. "Come on."

Henry ran at him, his sword raised in a battle stance. Blake thrust out his own gladius and parried it with what must have been a bone-jarring blow. The clang of metal echoed around the inn-yard. Henry pulled up at the edge of the stage and rubbed his elbow.

"Titus is supposed to engage in the fight," Style said huffily. "Not force Marius to the side."

"That's because Marius did two things wrong," Blake said. "First, he ran when he should have moved with more purpose. It's easy to force someone off course when they're coming at you fast. Second, he was holding the sword incorrectly." He beckoned Henry back. "The gladius is not like a rapier. Hold it like this," he hefted his own blade, "with your thumb here. If it's too heavy, use two hands. Now thrust again, this time without running at me."

Henry blinked at him. "Perhaps you should get a shield. Titus and Marius both have shields in this scene."

Blake sighed. "We don't need shields. We're simply doing this as an exercise."

"I'd prefer you didn't use shields anyway," Croft said from the curtain separating the stage from the tiring house. "The dents are nigh impossible to get out."

"And you need to be mindful of the costumes too," Alice said. "A rent in a sleeve means more work for me."

"We're striving for authenticity, are we not?" Blake said. "A rent here or a dent there is inevitable. Wells, come again."

This time Henry stood his ground and thrust his blade at Blake. Again Blake parried but at least Henry was still standing exactly where he should be.

"Wrist up," Blake said.

Henry repeated the move twice more, and each time Blake dashed the gladius away as if it were nothing more than a twig.

"Good. Now put some shoulder into it. Marius is a big, strong hero and he's defending his woman. Every strike of his blade needs to reflect that power."

Wells tried again and again. On the third thrust, Blake had to dance away to avoid the blade. Of course, Min didn't know that he'd moved aside until she re-opened her eyes.

The other players cheered. One of the servants, leaning on his broom in the courtyard, whistled.

"What's going on out here?" Shakespeare said, emerging from the tiring house.

"Blake is teaching Henry to fight like a man," Alice said.

"Oh dear," Shakespeare said with a laugh. "This could take a while."

"He already came close to injuring Blake," Min said. Far, far too close.

Alice laughed softly. "How could you possibly know with your eyes closed?"

"Blake had to move," Min said. A shiver shimmered down her spine. "If he hadn't..." The thought was too awful to put into words.

"I don't think you have much to worry about. Your friend

seems to know how to use that sword the way I know how to wield a needle."

"I hope you're right." Min blew out a measured breath. "But even so, perhaps I'll just go back into the tiring house and tidy up. I'm discovering I rather abhor violence."

"Ho! What's going on here?" the booming, slightly amused voice of Lord Hawkesbury, emerging from the taproom, halted her and the sword fight.

Henry dropped his weapon with a yelp. Blake's grip whitened around the hilt of his.

"We're practicing, my lord," Style said, rushing down the stage steps to join Hawkesbury. "Care to watch? It turns out our playwright has some experience with swordsmanship and has offered to show young Wells how to make the fight scene look more authentic."

"A writer who can also fight?" Hawkesbury inclined his head. "Intriguing. Carry on." He leaned against the wall on the far side of the inn-yard, arms and ankles crossed lazily. An ostler leading a horse moved past the stage and the dusty traveler who'd ridden in stayed to watch too.

Henry picked up his sword. Blake tossed his gladius from palm to palm and beckoned Henry forward. "Wrist up," he said.

Henry stopped, nodded. "Sorry." He rolled his shoulders. "I'm ready now." He tried again. As before, Blake had to move out of the way of what could have been an injuring blow. Henry continued to strike, again and again. After several attempts, his breath came in short bursts and beads of sweat popped out on his brow.

"Titus isn't supposed to get the upper hand," Style said, hands on hips. "You need to stop moving about, Blake. We have our steps already perfectly memorized. You can't change them now."

"Memorized?" Blake said.

"Yes. They're the same as every sword fight in every play that has one."

"Then you need new steps. What I've seen is sluggish at best. No swordsman who wants to preserve his life would move the way your players move up here."

"Ouch," Shakespeare muttered. Alice shushed him.

"Of course we want to be as authentic as possible," Style blustered with a glance in Lord Hawkesbury's direction. "But we have limited time in which to practice new moves."

"We're a little busy learning new lines," Edward said with an apologetic shrug.

"But we do appreciate what you're trying to do," Henry said with an encouraging smile. "At least now I know how to hold the sword like a real Roman. Well, an ancient Roman that is."

Far from looking disappointed, Blake simply shrugged and handed his sword to Croft. Min could finally breathe again. No more fighting.

"I'm off to the taproom," Edward announced. "Who'll join me?"

"Aye," said Henry. "I've worked up a thirst."

"The girl and I have work to do," Croft said, "but I'll join you later."

Alice sighed. Min gave her a sympathetic look. She too should be returning home to work on her father's paper and her new play, but she couldn't leave Blake without speaking to him first.

I'll come to you later.

Later *when*?

She tried to catch his eye but he wasn't looking at her. His gaze was fixed on Lord Hawkesbury. The earl hadn't moved from his position. He stared back at Blake, a slight frown troubling his handsome brow.

"Do I know you?" he said.

"Not directly." Blake pulled at the cuff of his doublet and Min wondered if he still had a dagger hidden there.

And if he would use it.

"You look familiar," Hawkesbury said. "What did you say your name was again?"

"Blake."

"Full name?"

The servants who had resumed their cleaning stopped once more. Even the traveler had halted again in his journey to the taproom. They, like Min, sensed that Hawkesbury was demanding, not asking. Where the earl had been entertained by the display only moments before, now he was rigid with tension.

"Just Blake," Blake said evenly.

"What is he doing?" Croft whispered. "He must answer his lordship! If he doesn't, he might cause trouble."

"If he *does* answer him," Alice muttered, "then there'll definitely be trouble."

Min swallowed and willed Blake to walk away, to get out before he said too much, did too much. But he wouldn't. She knew it like she knew her father could never give up his work. It wasn't in his nature. Blake wasn't about to abandon the confrontation now.

Lord Hawkesbury approached the stage, his cool gaze never leaving Blake. "Anyone would think you are deliberately trying to avoid giving me your name."

"Do you take wagers?" Blake said.

Hawkesbury hesitated. "If the price is right."

"Then I'll make you an offer. Join me up here and help me show these players how to fight. If you win, I'll tell you my name."

The earl's shoulders seemed to loosen, and a smile played around his lips. "And if *you* win?"

Blake shrugged. "I tell you nothing unless I want to. And I get the satisfaction of knowing I beat the great Lord Hawkesbury in a swordfight."

Hawkesbury threw his head back and laughed, a deep throaty sound that filled the inn-yard. But it lacked humor. Style joined in but no one else appeared to think it funny. Not a single person moved. Min couldn't even breathe let alone walk away.

Lord Hawkesbury climbed the stairs, his gaze on Blake. Always on Blake. They were of a height, Min realized when they both stood on the wooden platform, although Lord Hawkesbury was leaner but no less broad across chest and shoulder. Like Blake, he didn't wear the latest ridiculous fashions but his clothes had a simple yet elegant cut.

"And how," he said, the smile turning grim, "do you propose we determine a winner?"

"First blood," Blake said.

Min heard Croft blow out a breath. She exchanged glances with Alice. First blood was better than a fight to the death but it could still prove fatal. A small scratch could fester and see the injured party die several days later.

"This might get interesting," Shakespeare said in her ear. "Watch closely. There'll be a great deal a writer can learn from a fight between two beasts like we see standing before us."

"Beasts?" Min said weakly.

"Aye. And I suspect these two are not the sort to be tamed. Do you not agree?" He watched her with those dark, all-knowing eyes, not a hint of humor gleaming in them now.

"Yes," Min said weakly. "I was beginning to suspect that myself."

"You're an intuitive woman," he said. "I hope your friend knows what he's doing."

"So do I. Do you know if Hawkesbury is a good swordsman?"

Shakespeare shrugged one shoulder. Alice leaned towards them. "He's the best in London so I hear," she said.

A small moan escaped Min's lips.

"An interesting wager," Lord Hawkesbury said. "I accept." He stripped down to his shirt, tossing his outer clothing aside as if it had cost little, although Min suspect the beautiful black velvet doublet slit to reveal the gold silk lining beneath would have cost him more than she'd earned for her first play. Blake followed suit. "Sword!"

Croft threw them both a gladius.

They raised them and Min felt quite ill. Perhaps she'd sit the fight out in the tiring house. But when the first *clang* of steel on steel echoed around the inn-yard, she found her feet couldn't move.

"This will be an afternoon of entertainment," Edward said, uneasily.

"Let's hope he has the good sense to lose," Style said. No one had to ask who he was referring to.

Henry blew on his hands then winced when Blake missed Lord Hawkesbury's arm by the width of a hair. "That was close," he said.

"I hope your friend knows what he's doing, Min" Alice said. "If he injures our patron, his plays might never see the light of day again in this troupe."

Min closed her eyes and sent up a silent prayer. She knew more than anyone that Blake knew what he was doing. Injuring the earl was precisely what he had in mind.

Or worse.

The two swordsmen thrust and parried with apparent ease. It was like watching a dance—one would advance, the other retreat until they were courting each other around the stage. Sometimes one got the upper hand but then the other would change tactics and the dance shifted again. Min found she was as riveted to the fight as she had been to the first performance of her play.

"They're quite beautiful to watch," Alice murmured. "So graceful in their movements."

Min refrained from telling the seamstress she was mad. "I'm not sure those are the words I would use." Gut-wrenching, barbaric and heart-stopping sprang to mind.

And then her heart did stop. Blake's back foot teetered on the edge of the stage and Hawkesbury took advantage of his opponent's momentary distraction. He lunged. Blake just managed to deflect the blow but not before the blade snagged his shirt, tearing it open down the front.

Min buried her face in her hands. "I can't watch anymore."

Alice put an arm around her shoulders. "It's all right. He's perfectly fine."

"No blood," Shakespeare noted.

"His shirt is ruined though," Alice said with a hint of professional irritation.

The clash of metal proved impossible to ignore and Min looked up again. The fight had moved off the stage to the courtyard where ostlers and servants jumped back to make room. Blake appeared to have the upper hand with a series of quick jabs, sending Hawkesbury backwards out of reach.

The door to the taproom opened and Freddie emerged, surrounded by at least a dozen youths, all holding tankards of ale. "Whoa, what's happening here?"

The fighters didn't seem to notice him as they moved around the courtyard, using every inch of space, causing the crowd down there to flatten against the walls.

"Two to one on Hawkesbury," Freddie announced. "Who'll take it?" Five of his friends immediately put up their hands.

"That boy," Style muttered.

A grunt from Blake drew everyone's attention back to the fight. Hawkesbury had Blake up against a pillar. His blade descended.

Min felt faint.

Blake ducked at the last moment and the gladius rammed into the plasterwork. If Blake hadn't moved, he would have been killed.

"I thought this wasn't supposed to be to the death," Min said, more to herself than anyone in particular.

"Hawkesbury knew Blake would move," Shakespeare assured her. "Don't worry. There seems to be an odd sort of rhythm to their fight. It's like the one knows exactly what the other is going to do."

"Like our fight scenes," Style said.

"No," Croft said darkly. "Nothing like our fight scenes."

"If they're so evenly matched," Min said, "how will it ever end?"

"One of them will tire," Alice assured her.

Shakespeare nodded. "Or will do something unexpected."

As he said it, Blake picked up a bucket of water one of the servants had been using to clean away the urine and other muck left by the groundlings. As he ducked out of the path of Hawkesbury's blade, he swung his arm around and smashed the bucket into the side of the earl's head. Hawkesbury sank to the ground and grunted as water drenched him.

Freddie whooped from the sidelines. His friends applauded.

"You can't do that!" Style said, standing on the edge of the stage, hands on hips. "It's against the rules."

"I don't recall there being any rules," Alice said. She glanced at her father. His mouth was set into a grim line as he watched the fight.

Hawkesbury shook his head and droplets of water sprayed

in an arc around him. Then he had to leap to the side as Blake thrust his gladius at the earl's shoulder. He rolled, and as he did so, Blake lunged. Hawkesbury scrambled out of the way and jumped to his feet. As if he'd not just been about to have a blade pierce his body, he engaged Blake once more, glancing blow after blow and managing to get in a few thrusts of his own.

With a roar of frustration, Blake kept up the attack, his momentum backing Hawkesbury into the stage. Everyone except Min drew closer to the edge to get a good view of the action. She couldn't look.

Then suddenly Blake was on the stage. He'd hoisted himself up onto the shoulder-height platform and ran to the back of the stage where he pulled down the curtain hanging at the entrance to the tiring house. He was so close to Min she could see the beads of sweat on his top lip and the ice in his eyes. She shivered.

Hawkesbury leapt onto the stage too and sprinted towards Blake.

"Watch out!" she shouted. But her warning was unnecessary because Blake was already turning. He flung the curtain at Hawkesbury.

The earl caught it, but in doing so became tangled in the material. Blake seized the opportunity and swiped his blade horizontally at Hawkesbury's arm.

Both men grunted. The earl tried to free himself from the material. Blake raised his sword high over his head and changed his grip. His lips curled, his blade descended, aiming straight for Hawkesbury's throat.

Min gasped. "Blood! I see blood!"

Blake dropped his arm. His chest heaved, dragging in air, and sweat dripped from his brow, spotting the wooden stage. He stared at Hawkesbury with an intensity that terrified Min. She recognized it. She'd seen that look on Blake's face before but in its opposite guise.

Passion. The passion to kill.

"Who's bleeding?" It was Style, taking the curtain Hawkesbury shoved at him.

"I am." Hawkesbury indicated his forearm where blood

trickled from a gash. Damp, dark hair covered his forehead and he peered at Blake from beneath its clumped strands. "You win," he said with a brief nod and a quirk of his lips.

"Let me see to the wound," said Croft. The earl allowed him to study his arm. "It's not deep. But you need to keep it clean."

Hawkesbury nodded, his gaze not leaving Blake's. Blake glared back at the earl. His animosity towards him hadn't faded. He still looked like he wanted to run him through.

"You fight well," Hawkesbury said. "*Blake*."

Blake's eyes narrowed and his grip tightened around his sword hilt.

"Ah, perhaps you should hand those over to me now for safe keeping," Croft said. Hawkesbury gave his sword up and so did Blake, eventually.

The earl flicked his hair off his face with a toss of his head. Droplets of sweat sprayed over those nearest him but mostly over Blake. "It would appear you'll keep your mysterious identity a little longer," he said. "But give me time and I'll place you. You look familiar and I'm very good with faces."

Blake ignored him and turned to Henry. "Escort Min home for me, if you will. I have urgent business in another direction."

"Of course," Henry said, just as Min said, "It's not yet dark. An escort is unnecessary."

"Do it!" He blinked, as if surprised by his own vehemence. Then without looking at her, he gathered up his discarded clothing and jumped off the stage. She watched him walk through the arch leading out to the street beyond. He didn't look back.

The little group on the stage stared after him in silence. Freddie and his cronies on the ground were busy exchanging money and reliving the fight, blow by blow.

"Freddie!" Style shouted. "Fresh water and bandages for his lordship's wound. *Now* lad!"

Grumbling, Freddie returned to the taproom, unhurried.

"You would have won if he'd fought fair," Style said to Lord Hawkesbury. He retrieved the earl's doublet and brushed it down with the back of his hand.

Hawkesbury shook his head. "He was the better swordsman."

"No," Shakespeare said, "you were. But he was more creative."

"Well, he *is* a playwright," Henry said. "He's creative by nature."

Min glanced at Shakespeare then up at Lord Hawkesbury and caught him watching her. He seemed to be trying to read her, to get some answers about Blake from her. Hopefully her face gave nothing away.

"My lord," Style said, holding up the doublet for Hawkesbury to step into.

"He's a friend of yours," the earl said to Min.

"I barely know him."

"Who is he?"

She swallowed. The way he looked at her, with those near-black eyes and a presence almost as powerful as Blake's, he was hard to resist. She *wanted* to tell him. Perhaps he could speak to Blake and sort out their problem, whatever it was.

But, using a line of Blake's, the secret wasn't hers to tell. If he didn't want to tell Hawkesbury, then *she* wouldn't do it. That her loyalty was a little misguided hit her like a rock to the head. He was a pirate, a scoundrel, and a violent man.

But despite all that, despite logic, she cared for him. Perhaps *she* was a little mad.

"His name is Blakewell," Croft said. "I overheard them speaking in the tiring house."

"Father!" Alice growled. "How could you!"

"I owe him nothing," Croft said. "My loyalty is to this troupe and its patron."

"He is part of this troupe. A very large part. Without his plays, Lord Hawkesbury's Men would have soon become nothing."

"Enough, Alice! Go inside and tidy up."

She hissed then stomped into the tiring house, now without its curtain. No doubt her father would hear more of her ire later, but she had enough respect for him to do it in private, Min was sure.

"Blakewell?" Hawkesbury said. He looked a little green

beneath his tanned skin. The self-assured, slightly amused manner was nowhere to be seen. "As in Robert Blakewell?"

"Aye," Croft said.

Min held her breath but Croft didn't mention Blake's pirating. Thankfully. She couldn't imagine how Style would have reacted to that news.

"Who is Robert Blakewell?" Style said. "Is he important?"

Hawkesbury stared at the archway through which Blake had just left. "Yes. He is."

CHAPTER 14

Blake stopped at the Gracechurch Street conduit and splashed water on his face. Combined with the brisk afternoon breeze, it dampened his temper and soothed his aches, allowing him to think rationally for the first time since the sword fight with Hawkesbury had started. The thoughts that crept into his mind were cold. And violent.

The earl might not have won, but he'd put up a good fight. A bloody good fight. If he'd been less concerned about fairness, the outcome could have been different. If the fight achieved nothing else, it showed Blake the measure of the gentleman he was up against. A capable, clever man who could match swords with any pirate Blake had encountered.

He'd met quite a few over the years. Some he'd fought alongside, others against. So many... It was why violence had become second nature to him.

It hadn't always been that way. He'd been sick the first time he'd killed a man. He could still see the Spaniard's bloodshot eyes in his nightmares, and hear the prayer and the blood gurgling from the pirate's mouth. That death, like the others since, had been necessary.

Just like Lord Hawkesbury's may be necessary—if the devil didn't accept responsibility for his actions and marry Lilly. But first, Blake needed confirmation from her. Even with anger sizzling through his veins, he had enough sense to know he couldn't go about killing peers of the realm based on gut instinct alone.

But with her confirmation, he'd do whatever was necessary. He already looked forward to another confrontation with Hawkesbury—more proof that violence was never far from his mind. Up until today, he'd thought it limited to his seafaring adventures. Now it seemed it had spilled over into the rest of his life. He'd even snapped at Min and she was the last person in the world who deserved it.

Violence and Min were like thunderstorms and sunshine. They didn't go together. He regretted that she'd witnessed the swordfight, but at the time he'd been so consumed by hatred that he'd been blinded to her fear and abhorrence. It wasn't until the fight had ended that he saw on her shocked face what any man of sense would have seen earlier—that Min needed protecting from such violence.

And from men like himself. Men who no longer knew how to live without it.

That bothered him. More than he liked to admit.

He quickened his pace and reached home as the sun sank behind the rooftops of the livery halls opposite his Dowgate Street house. He handed his hat to Greeves and took the stairs two at a time to the second floor.

"Lil, it's me," he said, banging on Lilly's door.

She bade him enter and he pushed it open. "It *is* Hawkesbury, isn't it?" He tried very hard to keep his voice steady but failed miserably. If Lilly hadn't guessed he was angry from his knock, she would have guessed it from his words.

"I think we've already had this conversation, Brother." She reclined on the daybed, her feet tucked beneath her skirts. She looked like a piece of fine glassware, colorless and fragile. Her eyes were cloudy with sleep. He must have woken her.

His anger drained away. "Are you all right? You look even worse than usual."

"So tactful," she said faintly. "No wonder the women vie for your attentions."

"Don't jest." He knelt at her side and took her hand. It was cool and damp. "Can I get you something? Wine? Sweetmeats? Mother?"

"No! Please don't. She only just left. Ever since I told her of my condition, she's been unbearably attentive."

"More than usual?"

Lilly gave him a small, tired smile. "Much more than usual. You don't know how lucky you are to be able to escape every day."

"She's worried about you, Lil. She's only trying to do what's best for you."

"As are you?" Her teasing tone had vanished.

"Of course. You're my little sister. It's my responsibility to look after you."

"That's quite a task you've set yourself from the opposite side of the ocean."

He sighed. "Don't start that old argument again. I want to travel and see the world but that doesn't mean I care less for you or Mother."

"You've been sailing for years. Haven't you seen all there is to see yet?"

He managed a smile. "Not quite."

She sank lower into the pillows and stretched out her legs along the length of the daybed. "Then don't expect to be able to protect me while you're not here."

"I don't. I expect Leo to. Our older brother has a lot to answer for." He couldn't keep the snarl from his voice.

She sighed. "Don't blame Leo. He's got a great deal on his mind."

"Like how to marry well and ingratiate himself at court?"

"He has a title to protect and a career to forge, no mean feat in the wake of his father's behavior."

"I'd rather he was protecting you." He clasped her hand tighter and took his time choosing his next words. "The birth of your child will hinder his ambitions somewhat." More like devastate them entirely. If Leo wanted to elevate himself to the position he thought he deserved, he couldn't have the odor of scandal clinging to his person. It already clung to the Warhurst name like horse shit.

"Blake..." She tipped her head back and searched the ceiling. "Don't think I haven't considered that."

"It will all be well if you can marry your child's father. *Tell me,* Lilly." He squeezed her hand, as if that could force the answer out of her. "Is it Lord Hawkesbury?"

"Don't," she whispered.

"Never mind," he said, not caring that his irritability showed. It was time to give her the bald truth. "I know it is. People have seen you together."

Her eyes widened. "Who have you been speaking to?"

"You told me so yourself, in a way."

She half sat up. "I did what?"

"When I asked you if the man was married you couldn't meet my eyes. Yet I believed your denial. I was right to. You didn't lie. Hawkesbury is not married but he's betrothed. You knew that, didn't you? That's why you couldn't look at me."

She chewed on her top lip and her fingers twisted in her lap, but she said nothing.

He wanted to shout at her but she looked like she would shatter if he raised his voice. "Lilly," he said between several deep breaths, "it's over. I know he's the one." He rubbed her knuckles with his thumb. "Tell me what happened. Just give me the word and I'll set it right."

"You can't." Two fat tears slid down her cheeks and she bit her bottom lip but not before he saw it wobble. "Don't you see, Robert, you can't make it better. It's impossible. He's to be married to someone else. He can't break the engagement."

Blake's heart cracked. His sister was always the strong one, the one who tried to keep the peace between her two brothers, who knew how to soften up their mother. He meant what he said—he wanted to make everything right for her. Wanted to make *her* right.

"Can't or won't?" he said softly.

"He says can't." She tilted her chin, defiant. Something of the old Lilly. "And I believe him."

He scoffed. "You believe the man who did this to you? He's turned you into a shadow, Lil. He's set you up for a lifetime of loneliness and misery. He's done all that and yet you *believe* him?"

"Of course I do," she snapped. "Wouldn't you believe the one you loved?"

He sat back on his haunches and stared at her. She closed her eyes but more tears escaped from beneath her lids. "Love?" he whispered.

She nodded. "Have you forgotten what it is? You spend so much time away from the ones who love you most, it wouldn't surprise me." That she had strength enough, passion enough, to put a sneer into her words surprised Blake.

"But...how can you love the man who did this to you?" He didn't understand. She wasn't making sense.

"I had something to do with it too."

"You did?"

She opened her eyes and picked up a white lace handkerchief from the nearby table. "Surely I don't have to tell *you* how a child is made." She wiped her damp cheeks and dabbed at her nose.

"But...do you mean to tell me that you were..." How could he put this sensitively? "...willing?"

"Of course!" She stared at him. "Did you think I was forced?"

"Well, not exactly forced, but...coerced. You're young and he seems like the sort of man who gets what he wants, especially when it comes to the fairer sex. I've heard him called charming."

An odd little smile played around her lips. "He certainly is."

Blake didn't want to know any more. He held up his hands in surrender. "My poor brain can't cope with this. If you love him, and he didn't force you, why is the cur still planning on marrying the other girl? Is it her inheritance?"

She sank back into her pillows again with a deep sigh. "No, I don't think so. I've asked him and he won't say."

"Then I'll ask him."

"No! You'll only use your sword and that won't achieve anything."

Blake wasn't so certain. He thought their swordfight had achieved a great deal. He'd learned the measure of the man and worked off some excess anger in the process. Not that he'd tell his sister. He didn't think she'd want to hear how her brother cut the arm of her lover.

"Besides," she continued, "I've begged him to tell me. Pleaded with him. And if I couldn't get an answer, I don't think you will either."

Another thing he wasn't so sure about. Men had been known to divulge lifelong secrets when the pointy end of a blade pricked their nose.

"Whatever his reasons for marrying her, they must be important ones," she said.

"Why? Because he really loves you and not her?" When she wouldn't meet his gaze, he touched her cheek. "Oh, Lilly."

"Don't," she said, her face crumpling. "At least let me have that."

He said nothing. She was too vulnerable to hear the truth so blandly put—that Lord Hawkesbury didn't love her at all, that he had used her.

"The fact is," Blake said softly, "that he has left you to fend for yourself. I look at you now, so pale and sad, and I wonder how someone could do that."

"He didn't intend to get me with child," she said on a sob. "And I was a willing participant, remember."

"I haven't forgotten," he ground out. "But he should never have made advances towards you if he didn't have the most honest of intentions."

"Oh, Brother, don't be so naïve. Men and women couple all the time and don't expect there to be marriage at the end."

"That's not—."

Oh.

Hell.

Pain stabbed him in the gut. It felt like someone had tied his insides into a knot and was pulling the ends, tightening it.

"Robert? Are you ill? What is it?"

He stood but had to lay a hand on the back of a nearby chair to steady himself. "I, I have to go."

Min.

Lilly caught his hand. "You're not going to do anything foolish, are you?"

He stared down at her but instead of his sister he saw Min's face, blotchy from crying. Min lying on a daybed, her body weakened, her spirit washed away, a shadow of the vibrant woman she'd been. Min—carrying his child. All alone. Ignored by society and perhaps even those closest to her. At least Lilly had her family. Was Min so lucky?

"I don't know," he whispered. He blinked slowly and Min was gone. Lilly frowned back at him.

"I forbid you to go near him." It took Blake a moment to realize she was speaking about Hawkesbury. "Or write to him. Do you hear me?" She shook his hand with surprising force. "If you do, I shall never speak to you again, Robert Blakewell."

He nodded. That was a threat he understood. He pulled his hand away and nodded a farewell. But he got no further than the door. His mother's formidable personage blocked the exit.

"Where are you going?" she said.

"To do something I should have done last night."

"Can't it wait, Son?" She took both of his hands in hers. "You've been gone all day. I haven't seen much of you since your return. Stay. Talk with us." She tried to pull him into the room after her, but he withdrew.

"I can't. I have to go."

She took hold of his elbow. "Surely it's something that can wait?"

"No. It can't. Mother, I agree, we need to talk, but not now."

"Talk about what?"

He sighed. Escaping his mother had always been a difficult thing to do, even as a boy. "About the times you chaperoned Lilly to the White Swan to see the plays put on by Lord Hawkesbury's Men. And all the times she spoke to the troupe's patron after the performances."

If he didn't know her so well he would have missed the telltale signs of her guilt. The rapid flutter of her eyelashes, the closing of her fist. "Don't be absurd." The vehemence of her denial.

"You were there, Mother. You must have seen Lilly and Hawkesbury talking."

"Of course. But I didn't think him capable of..." She sat on a stool beside Lilly and clasped her daughter's hand. It would have been a loving family scene except Lilly was staring at her with something akin to horror.

"You *knew*?" Lilly said. "All this time and you already knew?"

"I saw you talking," Lady Warhurst said with the imperialism of a woman born to her rank, which she was not. "I did not think that he was the father."

"Bollocks!" He rounded on them both.

"Robert! Language!"

"You put the pieces together some time ago, Mother, just like I have now. There is no shrewder woman in England than you. You *knew* Hawkesbury was the man I sought, and yet you told me nothing. You let us all believe you didn't know."

"I..." But she seemed to have run out of fire. She heaved a heavy sigh. "Very well. Yes, I knew." She held up a hand to silence him. He obliged but only because he wanted to leave to go see Min. Interruptions only prolonged his departure. "Unlike you and your brother, I trust that Lilly knows what she's doing. She chose to...lie with Lord Hawkesbury, despite knowing the consequences. It's not what I would have wished on her, and it is certainly not something I would have encouraged had I known the connection had developed so far."

Lilly seemed to wilt beneath her mother's heated glare.

"But it has happened. And we must deal with it as best we can."

"That's what I've been trying to do!" Blake couldn't keep quiet any longer. "I could have done it faster if you'd helped me."

"Helped you to browbeat Lord Hawkesbury into marriage?" She clicked her tongue as if she were chastising a petulant child. "He is not the sort of man who can be easily forced. And I trust Lilly has done as much as she can in that department. If she could not get him to marry her, then I doubt anyone else can."

Lilly put a skeletal hand to her mouth, smothering a sob. Lady Warhurst stroked her cheek. "There now, you've upset her with all this sad talk."

Blake bit his tongue to stop himself reminding his mother that she was the one who wanted to have the conversation. He'd wanted to leave to find Min.

"I have to go," he said. "We'll discuss this further in the morning."

"There's nothing more to discuss," his mother said.

"No? Who shall we claim is the father? Who will introduce the baby into society when the time comes? You? Lilly? And then there's Leo. I don't think Baron Warhurst will be as...understanding when he finds out who the father is."

Lilly started crying again. Blake wanted to go to her and apologize but he was too oafish and didn't know the right words to make her stop. He didn't think false promises would work in her instance, and they were all he had to offer.

"We'll discuss what we're going to tell Leo tomorrow," Lady Warhurst said turning, presenting her back to Blake. "Now go. You're upsetting Lilly."

Gladly. There was something he needed to say to Min and it was best said as soon as possible.

But as he left, he had the sickening feeling he was abandoning the ship for a leaky rowboat.

CHAPTER 15

The fight scene was the best Min had ever written. It was so good she decided to put another one into the third act. Barnaby Fortune was turning into quite the swordsman. Of course nobody died in his fights. Just a few cuts to give the audience the blood they craved.

Min rested her pen in the inkstand and her head in her hands. The fight at the White Swan could so easily have turned fatal. Both swordsmen were capable of great destruction, and she was in no doubt that Blake had wanted to do more than wound Lord Hawkesbury. He'd wanted to kill him.

So why hadn't he? No one would have stopped him. No one watching *could* have stopped him if he set his mind to it. Perhaps Blake had experienced a sudden return of conscience. Or perhaps he wasn't the innately violent man she'd begun to suspect him of being.

With a heavy sigh and a heavier heart, she gathered the pages of her play together and put them aside. She'd best do some of her father's work before she grew too tired to keep her eyes open. It had been a long and arduous day after getting very little sleep the night before thanks to her nocturnal visitor. Her one and likely to be her only.

He wouldn't return ever again. Now that he'd got what he

wanted from her and revealed his hand, she wasn't fool enough to think she factored into his future plans.

She should have been content with that prospect. He was Trouble and Danger all rolled into one—he was a pirate for God's sake!—and she didn't need any further distractions or complications in her life. But her heart felt shredded at the prospect of not seeing those bright blue eyes again or feeling his breath on her throat, his mouth consuming her. She'd grown accustomed to having him in her life. She not only wanted to see him every day, she expected it. He occupied her waking thoughts almost constantly. To go from that to never seeing him again made her feel empty inside, as if she were starving and could not eat enough to fill her stomach.

And then there was the worry over her plays. Without Blake to act as their author, what would happen to them?

Most likely Lord Hawkesbury would ban all performances of her plays by the troupe, effectively ending her career. He knew Blake had a grudge against him now and no one would blame Hawkesbury for ending the association.

She picked up her pen again and dipped it into the ink. Then dropped it at the sound of a light rap at her window. Droplets of ink splattered her father's notes and the pen rolled off the desk onto the rushes. She stared at the silhouette of the man on her balcony.

Blake.

Her heart skidded to a halt.

He was here.

He knocked again, more impatient. She opened the window and stood aside so he could climb through.

"I thought you weren't going to let me in," he said, uncertainty threading through the gruffness. It was something she'd not heard in his voice before, nor had she ever associated it with his character. Blake always seemed certain of everything.

"I was taken by surprise, that's all," she said. "I wasn't expecting you.

He closed the window and seemed to take a very long time to turn around again. When he did, she was disturbed by the tiredness shadowing his eyes, the deepening of the lines across his forehead and around his mouth.

"You're unwell!" She took his arm and steered him to her desk chair, the most comfortable in the room. "Here, come sit down. Good Lord, did you get injured in the fight after all?"

"No, I am well, do not be alarmed." But he allowed himself to be led and he even seemed a little amused by her concern.

She let go of him and shoved him lightly in the chest, not enough to move such a big man but he sat down anyway. "That fight today was an utterly irresponsible and foolish thing to do! You could have been killed or hurt, and so could Lord Hawkesbury and where would you have ended up then? I don't think your money could buy your freedom if Hawkesbury's kin decided to pursue the matter. What were you thinking?"

"I wasn't thinking. Well, not with this." He tapped his temple.

Her gaze shifted lower down, to his hose. "Then what were you thinking with?"

The corner of his mouth lifted. This time she was in no doubt he was amused. "Not with that either." He tapped his chest. "With my heart. Min, sit down. There is something I need to tell you."

"There most certainly is." She pulled another chair closer and sat, concentrating on smoothing out the fabric of her housecoat because anything was better than looking at Blake. His blue eyes seemed to dance in the candlelight and there was something most odd about his countenance. It was as if his self-confidence had been given a tweak.

He leaned back in the chair and regarded her for a long time. She squirmed and waited. She would not hurry him. It wouldn't do to show him how impatient she was for an explanation and for...whatever might happen between them after that.

Her body warmed and loosened at the prospect.

"My sister Lilly is pregnant."

Min's jaw dropped. She didn't realize until Blake leaned forward, placed a finger under her chin and shut it. But instead of letting go, his finger traced the edge of her bottom lip to the corner of her mouth where it lingered.

Then he pulled away. She swallowed and continued to stare.

"She's just confirmed my suspicion that Lord Hawkesbury is the father."

"Oh?" She felt quite dizzy and it took a few shakes of her head to clear it. "That's good. All you need to do is tell him she's with child and he'll marry her."

"He won't. According to Lilly he's set on marrying the Enderby girl we saw him with this afternoon."

"Does he know she's pregnant?"

He lifted one shoulder. "I suspect so. It's not like Lilly to hold back a weapon available in her arsenal. My sister knows how to fight. I've the childhood scars to prove it."

"Oh." Her heart clenched. Poor Lilly.

"She loves him."

It just got worse and worse. "But he doesn't love her?"

"I doubt it. His actions don't sound like those of a man in love."

She had to agree they didn't. They sounded like a man who'd used a woman to sate his carnal desires. "No wonder you wanted to thrash him today."

"I wanted to do more than thrash him."

"I know."

Their gazes met and Min felt a deepening of the connection between them. It must have cost him a great deal of family pride to tell her about his sister. No doubt it was something they wanted to keep quiet until Lord Hawkesbury could be made to marry Lilly, but Blake had offered the secret to Min nevertheless.

Why? Blake was not the sort of man to do things without a very good reason.

"I'm sorry," he said.

"For what?"

"For..." he cleared his throat, "for showing you a side of my nature today not fit to be seen by a woman like you."

"A woman like me?"

"A gentle-hearted woman. You hate violence. I could see it in your face when you saw the blood on Hawkesbury's arm. That makes you somewhat of an oddity," he said with a half-smile.

"Most Londoners would have given up a body part to witness a sword fight between two gentlemen."

She wasn't sure how to tell him that it wasn't the blood but the wildness she'd seen in Blake's eyes that had so disturbed her. The uncontrollable beast lurking inside him had taken over his soul during the fight. And that scared her witless.

"I suppose my upbringing was unlike most," she said weakly.

"That's what makes you so unique. Precious."

Precious? He thought she was precious? Her face heated and she battled to contain a silly smile.

No! Oh no, Minerva Peabody, do NOT get sucked in by a few pretty words and a pair of blue eyes. Danger and Trouble remember? Pirates know how to get what they want.

She struggled to maintain her composure. When she'd won the battle, she said, "So what are you going to do about Lilly and Lord Hawkesbury?"

He removed his hat and rubbed a hand through his hair, making it stand out at odd angles. "I don't know. She doesn't want me to speak to him." He crushed the brim of the hat in his fist. "But I can't leave things as they are. She's my *sister*. The cur needs to be made accountable for his actions."

"Accountable how?"

He shrugged and looked down at his hat, loosening his grip but the brim was beyond repair. Was he deliberately avoiding her gaze? Avoiding her question?

She wouldn't let him. This involved her now too, whether he liked it or not. The ramifications of whatever action he decided to take affected more than just himself and his family. He needed to understand that.

"You used me to get into the troupe," she said, her jaw tight, "and now you want to jeopardize my dream by killing the patron!"

He fixed a hard, unyielding gaze on her. "You used me too. First to have your play performed and then to teach you about desire. I think we're even."

"You black-hearted, vile...*pirate*!"

Instead of rising to her challenge, he sighed and slumped lower in his chair. "Min—."

"Lord Hawkesbury knows who you are," she said, cutting him off. It was all she could think of to wound him. And she wanted to wound him, to prod him into seeing this problem from the point of view of others.

His face slowly changed. The hard angles softened, his cheeks hollowed and misery haunted his eyes. She wanted to reach for him, hold him, but didn't. She couldn't risk it leading to something more, something she couldn't stop. Not with this man, this wild beast. This pirate.

"I see," he said quietly.

"It wasn't me who told him." She wasn't willing to tell him who had given up his identity. She wouldn't risk his ire being turned on anyone else.

"I know it wasn't you or Alice." Which they both knew left only one other person. So much for keeping it a secret.

"How can you be so sure of my loyalty?"

He shrugged. "I just am."

"Someone once told me it's unwise to trust people so readily."

He offered a grim smile at her reminder of his own remark. "I think that person was referring to trusting blackguards like myself."

"You're not a blackguard."

"You don't believe that."

She didn't know what to believe anymore.

"I know I've not given you reason to like me today." He leaned forward and rested his elbows on his knees, his damaged hat dangling between his fingers. "But I want you to know that I've not lied to you, and that I don't want to hurt you."

"Then leave Lord Hawkesbury alone. Find a way to make him wed your sister but do not kill him or harm him or do anything that will jeopardize my plays."

The fact that it might be too late for that hung heavy between them. Neither spoke it but Min knew Blake must be thinking it. If Lord Hawkesbury wanted to disassociate himself with Lilly and her family, then he would want to sever Blake's connection to the troupe. That meant no more performances of his plays —*Min's* plays—now that Blake's identity was known.

"I have an offer for you that might go some way to alleviating your financial strain," he said.

She blinked at him. What was he talking about? What did her family's situation have to do with her plays or Lord Hawkesbury? Surely he didn't think she was writing them simply for the money. Although that certainly helped, it was not everything. Not in the least.

"I think you'd best explain yourself," she said.

He drew in a slow breath then let it out again. Just when she thought he would tell her, he suddenly stood and strode to the window. Was he going to leave already?

She stood too, but she wasn't sure how to stop him leaving. Beg?

Then he turned around, the hat brim suffering once more but this time it was wrung by both hands. He cleared his throat and opened his mouth to speak. But he appeared to have second thoughts and shut it again. Then he did the most odd thing. He knelt on one knee and took her hand in one of his. His thumb rubbed a calloused area of her palm as if he were trying to remove the hardened pad of skin.

"Blake, what are you doing? You'll snag your hose on the rushes if you're not careful."

"Min," he said and cleared his throat again. "Min, I've come here tonight to ask you to be my wife."

Time stopped. Blood ceased to flow in her veins. Her mind shut down. Was this what it felt like to swoon? She plopped down in a chair because her legs could no longer hold her up.

Then everything whirred to life with a vengeance.

He wanted to *marry* her?

Marry!

Her!

"Er." She couldn't get out a single coherent word without her throat closing.

"That's not quite the answer I was after." He smiled. Smiled! The dog.

"Is this your idea of a joke?" she said, pulling her hand out of his.

"N—."

"Because I don't find it funny."

"No! Min. I'm serious." He took her hand again. She removed it from his grasp once more. He sighed and stood up. "Min, I'm trying to do the right thing. You're not making my task any easier."

Task? The right thing? Was proposing marriage to her such a chore?

"We've only known each other a few days, Blake," she said, choosing her words carefully. "What has led you to this in such a short time? Particularly since I was quite certain we came to an understanding last night that there could be nothing more between us?"

He moved to the fire, reduced to a few flames clinging to a single piece of blackened wood. He stoked it and added another log. "I changed my mind. I'd like to marry you. I think it would be a good match."

"For me, certainly. I'd gain your fortune and your good name. But what would you achieve from the union?" She clasped her hands in her lap and a sense of calm soothed her frayed nerves. "I could bring no dowry and my family name has become synonymous with failure on a monumental scale. You'd be encumbered with a father-in-law who is eccentric at best, a candidate for Bedlam at worst, and a wife who writes plays and is prone to flights of fancy. So when you tell me it is what you want, forgive me if I don't believe you."

He wheeled on her, poker in hand. "None of that matters to me, Min!" He returned the poker to the tool stand and knelt before her. "You want to know what I'd gain from the marriage?" When before he couldn't quite look her in the eyes, this time he seemed to have no such problems. What she saw in his gaze unnerved her with its ferocity. "I'd gain *you*. I'd have you to greet me when I get home and warm my bed at night. I'd have you at my side, your strength and resilience, your passion and your loyalty. A woman I can be proud of. A woman I can trust."

More pretty words. They were heartfelt enough, perhaps even true, but there was something unbelievable about his proposal. It took her several anguished moments of alternating exhilaration and disbelief to put her finger on it—he'd not mentioned love.

She swallowed the lump in her throat and willed herself not to shed any tears. They would do her no good. What she needed now was inner strength to say what she needed to say.

"You mentioned having me at your side," she whispered, "but you and I both know that isn't possible. A ship is no place for a woman, Blake, and you're not ready to make a home here." She held up her hand to silence him. Surprisingly, he obeyed. "You are a man of the sea, you want to roam the world and experience more of what life has to offer. Those are your dreams and I am a great believer in following dreams."

He shook his head and his gaze shifted away from hers once more. "I'll give it up. We can buy a house wherever you desire. Your father can come live—."

"Stop! Enough, Blake." She stood and crossed the room to the fire. It was the closest she could be to him and not feel the pull of his powerful presence. "You don't need to feel guilty about last night. I am not your sister."

He stared at her, unblinking, unmoving. Oh dear, had she gone too far?

"I'm not offering marriage out of guilt." But it was a lie and she knew it. What's more, she sensed that he knew that she knew it. "I'll not abandon you, Min." It was enough to confirm her suspicions. He didn't love her. He didn't *want* to marry her, but his sense of duty was so great that he'd been willing to give up so much for her sake.

It only made her love him more.

That's why she couldn't accept. Couldn't tie him to a woman he didn't love with all his heart, couldn't tie him to England when he wanted to see the world. If she did, he would eventually resent her for it, perhaps he'd even come to hate her. She couldn't bear that.

It wasn't fair. She wanted him more than she'd wanted anything in her life, more even than she wanted to write, but not like this. She didn't want his pity or his guilt. She wanted his unconditional love in return.

"I'm not pregnant, Blake. There's no need to worry on that score. You took care of that possibility."

"That's not the point," he snapped. He was breathing heavily, his chest rising and falling as it had done after his fight with Lord Hawkesbury.

"It is for me."

He strode to her, closing the gap between them in a blink. "Min—."

She put her hand against his chest to stop him. His heart thundered against her palm. "Don't. This is awkward enough. Do not prolong it."

"Min." It came out as a sigh not a protest. His shoulders slumped and his head lowered. She dropped her hand. "You are one hell of a stubborn woman."

He didn't know all of it. It took every ounce of her willpower to ignore the screaming of her heart in protest at her refusal.

"I'm sorry," he said.

"There's nothing to be sorry for. You wanted to do the right thing and you should be commended for it."

He grunted. "You have it wrong there. The problem is, I don't want to do the right thing where you're concerned. The right thing would have been to walk away. I couldn't." He wiped his thumb across her cheek.

Don't do that. Don't go and do something so tender. Her heart was already fragile enough. She was barely holding herself together as it was. If he kissed her, she might take back her refusal. And then she'd probably take him to bed.

"Believe me when I tell you that you are the only woman I would wish to marry."

"It's just that you don't want to marry anyone right now?"

His nod was small but it was there. His thumb slipped from her cheek to the corner of her mouth. He leaned in and kissed her, his lips like feathers, his scent intoxicating.

She stood still so her soul wouldn't shatter. But then he released her and she would have given her soul, whole or not, to have him kiss her again.

He took up his deformed hat and opened the window. Cool air flooded the room and soothed her heated skin. Misty rain sprayed the sill and his cloak as he climbed through. He stood on the balcony and lifted a hand in farewell. *Goodbye,* he mouthed.

And then he closed the window and was swallowed up by the night and the rain.

CHAPTER 16

Min awoke late and out of sorts. She'd been up most of the night reliving Blake's proposal and agonizing over whether she'd done the right thing. Every possible scenario had played out in her head, from wedded bliss on a country estate to her own descent into piracy to follow Blake on his chosen path. Needless to say, all scenarios ended happily. And none of them were close to reality. They only served to make her feel more miserable and more certain of the hopelessness of a union between them.

She'd done the right thing. If only the right thing didn't *hurt* so much. The pain was like an arrow through her heart. Not even turning to her play could dislodge it. Her father's work certainly couldn't. It would take something time-consuming and all-absorbing to distract her.

So she went shopping. Alone. The last thing she needed was Jane's sympathetic yet probing questions. Min simply wanted to avoid the subject of Blake altogether.

Shopping turned out to be a very bad idea. Blake's name was on everyone's lips. It seemed vendors and buyers alike on Cheapside had either seen or heard of *Marius and Livia* and wanted to know more about its mysterious author.

The euphoria of hearing how much the play was enjoyed by so many was quickly dashed on the rocks of her disappointment when she recalled what had passed between her and Blake the night before. A deepening of her love for him. The absence of love in his feelings for her. Their final farewell.

It was like the script of a play. One that didn't end well for the hapless heroine.

She made it home without crying—except for the little sob she allowed herself at the onion stall after hearing his name yet again—only to find Ned lingering on her doorstep. Could the day get any worse?

"Allow me to help you with your basket," he said, relieving her of it before she assented. "Shall I carry it up to your rooms?"

No way was she letting Ned anywhere near her rooms and the privacy they offered. "The parlor will do. Thank you."

Inside, he deposited the basket on the small table but not before he lifted the corner of the cloth laid atop her packages, protecting them from the weather and prying eyes. She stopped him before he raised it further. He withdrew his hand as if she'd slapped it away. "So..." He cleared his throat. "You've been shopping."

"Yes. Hence the full basket you've just brought in for me."

"Ah. Yes. Of course. Where did you go?"

"Cheapside mostly."

"Did you buy any fabric? I would have given it to you at a considerable discount if you'd come to me. We've got an excess of fustian in stock at the moment thanks to an incorrect order placed by my inept apprentice. I could have given you an excellent price on it."

"No, no fabric." She hoped her face didn't give away her lie. She'd decided against buying from any of Ned's father's shops. She didn't want to be beholden to him for the favor, nor did she want him to know she had extra money for such a purchase.

Unfortunately he knew now.

"No fabric? Your basket seems quite full..." He stared at it as if hoping to see through the protective layer to all her purchases below.

"Meaning?"

He shrugged one shoulder. "Er, nothing. Nothing at all." A long silence sucked the air out of the room and Ned grew more agitated the longer it went on, fidgeting with his cuff and shifting his weight from foot to foot. Min refused to relieve him of his agony. She was quite content to see him war with himself. Eventually, his curiosity won out. "Has your father found a new patron?"

"No." It gave her a perverse sense of satisfaction not to tell him where the money for her purchases had come from. "Now if you'll excuse me, I should see if Jane needs me."

"Yes, of course." He didn't move. "One thing before I go..." The fidgeting got worse until she thought he might detatch the lace cuff altogether. "Have you thought any more about my offer of marriage?"

"Actually, I have. And I'm afraid I must decline."

"What!" Clearly that hadn't been the response he'd expected.

"I'm sorry, Ned. I simply cannot marry you."

"Don't be absurd." He shook his head in disbelief. "You cannot afford NOT to marry me, Minerva. Look at you." He waved a hand at her gown. "Your attire is shabby, your hands are worn and you probably haven't eaten a good meal in weeks. You cannot go on like this." He stepped closer and grasped her shoulders. "You need to marry me or you'll be out on the street soon."

"We'll be all right." She picked off his fingers and stepped away. "Thank you for your concern, Ned, but I can't marry for money."

He frowned. "Why not? Everyone else does."

"That's not quite true. People marry for love too."

He snorted. "Now you're talking like a woman again."

That's because I am! Instead of screaming at him like she wanted to, she clamped down her jaw and gave him a sour smile. "Love aside, my feelings towards you are not what they should be between a husband and wife."

"But that might change, given time."

There wasn't enough time in the world to make her want to share a bed with Ned. "I like you as a friend but that is all. I'm certain that won't change."

"You can't be certain," he scoffed. "Everyone knows the female sex is fickle. Your feelings could be different tomorrow."

"I can assure you they won't be. Now, if you'll excuse me, I've got to help Jane. Good day, Ned." She wasn't about to leave her basket and its goods to his prying eyes so she waited to see him out.

With another shake of his head and a last look at her basket, he left. Min breathed a sigh of relief and carried her shopping into the kitchen. Jane looked up from where she sat on a stool by the fire mending a hole in her spare netherhose.

"What's for dinner?" Min asked.

"Mutton pie. It's almost ready. What's that you've got in there?" she said, craning her neck to see into the basket.

Min placed it on the table and lifted off the cloth, followed by the flat parcel containing blank parchment for herself and her father. Then she pulled out three bottles of ink, two pens, a length of blue holland and another of black broadcloth, a pair of gloves and a good copy of the map her father wanted.

Jane gasped and stood suddenly, sending her sewing tumbling to the floor. "Oh, dear girl, what is all this?" She picked up the gloves and sniffed them. "I do love the smell of new leather."

"Good because they're yours."

"Oh no, I couldn't." She returned the gloves to the basket. "You already paid me—."

"That was simply what you were owed. This is extra for your continuing good service."

"Oh." Jane fingered one of the gloves. "They're very well made. Excellent stitching."

"Try them on," Min said.

Jane shook her head. "I couldn't. I shouldn't accept them. They must have cost quite a lot."

"Don't worry about the cost and just try them on. Go on," she said when the maid hesitated again.

Jane chewed the inside of her lip and picked up the gloves. She put them to her nose and closed her eyes as she inhaled. "They are lovely."

"It's settled then."

Jane pecked her on the cheek. "Dear girl, you're so good to me."

"Good Lord, Jane, you're acting as if I was giving you the moon. It's just a pair of gloves."

"But such a fine pair. I'll save them for Sundays." Jane wiped her palms down her apron and tried on the gloves, oohing and aahing as they slipped over her fingers. "Can we afford all this, m'lady? There's such an awful lot here."

"We can. And there'll be some left over for a nice piece of beef for next week."

"And cheese without mould?"

"Of course. And no black bread either."

Jane laughed loudly as if it were the funniest thing she'd heard. Then because Min needed a good laugh and Jane seemed so happy, she joined in. After a few inelegant snorts which only set them off again, they plopped down on stools, breathless and red cheeked.

Jane removed her gloves and returned them to the basket. "Aren't you tryin' to economize?" she said, dabbing the back of her hand to her cheeks.

"Oh, Jane, I'm tired of economizing. I've mended clothes until they've become nothing but patches sewn together. I'm trying to cram as much onto a page as possible when I write that I can barely even read it. Just for a while, I want to remember what it's like to not economize." Jane nodded but Min wasn't sure she entirely understood. How could she when she had even less than Min? "Besides, there's still the money from Lord Pilkington coming in. And we do *need* all these things."

"I suppose so. And there'll be another payment from Style for yer next play anyway," Jane said, gazing at her gloves.

Min nodded and plastered what she hoped was a confident smile on her face. She didn't want to destroy Jane's euphoria. Not until she knew for certain what Lord Hawkesbury planned to do regarding the performance of her plays by his company. The outlook might be grim, but Jane did look so happy with her new gloves and her hopes for the future. Min simply couldn't take that away from her yet.

She gathered up all the purchases and returned them to the basket. All except the map. "I'll take Father his gift now. I'll tell him it's for his birthday next month and he might not ask questions about the expense."

"He will when you present him with a new cloak," Jane said, tugging on a corner of the broadcloth.

Min sighed. "I'll cross that bridge once the cloak is made up." She headed to his study but stopped at the closed door. The last time they'd spoken, he'd shattered his spectacles and stormed off in anger. She had no idea how she'd be received but she had to find out. She couldn't avoid him forever. She knocked softly. On his order, she entered.

"Ah, my child, how are you today?" He removed his spectacles—his spare pair—and placed them gingerly on top of an open book. It would seem he wanted to pretend all was well. That suited Min.

"Fine thank you, Father."

"And what, pray, have you been doing with yourself on this pleasant morning?" He glanced out the window. "Is it a pleasant morning?"

"A little cloudy but I don't think it will rain." Min was under no illusions that his question had more to do with his concern over the completion of his own work than any interest in her activities.

"You've been out then?"

She nodded and handed him the rolled up map. "I bought you this. It's the map you wanted."

"Oh?" He looked at it as if it had grown wings. Then he cautiously took it. She chewed her lip as he unrolled it. "Minerva, my girl, this is marvelous!" He shoved aside books and papers on his desk and spread the map out. "Ah, yes." He mumbled to himself as he pointed to various features, then rummaged through several sheets of paper before finding one containing his own calculations. "Mmmm, ahhh, yes, yes." He pulled at his beard and muttered to himself, occasionally nodding.

He was completely engrossed so Min retreated to the door, one small step at a time so as not to catch his attention. She was almost out of the room when he glanced up. There was a light in his eyes, brighter than before, but also something else. Concern?

"Thank you, this is a wonderful surprise, but...what brought on this generosity of spirit?"

"I knew you wanted it so I decided to give you an early birthday gift. Do you approve?"

He nodded and spread his hand lovingly across the map. She should have taken that moment to turn and run. But she was just a little too slow and he spoke before she could escape. "Where did you find the money for it? You didn't go without candles did you? You couldn't write at night without them."

"I managed to save a little extra this week without sacrificing the candles."

"You did?" His beard trembled as he chewed over that piece of information. "Even after the mutton we've been dining on?"

Since when had he become so concerned with the household finances? He'd never once questioned her before. He'd simply allowed her to take over the task of budgeting the family's income when her mother passed away. He'd shown very little interest in monetary matters at all, as long as he had books, paper and ink. The fact that he'd noticed what he'd eaten for dinner was also rather alarming. Usually he didn't care about food, it was simply something Jane brought into his study, disrupting his work. All breads were equal, as were all meats. As long as an empty stomach didn't distract him, he was even known to miss meals entirely unless Jane or Min reminded him to eat.

"I got an excellent price on both the mutton and the map," Min said. The map had been purchased with a part payment, the rest to be paid when she had the funds. It had been a risk considering she wasn't sure where the funds would come from, but she was prepared to take it. Seeing her father happy confirmed that she'd made the right choice.

"Good girl. You always had a head for practicalities. Come here and appreciate this fine piece of cartography."

Crisis over, Min could breathe again. She made a show of looking at the map with him and listening as he eagerly described points of interest. But she really saw nothing except the land masses of England and the New World. So far away. So much ocean separating them.

How long did it take for Blake to sail from one to the other? Her father would know. But she didn't want to find out the answer. It wasn't only the physical distance between them it was also the personal one. She and Blake were oceans apart in experience, views and nature. A marriage could not flourish in those conditions unless someone was willing to compromise, and she didn't think either of them was prepared to, let alone capable of, doing that.

"I must be going," she said. "Enjoy your map. Will you be joining me for dinner?"

"Have Jane bring me something."

"Very well, Father."

"Are you going to finish my paper after dinner?" he asked, peering down his nose at her. So she had not escaped after all. "I would have liked to speak to you about it before the symposium but we've not got time now. It must be printed as soon as possible."

"Of course we'll have time. It's not finished but I will complete several pages—."

"Not finished! What have you been doing these last few days, Minerva?"

"I—."

He slammed his fist down on the map, making Min and everything on the desk jump. "I *told* you to have it ready for the symposium! If it's not finished this afternoon it'll never be printed by tomorrow."

"Tomorrow! But it's another two weeks before the Academy's next gathering." Oh dear, couldn't he even keep track of the days anymore? She patted his arm. "Tomorrow is only the eleventh, Father," she said gently.

He shook her off. "I know that. But the Academy is hosting a special symposium to honor Petrick van Rijn."

"Wh, what?"

He must have mistaken her sickened look for one of confusion. "He's a visiting Dutch scientist who wants to hear our ideas. Minerva, we spoke about this. I *told* you about the symposium."

Min's stomach plunged to her toes and a sense of dread

folded around her. There was no way she could write his paper and have it printed by tomorrow. "I'm so sorry, Father."

"You're *sorry*!" He squared his shoulders and straightened his usually hunched back so that he appeared taller than he had in a long time. "Sorry isn't going to get the paper ready on time, is it?"

Tears stung her eyes but she refused to take the entire blame. "I thought you were talking about the next meeting," she said, desperation making her voice high. "You didn't clarify—."

"You've been writing your poetry and plays again, haven't you! I've been warning you over and over that science is what matters, that it is the future, but you've not listened. Instead you've squandered your talent and time on...on *nonsense*!"

It was on the tip of her tongue to tell him that her plays had bought him a new map and the first decent food they'd eaten in weeks. That *their* immediate future depended as much on her plays as on his science. But she bit her tongue to keep the words to herself. He wasn't in a fit state of mind to hear her defense. She wasn't sure he was capable of hearing the blasts from a thousand horns let alone her small voice.

With a growl, he pushed past her and stalked to the door.

"Father, where are you going?"

He strode up the stairs. Min ran after him. Jane poked her head out of the kitchen as they passed.

"Is everything all right?"

"Yes," Min said without stopping, "I'll be down to dine shortly." But it wasn't all right. She had a dreadful feeling her father was about to do something that she'd not thought him capable of.

Destroying her dreams.

"Father," she said, catching up to him outside the door to her study, "please come back downstairs. You're over-exerting yourself."

But she knew he hadn't heard her. His eyes were wide and dilated, his mouth twisted into an ugly slash. He pushed open her door and stalked to her desk. "Where is it?" he snapped.

"Where is what?" She placed a tentative hand on his shoulder but he pushed it off and began rifling through papers—most of them his own work—scattering them over her desk and onto the floor.

"Father! What are you doing?" She knelt and gathered up the pages but more followed in a snowstorm of parchment. "Stop it! You're making a mess."

"Aha! Here it is."

She looked up. "My play!" He held up the latest version of *The Fantastical Lives and Loves of Barnaby Fortune* in triumph. She dropped all the rescued papers in her haste to stand. "Father, what are you going to do with it?"

"Help you, my poor girl. The sooner this time-wasting twaddle," he flapped the pages in the air, "is banished to the fireplace, the better off you'll be."

"Father, no!" She tried to seize the pages but he put the manuscript behind his back.

"I only have your best interests at heart, Minerva. Once I've relieved you of this cursed muck, the sooner you'll see that I am right." He moved to the fireplace. There were no flames but a puff of air on the glowing embers would see the pages catch alight in no time.

"No! Don't!" She grabbed his elbow and pulled hard. He winced and dropped his arm, allowing her to snatch the play out of his fingers.

He reeled on her. "Give it back to me!" His breathing labored dangerously.

But in that moment, she didn't care about anything except her manuscript. It was all she had left now that Blake was out of her life. She held it close to her chest.

"You ungrateful, irresponsible daughter! I am your father and I am demanding you give me those pages."

"Or what?" She barely recognized her own voice, clogged with emotion.

He'd never struck her in his life but from the raw anger pinching his face, she suspected that was about to change. She braced for the slap.

None came.

She took advantage of the hesitation to diffuse the situation by striking at the heart of their relationship—his dependence on her.

"If you burn or in any way destroy or damage my plays," she said, speaking every word carefully so that her voice wouldn't crack, "I will walk out of this house and never return. Is that clear?"

He blinked slowly, once. It was like a mask had been raised. One moment he was crazed with ire, the next he was the little old man who couldn't even remember to eat at meal times. Min resisted the urge to steer him to the nearest chair to sit down. As with teaching a child, she needed to stand firm or he would never fully understand the depth of his error.

"Forgive me, Minerva," he said, rubbing the bridge of his nose. "I let my emotions get the better of me. It'll not happen again."

She nodded, not trusting herself to speak.

"I'd best leave you alone to finish..." He left the sentence dangling, perhaps expecting her to complete it for him.

She did not. Instead she stood by the door and held it open for him. He shuffled out and his shoulders rounded, once more the meek old man. She closed the door against the urge to go after him. It would do no good. The simple fact was, she had work to do and very little time in which to do it.

Without his paper in proper order and printed up for distribution to the audience, her father would have to work from his own memory and notes for his lecture. And that was definitely not a good idea with the chaotic paths his mind took lately. With his reputation already hanging by a thread, he needed to put forward a professional and capable image to attract further sponsors. And to retain the one he had.

She sat at her desk and got to work. Jane came with a slice of mutton pie and left with strict instructions that Min wasn't to be disturbed.

Some time later, she put her head down on the desk and sobbed. Not only was the amount of work still to be done insurmountable, but it was becoming clear that her father's theory was poorly thought out. She'd known from the first paragraph that it was a wild conclusion, but now she'd come to realize he'd not backed up his interpretation with solid reasoning. His explanations were haphazard in places, vague in others, and relied upon untested theories and speculative data provided by unreliable sources.

It was awful. He'd be the laughing stock of the Academy by the end of his lecture. No disciple of the New Sciences could accept the theory based on this paper, not with her father's reputation already sullied from his last disaster.

Her only hope was that Lord Pilkington would not attend and that he wouldn't hear of her father's madness later. For it had to be madness. What else could explain his descent from brilliant scientist to the...the nonsensical failure he'd become?

But the scientific community being as close as it was, that was not a realistic hope at all.

CHAPTER 17

Blake didn't understand it. Min had rejected him, a man with a lot to offer a woman. He was wealthy, came from a respectable family and was reasonably handsome. What he lacked in charm he made up for in good personal hygiene and attentiveness to a woman's needs in bed. What more could she possibly want?

Even if she didn't love him, or like him overmuch, it wouldn't matter because he was away for months on end. He could stretch it to years if she preferred. Many women he knew would consider that the perfect marriage.

Not that he'd find it easy to stay away from Min for long periods. Knowing she was waiting for him in his home, his bed, would drive him to sail through the worst tempest the sea could throw at him. He was beginning to think she was like the Sirens of legend, calling to him, and he was unable to resist her song. He was certainly finding it difficult to stay away from her while in London.

He almost asked Alice Croft for advice but decided against it. Ever since he arrived at the White Swan to undertake his book-keeping duties for the afternoon's performance, everyone, including the seamstress, had given him a wide berth. All except Style. Unfortunately.

As soon as he saw Blake, he strode up to him and pulled the

prompt book out of his hands. "What were you trying to do yesterday?" the manager demanded. "Destroy this company?"

Like a herd of sheep, all heads turned as one to watch the drama playing out before them. Everyone stopped what they were doing, except for Croft who sat on a stool, polishing the blade of a gladius. The warning glare he gave Blake said more than Style's blustering words ever could—do not jeopardize the troupe's patronage.

"No." Blake could have said the incident had nothing to do with the company, but he doubted Style or the others would see it that way. Min hadn't. But then Min had more at stake. Style and his players could find another patron, but Min's fortune was linked inextricably with Blake's. If Hawkesbury forbade his troupe to perform Blake's plays, as their writer, Min would suffer.

It was the flaw in his plan. The reef in the bay, except he couldn't steer around it like he'd originally assumed. Min had got under his skin and inside his conscience. No easy feat considering he'd thought he no longer had one.

"No?" Style must have been furious because he hadn't noticed his toga slipping nor did he wipe away the spittle frothing at the corner of his mouth. "That's it? That's all you have to say? *No*?"

"Nobody died," Blake said, "so there's no cause for alarm."

"Nobody..." Style gurgled, turning an interesting shade of crimson. "No cause for..." He began to choke and splutter, his face turning redder and redder.

Blake slapped him on the back, perhaps a little harder than necessary. Style stumbled forward through the curtain—newly replaced—onto the stage. The audience massed on the other side roared, thinking the play was about to begin. Style said a few words to calm them then re-entered the tiring house.

He wagged a finger at Blake. "Do not think that your plays will save you, Blakewell, or whatever your name is. I don't care who you are or how good your poetry is, if you so much as approach Lord Hawkesbury again while he is patron of this company, you'll find yourself without a job. Is that clear?"

"Quite."

Croft grunted. "I'm not sure that's such a threat."

"Father," Alice said from beneath a swathe of crimson fabric, "can you help me with this?" She shot him a look which he either didn't see or ignored.

"What do you mean?" Style said.

"He's from one of London's most notable families," Croft went on, stroking the blade with his cleaning cloth. "Lady Warhurst is his mother and the current Lord Warhurst his brother."

Freddie, sitting on a stool with his legs apart showing more than a lady, even a fake one, ought to, whistled. "Bloody hell! He's royalty."

Edward clipped the back of the lad's head and Freddie swore at him. One of the hired players sniggered.

"Half-brother," Blake corrected as he'd been correcting people for years. He didn't want anyone to think the Warhursts and the Blakewells were one and the same. They were not. They shared a mother, that was all. Leo would be the first to correct the mistake if he was there right now.

"He also has a fortune in his own right," Croft said. "He doesn't need to keep our books. Or sell his plays."

"Not true," Blake said quickly. "My plays are important to me in ways other than financial."

"Then give me back my four pounds." Style held out his hand.

Blake picked up the discarded prompt book and placed it on the manager's palm. "It seems I won't be needing this any longer."

Style gave him a triumphant look, as if he'd called Blake's bluff and won. Blake was happy to let him think he needed the four pounds. It didn't matter. What mattered was the future of Min's plays. Style already owned *Marius and Livia* and could perform it or not as he liked. But any future ones needed a home.

They also needed someone to act as their author. With Blake setting sail soon now that the issue with Hawkesbury and Lilly was coming to a head, he could hardly remain as the author, even if Style was prepared to purchase them from him. Which, judging by his petulance, he was not.

"Are you going to buy his next play?" The question—the one

that everyone probably wanted to ask but didn't dare—came from Shakespeare at the back of the tiring house. The entire room became still, breathless. Not a pin dropped nor a hair moved. Blake had to hand it to the hired man—he knew how to get himself noticed.

Style stared down at the prompt book in his hands and for the first time since Blake had met him, the manager seemed less than completely sure of himself. "I need to think about it. I cannot support someone who would do injury to our patron and jeopardize our very existence."

"You mean you can't be *seen* to support him," Alice said. All eyes turned to her. She simply shrugged and returned to her sewing.

"Same thing," Freddie said. That earned him another clip. "What? I don't get it. We *have* to buy another play from him. Apart from Marlowe and maybe Greene, he's the only decent writer around."

"Not true," Shakespeare mumbled.

"I said," Style ground out, "that I'll think about it. Now get out there, Edward, and announce the play. The crowd's growing restless."

Edward strode past them and through the curtain to a roar of approval. It was an odd contrast to the heavy silence of the tiring house. The players prepared for their roles in hushed tones, as if they were in the company of the dying. Or as if the company itself was dying.

Unease settled within Blake. Style avoided him by fussing over his costume, Wells stood by the curtain and waited for his cue while Freddie and some of the hired men practiced their parts at the back. Alice gave Blake an encouraging smile but stopped when her father scowled at her.

Only Shakespeare came near him. He arranged the toga over one shoulder and inclined his chin in greeting. "We should talk."

Blake nodded. "Aye. I think you can help me," he said quietly. Being a budding playwright himself, Shakespeare might know someone suitable to act as the author of Min's plays. Of course he'd have to let the man in on the secret, but he seemed to have already guessed the truth anyway and had kept it to himself. It was the only way to help Min.

Edward came off stage and Wells replaced him. Croft handed out swords to the hired players while Alice painted Freddie's cheeks a darker shade of rose. The atmosphere began to return to normal as the audience's reaction filtered through to them. The players seemed to thrive on the cheers and applause. Even Croft appeared more buoyant.

Then Lord Hawkesbury entered the tiring house via the back door and once more the room chilled. Blake stiffened and reached for his sword but didn't withdraw it. There wasn't enough room to fight. Too many props and people.

Outside was a different matter.

"My lord!" Style pushed aside costumes, props and Alice to greet Hawkesbury. "What an unexpected surprise. But a pleasant one of course. It's been quite some time since you've graced us with your presence in the tiring house, my lord."

"Two months," Hawkesbury said, his gaze settling on Blake. There was no animosity in it. Only curiosity and a kind of desperation that didn't sit comfortably on the earl. "Blakewell, will you join me in the taproom for an ale?"

Blake nodded. "Might as well since my services as book-keeper are no longer needed."

Hawkesbury raised an eyebrow, a hint of amusement glistening in his eyes. "Nothing to do with our bout of exercise yesterday, I hope."

"Exercise?" Style spluttered. "The man tried to kill you!"

Hawkesbury laughed. "If he wanted to kill me, he could have done it easily."

Blake shook his head. Hawkesbury knew how to wield a sword. He could have beaten Blake if he'd loosened up a little and used his imagination instead of following the rules of gentlemanly conduct.

"Never fear, Style," Hawkesbury went on, "you can't be rid of me that easily."

Style gasped and pressed a hand to his heart. "I can assure you, my lord, we do not wish to be rid of you."

"Not even in exchange for a patron who comes to your performances more often than I?"

"Your presence is all the more precious because of its rarity."

Hawkesbury smiled an unreadable smile. Alice rolled her eyes behind Style's back. Blake joined his lordship near the door when Wells poked his head through the curtain from the stage.

"Freddie!" he hissed. "Get out here now!"

"Shit." Freddie gathered up his skirts and scrambled to join Wells.

"Let's go," Blake said to Hawkesbury.

The taproom was empty except for the serving girl and an old man asleep at one of the tables. Everyone else was out in the yard watching the play. Blake felt a swell of pride that Min had achieved yet another full house. He was a little surprised she wasn't there to see it, unless she was buried somewhere within the audience. Or perhaps she was staying away to avoid seeing him.

If circumstances had been different between them he would go to her that night and tell her about it, tell her how much her play was loved. It was wrong that he should receive all the praise. She must surely want to hear it too.

But he could not see her again. Not after her rejection. Walking away from her afterwards, without looking back and without regrets, had been one of the hardest things he'd done. To do it again would be nigh impossible.

"Are you with me, Blakewell?" Hawkesbury's voice snapped Blake's attention back to his present dilemma. It was almost a relief to think of something else.

"Aye, you have my full attention." They sat at a table in the darkest corner where their conversation couldn't be overheard. "So explain to me why you want to ruin my sister."

Hawkesbury signaled the serving girl for two ales then carefully removed both his gloves. He placed them to one side before finally answering. "First of all, I wish to do nothing of the sort. Second, my...relationship with Mistress Blakewell is not your business."

"Not my business! You—."

"It is between her and I. And it is over."

Blake could have run the man through with his rapier right there in the taproom, witnesses be damned. But he was aware that it would solve nothing, and would probably only make Lilly's situation worse. A corpse could not be made to marry.

And the future of Min's plays had not yet been resolved. Until then, Blake was still their apparent author and as such, he needed to refrain from killing or maiming the patron of Style's company.

"My sister is very much my business," he said, "and that of Lord Warhurst. If you and I do not come to a satisfactory resolution before my half-brother arrives in London, you'll have to deal with the both of us. And I can assure you, Leo's temper matches my own."

Hawkesbury accepted his ale from the serving girl. She placed the other in front of Blake then slipped away as quietly as she had arrived. "Let's not resort to threats just yet," the earl said.

"Then let's use reason."

"Gladly." Hawkesbury gripped his tankard between his hands and twisted it. "Blakewell, you need to understand that Lilly and I have already discussed the situation. As much as I want to marry her, she knows I cannot. I am already betrothed." He sipped his ale, went to lower the tankard then changed his mind and drained it.

Blake waited until the potential weapon had been returned to the table before he spoke. "Break it."

Hawkesbury didn't pick the tankard up and throw it. He merely sighed deeply. "I can't."

"Why not?"

"I can't tell you why."

"But you will."

Hawkesbury's eyes narrowed. "No, I won't."

Blake leaned forward. "Let's not make a scene, my lord, the poor serving girl doesn't deserve it. Now, tell me why you cannot break your betrothal or I will slit your throat." It would be simple enough to whip out the dirk hidden up his sleeve and slice the cur's neck open.

"If you're going to kill me then get it over with. Otherwise, let's be gentlemen and discuss this civilly."

"I am being a gentleman," Blake said. "You're the one who refuses to marry the woman who is carrying your child."

Hawkesbury's face went white then a vivid shade of green. His jaw dropped. He stared at Blake. "You jest."

"Not the sort of joke I find funny, my lord."

Hawkesbury made a choking sound in the back of his throat then rubbed a hand over his face. "Oh, Lilly."

Blake frowned. "You didn't know? I thought she told you."

The earl shook his head. "She didn't." With a sudden, violent change, he slammed his fist down on the table. The slumbering drunk at the other end of the taproom sat up then slumped back down again, snoring loudly. "Why didn't she write?"

Bloody good question. "Now that you know, you can break your engagement to the Enderby girl and marry Lilly."

Hawkesbury studied his empty tankard, twisting it between his fingers again but more vigorously, as if it were a throat and he wanted to wring it. It was a long time before the earl shook his head. "I told you, I cannot."

"What! My sister is carrying *your* child, Hawkesbury. Doesn't that mean anything to you?"

"Of course it does," he snapped. "I'll do everything I can for her and the babe. I'll take care of them. They'll want for nothing and the child will have the best education money can buy. Lilly would like my Hampshire house I think. They can live there and I'll pay her a generous annuity—."

"*Pay* her?" Blake spat. "She is not your *whore*, Hawkesbury. She is a lady. One of the best and—."

"Don't you think I know that?" Hawkesbury slammed his hands down on the table. "Christ, do you think this is what I *want*? Do you think I would willingly choose Patience over Lilly?" He scoffed and shook his head. "Your sister is...important to me. Very important. I would not wish this on her. But the fact is, it has happened and we must deal with it."

Blake closed his fingers around the hilt of his sword. Perhaps he should run the heartless scum through after all. If nothing else, it would make Blake feel better.

Hawkesbury's eyes narrowed. "Would you like to settle this with swords? It might make us both feel better."

Blake flexed his fingers and returned both hands to the table. "What I would *like* to do and what I *must* do are two entirely different things, my lord."

Hawkesbury acknowledged the sentiment with a sharp nod. "If there was any other way, you must believe me when I say I would gladly take it. No matter the personal cost to me."

A pretty sentiment. Or a guilty one. "Tell me why you can't break the engagement with the Enderby girl," Blake said. "Perhaps I can help you find a way out. Did you get her pregnant too?"

"No!"

"Is it money? I have enough—."

"It's not money." Hawkesbury pressed his thumb and finger into his eye sockets and sighed. "It is a secret. One I cannot tell and one with ramifications that affect people dear to me."

More bloody secrets. Blake was sick of them. They'd only got him into an ugly mess he was struggling to wade through.

"Your sister knows all of this which is perhaps why she didn't tell me of her predicament. She didn't want to make my decision any more difficult than it already is."

"It doesn't look too bloody difficult from where I'm sitting," Blake muttered. "You made it quite hastily."

"Believe me I'd rather walk through a burning building than hurt Lilly. She is—."

"Important to you. Yes, I heard you the first time." Another pretty sentiment. Blake was tired of them. He stood. "She's important to me too."

Hawkesbury nodded. "I know. You've gone to great lengths to ensure her reputation remains in tact."

Anger, hot and sharp, grated along Blake's skin and ripped his self-control to shreds. "And you can be assured I will go to even further lengths." It took every ounce of willpower not to draw his rapier on the cur right there in the White Swan's taproom. He wanted to. God, he ached with the need to do it.

But the thought of Min kept him from committing murder. If Blake destroyed Hawkesbury, he would destroy Min too, or at least her dreams. He couldn't do that to her.

"I know," Hawkesbury said heavily. "But I cannot stress

enough that there are other people who will be hurt if I break my engagement to marry Lilly."

"Patience Enderby?"

Hawkesbury huffed out a breath. "She would be the least injured party."

"Then who?" He pressed his hands onto the table. "Tell me so that I can help."

For one fleeting second Hawkesbury seemed to consider the offer. But then he shook his head and stood too. "It's not possible. But please, Blakewell, for Lilly's sake and for the others I speak of, do not pursue this matter further."

Blake said nothing. What more could he say against such a plea? He had to get out, get away from Hawkesbury, Style, everyone, and seek some comfort elsewhere. With Min. She would at least distract him with her warm eyes and soft heart.

He turned and made for the door, feeling strangely empty, as if a hole had been carved into his gut and a piece of him had fallen out.

"Wait," Hawkesbury called after him. "Lilly...is she well?"

He regarded the earl through lowered lashes. Hawkesbury truly seemed to have feelings for Lilly. He certainly appeared interested in Blake's answer, straining almost.

"She is pale, thin and tired," Blake said, not wanting to shield the earl from the truth. Nor did he want to feel empty anymore. He wanted the anger to return to fill the void, and this reminder of Lilly's health would perhaps rally his own hatred of Hawkesbury again. "She keeps to her room, speaks only to her maid, our mother or myself if I force my way into her presence. I haven't heard her laugh since my return to London, nor have I been able to distract her with stories of my adventures abroad. She is miserable."

Hawkesbury turned away so Blake couldn't see his face. His shoulders hunched and his head lowered. And then he went very still, as if moving would shatter him. Blake knew what that was like.

Applause erupted from the yard beyond the taproom door. The drunk lifted his head again and wiped his mouth with his sleeve. He looked around then promptly put his head back down on the table and fell back to sleep.

"Thank you for telling me about her predicament," Hawkesbury said without turning around.

"You should never thank the man who wants to kill you."

CHAPTER 18

Blake didn't want to go home and face his sister. Not yet. If he went home he'd have to tell her about his conversation with Hawkesbury and then she would berate him. It would end in an argument which would make her feel weaker and him guiltier. So he avoided going home altogether and went to the Mermaid's Tail where he was sure of a drinking partner and lively conversation.

What he really wanted to do was see Min but it was not yet dark and he could not risk a daylight visit. Nor could he be sure of the reception he'd receive, and he wasn't a man who wagered on long odds.

His quartermaster and two of his sailors did their best to distract him with tankard after tankard of the inn's strongest ale, and regaling him with dockside gossip. After two hours he knew which ship was carrying what cargo to where. If he really was a pirate the information would have been useful, but it was only the Spanish ships that interested him now and none of those dared go near London.

He informed his quartermaster to be prepared to sail within a few days then left his crewmen to seek Min's company. He'd had enough of masculine conversation for the night.

It took him nearly an hour to find her Knightridge Street house after trudging across half of London. It seemed to have moved. Since that wasn't possible, he must be drunk. Good. Drunk was definitely an improvement. It meant he didn't have to think. Thinking was bad.

When he finally stumbled across Knightridge Street and Min's house, he peered up at her window. The balcony was a lot higher than he remembered. But he'd climbed masts that were higher still.

So he jumped, grabbed an overhanging beam and hoisted himself up. But the beam was slippery and he slid off, landing on his arse on the ground. The muddy ground.

He swore. Loudly. A man from a nearby building came out and swore back at him. Blake gave him one of his most formidable glares but the effect was probably wasted in the dark. The man left and Blake picked himself up, brushing as much loose muck off his clothes as possible. One thing was for sure, Min lived in a less than desirable neighborhood. She should be in a grand house in a good part of London. Or better yet, a castle. Yes, she definitely deserved a castle, complete with turrets and a moat and possibly a dragon to eat any undesirable knights who wanted to ravage—er, rescue—her.

He looked up at her window again. "Min," he whispered loudly. "Min, come out, it's me."

The window flew open and a man appeared on the balcony. A young man dressed in nothing more than his shirt. What the hell was he doing in Min's room? Blake was about to climb up and ask him face to face when a voice called him from the other side of the road.

"Good eve, sir!" A woman holding a candle stood inside the doorway to the house opposite. "Are you after my mistress?"

"Is your mistress Minerva Peabody?"

"Are you Captain Blakewell?"

Blake bent and picked his hat out of the mud. "At your service."

The woman stalked across the road, grabbed Blake by the arm and pulled him back to her front porch. Ah, so *this* was Min's house. *Now* he remembered. He waved an apology to the other man opposite who returned inside the house that definitely wasn't Min's.

"Is she home?" he asked Min's maid.

"Shhh or you'll alert her."

"Good. I want to speak to her."

She shushed him again. "Not tonight you don't."

"Yes. I can assure you I do."

The maid held the candle up to his face. Its heat warmed his nose. Any closer and his eyelashes would be singed. "You're quite handsome."

"Thank you."

"For a drunk."

"Ah. That. I don't usually get this drunk. But tonight was a special occasion." He winced. Perhaps he should stop talking until his mind was working properly again.

"I don't care about the 'casion. You must leave *now*." She gave him a shove in the arm. He managed not to topple over despite the tilting of the earth.

"Not until I've spoken to Min."

"You can't. She's busy."

"Doing what?"

"Work for her father. Thanks to a few distractions of late," she pinned him with a sharp glare, "she's behind in her tasks."

"I just want to see her. Only for a moment."

"No. Anyway, I'm not sure that's a good idea. Look at you. You're drunk, filthy and..." she sniffed him, "you stink. Sir."

"I do not!" He drew in a deep breath and his stomach heaved. It wasn't mud he'd landed in. "You're right, I reek. Is that any reason to ban me from your mistress's rooms?"

She put a hand on her hip and her gaze grew sharper. "If you'd like me to pass on a message, I'd be happy to."

"I can deliver the message myself." He stepped past her onto the road and cupped his hands to his mouth. "Min!"

The maid jerked hard on his arm, dragging him back to the front door where Min couldn't see him if she peered out her window. "Shhhh! Sir, not tonight! She's too much to do. If you go to her, she'll be sure to—."

Both looked up as they heard the window above open.

"Jane?" came Min's voice. "Is that you?"

Simply hearing her had a sobering affect on him. She was so

close. All he had to do was step back onto the street and she'd see him.

"You'll get her in awful trouble with her father," Jane whispered to Blake. "Please, sir. Don't."

Blake closed his eyes and the world lurched. He had to lean against the house to steady himself. Christ, he was in no state to call on Min. She'd be appalled at his drunkenness and count herself lucky to have escaped marriage to him.

"Jane?" Min called again.

He rubbed a hand over his eyes and nodded at the maid.

"Aye, it's me, Mistress," Jane said. "Just checkin' everythin' is shut for the night. G'night."

A heavy sigh floated down from the balcony. "Goodnight, Jane." The click of the closing window signaled her departure.

Blake gave the maid a grim smile. "Don't tell her I was here."

She frowned. "Why not? She'd want to know."

He shook his head. "No, she wouldn't. It would just make things...very awkward for her. As you said, she's got enough on her mind. Promise me?"

He thought she'd refuse his request but then she nodded. "Very well. 'Night, sir."

He slapped his hat on his head then remembered what it had fallen in and wished he hadn't. "Goodnight."

CHAPTER 19

"Minerva! Minerva, is it ready?"

The pounding on her door shook the cobwebs from Min's mind. She realized she'd been staring at the opening paragraph of her father's paper for quite some time, but had long ago given up trying to improve it. It was hopeless. There was no way to explain her father's theory to the satisfaction of the scientific world.

"Aye," she said, opening the door to him. "It's ready."

He nodded once. His thin white hair, unadorned by hat or cap, floated about his head like reeds in a lake. He'd not had any sleep either if the circles shadowing his eyes were anything to go by.

"It's too late to have it printed now," was all he said.

She handed him the stack of pages. "You can promise the attendees that you'll have a copy made and sent to them. I'll see to it myself tomorrow."

He took the pages and gave her a tentative, enquiring smile. "Well? What do you think?"

"I..." Oh, lord. What a dilemma. Should she tell him the truth and suffer his temper—or worse, his disillusionment? Or let him make a fool of himself in front of his peers?

It wasn't really a choice after all. She held his elbow and steered him to a chair. "Father, I think it needs a little more work before you present it today. Can you postpone—?"

"Nonsense!" He'd no sooner sat down than he stood again, once more the domineering parent. The color rose in his cheeks and his eyebrows drew together to form a single angry line. "I've worked on it for months. I've been over and over *every* calculation and *every* variable several times." He pointed the papers at her. They shook uncontrollably. "If you'd been helping me these last few weeks instead of writing your plays I would have discussed my conclusions with you in more detail and you would have a deeper understanding."

"But it's not a case of *mis*understanding—."

"You're wrong, Minerva. I wish I had time to explain it to you in detail but we've run out of that commodity." He stormed off to the door, huffing and puffing like a bull in the baiting ring. She ran after him. Perhaps she was just as mad as he was, but she couldn't let him destroy years of valuable work in a single day by presenting that lecture as it stood.

"Father, wait! Please, don't dismiss my concerns so hastily." Thankfully he paused, although his tapping foot spelled out his impatience. "It is true I may not understand it, but if that is the case, then perhaps other members of the Academy won't either. Not from your lecture." She winced at her tactlessness. "Er, what I mean is, such a...unique theory needs more time than you can devote to it today."

"You doubt me on this?"

"No, I doubt them. As I doubt myself. If I fail to grasp all the complexities then perhaps some of them might too." She'd failed to completely grasp *any* of the theory's facets but it wasn't in his best interests to know that, or hers. Not now when his temper could snap at any moment. And his mind too.

He shook his head and sighed deeply. The raging bull was gone and the tired old man returned in its place. "Science is an ever-changing beast, Minerva, and you've been too busy with your plays to keep abreast of new developments. I wish it were not true, but alas...you've changed too."

It *was* true. He was right. She no longer read the pamphlets he brought home or listened with a scholar's ear to his accounts of the Academy meetings. She simply wasn't interested anymore in scientific things. She wasn't entirely sure if she ever had been.

She'd been hungry for knowledge while being tutored in the sciences and mathematics, but in recent years those subjects had failed to hold her attention as much as plays and poetry.

She didn't really know when her interests had changed. It must have been gradual—a new play that had her returning to the theatre, a discovery of the art of poetry, her first forays into writing plays—until it slowly overtook everything else in her life, including science. Especially science. Looking back, she wasn't even sure if science was *her* interest or whether it was her father impressing it upon her young mind because he so desperately wanted...what? Someone to help him? No, that's not how it had begun. Involvement. Inclusion. Someone to share his joy and his passion because his wife had not.

But it wasn't entirely his fault either. She had grasped his work with both hands because it was a way to get closer to him, her only surviving parent.

It was difficult to say now, but she knew one thing for certain—she was a grown woman and her thoughts were her own. Even if her mind was capable of understanding a complex mathematical formula, she didn't have to *be* a scientist if she didn't want to.

"Such a waste," he said with a shake of his head.

"Father." She stopped him from walking off with a gentle hand on his arm. "There is something I should tell you." It was time he knew the full extent of her commitment to writing plays. If he knew about Style buying *Marius and Livia* it might help him to see that her new interest was not such an unfortunate one after all.

"Can't it wait until later?" he grumbled. "I must go or I'll be late." He shuffled off without waiting for her answer, his shoulders stooped, his papers folded against his chest.

Against every instinct, Min let him go. No amount of pleading or reasoning could have persuaded him against his mission. He might be losing his mind but he was certainly as driven as ever.

She trudged back to her room and lay down on the bed. It

was still unmade from the morning but she didn't care. She'd never felt so tired. It was like something had sucked out the life from her body and left her flat and empty. Perhaps if she closed her eyes for awhile, she would feel refreshed when she awoke and all her ills will have disappeared...

* * *

"MISTRESS, WAKE UP. MISTRESS."

Min shot up out of bed and caught Jane by her shoulders. "Is Father all right?" She shook the maid and Jane's eyes widened in alarm. "Has something happened to him?"

"No, I've not seen Sir George since this mornin'. It's naught to do with him." She wrung her hands in her apron and gave Min a forlorn look. Jane, always practical and steady, never looked forlorn. Something terrible had happened.

Blake. No, don't let it be him.

But Jane had never met him so that couldn't be it. "Oh, do get on with it," Min said, trying very hard not to appear any more anxious than necessary. "My nerves are frayed enough as it is. What has happened to send you in here like a skittish cat?"

Jane lifted her chin and Min could almost see her maid concentrate as she gathered her words together.

"I've just come from the market, Mistress. And people there were talkin' of yer play again. Now, that's not such a hardship to listen to, but it's what *else* they were sayin' that's got me worried. It had them all in such a twitter."

"Well? What were they saying?" The suspense was almost painful.

"They were talkin' about the play a *woman* wrote."

Min blinked at her. It took a moment for the maid's words to sink in. Or really, one word. The air escaped from Min in a rush. "Who spoke of it?" she barely managed to whisper.

"Everyone from the fishwife to the lady's maid. It had them all in a huddle. I asked how they knew but it was always someone else who'd said somethin' and no one really knew where the gossip started. I scoffed at 'em all but I don't think anyone heard me. They just wanted to spec, specula..."

"Speculate."

"Aye, speculate on who the woman may be."

Min rubbed her temple where an ache was blooming. What ill timing! Why now when her life was coming apart at the seams? This disaster might as well rent it asunder.

At least if they were speculating about the author, they didn't know it was her. She hoped. "Who were some of the suggestions?"

"Everyone from Henrietta the half-wit flower seller to Her Majesty herself. I'm not sure which was sillier. To think of the queen botherin' with the lowly Lord Hawkesbury's Men. She'd use her own company for certain."

"So my name wasn't mentioned?"

Jane's fingers twisted her apron until it finally tore. The maid didn't appear to notice. "It was, several times by those who know you."

Min gasped and clapped a hand to her mouth. Oh Lord! How could this be happening?

"Oh, Mistress, what are we to do? Surely Mr. Style will hear."

"Yes," Min whispered against her fingers, "I'm sure he will." If the entire market was alive with the talk it wouldn't be long before Style and the others found out.

She put her head in her hands and tried to think through the ache chipping away at her skull. She could speak to Style before he heard it from someone else and pray he wouldn't mind now that the play was a success. Or she could find Blake and together form a story to blame some other nameless woman...

Blake. Aside from Jane who was utterly loyal, no one else knew she'd written *Marius and Livia*. Not even her father. Blake must have told someone...

She dug her fingers into her scalp but it was her heart that hurt like the devil now. She closed her eyes and willed the pain to go away but it remained, piercing and unrelenting.

No. No, *no*, NO! She couldn't believe it. It wasn't possible. She wasn't such a poor judge of character that she'd not seen how cruel he could be. Was she?

He'd called himself a blackguard. He'd warned her more than

once not to trust him. Perhaps he'd been alerting her to the blackness of his heart, the real Robert Blakewell. The pirate.

Besides, who else knew her secret? Who else could it have been?

She let out a low, primal groan. She'd given him everything, from her maidenhead to her trust and he'd thrown it all to the wind as if it were merely dust. Nothing. That's what she meant to him. He'd used her to get into the troupe and he'd taken advantage of her desire and used her in bed too. And when he'd finished with her, he'd given away her precious secret.

She wanted to throw up.

Jane's strong arm came around her shoulders and pulled Min to her bosom. But Min wasn't ready for comfort. A sudden wave of anger swept her up. She wanted to fight.

She stood and straightened her skirts. "Fetch my cloak, hat and gloves, Jane. I'm going out."

CHAPTER 20

Min decided it would be easier, and safer, to learn where Blake lived by asking at the cloth trading center on Basinghall Street than venturing down to the docks. By questioning a kindly servant at the hall that served as a depot for London's merchant adventurers, she discovered Blake's father had been the pre-eminent merchant adventurer of his time, a good man and fortunate in his choice of wife, the widow of a baron. She also learned the family lived in the largest house on Dowgate Street.

The largest house on Dowgate Street turned out to be a grand *mansion*. And the blackguard was "indisposed" according to his steward. All that walking and worrying about what she would say for nothing.

She was about to ask his steward if she could wait but she changed her mind. The house had a hushed, grim feel to it, as if it were in mourning.

She spared a prayer for his sister and her unborn babe then headed back toward Gracechurch Street. But she couldn't go home. She was too restless. She needed to do something to cut off the looming disaster before the rumor spread to Lord Hawkesbury's Men. And she needed to do it *now*.

She headed to the White Swan inn only to find the players in the taproom nursing tankards and their misery as if they too were in mourning. Blake wasn't among them, nor were the Crofts.

Min cleared her throat. They glanced up as one.

"You," Style snarled. He rose and Min backed away from the sheer force of his hatred. "You...you vile creature, you witch, you...*wanton*!"

"Easy there," said Henry Wells. He stood and edged his bulkier frame between Min and Style. She silently thanked him for it. "We don't know for sure she wrote it." He shot a glance at Edward. "We don't, do we?"

"You thick-headed dolt," Style growled. He no longer came towards her but he still looked like he had murder on his mind. Hers. "Of course she did it. If you used that pea-brain of yours, you'd realize it couldn't be anyone else." Instead of appearing injured by the insult, Henry simply shrugged at Min. "She ruined us," Style said. "Her and that Blake fellow she has under her spell."

Min drew in a deep breath to steady her sizzling nerves. It wouldn't serve her purpose to show anger. Style wouldn't respond to counter-insults. Although she wasn't sure he'd respond to reason either, but she had to try. "I see you've heard. Please, it's not what it appears."

Style snorted and folded his arms. The rest waited for an answer but with slightly more forgiving expressions. Only Freddie seemed not to care as he wiped his mouth with the back of his hand.

"It's not?" said Style, cynicism dripping from his words. "You didn't write it? Oh, pray tell us, who did?" He ended with a flourish to encompass not only the other players but the entire taproom. Everyone was listening. Even the drunk in the corner.

"I, uh..." Min wanted to turn and run. She probably should have. Instead, she dug in her heels and crossed her arms and turned on Style. Perhaps this *was* a time for anger, a little anyway.

"Yes, I wrote it. So? What's wrong with that?" Style made a choking sound but she kept talking to ensure he couldn't get a word in. "I proved I could write as well as any playwright. You thought I was a scholar, that my education rivaled Marlowe's.

Well," she said, triumphant, "it does. I have a mind as good as any man's. Londoners have been flocking to the performances of *Marius and Livia*. You should be thanking me, Mr. Style. Without my play your company might not exist."

His face went a rather violent shade of crimson. "Thanking *you*! You vile creature—."

"Yes, I heard the insults before," she said, raising her hands palms out. "They do not concern me. What does concern me is who told you?"

"Who told me?" he spluttered. "Who told me? Why, *everybody*! My wife's maid, my neighbor, the cripple who delivers my water! I've never been so humiliated in my life."

So that's what it was about. Humiliation. Well, he should step out in her shoes some time and know what it was like to be called a wanton. And to be betrayed by someone she'd given her heart to.

Lord, it hurt so much.

"You have ruined this company," he spat. "Lord Hawkesbury will be sure to withdraw his patronage now."

"We don't know that," Shakespeare said.

"He would not want to become a laughing stock," the manager said with authority. Of all of them, Style knew Hawkesbury best—perhaps he was right.

"No," Shakespeare said. "But depending on how he handles this situation, he may not *become* a laughing stock."

"Quiet," Style snapped. "No one is speaking to you."

"Brother," Edward said, "perhaps we should talk in private with Mistress Peabody. We need to discuss our immediate and long term plans regarding her plays."

"I can tell you what our plans are. We cancel this afternoon's performance and all future performances."

"What!" everyone chorused. Even Freddie looked up from his ale.

"B, but we have to put on something," Edward said, eyes widening and voice pitching high. "No. Please no. We can't go back." He could have been speaking of returning to hell rather than putting on an older play.

"We have to. *A Day and a Night in Venice*," Style announced. A chorus of groans echoed around the taproom. "It's our most recent play and thus freshest in our minds. There'll be little preparation in the way of costumes. Someone take the message to the Crofts in the tiring house."

No one moved.

"I *hate* that play," Freddie muttered.

"But all the handbills are printed announcing *Marius and Livia* as today's performance," Edward said. "It's too late to change them now. We start in less than two hours."

"I don't care," Style said without taking his eyes off Min. "We will not be putting on *her* play. I'll not suffer any more humiliation than I already have."

Freddie rubbed his left eye with his fist. "Last time we did *Venice* I nearly lost an eye from an apple core one of the groundlings threw at me."

"Expect worse than apple cores if we put on something other than *Marius and Livia*," Edward mumbled. "Please, Brother, can't you allow this one performance? We can have different handbills drawn up for tomorrow. That way no one can complain we misled them."

"*Marius and Livia* might be an even bigger sensation now," Shakespeare said, hopefully. "Everyone will want to see the play a woman wrote and judge its quality for themselves."

"Everyone will laugh at the play a woman wrote," Style said, "and then they'll laugh at us for being duped by a witless female."

"Have you quite finished insulting me?" Min said. She took a step forward. Style wasn't so much taller than her that she felt threatened by him. However, she didn't want to get too close to him either. Not while his anger oozed from every orifice.

"Are you finished humiliating *me*?" Style shot back. Then he suddenly sat down again, causing the feathers in his hat to jiggle. "What am I going to say to Lord Hawkesbury?" He pressed his fingers to his temples and rubbed in a circular motion. Min could sympathize. Her own ache had gone from dull to sharp since she'd entered the White Swan.

"Tell him you were not aware of the sex of the author,"

Edward said with an apologetic shrug at Min. "He'll not blame you, Roger."

"Tell him it won't happen again," Wells suggested. He sat down on a stool and rested his chin in his hands.

"Why not tell him to judge the play on its merits and not by who penned it?" Shakespeare said.

Style glared at him. Freddie snorted. "Everyone knows a woman couldn't write this sort of thing," the lad said with all the assurance of a youth who thought he knew everything. "The devil's inside her. Must be."

Style nodded and Edward shifted in his seat, suddenly avoiding Min's gaze. Henry Wells and Shakespeare were the only ones who didn't look convinced although Henry seemed to at least consider the idea.

Min's jaw dropped. She stared at them all. Is that what they really thought? That she was some kind of witch and *that's* how she'd written the play? Good lord, how was she supposed to reason against such notions? It was impossible. Futile.

And rather frightening. If they believed she was the devil's agent, then who else might? The audience? Lord Hawkesbury? The authorities? She could be imprisoned on suspicion of witchcraft. Or worse. It explained Style's reluctance to put on her plays again. Perhaps it had nothing to do with humiliation at all and more to do with his own fears. He was afraid of being tainted by her play, of consorting with the devil's earthly incarnation. A shiver crept up her spine and she folded her arms against the sudden cold.

Then she turned and ran through the taproom. People moved aside to let her past. She saw fear in their eyes, and awe too, a combination that assured her safe passage to the door.

Outside, she sucked in the cold air. It cleansed her throat and cooled her heated cheeks but not her temper, or the fear. She should have known this would happen. A woman's place was not in the theatre. Even Alice stepped a fine line by being backstage. But she was at least doing an acceptable woman's trade. Min was not.

To watch a play was one thing, but to write one was entirely another. It was corrupting to her gentle nature. To see her *will-*

ingly subject herself to that corruption was quite a disturbance on the average man's conscience. No wonder the Style brothers and many others blamed her behavior on the devil. They could see no other explanation for it. For a gentlewoman would surely not *choose* to write a play any more than she could be capable of it.

A pox on them! It was all too vexing and...impossible!

"Wait! Min." It was Shakespeare. He trotted up to her, a hand holding his hat in place against the stinging wind, the other pressed to his chest. He breathed heavily. "Good lord, but you're a fast walker."

"Only when I'm angry."

"I understand your anger," he said. "I have experienced prejudices too, but mine are more to do with my station and my lack of a formal education rather than my sex."

Min cocked an eyebrow. "Yes, I can see that wouldn't be an issue." She spoke freely with more than a hint of irritation but she didn't care. Although it occurred to her that she wasn't being fair. She wasn't angry with Shakespeare. She was mad at Style. And she was furious with Blake.

"What is it you want?" she said. "I have someone I need to find."

"Ah, your friend, Blake," he said.

She strode off. "He is not my friend."

He fell into step alongside her. "I see. Well, may I suggest that when you do find him, that you be gentle with him. I believe he cares for you and wouldn't wish to hurt you."

It appeared Blake had duped more than just Min. He even had others thinking he had feelings. "If that were the case, he wouldn't have put me in this position."

"Perhaps it came about through a mistake, a slip of the tongue."

"I'll cut out his tongue if he tries to defend his actions to me."

"I see you are hurt," he said dryly. "So I shall get to the point. I simply wanted to wish you well."

She swallowed. "Thank you," she said sincerely. "That is kind."

He doffed his hat and bowed. "Now I must go and speak to

Burbage and beg him to look at my newest play. I have a suspicion I'll not get anywhere with Lord Hawkesbury's Men." He said it with a laugh and Min almost smiled.

"Then I wish you well too, Master Shakespeare. And thank you for your defense of me in the White Swan."

"I consider it a privilege to assist a fellow playwright. Goodbye."

She didn't watch him go but spun on her heel and kept walking. She had a villain to confront.

CHAPTER 21

Blake lifted Lilly's cool hand to his lips and pressed a kiss to the knuckles. Her eyeballs rolled beneath closed alabaster lids but she made no other response. Her maid dabbed a damp cloth to Lilly's already moist forehead and murmured soothing words which fell on deaf ears—Lilly could hear no one and see nothing with the fever upon her. Blake, in perfect health, could *feel* nothing. He was hollow inside, an empty vessel. He should feel angry. He *wanted* to be angry. Lilly was too young to die. Too beautiful. And he needed her, especially now. She would know what to do about Min.

He lowered her hand to the bed and rose.

"Ah, there you are." His mother came up behind him, her slim frame emanating a surprising amount of strength at his back. He found comfort in it, and was a little surprised by the fact that he wanted to be comforted.

"When did she fall ill?" he said without turning.

"She's been like this since you told her of your confrontation with Lord Hawkesbury."

Meaning it was his fault.

He'd awoken to hear the news of Lilly's illness only a short time ago. After Min's maid sent him away from her house he must have wandered London's streets until he eventually wound up at his own home near dawn. He'd slept most of the morning and arisen to find the servants looking mournful and his mother crying. She never cried.

He cursed silently. Although he didn't blame himself for Lilly's illness—the blame for that lay firmly at Hawkesbury's feet—he did feel guilty. He should have been at her bedside, watching over her. Just as he should have been in London all these years instead of only when it appealed to him. Obviously Leo could not be trusted with the task of protecting their womenfolk.

"What did the doctor say?" he asked. The maidservant had already informed him of Dr. Seymour's earlier visit but she'd not known the diagnosis.

"That there is nothing we can do." Lady Warhurst sat on the chair Blake had vacated and touched her daughter's glistening, creamy cheek with her fingertips. "He said we must wait."

Wait. He let out a long, measured breath. Waiting was not something he was good at. The things he was good at included sailing, ordering men and killing. Not necessarily in that order. "If she dies," he said, flatly, "I am going to kill him."

"He didn't give her the fever." It seemed she didn't need to ask who he was speaking about.

"No, but she wouldn't have caught it if she wasn't already weakened by the babe inside her."

"Excuse me, sir," said Greeves the steward from the doorway. "There is a Mistress Peabody here. Do you wish to see her?"

Min? Here? Had Jane told her of Blake's late night visit after all? Or had Min changed her mind and wished to accept his proposal now that she'd had time to think it through? His chest swelled and he realized with a jolt that the idea made him happy. He shouldn't be happy. Not with Lilly lying lifeless in her bed. He should be angry and vengeful and afraid for her. And he was, but the happiness towered above all those emotions, a triumphant conqueror waving a flag in victory.

"Show her to the Rose Room."

Greeves left and Blake made to follow him, but his mother called him back into Lilly's room. "Who is Mistress Peabody?"

"A friend."

She arched one brow. "I've not heard you mention her name before."

He sighed. Not even Lilly's illness could keep his mother from attempting a match. And here he thought she'd given up and turned her powers on Leo. It almost explained his brother's permanently bad mood these days. "That's because I've not spoken of her before."

"Is she young? Eligible? Are her connections—?"

"Mo*ther*. Enough. Not now. If Min has come here it must be important. Please allow me to speak to her without interference."

She held up her hands in surrender. "I shall be here if you wish to introduce us."

If Min had changed her mind about marrying him, meeting his mother might change it back again. But he nodded and cast another look at Lilly's limp form before he left.

Outside the Rose Room, he gave Greeves orders to bring sweetmeats and wine. Then he entered. Min sat stiffly on a chair by the fire, staring at the grate. She looked up when he entered. He was shocked by how her face had changed since he'd last seen her. Her eyes, usually so bright, had dulled and hardened like a well-worn pebble. Her body tensed but there was a stoop where before there'd been none, and that alone made her seem older, her tender years behind her. And her hands moved constantly. The long, elegant fingers twisted over and over until they abruptly stopped, as if she'd suddenly become aware of her fidgeting.

So. She had experienced life after all, and not just the side of it that he'd wanted to show her, but the grim reality. Poor, tender Min, no longer the innocent. He wanted to enfold her in his arms, press her cheek to his chest and kiss away her ills. He wanted to protect her from whatever had upset her.

He wanted to put back the light in her eyes.

But he had the crushing feeling that it was a task beyond his capabilities.

And that his attempts would not be welcome.

Nevertheless, he knelt before her and felt the full force of her anger. As always, he reacted to her in the most basic manner. She affected him the way no woman had ever affected him. She made something inside him lift, tighten.

"What is it?" he said, taking her hand. She recoiled. "What has happened?" he pressed.

She nodded at the door. "I should ask you that. There's a feeling of...unease here." She looked uneasy herself, wary. "Has something happened to your sister?"

She was perceptive. He was about to tell her Lilly was ill but changed his mind. Min seemed to be carrying a heavy enough burden. She didn't need another one, one that might affect what she was about to tell him. She might be inclined to be sympathetic towards him and he didn't want her sympathy, he wanted her honesty. He wanted to know what was wrong so he could help her, even if the only way to help her was to let her be angry with him.

"No. All is well. My mother just likes to keep a quiet household." He smiled what he hoped was an optimistic smile and sat on a chair opposite. The room felt suddenly too small even though his mother liked to boast that the Rose Room was as grand as any parlor at Warhurst Hall, his brother's Northumberland seat. All those damned pink flowers painted on the walls and the ceiling plaster. It felt as if they would reach out and twine around his neck.

"Now," he said, struggling for breath, "I don't suppose you are here to accept my proposal."

She glanced at the door again and her entire body shrugged, as if she'd chosen to accept his explanation about his mother. "You're right. I'm here to tell you that you are a fiend. A scoundrel. A heartless wretch with no more feelings than a puddle of muddy water." With every accusation her eyes narrowed a little more and she edged forward until she was perched on the edge of the chair.

Every accusation sent him further back until he was sitting as rigid as a pole. He felt completely witless—he hadn't any notion what had brought on her anger. Nor was he sure how to handle it. Min wasn't the fierce type. She was gentle and sweet and kind.

Not anymore. His kitten had turned into a tiger.

"I'm not sure I understand what I've done to deserve such vehemence," he said carefully. Living with two volatile women, he'd learned early in life to approach these sorts of conversations with the utmost caution. That's if he couldn't flee. He looked to the solid oak door. It was open. In Min's present state of tension, he wouldn't be surprised if she sprang up and reached it first.

"You betrayed me," she said without moving her jaw. Her fingers went white as each hand pressed against the other. "You. Be. Trayed. Me."

Betrayed her? The only way he could ever betray her was to tell Style that she was really the author of her play, but he'd not breathed a word of it to anyone. Not even Shakespeare, although he'd intended to before he got side-tracked by Lord Hawkesbury at the White Swan.

"Min," he said with all the care of a man about to put his arm into the tiger's mouth, "you must believe me when I say I have not. I would never—."

"Liar!" Half the house must have heard her raised voice. "No one else could have done it. Not a single soul except for Jane knew. And do not accuse my maid," she said, stabbing her finger at him. "She is the most loyal of servants. A better friend to me than *you*."

"Min," he said, his voice also rising, despite every attempt to remain calm, "I did not do it. I wouldn't do that to you. I—." He stopped himself before he said something foolish and inappropriate. Something he couldn't take back. Something that would upset the delicate balance of his world.

"Don't lie to me." She got up and stalked to the window then swung round to pin him with a freezing glare. "You wanted to bring down Lord Hawkesbury to seek your sister's revenge." This she said more quietly. "Well? Deny that!"

Christ, what a mess. He seemed to be good at making messes for the people he cared about. He stood and got as close to her as he thought she'd allow, and as close as he could get without being affected by her to the point of becoming foolish. He needed to keep his mind focused so as not turn into a blathering half-wit who'd say anything to see her smile again.

He drew in a deep breath and wished he hadn't. Even from

where he stood he could smell her intoxicating scent. "I admit I want to get my revenge on him for his behavior towards my sister. But I would confront him directly to make him pay for his sin, not use you."

She crossed her arms and tilted her adorable and very stubborn chin. She didn't look convinced.

And that hurt. He took a step closer and almost lost all his sense of propriety right there in the Rose Room parlor. He wanted to kiss those pursed lips. Hell, he wanted to kiss her everywhere from her rosy nipples to her knees and everywhere in between. Make her squirm with desire. Make her—.

Damnation! He took a step back, out of her sphere. *Focus*. But not on her lips. Or her chin and definitely not on the freckle at the corner of her mouth. It didn't leave too many places because her eyes were equally as distracting.

He cleared his throat and tried again. "Do you think I would care so little for you after taking your maidenhead that I would use your secret for my own revenge?" He paced the room. The continuous movement hopefully meant there was less chance of pulling her to him and kissing some sense into her. "Is that the value you place on our love-making?"

"I..." She looked at his ear, his shoulder, his chest, everywhere but his eyes. "I don't know." He began to protest when she cut him off. "You said it yourself. You're a blackguard. You can't be trusted."

All protest died on his lips. She was right. He'd warned her using those exact words.

Her mouth formed an 'oh' as if she would say something but the only thing that came from her lips was the release of a long breath. "I don't know you, Blake. I only learned you were a pirate two days ago."

He didn't bother to correct her. It seemed she'd already made up her mind about his profession, and therefore his heart and soul were placed into the box marked 'pirate' too.

"I've learned my lesson," she went on, the gray of her eyes turning the shade of flint. "You were right. I shouldn't trust you. So now I don't."

"Did it mean nothing when I said I wouldn't hurt you?" It

was a final, pathetic attempt to save something of whatever it was they'd experienced. But he knew from the unyielding set of her jaw and the straight, forbidding line of her brows that she would not give in.

"Sweet words," she whispered, as if it hurt her throat to speak them. "But they are just words." She closed her eyes. As with his sister, he could see her eyeballs moving beneath the lids, as if she were reading the insides of them. He waited for what felt like an age until she finally opened them again. Tears puddled and her lower lip wobbled.

She was going to cry. The only way he knew how to stop a woman from crying was to kiss her.

So he did.

She tasted of salty tears and...Min. He brought his other hand up to the back of her head and tangled his fingers in the stray wisps at the nape of her neck. Her mouth opened and her tongue explored. His groin grew heavy. He wanted her.

Min wanted him. Wanted to feel his thumb brush across her cheek, taste her own tears on his lips and feel the very solidness of him. Everything inside her melted with that kiss—her anger and hurt—and yet she knew it was beyond foolish to release those emotions. They were what kept her safe and sane. *This* was craziness—the kiss, the thudding of her heart, the desperate desire for him to hold her. And yet she couldn't end it.

God help her, she was clutching the man who'd used her and betrayed her. And she never wanted to let him go.

But a strangled gasp sent them springing apart. Blake's steward, hovering in the doorway with a tray of sweetmeats and a reddening face, quickly recalled his duty and placed the tray on the small side table. Thankfully his gaze didn't meet Min's so she didn't have to hide her own blush.

"Will there be anything else, sir?" the steward said.

Blake shook his head. He didn't look the least concerned that they'd been caught by his man. "Thank you, Greeves," he said, "that will be all. Please ensure we're not disturbed again." The steward backed out with his head bowed low.

Blake took a very long time to turn around. Perhaps he too had a blush to hide. Or he was considering his next words. An apology? A confession? A declaration? Any would be a perfectly acceptable start.

When he finally turned, she was disappointed. There wasn't a hint of pink cheeks and the only thing he said was, "Sweetmeat?"

She had to leave. Now. Before he kissed her again and she found herself forgiving the unforgivable. "I must go." She moved towards the door.

He blocked her exit. "Not yet." His body filled the doorway, a solid, scowling presence among the cheerful roses covering the parlor's walls and ceiling. It was a remarkably feminine room for a pirate. "Tell me how it all unraveled."

She thought about refusing but where would be the sense in that? It was in her best interests to tell him about her miserable day. So she took a deep breath and told him about the rumor Jane had passed on, and about her visit to Style and Style's ban on her plays. She told it matter-of-factly, as if narrating the beginning of her play as Edward did, only with much less exaggeration. All the while her stomach tied itself into knots, waiting for his interruption, for him to say something or even show guilt or remorse or at least a little regret over his actions. But he said and did nothing, just watched her passively beneath half-lowered lids as if he were bored.

"I'll kill him."

She blinked. "Pardon?" He'd said it as if it were as inconsequential as choosing which pair of gloves to wear. She swallowed. He wouldn't. Would he? "You can't kill everyone." She rubbed her arms against the sudden chill in the room.

"Don't do that." His hand closed over hers and she felt a responding jolt inside her. The one that always occurred when he touched her. The one that frightened her now as much as thrilled her. "Your cloak sleeves are wearing thin from all the rubbing. You should buy a new one."

"I, uh..." His thumb caressed her knuckles and something flared in his eyes. A responding heat pooled in her lower belly. The air was thick with her awareness of him. All she could think about was what he could do to her—make her want him, make her forgive him.

She pulled away. If she hadn't...she didn't want to contemplate what might have happened.

"As far as I can see," she said, re-arming herself with her wits and her anger, "there's only one way to decrease the damage that's been caused by my exposure and that is for you to tell Style there's been a mistake. That the rumors are wrong and that you really are the one who wrote *Marius and Livia*."

"Agreed." His voice rumbled low in his chest like ominous thunder. She was reminded of when they first met and the danger she'd felt within him then.

First impressions are often correct.

She pressed on, down the path she had carefully thought through on her way to Blake's house. "And then we must find someone else to act as the author of my next plays. You can't continue to do it from the other side of the world."

"Aye," he said quietly. "I'll ask Shakespeare if he knows anyone or wishes to do it himself."

She nodded, knowing she should feel relieved that he readily agreed with her and yet not feeling relieved at all. Her reaction was rather vexing and quite overwhelming. "I thought of him too. He seems like a decent fellow."

"You thought I was a decent fellow."

"Did I?"

"Enough to relieve you of something precious."

Her knees went weak at the memory. "As I said at the time, it wasn't such a precious thing to me. Not as much as everyone thinks." She swallowed hard and concentrated on not blinking, not giving away her lie.

"Wasn't it?"

The room grew hot and she felt a little dizzy. All those pink petals. It was enough to make one's head spin. "I... I was taken in by your good looks and..." She was going to say charm but he'd know she was lying. "...and your sense of fashion."

He bent down to her level. "Liar." He said it softly, a smile teasing his lips. "You liked me, despite every piece of common sense warning you otherwise. Your instincts told you I could be trusted, Min." He tapped her forehead with his finger. She swatted it away. "You should stop listening to this..." His finger tapped her just above her left breast. "...and start listening to this more. Like you did when you gave yourself to me."

She went to grab his finger with the idea of snapping it but he was too quick and she caught nothing but air. "You are arrogant in the extreme, Blake, and a black-hearted cur." She prodded him in the chest. He bore it with a raised eyebrow. "I do not like you and never have. I used you to get my play performed and to improve my...understanding of carnal matters. And you used me which is only fair. What is *not* fair is that you *betrayed* me to get what you wanted."

"That is your head speaking again—."

"No, it's my tongue."

"And a very loud one it is too," said a woman entering the room with an expression as dark and forbidding as her clothing. Of middling age, she was covered in black from her cap to her rich velvet gown embroidered in a lighter shade of the same color, and on to her delicate buckled house shoes. The only color breaking up the severity of her clothing came from her fingers, every one adorned with a ring set with an exquisite emerald that caught the light as her hands moved. She inclined her head and looked down her straight nose at Min.

Blake stiffened. He didn't look in the least happy to see the newcomer.

Min bit back any retorts she was about to let loose at him. The woman must be his mother. She certainly had walked in as if she owned the house and everything in it. In truth it all belonged to Blake, but as he was unwed, his widowed mother would manage the household for her son.

"Robert, who is this?"

Blake cleared his throat and shot a warning glance at Min. Clearly he didn't want her to cause a scene. She wouldn't but she had no inclination to relieve him of the suspense. "Mother, this is Minerva Peabody, daughter of Sir George Peabody."

"*Sir* George Peabody?" His mother's eyebrow rose in a direct replica of her son's. "The daughter of a knight?" She turned her enquiring eyebrow on Blake.

"Min," he said, sounding irritable, "this is my mother, Lady

Warhurst. Mother, Min and I are having an important discussion."

"About what?"

"Business."

Lady Warhurst turned back to Min and openly scanned her from head to foot. No doubt she saw the threadbare cloak, the worn boots, the coarse fabric of her skirt. Min resisted the urge to run when every instinct was screaming at her to get away from both mother and son. Instead, she curled her toes inside her boots in an effort to root herself to the spot.

"What sort of business could you possibly have with this girl?" Lady Warhurst said.

"That is not your concern," he said.

"It can't possibly have anything to do with your adventuring."

He sighed heavily. "Mother. Is there something you wanted?"

"Yes." She drew her gaze up, off Min's clothes and to her face. Lady Warhurst's lips pursed and twisted, as if she were considering something. Finally, she gave a *humph* and turned back to Blake.

Min began to breathe again.

"It's Lilly. She wants you."

Blake, who'd also been watching Min uncomfortably closely, snapped his entire focus onto his mother. "She's awake?" The urgent hope in his voice told Min he'd lied to her earlier. His sister wasn't well at all.

And Min had intruded, perhaps during a time of utmost peril for the girl and her family.

Shocked at her own selfishness, she hastily bowed her head at Lady Warhurst. "Excuse me, I must leave." She dared not look at Blake. She wanted to reproach him for lying to her about his sister but she still couldn't forgive him for what he'd done to her.

"No," he said, blocking her path once more. "Not yet. We haven't finished—."

"Lilly's waiting," Lady Warhurst said with all the authority of a woman not used to being dismissed.

"Good bye, Blake," Min said. She side-stepped around him and this time he let her go. She hurried out of the parlor and was met near the front door by the steward who let her out. No one came after her.

* * *

HIS MOTHER'S grip on Blake's arm would probably leave a mark. She didn't let go even after Min left.

"Mother," he said with exaggerated politeness, "I'm not going after her, I'm going to see Lilly."

Her grip finally loosened enough so he could pry her fingers off his doublet sleeve. "You can't," she said, walking to the window. "She's still in the grip of the fever and the doctor is with her."

"But you said she was awake!"

She lifted one shoulder.

"You lied? Why?"

"I was rescuing you." She turned and fixed him with one of her glares. The sort that saw deep into his soul and was capable of sniffing out his innermost thoughts.

He braced himself for what was to come. "Rescuing me?"

"It seemed like you needed it."

"What do you mean?" A sense of foreboding crawled beneath his skin like an itch.

"That girl...she's pretty in her way. And the daughter of a knight would make an acceptable match."

The itch intensified. "But?"

"But she's not for you."

He shouldn't be having this discussion with her. Although as a mother she had an understandable interest in the matrimonial future of her son, he wasn't the sort of son to share his feelings on the matter with her. His feelings for Min were decidedly his own affair. And therein lay the crux of the problem. He had feelings for Min. Awkward, uncontrollable, urgent feelings.

"Why?" he said, taking the bait even though he knew a trap lurked just ahead.

She stood behind the chair Min had vacated and rested her hands on the back. The gems in her rings flashed in the sunlight like a warning signal. "I don't know why." She shook her head and looked down at the chair as if she could see Min sitting there. "It's a feeling I have. A sense that there's something about her that sets her apart from more eligible women. Something...different and not in an altogether good way."

"It's her poverty, isn't it? Mother, I'll have you know her lack of fortune—."

"No." She silenced him with a raised hand. "It's not that." She shook her head and sighed. "Whatever it is, listen to your mother when I tell you to leave that girl be. She'll cause you trouble."

That was the first thing of sense his mother had said since she walked in.

CHAPTER 22

On the walk back to Knightridge Street, Min came to two conclusions—Blake was ruining her life, and that he was quite possibly the devil himself. It was the only way to explain how she could hate him on the one hand and yet desire him with every fiber of her being on the other.

For both those reasons, she vowed never to see him again. She repeated the declaration over and over all the way home but was still unconvinced by the time she reached the house. He could break her heart a thousand times and she would still want to see his face on her pillow, brush a kiss across his eyelids, feel him move inside her.

"Ned Taylor's here," Jane said when Min opened the door. "He's in the parlor with Sir George."

It seemed Fate was out to take its pound of her flesh too. With heavy feet, she trudged to the parlor and tried to put thoughts of Blake to the back of her mind. Now was not the time to be distracted by him.

Her father and Ned stood when she entered. Both had faces as forbidding as thunder clouds. She turned her sweetest smile on them.

"Where have you been?" her father demanded. She stopped smiling.

Ned, standing by the unlit fireplace, folded his arms. "Yes, where have you been, Minerva? We've been waiting for you."

She ignored him and turned to her father. "I had some errands to run. How was your lecture today?"

But she didn't need to hear his answer. She could see it in his manner, how he held himself. The stoop had returned, his cheeks were gray and his eyes hollow and ringed with deep wrinkles. He'd aged ten years since Min last saw him. Her throat closed and she moved towards him.

He held up his hand to halt her. "How was it?" There was nothing of the old man in his voice, not a hint of frailty. "Minerva, I have never been so disappointed! Does that answer your question?"

She recoiled as his words whipped her, and glanced at Ned. He shouldn't be here, hearing a conversation that didn't involve him. But he made no move to leave. In fact, he looked like he had a right to be precisely there—leaning against her father's fireplace as if he owned it.

"Oh, Father, I'm so sorry," she said, doing her best to ignore Ned. "But I tried to warn you. Your paper needed much more than one lecture to—."

"I'm not talking about my paper or the lecture! I'm talking about your betrayal."

"My—." Oh. Oh no. The gossip really had reached everywhere. She clenched her fists about the same time her heart constricted. "I suppose you are talking about my play?"

"Is it true?"

She tilted her chin. One could not outrun a storm and the best way to weather a storm was to face it head on. "It's true. I wrote the play and found a company to perform it."

"Oh, Minerva." Her father sat heavily on a chair by the window and pulled off his cap. His freed hair floated up as if it wished to fly away. "I had hoped it wasn't true." His voice faded to a thin, weak whine. It was a dramatic and disconcerting change. She almost wished for his ferocity again.

She knelt at his side but didn't dare touch his arm. The simple gesture could fan the flames of his ire. She knew from experience it only took a mere breath. "Tell me what happened, Father."

But it was Ned who spoke. "*Willingly* perform it?" Ned said. "You found a theatre manager who wanted to perform your play, knowing it was written by a *woman*."

Min gave him a tight smile. "Ned, why are you still here? This is a private family matter and as such, Father and I would appreciate a little time to ourselves. Perhaps you can return later—."

"He can stay," her father said wearily. "It concerns him too."

"In what way?" Min looked from one to the other. Her father avoided her gaze but Ned's fox-like smile made her uneasy. No—made her decidedly *anxious*. "What's happened?"

"As you say," Ned said, "this is a family matter. And since we are about to become family, it is only appropriate—."

"What!" She looked from one to the other but neither spoke so she gripped her father's hands. "What have you done?" she said, shaking him.

"I have saved us from poverty." Sir George removed his hands from hers. "It was the only way."

"What your father is trying to say," Ned said, "is that he has given his permission for us to marry."

Min's first instinct was to fly at him and knock that triumphant smirk from his face. Then disbelief and disillusionment chased away her anger. This was too much. After her horrible day, she could not endure this too. *Would* not endure it.

"I'll not marry him," she said to her father.

He blinked slowly at her and she was afraid he hadn't heard her. That he *couldn't* hear her. That something in his head had melted or rotted away from age or overuse. She squeezed his fingers again, more reassuring this time.

He gasped in a breath, as if he had forgotten to breathe for several moments and then suddenly remembered. "You have to. I have given permission. There is no more to be said."

"There is! Father, why the change of heart? You said you were happy for me to remain here with you. I don't understand. Is it because of my play? Do you...do you want to be rid of me?" Tears welled as the depth of her problems became clear. The no-longer dutiful daughter had gone from troublesome to embarrassing. It was too much for him and so he wanted her gone.

"Of course I don't want to be rid of you." It was the kindest thing he'd said to her in days. She couldn't help the single tear that slipped from her eye but she allowed no more. She wasn't sure he deserved them. "But I simply cannot afford you anymore, my girl."

"Afford me? What are you saying?"

"Or Jane. In fact, I cannot afford myself now. Not with Lord Pilkington's funding gone."

Min rocked back on her haunches as if she'd been struck. "Lord Pilkington has withdrawn his patronage? Oh, Father, *no*." It was quite possibly the worst thing that could happen, at a time when she thought nothing worse *could* happen. Without the money from her father's work or her plays, they had nothing. They couldn't even afford to eat.

No wonder he had accepted Ned's offer. It must have seemed like a gift from a higher power.

More like a lower one. Ned, the pond slime, had taken advantage of the dire situation and pressured an agreement from her father.

"It seems Pilkington doesn't think highly of women playwrights either," Ned said. He smiled down at her. Two days ago she'd have called his smile kind. Now she thought it condescending. "Come sit with me, Minerva. There's much to discuss." He held out his hand.

She screwed her nose up at it. "What are you talking about? Surely his withdrawal has nothing to do with me."

"Lord Pilkington believes the fairer sex should remain just that...fair," Sir George said calmly. His voice had a sort of sing-song quality to it. He didn't sound like himself at all. Min held his hand tighter. "He doesn't like women to attend the theatre let alone write for it. He says it makes them heathens."

"Heathens!" Good lord, he must have been born beneath a rock. For a man with an interest in the New Sciences, he had a decidedly ancient opinion of the theatre. Didn't he know that his queen adored plays? Didn't he see the benefits of it for the masses and gentry alike? "Father, that is ridiculous. Go back to him and plead for his patronage."

"He'll refuse it." He looked at her but didn't seem to *see* her.

His eyes were vacant. Min's heart lurched into her throat. "He was quite angry," he went on in that strange manner of speaking he'd adopted. "He said I didn't know what I was talking about."

She frowned. Why would he say that? "Father, are you sure Lord Pilkington didn't withdraw his funding because of your paper and your...unusual theories?" It made far more sense for that to be the reason than her being a playwright.

He blinked rapidly and he seemed to focus on her once more. His features, gone slack only moments ago, stiffened again. "Of course not," he said. "He says he's looking forward to reading a copy of it. You must remember to go to the printers tomorrow, Minerva. And then visit Lord Pilkington to explain that there has been a mistake. You must make him believe you didn't write that play." He nodded and pushed his spectacles up his nose. "If you can convince him it had nothing to do with you, he might resume his patronage. Yes, yes. Good idea."

No, bad idea. "Father, what exactly did he say after your lecture?"

He waved a hand in the air. "Nothing of consequence. Something about needing time to think my theory through."

She groaned. Oh dear. Lord Pilkington hadn't understood the lecture at all. If they did give him time and a copy of the paper, the only thing he would understand was that her father's theory had been plucked from thin air. Or an imagination as active as her own.

Ned cleared his throat and stepped forward, making his presence felt. As if Min could forget he was there. "If this Pilkington is a clever man," he said, "surely he will require a great deal of convincing of Min's innocence. After all, her name is on everyone's lips."

"Ned," she snapped. "I do not—."

"He's right." Sir Geroge nodded. "Lord Pilkington will want an assurance from you that you will write no more poetry. And I'll require the same. Well, Minerva? Do you promise to stop writing plays? Will you stay away from the theatres?"

"My plays might be the only things that can save us." If she could find someone else to act as their author. "The last one earned me four pounds."

"Four pounds is not going to save us. Only my work will save us." He crossed his arms, but not in anger. It was almost as if he were embracing himself. He muttered something under his breath.

Min leaned closer. "What did you say?"

"Save them."

She looked to Ned for an answer but he shook his head and lifted his shoulders. "Them? Who?" she prompted her father.

"The lost ones," he mumbled. "Just boys. All gone. Taken by the sea."

He meant the seamen from the *Lucinda May*, all drowned on her maiden voyage. All lost, as he said. Something inside Min shattered. "Oh, Father."

She touched his cheek but he was gone again. His eyes were empty of life as they stared at something in the distance. Did he see their ghosts? Is that what haunted him? Is that what drove him to find another method for calculating a ship's location? Is that what had eaten away at his conscience until there was nothing left but an empty shell where once a brilliant mind had lurked?

She should have seen it coming. She should have spent more time with him, helped him, comforted him. But she'd been too busy with her own dreams to care about his. The bitter reality twisted like a knife in her gut.

"My work is important," he muttered.

"I know."

"We must help them. Bring them back."

She kissed his forehead. "Come, Father, you need to lie down now." She helped him to stand and he allowed himself to be led to the door. She called for Jane. The maid came running and Min gave instructions for Sir George to be taken to his rooms.

When they were gone, Min turned on Ned. She threw back her head, tossing off her grief and her fears. There was no space in her for those emotions right now. She needed to be strong for her father and Jane, but mostly for herself. "I'll not marry you, Ned Taylor. You've taken advantage of Father's ill health to force his agreement. It won't be binding."

He'd been watching her father and Jane retreating up the

stairs, his eyebrows knotted together in thought. Now he turned to her and the knot cleared. He looked...satisfied. "Why not? Do you doubt his state of mind?"

"Of course! You witnessed that scene. He didn't know what he was talking about. No law will hold me to a promise made by a man in that state." They both knew it would come down to her word against his, and perhaps that of a doctor if the money could be found for one, but she would fight him if she had to.

"How will you live?" Ned said. "Your father has no hope of patronage and no one will touch your plays. Nor would a sensible man partner you in such a scheme now. He would be foolish to. So," the smirk returned, "how do you propose to keep yourself and your father off the streets if you do not marry me?"

"I will marry someone else."

He pushed his chest out and laughed. "Don't be ridiculous. You were unmarriageable before this debacle. A man would have to be a candidate for Bedlam to accept the woman who writes plays and has a mad father."

Min drew in a long breath and considered saying nothing. But it wasn't in her nature to lie down and be stomped over, not when a sweet triumph was within her grasp. "As it happens, someone has made an offer. And he has more than enough money to take care of myself, Father and a house full of servants."

His eyes briefly flared but then he burst into a raucous, humorless laugh. "You really do live in a land of fantasy."

She smiled benignly, sympathetically. "Good day to you, Ned. If you would be so kind as to see yourself out."

The harsh laughter suddenly stopped. His Adam's apple bobbed furiously. Her calm condescension must have rattled him. Without a word, he strode out the door.

Min let out a long breath and collapsed onto a chair. Oh lord, what had she said that for? She couldn't very well marry Blake, even though he'd not recanted his offer. He might have denied his betrayal, but who else could have done it? No one else knew her secret. It *must* have been him. He was still a blackguard. A lying, heartless pirate.

Perhaps not so heartless where his sister was concerned, but certainly he cared for no one else. He didn't even speak gently to his own mother. What sort of man did that?

No, she wouldn't marry him. Couldn't.

So what then? She'd rather starve than marry Ned. She could beg Lord Pilkington to reconsider, right after she lied and told him she would never write again. And then she would seek out Will Shakespeare and ask him to help her find someone suitable to act as the writer of her plays. Perhaps he would even do it himself.

There. It was a plan and it might even work. She felt relieved.

And yet miserable. Blake had broken her heart, and her father had broken his mind. Worse still, she had no idea how to fix either.

She buried her face in her hands and finally let the tears flow.

CHAPTER 23

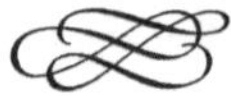

For the first time in many nights, Min didn't sit down at her desk and write. She couldn't. The words had all shriveled and died within her. She sat by the window and ran through what she would say to Lord Pilkington in the morning. It depended very much on what exactly was the reason behind his withdrawal. Was it truly because of the rumor that she was a playwright, or was her father's lecture a major contributing factor? Nevertheless, she eventually had a speech to cover both scenarios.

Now, what to say to Shakespeare. Would he—?

A shadowy figure suddenly swung onto her balcony from below, halting her thoughts and her heart. She jumped up, toppling her chair, and let out a small yelp. Then she saw it was Blake and was glad she'd not screamed loud enough for Jane to hear. This intruder was one she needed to manage on her own.

She opened the window and he climbed through. "What is the meaning of this?" she demanded, pressing a hand to her heart which had re-started with a vengeance. Whether it was beating rapidly from the fright of his sudden appearance or from his mere presence, it was difficult to tell. "You scared me half to death."

"I'm sorry," he said, studying her face with a concerned frown. "Have you recovered?"

"Quite." She crossed her arms beneath her bosom, feeling a little exposed dressed in only her shift and housecoat. She wished she'd left her hair up because he seemed to be fixated with it. His gaze had shifted to the tresses flowing over her shoulders and had not moved. "Blake, why are you here?"

"Um..."

"Is there something in my hair?" she said, running her hand through it.

He finally met her eyes. "No. It's just that...I like it unbound." He cleared his throat. "Why am I here? To speak to you of course. We didn't get to finish our conversation this afternoon."

"That would be because your sister was ill," she said tartly. "Why didn't you tell me?"

"Would you have stayed if I had?"

"No."

"That's why."

She sucked in her top lip then let it go with a *pop*. "You should have told me."

He watched her for several heartbeats then nodded. "You're right. I would have wanted to know had our positions been reversed. I'm sorry. And I'm sorry about my mother. She can be...difficult."

"She's enduring a difficult time. It must be awful watching one's child fall ill and not be able to help her. Is your sister better?"

He lifted one shoulder and let it drop heavily. "The fever has broken. She's still weak but the worst is over."

"That's a relief." She turned her back on him so she didn't have to see those penetrating eyes. Their blueness might be dulled by the lack of light—only a single candle burned on the desk—but their effect on her was not diminished.

He came closer and stood behind her. She couldn't see him but every sense was heightened by his nearness, her body alert to every twitch of muscle, every breath. She shivered, not from cold but from the pleasure rippling through her, raking across nerves already raw from a most trying day.

"You need a fire, Min," he said, mistaking the cause of her shivers. He stepped around her and she felt the loss of his nearness immediately as cool air replaced him. He opened the tinder box beside the fireplace and removed some tinder and a flint. "If you don't keep warm this winter, you'll get ill." He struck the flint and a spark lit the dry tinder in the grate. "If you can't afford—."

"We can."

He glanced at her over his shoulder. "If you can't afford wood then come to my house. I'll leave instructions for Greeves to supply you with some from our stores. In fact..." He rose and faced her squarely. "Why don't you just marry me. That way I'll know you've got everything you need."

She blinked at him. But he appeared to be entirely sincere. She sighed. It wasn't fair. He wasn't supposed to be kind. It made her answer so much more difficult to say.

Until she remembered what he'd done.

"I went down to the docks before I came here," he said before she could speak. "Many of the captains of my acquaintance had heard about your father's lecture and Lord Pilkington's cancellation of his patronage." His fingers lightly brushed hers until she closed her fist, blocking him. His fingers curled and withdrew. "I can take care of you. And your father. You *need* to marry me now more than ever, Min."

"I am very aware of my family's perilous situation. But that changes nothing. I cannot marry you." She said each word carefully, concentrating on each syllable because if she allowed herself to think of what she was refusing, she might crumble and give in. "We've already discussed this, Blake. You don't belong here and I don't belong on a ship. One of us has to give up something dear and neither of us is prepared to do that. In my case, my father and the theatre, and in yours the adventure."

He said nothing. Because he knew she was right? His face shut down, his features became sharp, rigid, and his eyes hooded as they looked at her ear instead of directly at her face. It would seem he *did* agree with her.

It was very far from being a relief to know it.

She drew in a shuddering breath and tried to ignore the gaping hole opening up inside her. There was something else to say. "And then there's the matter of your betrayal."

That got a response. His eyes widened and he stepped towards her. No avoidance now, he simply bored right through her with his piercing gaze. "I didn't do it!" He caught her shoulders and shook her. "You must believe me!"

"Why must I?" Her voice was far steadier than her nerves.

He stopped shaking and simply stared at her. "Because it pains me that you think I could do that to you. I've grown to like you, Min." He made a gruff, derisive sound in the back of his throat—directed at himself she felt sure. "And I want you to like me."

"A pirate who wants to be liked? Good Lord, that'll be a challenge, what with all the killing and pillaging."

His jaw shut with an audible *snap* of back teeth. "Does my sincerity mean so little to you that you'd sneer at me?"

"I'm finding it difficult to tell sincerity from half-truths." Her words came out clipped. She couldn't look at him but he caught her chin and stopped her from turning away. Her blood throbbed along her veins, heat melted her insides. Anger and hurt still edged her heart but it was Blake's presence that filled it, swelled it.

She ripped herself free from his grip and stepped back, clear of his power.

He stepped forward and closed the gap once more. "Let's discuss what is truth and half-truth," he said. She took another step away but he matched it with one of his own towards her. "The first truth you need to understand is that I did not tell a soul that you wrote that play."

"But—."

"I didn't." He said it with such finality, such...urgency, that she believed him. Almost.

Nevertheless, she stepped back once more, away from his influence and a glare so intense it burned.

But he followed her again, a predator stalking its pray. "The second thing you need to understand is that your situation is dire. You have no income and no prospect of one."

"Not if—."

He clamped a hand over her mouth.

She bit it.

"Ow!" He shook his hand. "You bit me!"

"You tried to stop me from saying my piece."

He rolled his eyes ceiling-ward. "I am surrounded by women with something to say."

She shifted her weight. "All is not yet lost. I intend to speak to Lord Pilkington and Shakespeare tomorrow. It might not to be too late to find a solution."

"Shakespeare cannot act as the writer of your plays. Nor can anyone else."

"Why not?"

"After the docks, I went to see Style to plead your case. He says if he ever finds anyone pedaling your plays as their own, not only will he not employ them, but he'll ensure they'll not be employed by anyone else either. By that I assumed he meant he'd spread rumors about them. Nasty ones."

Good lord! Style had turned out to be a most monstrous person! Shakespeare couldn't afford to help her, even if he wanted to. The man had his own career to think of. "But how would Style know if a play was mine or really Shakespeare's or someone else's?"

"Style claims he'd know a play of yours. He says he'd recognize your writing style."

"He did? Oh." She swallowed back her disappointment. "Well." She suddenly felt very tired. Tired of fighting, tired of reasoning, tired of nothing going her way. What had she done to deserve such ill luck? "Is that all you came here to say?" she asked.

"No. There's a third truth that I think will convince you to accept my proposal." His eyes turned the color of a stormy sea.

His self-assurance rallied her. It was far easier to refuse an arrogant man than a kind-hearted one. She planted her hands on her hips. She would not be intimidated. "And that is?"

He traced the corner of her mouth with his thumb. "That I care about you."

"Care." Her hands slipped to her sides again. She went numb. His tender touch began shredding the last remnants of her resolve. He wasn't playing fair.

"There's more," he said huskily.

"There is?"

"Yes. I want you, Min."

"Oh. Care and want. I see." But she didn't. All she saw was a man who desired her but wasn't prepared to give up anything for her. He didn't love her. Not enough to be with her always.

"No," he said, thickly, "I don't think you do." He kissed the corner of her mouth. Tasting, searching. "You drive me to distraction." Another teasing kiss and then he retreated and looked down at her. His eyes simmered. "I *need* to have you. Now. Here. The way I need air to breathe." His hand spread across the small of her back, pressing her to his hard body. "It's wrong." His hands rubbed her arms, as if he were trying to warm her. But she wasn't cold. Not when his heat surrounded her, stroked her, caressed her until she was lulled and ready. "So very wrong to take you like this." He buried his face in her hair and inhaled. "But I can't help myself." He nipped her earlobe, her throat.

She felt him shudder. Something tugged deep within her in response.

"Say something," he whispered. "Tell me to get out before I..."

Make love to you. He didn't need to say it—she knew. "It's not wrong," she murmured. His tiny kisses tracked the heat rising up her throat, tickling and tempting. She tipped her head to the side to expose more of herself. "Not when I want you too."

"Are you sure?"

She was already removing his cloak when she said, "I'm sure." He helped her with the rest of his clothes and when he was finally, *finally* standing naked before her, she pressed against all that skin. He smelled of the exotic flavors of his travels, fresh and spicy and delicious. She licked his nipple and he inhaled sharply.

"Lord, Min." His hardness pressed against her belly, begging to be petted. Feeling wicked, she reached down and stroked. He sucked air between his teeth and a groan rolled in his chest. "I'm addicted to you." She heard the slight growl in his voice, the hint of anger. She supposed he was angry at himself for coming to her, for wanting her, for allowing her another chance to break down his resolve.

Just as she was angry with *herself* for the same reasons. He was capable of leaving her a shattered mess.

But the part of her that was desperate to take what she could of him while she still could, took control. And that part was a wanton.

She pushed him down onto a chair and removed her housecoat while he watched. He sat back, legs slightly apart, a mysterious smile teasing his lips. She began to remove her netherstocks but he caught her foot and placed it gently on the seat between his thighs. Her toes nudged his thick erection and his eyes fluttered shut as another groan escaped his lips.

She removed the netherstock completely and was about to drop it on the floor when she had another idea. She placed the strip of silk beneath his thick penis and slowly moved it from side to side. More groans. A low chuckle. "You've learned fast."

"I had a good teacher."

He stilled her hand. "Enough. I want to see you now. All of you." He tugged at the laces fastening her nightshift. "Take it off."

She did.

"Come here." He gently pulled her closer and settled her onto his lap. Her bottom slid forward over his thighs so that his member stood up between them. His hands pressed against her back, pushing her chest out. He licked a nipple the way she had done to him and everything inside her tightened.

"You taste sweet," he said right before he took her breast into his mouth. His hot tongue stroked. His hand closed over her other breast, his thumb teasing her nipple until the tension inside her rose higher.

Just when she thought she could no longer stand it, he stopped. "This is madness," he said, breathing like he'd run the length of the City. "I told myself I wouldn't do this again. Not with you."

His words stung. He was already thinking about making love to someone else? She'd heard the rumors about sailors—there was always a woman in the next port. It was a rude reminder of his life at sea, the life he'd had before he met her and the one he'd have again.

The one without her in it.

"Then perhaps we shouldn't," she said. She climbed off his lap but he stood and caught her waist.

"You're changing your mind? *Now*?" Something close to panic strained his voice. He cupped her waist. Holding her to him.

"I, uh, I'm not sure." She should get dressed. She really, really should...

Then he kissed her and she was sure that she wasn't going anywhere. Not when this man was making her limbs turn to water with a searing kiss. Imagine what he could do with—oh!

He cupped her between her thighs and slid a finger into her moist folds. The finger slid in and out. Slowly. Maddeningly. "Convinced yet?" he said.

"Mmmmmm." Then he strummed her swollen nub and she gasped. He kissed her again and she forgot all the reservations she'd had about making love to him one last time. She needed this. There were a lot of lonely nights ahead of her but at least she'd have this memory to keep her company.

"I can't," she muttered, "stand it. Now. I want you inside me *now*." He withdrew his finger and picked her up. She wound her legs around his waist and guided his erection into her. He slid in easily. "Bed," she said.

He shook his head. "Too far." Their bodies twined, he carried her to the wall and pressed her back against the square paneled wainscoting. With a thrust of his hips, he buried himself deeper.

Their groans were swallowed by a thorough kiss. She splayed her hands across his back, feeling the muscles working beneath her palms. So much power, so much strength of will and control. But not tonight. Tonight he was losing his control in her study. He was hers. For one last time.

The pressure mounted in her loins, spreading through her like wildfire until she could stand it no more. She cried out against his mouth and heard a responding growl from Blake. He pounded into her and she dug her nails into his back. The pressure rose. Higher. Harder. Faster.

Until release came and her body exploded.

Throwing his head back, he pulled out of her and spurted his seed over her stomach. When he was done, he pressed his forehead to hers and together they waited until their breathing returned to normal.

Then he gently lowered her to the floor. Her feet scrunched on the rushes and her legs nearly buckled. She felt loose and soft and so very feminine. A wanton. She smiled to herself.

"Min," he said, backing away. He buried both hands in his hair and heaved a sigh. "Min."

"Don't," she said, barely holding the pieces of her heart together. "Don't trouble yourself. I knew what this meant, or didn't mean, and yet I chose to do it anyway. You're not to blame."

He rubbed his hands over his face and shook his head. He said nothing but she got the feeling he was blaming himself despite her attempt to reassure him.

She swallowed back her tears and picked up his shirt. "Good-bye, Blake."

His hands dropped away from his face and he studied her. "You no longer believe I betrayed you, do you?"

She didn't know anything for certain anymore but how could she tell him that after making love to him? She nodded anyway. "I'm still asking you to leave." It was the best thing to do. The only thing. If she kept telling herself that, she might eventually believe it.

He nodded and took his shirt. She wiped herself clean and put her clothes back on while he dressed then handed him his cloak. He paused at the window and opened his mouth to speak.

"No poetry," she said. "Just go."

The corner of his mouth lifted. "No poetry."

He stepped out through the window and leaped over the balcony. She heard the soft thud of his boots landing on the street then closed the window and blew out the candle.

CHAPTER 24

Screaming. Someone was screaming.

Min leaped out of bed and threw on her housecoat. She raced out of her rooms and nearly ran into Jane coming up the stairs. The screaming came from the maid.

"Jane, what is it?"

Jane, dressed in nothing but her nightshift and cap, grasped Min's hand and pulled her towards the stairs. "Oh, Mistress, come quick! They're takin' him!"

"Who is taking whom?" Min stumbled down in the dark—neither possessed a candle—and tried to slow the maid's progress but Jane was strong and unrelenting.

"The master." Jane headed for the front door but Min, her heart racing, overtook her. The door was already open.

Outside, dawn had begun to chase away the night shadows, illuminating Knightridge Street just enough for Min to see a horse and cart parked outside the house. Four men climbed onto the cart—one of them was Sir George. Two of them held him under his arms, lifting him up, another stood on the ground, giving instructions.

"Stop!" she shouted, bunching his cloak in her fist. "What are you doing with my father?"

He caught her arm in a bruising grip. She let go of his cloak and tried to pull free but despite his wiry frame, he was strong.

"You're the daughter," he said. His voice was as thin as his body, but what it lacked in strength it made up for in authority. He licked his lips, his tongue flicking out and back at the speed of a blink.

"Let me go!" she snapped, trying again to free herself. She might have succeeded on her own but Jane intervened. The maid landed a blow with her fist between the man's shoulder blades. He grunted and arched his back. His grip weakened enough for Min to break free.

"Father!" She ran to the cart but her father was already settled on it between the two men.

"Minerva?" He turned but the men held him. They looked like they wouldn't be easily moved with their thick-set shoulders and fists like rocks.

"Father, what is going on?"

But he simply stared back at her, his eyes empty and distant as they had been that afternoon in the parlor. The sharp mind she'd known all her life, and battled against in more recent times, had ceased to function. "Where are you taking him?" she asked the man in charge at her side.

He licked already moist lips. "The Hospital of St. Mary of Bethlehem."

Jane gasped. "Bedlam!" Her next words were lost in a whimper smothered by her hands.

Min drew her close. She needed comforting—they both did—and the reassuring touch of another human. Bedlam might be a hospital for those sick with madness rather than physical illness, but it was not a place for healing. It was a place of filth and cruelty where the patients were kept in squalid conditions, sometimes chained up and often ill-treated. Everyone in London had heard about the institution. No one willingly sent their loved ones there.

Min held onto Jane tightly. "Are you the Keeper?" she asked the wiry man. He clicked his heels and bowed his head. "And by whose authority are you taking my father?"

He looked at her askance. "By the authority of the man paying me, of course. Now, move aside. I have a schedule."

Min and Jane moved as one and blocked his way. "Tell me who's paying you? The parish?"

The Keeper's cheek twitched. "His son-in-law."

"He doesn't have a son-in-law! I'm his only kin. You can't take him away!" The pitch of Min's voice rose alarmingly. A neighbor across the road emerged from his house and leaned against the door frame where he watched the proceedings as if he were at the White Swan viewing a play. Neither he, nor any of the other people peering out of their windows, intervened.

The Keeper's tongue darted out and licked his lips again. "I've been paid by a man presenting himself as Sir George Peabody's son-in-law. I suggest you take it up with him. If there's been a mistake, he can clear the matter up with me later today."

"Who?"

"Me."

She swung round. Ned approached, a triumphant smirk planted on his cold features. For someone who abhorred violence, Min had some very brutal thoughts of what she wanted to do to him. Most involved removing his genitals.

"*You*...you devil spawn!" She charged at him and managed to scratch his face before he and the Keeper removed her. She tried to free herself but they held her firm.

"Careful, my dear," Ned said, dabbing at the stripe of blood on his cheek, "or I'll have them take you too."

Jane's arm slipped around Min's waist. Solid. Assuring. Warning her not to be impulsive. It took several deep breaths before Min could see the sense in that. It was nigh impossible to set aside her anger and her hatred of the men before her, but she managed to hide it.

"Why are you doing this?" she asked Ned.

He nodded at the Keeper. The little man bowed and climbed onto the back of the cart. It drove off. Tears stung Min's eyes as she watched, the weight of helplessness heavy in her heart. Her father hung his head and didn't look up as the cart rounded the corner and disappeared.

"Explain yourself," Min said to Ned, dashing away a tear.

"It's simple. I'm surprised your brain hasn't worked it out

already. Perhaps the theatre really does destroy a woman's mind. It certainly destroys her morals."

"What are you saying, you cur?"

He patted the protruding stomach of his peascod-bellied doublet and smiled. "It's all your own doing, really."

"What?"

"Your father offered your hand to me yesterday, but you said his mind was too feeble to make such a promise." His hand flattened across his chest. "I disagree, but if you insist he was not of his right mind, then I had no choice but to have him committed to Bedlam."

"You're the insane one, Ned. Now go after them and order my father's release."

"Not yet. You see, I want to marry you. Despite your tempestuous nature and your...willfulness, I find I'm rather taken with you." He touched her chin. She jerked away. "Bedding you could be rather entertaining."

She spat in his face. He wiped the glob from his cheek with his sleeve and laughed. "Now that is exactly what I'm referring to. Besides, I do so want to have a knight's daughter for my wife. You, my dear Minerva, will be an asset if I am to become Master of the Mercer's company and then mayor of the City."

"Ah, so that's why you chose me. I did wonder. But surely your career would not be advanced by having a father-in-law in Bedlam."

He shrugged. "I'll get him out. Once we are wed."

"You seem to think that's a foregone conclusion."

"Oh, it is. You see, if you say your father was not of sound enough mind to agree to my marriage proposal then he must stay in Bedlam. That is only right for a man in his condition. He needs their expert help."

She swallowed back a sob. Her father would get no help in Bedlam. He'd be lucky if he survived a year.

The full extent of Ned's plan was becoming horribly clear. "And if I say he *was* of sound mind at the time, then the marriage promise is binding," she finished for him.

His face split into a smile. "Good girl. It appears you are reasonably clever after all."

"I hate you, Ned. I could never care for you."

"Then our marriage will be like most others. It matters not." He shrugged. "So the choice is yours. Let him rot in Bedlam and you live your life in poverty or you marry me and I'll have him released into your care."

"Can he do that, Mistress?" Jane whispered.

Min held her hand. The maid was shaking. Or perhaps that was Min. "No. He can't. I'll prove in court the proposal was made under duress and that he is not legally allowed to have Father committed."

Ned's smiled widened. "The courts take time and money. Do you have either commodity, Minerva?" She closed her mouth firmly. "No. I didn't think so. And I've paid the Keeper exceptionally well. He'll not release your father to anyone but me unless legally bound to do so. Now, let's be sensible about this and discuss the terms of our marriage inside where we can be more comfortable. I have certain conditions you need to agree to—."

"I'll not agree to anything!" And she sure as Hades wasn't allowing him into her house. She might be freezing and the subject of neighborhood gossip, but she still had control over who she let into her house.

Ned stiffened. "Be reasonable, Minerva. You have no income and no likelihood of any, especially when it's discovered that your father is in Bedlam. Even if he was released, who would be his patron? And your plays..." He laughed. "Not a single theatre manager would touch them now. Isn't that what you've been told?"

The horrible realization that he was right washed over her like a tide, overwhelming and relentless. She had no choice. She had no money, no prospect of getting any, and she had to get her father out of Bedlam before he breathed his last in that Hell. Her problems had just become insurmountable. They were bigger than her. Her own feelings no longer mattered. It was her responsibility to take care of her father now, and Jane too. Min was not at leisure to refuse the lifeline Ned offered.

"I want a guarantee that my father and Jane can both come and live with us," she said, stomach roiling at the future unraveling before her. A future governed by a man proving himself to be immoral and even cruel. A future without love or the prospect of it.

"Mistress!" Jane dug her elbow into Min's ribs. "You can't do this. What about...you know?" More digging.

"The offer from the other man?" Ned cut in with a sneer. "I doubt it even existed."

Min stared straight ahead, looking at neither Ned nor Jane. The maid's fingers curled tightly around Min's arm but she ignored the plea. In a way, Ned was right. Blake's offer of marriage wasn't a real one. It was done out of duty. He might desire her but he didn't love her.

Not that love mattered anymore. The only thing that mattered was getting her father out of Bedlam. And Blake couldn't do that. Only Ned could.

Min held onto Jane and blinked back her tears. "There is no one else," she said. "I'll marry you, Ned."

CHAPTER 25

"You're a fool, Robert." Lilly might still be as pale as snow but her accusation lacked nothing of the vigor Blake expected from her. It gave him hope that she would soon be out of bed and on the path to a full recovery.

"You'll get no argument from me," he said on a sigh.

Lilly, as always, had his measure—and she didn't even know about his mistake with Min. Two mistakes. His first was to make love to her, his second was to offer marriage, yet again, to rescue her from her plight. It seemed he hadn't learned his lesson from the last rejection.

"Is there any event in particular that led you to that conclusion?" he asked.

She rubbed a hand over eyes shot with red. Blake wasn't sure if they were that way from crying or illness. He didn't dare ask in case his question caused another outbreak of tears.

"Your conversation with Lord Hawkesbury about..." She placed a hand over her still flat belly. The doctor had said he didn't know if the babe lived, but Lilly was adamant it did. Only time would tell.

"Oh," he said. "That."

"That? Is there something else?" She looked intrigued, and slightly amused. He frowned at her. This was the Lilly of old, the Lilly he'd hoped desperately to see again during her illness, but now he wasn't so sure he wanted her back *exactly* the same. He wouldn't mind if she was a little less perceptive and much less direct.

"Nothing I wish to divulge to you, my nosy little sister." He tapped her lightly on the end of her nose.

"Ah. So it involves a woman." She was smiling now. He couldn't help smiling back at her, even though the teasing was at his expense.

But then he sighed. There was nothing amusing about his feelings for Min. Everything inside him hurt when he thought about her. And he thought about her all the time. Damn it, but he should have been glad she rejected him. Marrying Min meant staying in London and taking care of her. He'd miss out on adventure, the thrill of the ever-changing sea, the discovery of new places. The very idea of marriage *should* send him running back down to the Legal Quays until the *Silver Star* sailed.

Oddly, it didn't.

Perhaps he needed to speak to his quartermaster and have him postpone their departure another few days. Good idea. He'd see to it that afternoon. Another week in London would have Lilly on her feet again and Min...

He couldn't finish the thought. He had no idea what would happen to Min if she didn't wed. Her situation was hopeless. If the rumors he'd heard could be believed, Sir George was unlikely to find another patron.

So why didn't she just marry Blake?

Did she despise him that much that she couldn't put her reservations about his character aside and marry him for the good of herself and her father?

Or did she still believe he'd betrayed her?

"We were talking about Hawkesbury," he said to steer the conversation back to safer territory.

Lilly reached out to the table near her bed and picked up a folded letter. She handed it to him. "It's from Lord Hawkesbury, offering me a sum of money for my future and the baby's."

"A generous sum," Blake said, reading. "And a house."

"You told him." Her voice went cold. If her lips could turn any whiter they would have with all that pursing.

He folded the letter again and handed it back to her. There was nothing of a personal nature in it. No apology, no pleading of Hawkesbury's innocence and no mention of his betrothal to Patience Enderby. It was a statement of fact and an offer of a long-term arrangement that would see her and the baby set up for their lifetime. It was generous. But it was remote, detatched. It could have been written by anyone for all the lack of feeling expressed in it.

Blake met Lilly's gaze levelly. "I stand by my actions."

"You had no right!"

"I had every right. I am your brother. I had to at least try and talk sense into him."

She waved the letter. "Oh, you did. This letter is nothing if not sensible."

"It's not my fault the man you chose to love is an idiot and can't see what a wonderful wife you'd make."

"Stop it." She sank into her pillows and turned on her side. The letter lay beside her on the bed, her fingers covering it. "You may think you did the right thing, but you didn't. You betrayed me, Robert. And I'll never forgive you."

Betray. It seemed he was destined to hurt the women he cared about, even though he was doing his best to protect them. "He needed to know you were carrying his child," he said. "I would want to know if I was to become a father, even if I couldn't publicly acknowledge that child."

"I would have told him," she said. "But only when I was ready."

He took her cool, weightless hand. "I'm sorry," he said. And he was. More than that apology could ever indicate. "Will you take up his offer?"

"No," she said flatly.

"Not even the money?"

"No."

"Why? This is his only way of making amends, so why not accept it?"

She sighed and closed her eyes. The dark lashes contrasted starkly with the white pillow and her even whiter skin. "You men are so thick-headed. You don't see what is so obvious to us women."

He snorted softly. "Aye, you'll get no argument from me. Tell me, Lil, what don't we men see? Educate me."

Her eyes opened. Where before they were cold, now they were warm, soft and distant. "That we want you. We want the man our heart has chosen for us. Not money or whatever it is you men offer us out of a sense of duty. We want *you* and we want you only on the condition that you want us just as much."

He watched her for a long time, his heartbeat growing louder in his ears, his scalp tingling.

"We need to know that our chosen mate loves us as we love him," Lilly went on. "Do you understand, Robert?"

He stared. And stared.

Then he blinked.

He felt like he'd been given the key to unlock a treasure chest. "Yes," he murmured. "I think I do."

"Good." She waved at the door leading to her inner chamber where she kept a small desk and writing implements. "Please be so good as to fetch me paper, pen and ink."

He stood and did as bid. "You're going to write to Hawkesbury?" he said when he returned.

She nodded. Blake helped her to sit up a little and found a tray atop a nearby table. He upturned it on her lap and set out the writing materials. He sat on the chair next to the bed while she wrote her letter. When she finished, she gave it to him.

"Blot it and seal it for me, please," she said.

He took it into the inner chamber and carried out her instructions then brought the letter back to her.

"No," she said, refusing it, "I want you to deliver it."

He nodded. "I'll take it to him directly."

"You'll not harm him, I hope."

He bent and kissed the top of her head. "He doesn't deserve your fretting."

"Robert," she said, taking him weakly by the shoulders and giving him a glare that mimicked their mother's. "Promise me you'll deliver the message and that is all."

He sighed. "Yesterday I could not have made that promise.

Now...well, I've learned that making Hawkesbury pay for his sins will only harm those I love. So I've decided he can live."

She laughed. "I won't assume this new opinion is my doing. I can see that something in you has changed, Robert. And I know why." She kissed her fingertips and touched them to his cheek. "I hope she is worthy of you, Brother."

He raised an eyebrow. "Even when you're ill, you know everything."

"Not in this instance. Mother told me about Mistress Peabody. I have to say I'm most pleased someone has caught your roaming eye."

"Mother isn't so pleased."

"She'll change her mind when she realizes the lady is the one keeping you in London. Forever, I hope."

"She isn't the only reason I've decided to stay." Until he said it he hadn't known he would. But hearing it out loud made it real. And absolutely necessary. He wasn't leaving Min for all the Spanish gold his ship could carry.

"No," she said, "but she is the main one."

"Aye. She is." She was more important than any adventure, more important than getting revenge on Hawkesbury and more important than his mother's displeasure. He would never find a woman like Min. Ever. If he let her slip through his grasp now, he was a bigger fool than even Lilly thought him. "Only she doesn't know how important she is to me and I must tell her." He slapped the letter against the palm of his hand. "After I deliver this." He kissed her forehead again. "Wish me luck."

"Good luck."

He left the house via the servants' entrance to avoid Lady Warhurst and ordered the stable boy to saddle his horse. The sooner he delivered the letter, the sooner he could see Min. He rode through London and out along The Strand to Hawkesbury Hall.

The earl was at home and received Blake in his study. Alone. A brave move considering Blake's previous intention to do him harm. Hawkesbury rose from behind a large desk partially obscured by crooked stacks of papers and books. He set aside a sheet of parchment and placed a quill in a fine silver inkstand near his right hand. He greeted Blake with a hesitant smile which didn't reach his eyes.

Blake handed over the letter. Hawkesbury stared at it but didn't open it. "I'll give you your privacy in a moment," Blake said. "But first I want you to do something in exchange for me not forcing your hand where my sister is concerned."

The smile faltered. "As I've said previously, my hand is not available to be forced. I have promised to wed another and breaking that promise would have...consequences for those I care about." He glanced down at the letter. His thumb caressed the paper. "I wish it were not so." This last he said so quietly, Blake almost didn't hear it.

"No," he said. "Your explanation is not good enough for me and it certainly won't be good enough for my brother. He's got a reputation for bloody-mindedness." When Hawkesbury said nothing, he went on. "It may be within my power to help you but I need to know what I'm up against."

"You can't—"

"Tell me! "

Hawkesbury gave him a rueful smile. "Very well. I can tell you some of the situation—so that you know what *I* am up against as you put it." He drew in a deep breath and let it out slowly. "My bride-to-be is expecting."

Blake's fists clenched. "So you lied to me when you told me you hadn't got her with child."

A muscle in the earl's jaw pulsed. "I didn't lie."

"You mean you're taking on another man's whelp? What in God's name for?"

Hawkesbury looked away but not before Blake saw pain etched deep into the shadows around his eyes. He was being forced into the marriage then.

"You're being blackmailed?" Blake asked. "By the girl?"

Hawkesbury shook his head. "Patience wants this marriage as little as I do. She loves the babe's father."

"Then it must be her father forcing you."

Hawkesbury moved a few steps to the fireplace and rested his elbow on the mantelpiece between two slender silver candlesticks. Without turning to Blake he inclined his head in a curt nod.

"But...why? Why does he not wed her to the man she loves?"

"Because he is a farmer and I am an earl. It's economics, pure and simple."

Blake doubted it was either pure or simple. Hawkesbury was a powerful man, a favorite at court. Of course he would have more money and land than a farmer but he also held more power. Patience's father, Lord Enderby, must want some of that power for himself.

"And to achieve this he's blackmailing you," Blake said. "How?"

"I've told you, I cannot say." Hawkesbury fingered Lilly's letter. "It affects my loved ones."

"He's threatened them in some way? Then threaten him in return. Does he have any trade investments? I can get my seafaring contacts to block any shipments—."

Hawkesbury shook his head. "The threat comes from information that's in his possession. Damning information. Something to do with my father. Something that if it is revealed, will not only devastate my mother and sister, it may well destroy them. I wish to say no more than that." He cleared his throat and straightened. "Now what is your request, Blakewell? If it is within my power to accomplish it, I will."

Blake knew he'd get no more out of the earl on the subject. If Leo wished to try then so be it, but Blake didn't think Hawkesbury would divulge his secret. If the situation was reversed, Blake wouldn't. "It is well within your powers. Have you heard the rumors about Minerva Peabody?"

"That she is the writer of *Marius and Livia*? Yes. I was sorry to hear of it."

"Sorry?" Blake's hand fluttered at his sword hilt. If Hawkesbury slandered the name of the woman he intended to marry, he'd have to challenge him.

"Put your anger away," Hawkesbury said. "I meant I'm sorry for her. She's the one suffering from the rumor. It's true then?"

Blake flexed his fingers. "Aye. And Style is refusing to perform the play."

Hawkesbury inclined his head. "Ah. So you want me to order him to return it to the stage."

"Yes. And to not exclude any future plays of Min's simply because they are written by her."

Hawkesbury drew in a breath. "You ask a great deal. Knowingly putting on a play written by a woman is scandalous to say the least."

"I'm aware of that."

"There'll be those who don't like it. Some of them will be very important men. They might make life difficult for all involved, including Mistress Peabody."

"And for you?"

He lifted one shoulder. "The simple fact is, Blakewell, we don't know what the public's reaction will be. I would hate to see more damage caused by performing her plays than not."

To Hell with this. Blake wasn't leaving Hawkesbury Hall until the bloody-minded lord of the house agreed to his request. It was time to use whatever weapons he had at his disposal. And the biggest weapon was in his opponent's hand.

Blake nodded at the letter. "Read it."

Hawkesbury's face changed from a man sure of his power to one unsure of everything. His hand began to shake a little as he opened the letter. He turned his back to Blake and read.

It had not taken Lilly long to write but it took Hawkesbury several minutes to read. He leaned heavily on the desk, his head bowed. It seemed to get lower and lower as time wore on. When he finally turned around, he looked nothing like Blake expected. There was no feigned friendliness in his features, no hint of sorrow or regret at Lilly's refusal. No reaction to the letter whatsoever.

"Very well," Hawkesbury said. "I'll speak to Style today. Is there anything else?"

"No. Our business is concluded."

"And you'll not speak of my troubles to anyone except your brother? Not even your sister?"

"Especially not my sister." It would only hurt her more to think that Hawkesbury might really care for her. Perhaps he did, but it wasn't enough or he'd have tried harder to extricate himself from the marriage to Patience, blackmail or not.

They shook hands as if securing a business transaction then Hawkesbury turned away again to look out the nearby window. In the reflection, Blake could see the earl lift the letter to his mouth and nose. His deep, deep breath was the only sound in the room.

"Good day, my lord," Blake said.

Hawkesbury said nothing. Blake closed the door and left.

CHAPTER 26

There was a man at Min's house when Blake arrived. He was ordering a laborer to load furniture onto the back of a cart with a great deal of gesticulation. When the laborer—a hunchback dressed in a graying shirt and leather jerkin—dropped a chair, the man in charge smacked him across the face with the back of his gloved hand. The hunchback ducked but not fast enough.

"What is this?" Blake said, dismounting. "Who are you?"

The man, a foppish, dour-faced individual, nodded a greeting. "My name is Ned Taylor. I'm overseeing the safe transportation of Sir George Peabody's belongings to the house of my father. And you are?"

Blake ignored his question. He had a bad feeling about this. "By whose authority are you here? Where's Min?"

"You mean Minerva."

"I am not a patient man, Taylor, and if you fail to answer either one of my questions by the time I have drawn breath, you'll find yourself being introduced to my rapier. Understand?" He was perhaps being prematurely dramatic but Blake's gut was telling him something was very wrong. Besides, his threat achieved the desired result.

Taylor gulped. "I'm here on my own authority." He poked his thumb at the front door. "Minerva is inside. But you can't see her."

"Then you'd better stop me." Blake wanted answers and this fool wasn't providing them fast enough. He strode past him, measuring him out of the corner of his eye. He wasn't overly tall or large and his sword hilt shone with disuse—Blake could overpower him without much effort if the need arose.

"Stop. Stop!" Taylor trotted alongside him but didn't hinder Blake's progress. Not a complete fool then. "You've no right to enter that house."

"And what right do you have to enter it?"

"I'm Sir George's future son-in-law. And with Sir Geor—."

"What?" Blake halted. Turned. His mouth went dry. Min was going to be wed? To this man?

She couldn't. Wouldn't.

But instinct as brutal as any body blow told him it was true.

Taylor planted his feet on the ground. "I said—."

Blake didn't wait for him to finish. Ferocious, blinding emotion took over. He grasped the blathering turd just above his ruff and squeezed. The frantic attempts of Taylor to remove Blake's fingers only fueled his anger.

The door opened and Min stood there. She let out a strangled cry and ran at them. "Stop it! Blake, stop!" He let go. He was always going to. Probably. "What are you doing?"

Taylor spluttered and rubbed his throat. He edged along the wall, away from Blake. "He tried to kill me," he croaked.

"Yes," Min whispered, her wide eyes fixed on Blake, "I can see that."

Blake caught her hands. "Look at me and tell me it's not true." She withdrew her hands and said nothing. He gripped her shoulders. "Tell me, Min!"

She nodded. "It's true. Ned and I are to be married as soon as a special license can be bought."

His hands dropped to his sides and the ground beneath his feet rocked. He pressed a hand against the wall for balance and found he was doubling over to catch his breath too. His chest hurt. Everything hurt.

"Are you all right?" Min asked, inching closer.

"No." He straightened and their gazes locked. Until she

looked away. "Why are you marrying him? Is your father forcing you?"

She shook her head and rubbed her arms. The maid emerged from the house and drew Min to her. The pleading eyes she turned on Blake were red and swollen. Min's were dry as they stared at the wall.

Despite the audience, he had to ask Min a vital question. One he almost couldn't speak. "Are you..." He swallowed and tried again. "Are you in love with him?"

A short distance away, Ned snorted.

She squared her shoulders. "No. But love and marriage rarely go together, don't you think?"

"No. I think it's possible to have both. My parents were a fine example." He wanted to reach for her, hold her, kiss her all over and *make* her see sense. But he didn't think she'd want his kisses at that moment. "And I think you, Min, agree with me."

The fingers clutching the maid whitened. She continued to study the wall.

"Min, speak to me! If you're not marrying him for love or because your father has arranged it, then why? I don't understand."

"It's not your business to understand," Taylor said. He came up behind Min and the maid. Out of reach. For now.

"I am making it my business," Blake said as much to Min as to Taylor.

Min's lips formed a tight, straight line and her jaw went rigid. If he didn't know her, he'd have thought she was angry. But he did know her—she was barely holding herself together. And that surprised him more than anything.

Something quite shocking had happened to her since he came to her last night. Something had forced her to agree to wed Taylor. Her family's lack of money was certainly a problem, but it hadn't been enough to convince her to marry Blake. And, he liked to think, he was a better prospect than the foppish fool cowering behind her.

What would force her hand? What did she care about?

Her plays. Her father.

"Where is Sir George?" he asked. Min's lower lip trembled. She bit it. "And why is your furniture being moved?"

"This is nothing to do with you," Taylor said, puffing out his chest.

Blake's hand went to his rapier hilt. Taylor took a step backwards.

"Min? What's happened?"

She half shook her head and closed her eyes. "Please don't. It's difficult enough already."

If he could just hold her...

"He's in Bedlam," the maid blurted out. "This *swine* paid the Keeper to come get him this mornin', so early we weren't even out of bed."

"Bedlam!" The full horror of Min's situation sank in slowly. If his close relation was in that hell, he'd do anything to get them out. He'd sell his soul if he had to.

Min, it seemed, would too.

"Tell me," he said to the maid.

"Say nothing," Taylor ordered her.

Blake drew out his sword and darted around the women. He pressed the blade against the reddened stripes marking the spot where his fingers had gripped Taylor's throat. "You speak only when I order you."

Taylor nodded quickly. Despite the cool day, sweat popped out above his upper lip.

Blake looked to the maid. She gulped in air before saying, "Mr. Taylor here believes Sir George is not in his right mind." She went on to explain how Taylor had come to that conclusion and how he'd used it to force Min into marriage. "The only way Sir George can leave Bedlam is by Mr. Taylor's word."

"And Taylor will only give his word if you marry him." Blake's gaze never left Min's. She hadn't blinked once during the maid's speech but now she nodded.

"It's the only way," she said. "Father won't survive a long legal battle, even if I had the money to pay for one. So you see...it's hopeless."

"No. No, it's not. Whatever Taylor is paying the Keeper, I'll double it. We can have him out tonight."

Taylor cleared his throat. "If you'd be so kind as to remove your blade I'll tell you why that's not possible." Blake lowered his sword. Reluctantly. "My father is Master of the Mercer's company. He owns this City and many of its inhabitants owe him favors. You'd be surprised who." His grin was as slick as a greased pole. Blake nearly put his fist through the turd's face. "One of them is the Keeper of Bedlam. He won't release Sir George unless I say so."

"Forget it," Min said bitterly. "Forget about me, forget about this...just forget it!"

Blake sheathed his sword, cupped her face and kissed her. It wasn't gentle or sweet. He didn't want it to be. He simply wanted to show Taylor that Min was *his*. And show Min that he hadn't given up.

But he couldn't help himself. He deepened the kiss and felt Min respond. Her fingers curled into his cloak and a tiny sigh escaped her lips as she leaned into him.

"'Ho there, unhand my betrothed!"

Blake broke the kiss but didn't remove his hands from Min's face. He caressed the soft skin of her cheek, the elusive freckle at the corner of her mouth. "If you can forget me," he said to her, "then I will forget you."

Tears welled in her eyes and she shook her head. "You know that's not possible. I could live a thousand years and you'd still be as real in my mind as you are standing before me now."

He knew now that he'd been waiting to hear her say that ever since they'd met. His hands began to tremble. He pressed a kiss to her forehead and breathed, filling his body with the scent of her.

"I *said* unhand her!" Taylor pushed Blake's shoulder.

Blake let go of Min, pulled back and landed a punch on the maggot's nose. Taylor fell to the ground, clutching his face. A spray of blood decorated the wall behind him.

"You'll pay," Taylor spat. "I'll—."

Blake picked him up by his doublet and punched him again. He was about to land another blow when he saw Min out of the corner of his eye. She'd turned her face into the maid's shoulder but he could still see the wince, the abhorrence at his violent outburst.

Blake regarded his opponent, sheltering his shattered nose with both arms. Violence. It was so much a part of Blake's life, he wasn't sure he could find a solution without it.

But he had to, or Min would never be his no matter the outcome of this day.

He lowered his fist but didn't let go of Taylor. Instead, he felt the doublet between his fingers. It was made of a very fine blue velvet, exactly like some he'd carried on his ship after trading at a Flanders port. It gave him an idea. "I have a proposal," he said, letting go of the doublet. "You have Sir George released and I won't ruin you."

"Pardon?" Taylor stopped attempting to mop up the blood with his sleeve and instead turned his attention to Blake.

"Let me put it another way. If you do not have the Keeper release Sir George by the end of today, I'll refuse to trade with you. And I'll have every captain I know also refuse to trade with you. Perhaps you're not aware that I'm Robert Blakewell and I know every captain of every ship that has sailed from here in the last five years." He crossed his arms and watched as Taylor digested the information. "Now, is there any part of that you don't understand?"

Taylor's Adam's apple bobbed. "You can't! Minerva..." He turned to her, his eyes wide and desperate. "You've got nothing. No money, no patron—."

"You're wrong. I have my pride. And my friends." She held the maid's hand but looked directly at Blake. His heart flipped in his chest. "And my plays," she added.

"Ha! Who will buy them now after I—?" He stopped and backed away.

"You!" Min let go of Jane and curled her fingers at her sides. "You did it!" She stepped forward and punched Taylor on the chin. He reeled into the wall, swearing loudly. A spectator from across the street cheered.

"Blake," she said, shaking out her hand, "I'm sorry. I thought it was you. Can you ever forgive me?"

He took her hand and pressed his lips to the red knuckles.

"There's no need. It's over now. Let's not speak of it again."

Relief briefly flickered across her face. She drew in a deep breath and a small smile brightened her entire face. "Do you mind if we release my father now?"

He smiled back. "Of course. Taylor? Do you agree to my terms?"

"How can I not?" he mumbled, rubbing his chin.

"Good. Then let's go."

The party walked up Gracechurch Street, past the White Swan Inn where Lord Hawkesbury's Men would soon be putting on a play which was not written by Min, and continued along Bishopsgate Street through the gate itself. Min, walking beside Blake who led his horse, was the happiest she'd been for days. Her father was about to go home with her, Blake hadn't betrayed her, and despite the way she'd treated him, he still seemed to care for her.

Perhaps, just perhaps...

No. There was no point in speculating. She would take the next few days as they came, minute by minute. She would not look too far ahead.

They entered the grounds of Bedlam, made up of a few stone buildings hunkering around a courtyard on Bishopsgate Street Without. The wind swirled around the yard and buffeted against the hospital, playing havoc with hats and skirts. A moan carried on the breeze sent a shiver down Min's spine.

"Here," Blake said, "take my cloak."

"I'm not cold," she said but smiled her thanks. He smiled back. He had the sort of smile that quickened hearts. It was a wonder he didn't use it more often.

Ned, who'd been too busy stopping his nose from bleeding to say anything as they walked, pointed to one of the buildings. "The Keeper's office is in there."

The formalities were over within minutes. Ned ordered Sir George's release and the Keeper, after pointedly raising an eyebrow at Ned's bloodied face, sent for two servants to fetch him without comment.

When her father shuffled in between them, Min raced to his side. He smiled when he saw her and drew her into an embrace.

"Ah, my girl," he said, "I knew you'd find a way. You're too clever not to."

"Not me, Father, my friend, Captain Robert Blakewell."

It was an uncomfortable place and circumstance for introductions and Sir George, dressed in the loose-fitting clothing of the Bedlam patients, shifted uneasily. "Thank you," he said with a bob of his head.

Blake clasped her father's hand in greeting. "It's the least I could do for you. You've been such an important part of my life for years, I should be the one thanking you."

Sir George frowned. "Oh?"

"I'm captain of the *Silver Star*. I've been following your career and waiting for your new theory with anticipation."

Sir George's frown deepened. "Oh."

Ned snorted. Min shot him a glare.

"I hear it's coming along nicely," Blake continued. "My quartermaster reported much talk of it down at the Legal Quays."

Her father's face lifted, his focus sharpened. He smiled and Min put her arm around his waist, drawing him closer. *Thank you,* she mouthed to Blake. It didn't matter if he was lying. In her father's present state, the words of encouragement could be the difference between a stable mind and an unstable one.

"Come, Father, let's go." She steered him to the door, Blake following. Ned stayed behind.

"You go ahead," Blake said quietly to her when they stepped outside.

"Why, where are you going?"

He glanced back to Ned and the Keeper. "I want to make sure Taylor understands the full implications of what will happen to him if he tries to harm you or your family."

Oh. Oh no. He meant he was going to hurt him. Again. She chewed on her bottom lip and refused to face him. She didn't want to see the violence in the blue eyes she loved so much. Not that she was completely against hurting Ned—he deserved to be hurt after all—but she wasn't sure another punch would be enough for Blake. If only he could see that his earlier threat had been far more productive. She took her father's arm and began to walk away.

"Wait." Blake pulled Min aside and tilted her chin up, forcing her to look at him. The blue eyes smoldered. "I'm simply going to talk to him. I know what his father's company imports and I want to make sure he realizes the depth of my...resources."

"He's very rich. Do you think you really could ruin him?"

He gently squeezed her chin. Her father, bless him, pretended not to notice and sidled away to stand near Blake's tethered horse. "I know I haven't your faith in me, but believe me when I say I can make him miserable. And if I need to call in some favors, I will. You're important to me, Min. I want you to be happy."

She smiled. She couldn't help it. Every piece of her felt alive with happiness. The part of her that believed in the romance she wrote about in her plays *knew* it would all end well. She ignored the other part that warned her to tread cautiously, that nothing had truly been resolved between them. For now, she wanted this feeling all to herself.

"I'll come see you when I've finished," he said, touching her cheek. "I need to talk to you."

She nodded and leaned into his hand. "Until then."

Blake left her and joined her father. "Take my horse," he said. "He responds well to commands and is used to traffic." He then proceeded to remove his cloak. "And you'll need this, Sir. I'll bring your belongings back with me."

"Thank you," Sir George said, patting the horse's nose. "He's a fine steed. I used to ride one just like him in my youth."

Min couldn't imagine her father ever riding a huge beast like Blake's horse but she simply smiled and clutched the bridle in a firm grip. Blake helped her father to mount then stood aside and watched them leave.

"He's a fine man," Sir George said when Bishops Gate was long behind them. The hordes of travelers entering the City proper had dispersed and conditions were less dangerous for horse, rider and leader. "Are you going to marry him?"

"Father!"

"Well?" His brows lifted. "I don't mind. I think it's time you marry."

"You do?" This was most unexpected. Her father needed her now more than ever. "What about helping you with your work?"

He took a long time to answer and she thought he might have gone to sleep in the saddle. But when she squinted into the sun, she saw that he was looking into the distance.

"I think I might work a little less," he suddenly said. "I know my mind is not what it used to be." He sighed. "Sometimes I can't grasp a single thought. I can see it, I can *sense* it...but I can't hold onto it. It's like trying to catch a fish with your bare hands." He dropped the reins and lifted his hands, holding them in front of his face.

She yelped. "Father! Hold on."

He picked up the reins again. "I used to try to catch fish in the stream when I was a boy. Perhaps I'll go fishing again."

"You probably need a license to do that in the Thames."

"More fishing," he said, "means I'll be needing your assistance less. That'll give you time to write your plays."

Min's breath caught. Was he merely pretending to appease her? Or did he truly want to slow down? "I...I'm sure you'll still require me a great deal. There's your new theory you must expand upon—."

"Minerva, I'm tired. My theory is in good shape to be expanded upon by the next generation of scientists. I've left my legacy upon the world, for good or ill, now it's your turn." He turned watery eyes on her, but they weren't sad. Quite the opposite. "You are an intelligent girl, my dear. I've always told you to use your brain wisely."

"Yes," she said, unsure where the conversation was going.

"Now I'm adding to that advice. I wish you to use it on something you love. Your plays. I've been a fool to hold you so close to me, making you work on my dream when you had dreams of your own. I know that now, and I'm sorry." He sighed and it seemed to fill his entire body.

Her heart expanded and contracted with a rush of love for him. But she wouldn't tell him her plays would never again appear on the stage. There were some things he didn't need to know yet, if ever. "Thank you, Father. I'll try to make you proud."

"You already have."

CHAPTER 27

"Mistress! Mistress, come quick!"

"Shh, Jane, don't wake Father," Min said, rising from the stool by the kitchen fire where she'd been warming her knees. "What has set you in such a spin?"

"Lord Hawkesbury is here!" Jane, quite breathless, ushered Min out of the kitchen with a flap of her apron.

"Hawkesbury?" Min couldn't have been more surprised if Jane had said she'd flown to the moon.

"Aye. I've put him in the parlor. Quickly, don't keep him waitin'."

Min dutifully hurried to the parlor and greeted the earl with a curtsy. "This is quite a surprise," she said. "A pleasant one. I'm honored by your company, my lord. I'm sorry my father cannot greet you himself but he's ill at present."

He bowed formally. He looked quite out of place in her unprepossessing parlor with his immaculate clothes and impressive frame. But he wasn't disdainful of the meager furniture or the shabby cushions. In fact, he didn't appear to notice any of it. "I hope it's nothing serious," he said. "I'm sorry to disturb you but there's something I wanted to tell you. Actually, there's something I wanted to show you. He held out his hand. Care to walk with me?"

"I, uh..." It was all alarmingly sudden. And Blake had not yet arrived. "I'm waiting for someone."

"It's not far," he said. "I'm sure your maid will make your visitor comfortable if he or she arrives in your absence." And then he smiled, a brilliant, disarming and quite beautiful smile.

She took his hand. "Of course. I'd be delighted to walk with you." He wasn't the sort of man one refused. Not when he smiled like that, as if her presence on his arm was the most important thing in his world. Blake too made her feel that way, and more. Much, much more.

Where was he? Was he still bent on revenge? Would he be dismayed to find her walking about with the earl when she should be waiting for him?

"Jane," she said as the maid helped her into her cloak, "if Captain Blakewell arrives in my absence, please see to it that he waits. I won't be long." She glanced at the earl to see if he'd heard her. He inclined his head. It seemed he had.

They stepped out just as a stranger with the longest, reddest beard Min had ever seen approached. "Are you Mistress Peabody?" he asked.

"I am."

"I'm John Stokes, ma'am, quartermaster aboard the *Silver Star*." He rubbed his palms down his long, loose breeches as if he were nervous about something. Talking to her perhaps? "I was informed at Blake's, that is, Captain Blakewell's house, that I'd find him here."

"Oh, I'm sorry, he's not but he should be back shortly. Is there a message to pass on to him?"

"Aye. If you'd be so kind to say I was here and that the *Star*, that's his ship, ma'am, is ready to sail at next high tide. He needs to be aboard before nightfall."

"Tonight? Are you certain?"

"Aye. We sail at first light in the mornin'."

Min felt everything drain from her, like a river suddenly running dry. She must have gone white because both Stokes and Lord Hawkesbury came to her side.

"Are you ill?" the earl asked, taking her elbow.

"No," she whispered. Yes. She wanted to throw up. Blake was leaving? Tomorrow?

God. Oh God oh god. She'd known it all along, but she'd denied it ever since he'd rescued her father. She'd hoped he'd given up his seafaring to be with her, but those hopes now lay shattered at her feet.

Foolish, foolish girl. He'd given her no indication he was prepared to put her before his adventuring. Indeed, he'd given her no indication he cared for her more than his sense of honor dictated.

"Ma'am?" Stokes prompted.

She cleared her throat and rallied her nerves. "I'll pass the message on," she assured him.

He nodded and bowed as he backed away. Min watched him until he left Knightridge Street.

"Shall we?" Hawkesbury said.

She nodded and walked alongside him, trying not to think about Blake. She failed miserably.

"I saw Blakewell earlier," he said as they made their way along Gracechurch Street, the same way Min had gone to Bedlam. She half expected to run into Blake coming in the opposite direction. She was no longer sure if she wished to or not. She certainly didn't know what she'd say to him.

She had no right to say anything that was in her heart. She'd rejected him, more than once. Of course he would leave London, leave her—it was always an inevitability. He belonged at sea.

And he'd not once said he loved her...

"Oh?" she said. "He didn't try to..."

"Kill me?" He laughed. "Not this time. I think he's decided to put aside his revenge."

"Really?" She frowned. "But he was so bent on it. Are you sure?"

"He told me so himself. He'll not seek to marry me to his sister as long as I fulfill a promise to carry out a service for him."

Blake sold his sister's honor for a promise? That certainly didn't sound like him. "But...she's been ill," she said pathetically, her illusions about Hawkesbury shattered. His charm was simply a façade and he was really the sort of man who didn't take responsibility for his actions. Poor Lilly.

"Do not blame him," he said. It took a moment for her to realize he meant Blake. "If I know Lilly, she would have made his life miserable had he continued to pursue me."

"Oh? That sounds most...unusual." She frowned. She was understanding the Blakewell siblings less and less. Did Lilly not want her child to have a father? Did she not want to marry Lord Hawkesbury?

Or, like Min, perhaps she did but she didn't want to force him.

Min suddenly understood Lilly Blakewell very well.

"She is a most unusual woman." By the quiet way he said it, she understood him to consider such uniqueness to be admired, cherished even. If he thought that way about Lilly Blakewell, why didn't he marry her? It was most perplexing.

They stopped outside the White Swan. Instead of going into the taproom, they went through the arch to the inn-yard. But they could get no further than the entrance. The crowd was too thick. Min couldn't see over their heads but she could hear a single voice above the unnatural silence. It was Henry Wells, speaking a line she recognized as Marius'.

"My play," she whispered. She stared at the back of the man in front of her. "But...but Style said he'd never show it again."

The man turned around and glowered. "Shut it," he hissed. "I can't hear."

Hawkesbury led Min outside to the street again. "You did this, didn't you?" she said, blinking up at the man she understood less than Blake. "Thank you."

He shook his head. "Thank Blakewell. He organized it."

"This was what he exchanged Lilly's honor for?"

Hawkesbury's head jerked back and Min realized with horror that she'd insulted him.

"I, I'm sorry, I didn't mean—."

"Don't trouble yourself." He smiled but it was thin and unconvincing. "I was glad I could do this for you. You're the best thing to happen to Style and his ilk since I've known them. You have my word that you can continue as their playwright for as long as you wish."

"But...what if the audience is repelled by a woman writing plays? They'll not come and your company will suffer."

He indicated the inn-yard and its audience. "Every one of them knows a woman wrote that play." He pointed to a handbill nailed to the wall near the entrance. Beneath the printed announcement of the play were the handwritten words: *Penned by a Lady of Virtue.*

"There wasn't time to have new ones printed up for today's performance," he said. "I watched Style write that himself."

"A Lady of Virtue?" Min chuckled. "I like it. Style must hate it."

He laughed. "It almost killed him to write it but he'll grow used to it. He'll certainly grow used to the profits your play brings. Tell me, is the next one as good?"

"Oh, it's better. Much better."

"Humorous?"

"I hope so." But the one after that would be full of sorrow and love lost. Her heart sank and her good humor with it.

"Min? Min, what are you doing with him?"

She spun around. "Blake? I..." His murderous expression made her pause, swallow. His hand flirted with his sword hilt but he didn't draw. At least his anger hadn't completely obliterated his common sense, although she wasn't sure for how long.

"Get away from her, Hawkesbury. I might have relinquished my revenge where Lilly is concerned by I will not countenance you being anywhere near Min unchaperoned."

"Blake!"

"You are here now," Hawkesbury said with a bow. "Timely. You can escort Mistress Peabody home."

"I demand to know what you are doing here with her!"

"He was showing me this afternoon's performance," Min said, perhaps a little too ungraciously. But...honestly! To think that she and Hawkesbury were... "I believe I have you to thank for this." She indicated the handbill.

Blake read it. "He told you."

"Was I not supposed to?" Hawkesbury said. "I thought it would assist you with..." He glanced at Min. "...er..."

"I don't need assistance," Blake said through his teeth.

"Quite," Min said. She curtsied a farewell to Lord Hawkesbury. "I've a mind to take my leave of you both now. Good day, my lord. And thank you."

He took her hand and kissed it but quickly dropped it when Blake moved closer. "It's been an honor to make your acquaintance, Mistress Peabody."

She turned and left. Blake strode up alongside her. "Contrary to his lordship's suggestion, I am not in need of an escort," she said. "I know the way and it is quite safe at this time of day."

"Min? What's wrong?" When she didn't answer, he halted her with a hand to her arm. His grip was too firm to shake off. "Min, what did that self-important prick say to you?"

"He was a gentleman. I like him." She realized a heartbeat too late that she'd crossed a line. The wounds caused by Hawkesbury abandoning Lilly were still raw for Blake, and he didn't deserve her rubbing salt in them, not after what he'd done to help her. "Blake—."

"You *like* him?" He walked off but doubled back and thrust his face into hers. "You like *him*?"

"He has some good points. Although he is a little...unfathomable," she added hastily.

"Min." He rubbed a hand over his mouth and chin and expelled a breath. A man and woman passed nearby and he waited, impatiently, for them to be out of earshot. "I may have given up my revenge on Hawkesbury but I can assure you, my brother will not. And I can't say I'm not unhappy about that. The earl is a snake. He hurt my sister and he'd not hesitate to hurt you too."

"I do not care for him in that way, Blake! Good Lord, I simply meant he is not the heartless wretch you think him. I know he only spoke to Style because of his arrangement with you, but it was considerate of him to bring me here himself."

"You do not..." He shifted his weight and crossed his arms over his chest. "You have not developed an... an affection for him?"

"No!"

His arms dropped to his sides and he cleared his throat. "Ah, well, that's—."

"But if I had, it would not be your business."

He winced as if stung. Good. Let him see how much his impending departure had hurt her. She couldn't pretend that she didn't love him anymore, and that she wanted him to love her in return. Wanted him to think of her before he thought of anything else. Wanted, so very desperately, to be not only his wife but also the love of his life.

"Min, what's wrong? Is this about Hawkesbury or something else?"

She walked off, acutely aware that he was staring at her back. "Good day, Blake." The quartermaster's message hung heavily around her neck but she didn't stop to impart it. Let him find out for himself. His own ship would hardly leave London without him.

Miraculously, she made it home in one piece and without shedding a tear. It was an entirely different story when she shut the door. She leaned against it, all the breath knocked out of her, and sobbed.

Jane emerged from the kitchen and rushed to fold her into her arms. "What's wrong, dear girl? What's happened?"

Min was too overset to speak so she simply shook her head. Then the door at her back banged as if someone had swung an axe at it. The banging turned to rapid pounding.

"Who is it?" Jane called out.

"Blakewell. Open up! I wish to speak to Min."

Min shook her head at the maid. "She's not here," Jane said through the door.

"I saw her enter!" An almighty thump made the door shake. The women stepped away from it just as another thump caused the door to spring open. "Min!" Blake stormed inside, all massive and powerful and...desperate. "I demand to know what is the matter. And do not attempt to shrug off my concern because I know something has set you against me."

"Jane, you may go," Min said.

"But Mistress—." At Min's stern look, Jane nodded and headed to the kitchen.

Min gathered her courage and faced up to the towering presence blocking her doorway. "Blake, I've been remiss. I should have given you a message earlier but I failed to do so."

"Message? What message?" He shook his head and stepped closer. He was so near she could feel the heat emanating from him in waves. "It's of no concern right now anyway, whatever it is. If you'll not tell me what is the matter, then I must tell *you* something. Something I should have said days ago. You affect me, Min, in a way that no one has done before." The firm jaw softened, shuddered, and he blinked.

She put her hands behind her back and clasped them hard. "Do I?" she said, managing to sound quite cool when all she felt was heat sliding through her body.

"Yes." His thumb touched the corner of her mouth. "Do you know you have the most beguiling freckle here?"

"No." Her traitorous heart almost thundered right over the top of her answer.

"Ever since I saw it," he said, "I've tried to ignore its allure."

Oh. "You have?"

He nodded. "But I've been a fool. Ignoring something so tempting as your freckle is fruitless. It has invaded my every waking thought, and most of my sleeping ones, ever since I set eyes on it. So I've come to a conclusion."

Ah. This was it. The announcement of his departure. She steeled herself. It wasn't going to be easy to hear.

"I've decided I must possess that freckle or keep trying for the rest of my days. And so, since you and your freckle are not to be parted, I'd like you to accept my proposal of marriage."

She closed her eyes. It was much easier than looking at him—his handsome face, his kissable mouth.

She shook her head. "Blake—."

He placed the tip of his finger over her lips. She opened her eyes to see the most intense expression she'd ever seen him wear. He wasn't being fair. He simply wasn't...

"You haven't let me finish." He cupped her face in his hand, his thumb caressing the corner of her mouth where the freckle resided. "I love you, Min. You are...everything to me. More than everything."

"Everything?" she whispered.

He nodded. "You mean more to me than sailing, more than the New World, more than treasure."

Her bodice was much too tight. She couldn't breathe. "More than adventuring?"

He smiled. "The only adventure I wish to embark upon is with you, here. I don't want to be anywhere else. Besides, I've decided I can't live without you, Min. So you simply have to —*have* to—accept me this time."

A tingling thrill skittered through her, making every nerve stand up and sing. "Yes," she said, breaking into a silly grin, "I suppose I do."

He cupped her face and kissed her. Hotly. Deeply. A kiss that she felt all the way down to her toes. She would remember it forever.

But he broke it all too suddenly. "Now," he murmured against her lips, "you said you had a message to give me."

She did? What...? "Oh. Yes. Your quartermaster..." Good Lord her mind was so addled she couldn't remember the fellow's name.

"Stokes," Blake said with a smile that told her he knew exactly why her memory had failed her.

"Yes, Stokes. He was here."

"Here?" He pulled away and frowned. "Why?"

"He was looking for you."

"But... Oh." He chewed on his top lip. "That's why you were...upset with me." He circled his arms around her waist and pulled her close. "He told you my ship was leaving tomorrow and me with it?"

"So it's not?" Despite his heartfelt assurances and his hot kisses, Min still held her breath for his answer.

"Yes it is."

Her heart stopped beating. She stared at him, not sure if she wanted to shout in anger or burst into tears. He still planned to sail? But—.

"But I'm not going with it," he said. "Of course you already knew that." His mouth tipped into one of his crooked smiles. The tease. "Didn't you, my love?"

"Uh, yes, of course I knew. You told me so."

He squeezed her and chuckled. "In my rush to get here to see you earlier I forgot to send new orders to Stokes, telling him he's the new captain of the *Silver Star* and that he's to sail as planned. Without me."

She beamed. She couldn't help it. He was staying—for her.

"I adore your smile." He let go of her and held out his hand. "Now, will my blushing bride join me in telling the world of our marriage plans? We'll start with our families and end with Lord Hawkesbury's Men."

Min placed her hand inside his and tugged him closer. He didn't resist. "First, I want another kiss."

He grinned and dipped his head. "Whatever the lady wants, the lady gets." He pecked her on the lips but, frustratingly, withdrew. "Always." Then he pulled her into his chest and took her breath away with his searing kiss.

EPILOGUE

Jane cried when Min told her she was to marry Blake and live at his house, and that she was to be Min's maid of the chamber. When Sir George awoke, Blake asked for his blessing. Her father gave it then returned to the book he was reading. Min was surprised to see it wasn't a scientific one but one she'd used to research her plays—a translation of Plutarch's *Lives of the Noble Grecians and Romans*.

"That's your family seen to," Blake said as he planted yet another kiss on Min's lips that thoroughly rattled her senses.

She smiled against his mouth. So this was what happiness truly felt like. A lightness of being, a sense that she could conquer any obstacle, achieve anything she desired. It was quite a heady experience.

"Now onto yours," she said.

"Yes." He drew in a deep breath. "But I must warn you, my mother can be...taxing."

They arrived at the house just before supper and entered a hive bustling with activity. The servants scurried about and not even the steward was present to greet them.

"My brother must be home," Blake said. He took Min's hand. "I'm sorry."

"Why?"

"You'll find out soon enough. But first, come and meet Lilly."

He led her to a large bedchamber at the top of the stairs. All around the walls hung embroideries and cloths of the finest workmanship, lending warmth and comfort to the room. Occupying the centre was a canopied bed where a young woman of ethereal beauty lay. Dark eyes shone with determination inside the shadows of illness, and inky black hair framed pallid skin and sunken cheeks. Her lips, rosy and full, were the only thing of color on her. They curved into a smile when she saw Blake and Min.

"This must be Minerva Peabody," she said.

Min approached and took the hand the woman offered. "I'm pleased to meet you, Mistress Blakewell."

"Call me Lilly." Lilly held out her other hand for Blake.

He took it and sat beside her on the bed. "Min has consented to be my bride."

Lilly's smile widened. "Congratulations! I'm so glad someone has finally seen my brother for what he is."

"Oh?" Min said, intrigued. "And what is he?"

"A puppy."

"Puppy," Blake scoffed.

"Of course," Lilly said to Min, ignoring her brother. "He *pretends* to be mysterious and brooding but really he's the most playful creature. Don't you think?"

Min smiled. "I'm not sure playful is quite the word I'd use."

"Precisely," Blake said.

"Stop being so childish," Lilly chided. "Or I'll have to tell Min all your secrets."

"I knew bringing her here was a mistake," he said. "You'll make her change her mind and she hasn't even met Mother yet."

Min laughed. Brother and sister certainly liked to tease each other. It was so refreshing. Having never had a sibling, she would like to have a sister. And a brother. Perhaps.

"Or Leo," Lilly said grimly, reading Min's thoughts.

"Has his lordship been in to see you yet?" Blake asked, letting go of Lilly's hand and taking Min's.

"A quick visit when he arrived to check on my health. I expect him back any moment."

She sounded less than enthusiastic by the prospect. Blake commented as such.

"It's your fault he's here at all," Lily said sourly. "If you hadn't summoned him from Warhurst Hall he would have left me alone."

"My fault?" Blake said. "Funny, I don't recall sleeping with Hawkesbury."

Min's eyes widened but Lilly simply snorted softly and Blake didn't try to retract his observation. It was going to take a lifetime for Min to understand their relationship. Fortunately she had one.

Just then a breeze swept through the room, followed by a man with Blake's imposing stature, dark hair and sharp good looks. Lord Warhurst. But where Blake's mouth was full, made for kissing, his brother's was tight, severe. And his eyes were the most vivid green Min had ever seen and when they flashed they resembled his mother's emerald rings.

He stopped in the doorway, assessed the newcomers and bowed stiffly at Min. She stood suddenly and smiled a greeting. "Lord Warhurst, I believe. My name is Minerva Peabody. I am to be your new sister."

The baron's mouth dropped open, just a fraction, and he turned to Blake. "You're getting married? Did the sky fall down in my absence or is this a miracle?" He turned back to Min. "You have my best wishes, madam. You're going to need them."

It was Min's turn to let her mouth fall open.

"Ignore him," Lilly said, giving her eldest brother a glare that could shatter glass. "He's being rude and disrespectful. As usual."

But Blake didn't seem to be in the least perturbed as his brother strode past him to his sister's bedside. "Nice to see you too, Leo."

Leo stood stiffly by Lilly's bed but eyed his brother up and down. "You're not going to roll up your sleeves and attempt to flay me over my comment? Well, it would seem the prospect of marriage has knocked some wind out of your sails where I failed. It's about time." He inclined his head at Min. "Thank you for taking on the challenge that is my brother, Mistress Peabody. You are obviously a good influence."

Blake rolled his eyes. Min simply blinked at them all. What an odd family.

The doorway darkened again, making everyone turn. Min gulped. Lady Warhurst stood in a fine black mourning dress with an equally bleak expression on her face.

"Are you all squabbling again?" She entered the room and pointed her chin at Min. "And in front of our newest member too."

"She's not yet," Leo said. "She still has time to run away."

"If you don't all shut up," Blake said, forking one eyebrow at his brother, "she probably will." Then he frowned and turned to his mother. "How did you know Min had accepted my proposal?"

"She's here isn't she?" Lady Warhurst took Min's hand and squeezed affectionately. "Welcome to my family."

"Thank you, my lady," she said, bobbing a curtsy and trying to decipher why Blake's mother was being so nice to her. She'd been braced for antipathy.

"Call me Gwendolyne. And I shall call you Min since that is what Robert calls you. I must say, I'm glad you accepted my son, faults and all."

"There aren't that many," Min felt obliged to note. Honestly, what else could she say? She was completely taken aback by the woman's change of heart. Only yesterday she'd virtually run Min out of the house.

"Mother," Blake said, frowning and crossing his arms, "I have to say your welcome is somewhat...unexpected."

She waved a hand laden with jeweled rings. "Oh, that. You always did do the opposite of what I said, so I simply devised a little trick to push you along. Did it work, I wonder?"

Leo snickered and Min had to purse her lips to stop smiling. Lady Warhurst—Gwendolyne—was nothing like she'd been at their first meeting. She was quite pleasant and polite with an impish streak Min liked. It was no wonder her children treated each other so wickedly with her as their example.

"Is there any other times you've employed that line of

reasoning on me?" Blake said, his head tilted to the side as he regarded his mother.

"No, that was the first. Now, can I point out that it is my dearest wish that you and your lovely bride will find a house of your own, preferably on the other side of the world, and leave me in peace?" She winked at Min.

Blake snorted. "Very amusing," he said.

"Yes," said Leo, "there's no time for this foolishness. I've come home for the express purpose of finding out who got my sister in this state." He waved a hand at Lilly's belly. She folded her arms over it.

"It's all been taken care of," Gwendolyne said. "Robert has seen to it." And with that, the topic ended.

Except Leo didn't heed his mother's instruction. "He has?" He turned to Blake. "Well? Who is it? Who did this?"

"*This* is not a disease," Lilly said, hotly. "He or she is a child."

Leo cocked an eyebrow at Blake.

"Hawkesbury," Blake said. "Do you know—?"

"Hawkesbury?" Leo spluttered. "The earl of bloody Hawkesbury? The slippery cur!" Lilly smoothed the bed covers at her sides and failed to meet her eldest brother's glare. "You say it is all taken care of," he went on. "Does that mean he's going to marry her?"

Min looked away, not wanting to witness the crash she could sense approaching.

"Not quite." Blake explained the events leading up to his last meeting with Hawkesbury. He left nothing out as far as she knew. "And since he's set on not marrying her, I've decided to leave the situation as it is. There's nothing further to be done."

"Leave the situation! Nothing further to be done!" Leo shook his head, over and over. "Love has softened you, Blake. There is much still to be done. I'll challenge him to a duel."

"I did that. Nearly killed him."

Lilly's sharp intake of breath filled the room.

"Robert," Gwendolyne said, sitting on the edge of the bed. Do you have to speak of such things around your sister and your betrothed?"

"The whole point of a duel," Leo said with a sneering lift of his top lip, "*is* to kill your opponent."

"Killing Hawkesbury would serve no purpose," Blake said, squaring up to his brother. They were a match in height and bulk and anger. Min took hold of Lilly's hand and squeezed. "Enough, Leo," Blake said. "Our sister doesn't want us to kill him, nor does she want his money. It is our duty to protect both her and the baby. We must focus our attention on that now."

Leo took one step closer to his brother so that they were nose to nose, chest to chest. "You are a fool, Blake." Seconds passed and neither moved. Then Leo stepped back. With a curt nod to all the women in the room, he spun around and left.

Everyone let out a breath. Blake put his arm around Min's waist. "He's the fool. I'll speak to him later when he's calmed down and make him see sense."

"I doubt he will," Lilly said, rubbing her temple.

Gwendolyne patted Min's arm. "I'm sorry you had to meet us under such trying circumstances. Everything will settle back to normal as soon as Leo realizes he's on a futile errand."

It seemed everyone else in the room had already decided that getting Lord Hawkesbury to marry Lilly was indeed futile.

"Let us talk about more pleasant things," Gwendolyne said. "Like your wedding feast. We'll have it here of course."

Lilly instantly brightened. "You must wait until I'm better of course."

"Of course," Min said with a tentative smile. She was still a little shaken by Lord Warhurst's outburst but everyone else seemed to have cast it off already, as if it were nothing.

"And you've decided to stay in London to be with your wife, Robert?" Gwendolyne asked. "For good?"

"For good," he said, drawing Min into his arms.

"Then we owe you much, Min," his mother said. "We've tried everything from pleading to blackmail to get Robert to remain here but he's always refused."

Min tried to smile but suddenly felt a little out of sorts. She wasn't sure she wanted their appreciation. It was quite a burden to keep him here for everyone's sake.

Blake pecked her on the cheek. "It's not just Min," he said.

"Lilly's baby will need one sensible male figure in his life because his other uncle doesn't know the meaning of the word love. But I do," he said softly, capturing Min's gaze with his own bright, bright blue one. "I do."

Now Available
A TEMPTING LIFE
the 2nd Lord Hawkesbury's Players book

Read on for an excerpt

A TEMPTING LIFE

(AN EXCERPT)

About A TEMPTING LIFE

Cold, ruthless Lord Warhurst needs to distance himself from scandal if he's to marry an heiress and save his decaying estate. But with his unwed sister pregnant and his father's past indiscretions still haunting Leo, scandal threatens to erupt in an explosive way. Especially when he begins to desire strong-willed and low-born Alice Croft, the seamstress to Lord Hawkesbury's Players and the woman helping him spy on his sister's lover. If anyone finds out, Leo's chance of marrying well will be ruined.

However the scandal will be nothing compared to what happens when Alice cracks through the hard shell around his heart. Because how can Leo afford to love a woman who only wants him for the fortune she thinks he possesses?

CHAPTER 1

The White Swan Inn was the last place Leo, third Baron Warhurst, wanted to be on a Friday morning. He should have been at court, greasing the palms of the queen's favorites, or better still, having a drink in the taproom. But no. Thanks to the mess created by his siblings, he had gone to the Gracechurch Street inn to speak to a seamstress. A bloody *seamstress*!

He climbed the steps up to the wooden stage at the back of the cobbled innyard and lifted the curtain to peer into the tiring house beyond. Inside, several chests, some opened, occupied most of the floor space. A row of stools dotted one wall and a central bench almost disappeared beneath piles of neatly folded costumes. A massive pair of wings made of feathers hung between two hooks, and what looked like a cauldron was slotted beneath the bench. The room was crowded but not chaotic. Someone kept it orderly.

Whoever it was, they weren't there. Leo squeezed the bridge of his nose. God, he was tired. He'd traveled like the devil for a week to reach London and not been able to sleep since. And now the woman his brother had sent him to couldn't be found.

He was about to release the curtain when he heard the swish of lush fabric, velvet perhaps, coming from behind what appeared to be an unhinged door propped up in the middle of the tiring house.

"Damnation!" The voice, a woman's, came from behind the door screen. With language like that, she must be the one he sought.

"Hail!" he called out. "Is someone here?"

A pale, heart-shaped face topped with a tall hat popped out from behind the door. "Oh! I didn't know I had company."

"I'm sorry to startle you," he said.

"You didn't. I'm simply surprised."

He failed to see the difference and was about to say as much when she stepped out from behind the door and his words were sucked away along with his breath. She couldn't be the seamstress. This lady wouldn't have been out of place at court with her tall, slender frame, striking cheekbones, and imperial set to her shoulders.

"Madam, I am Lord Warhurst." He bowed.

She stepped forward and the swish of her crimson gown was soon drowned out by the drumming of his heartbeat in his ears. Her simple movement had caused the exposed flesh above her too-tight bodice to wobble most...ah, delightfully.

"Perhaps you could step a little closer," he said when she hesitated. "I would like to have a better look at your...face."

She did, with hands firmly on her hips, and stopped directly in front of him. "My face is *above* my neck, my lord."

He glanced up and got an icy blast from a pair of pale blue eyes. He bowed again, partly to hide his embarrassment and partly because it afforded him another view of her bounteous flesh. If God gave her a pair of luscious breasts like that, surely He meant for man to gaze upon them. Otherwise why create such low-cut gowns?

But on second glance, the gown seemed a little too low-cut for this lady. Although exquisitely made from what he could see, and certainly beautifully—and expensively—embroidered in gold thread, it was a poor fit.

"If you are looking for the players then I'm afraid they're not here," she said. Although her glare was still cool, her mouth curved into an intriguing smile.

"You are all alone here, my lady?" He could have bitten off his tongue after the words tumbled out. He sounded like a villain assessing the likelihood of having his wicked way with a defenseless woman.

"Lady?" She blinked at him. Then looked down at her sleeves, the crimson velvet slashed to reveal the gold of the lining beneath. "Oh."

He frowned. She had not seemed to grasp the crude yet unintentional meaning of his question. Thankfully. But…why *was* such a woman alone in the tiring house? What gentleman would allow his wife, sister, or daughter to fend for herself at, of all places, an inn—and a theatre at that? Guilt twisted his stomach at the similarity to his own situation but he cast it off. It was too late for guilt. Besides, his sister's pregnancy was not his fault although it was a weight that had landed on Leo's shoulders like a canker. He needed to remove it before any chance of restoring the honor of the Warhurst title was lost forever. Since the perpetrator of the problem had not been at home that morning, or last night, or the day before, Leo had come here on his brother's suggestion.

"Madam, I am—"

"Mistaken." Her laughter seemed to rise up from deep within her and burst forth like a sudden gust of air.

He tried not to notice how the laugh made the flesh above her bodice jiggle. "Mistaken?"

"Quite, quite mistaken. I am not a gentlewoman. It must be this dress..." She caressed the velvet of her gown as if it were her lover's skin. "It used to belong to Lady Dalrymple. She and I are of a height which will also suit Freddie, but the similarity does not extend to the chest area." She smiled that smile again, the one that wasn't quite a smile. This time it was accompanied by a wicked gleam in those clear eyes. "As you noticed."

Whatever was she talking about? "Freddie?"

"Freddie Putney, the company's boy actor. He plays the lead female roles."

"And that gown once belonged to Lady Dalrymple?"

"As I said." She looked at him as if he were a half-wit.

His limbs tensed. He had a bad feeling about this. "And you are wearing the gown because..."

"Because I'm adjusting it of course." She shrugged and the gown slipped off one shoulder. He stared at the smooth, white skin and wondered if it felt like silk, because it certainly looked silken.

She fixed the gown and he tried to focus on the conversation again. What had she been saying? Adjusting it...adjusting...the gown!

The bad feeling slammed into his gut with the force of a hammer blow. "You're Alice Croft," he said heavily. "The seamstress for Lord Hawkesbury's Players."

She nodded. "And you're Lord Warhurst, brother to Robert Blakewell."

"Half brother," he said without thinking.

"What can I do for you, Lord Warhurst? I assume you're looking for me since you know my name. Did Blake send you?"

She didn't seem in the least surprised or in any way alarmed by his presence or by the prospect of being sought. Women of her station usually lowered their eyes and spoke only when he asked a direct question of them. Unless they were whores or drunk. This woman certainly wasn't a whore—readjusting the gown to cover her bare shoulder was proof of that—and she didn't seem drunk.

Most unlike another seamstress he'd had the misfortune to meet. The slack-faced woman reeking of cheap wine had accosted him in the street years ago demanding Leo pay for the gown his late father had commissioned her to make for his mistress. The seamstress had threatened to tell Lady Warhurst about the other woman if Leo didn't pay the debt. He'd told her she was welcome to speak to his mother since she already knew, as did the better half of London. The seamstress had scampered like a rat back to the gutter out of which she'd crawled.

At least Alice Croft had all her teeth. And other…assets, besides.

"Blake did send me," he said in an attempt to keep his thoughts on the task at hand. "He said I should seek you out and that I'd find you here."

"As indeed you have."

He cleared his throat. "I'll have you know this goes against my better judgment."

Her eyes narrowed. "You haven't told me what 'this' is yet."

"If there was anyone else, I'd ask them first. I'd rather not involve someone else in our family dilemma but Blake assures me you'll be discreet."

"Discreet?" She shook her head. A frown furrowed her pretty brow. "My lord, is this about making a gown for your mistress? Because if it is—"

"No!" He shouldn't have come. Whatever was Blake thinking to send him to such a woman? How did he even know she could be trusted? He was wasting his time. Leo pulled back the curtain leading out to the stage.

"My lord, wait!" The seamstress placed a hand on his arm. There was no pressure, no attempt to halt his progress, yet he stopped anyway. There was something compelling in her touch, something far more forceful than mere strength. "If Blake sent you then it must have something to do with Lord Hawkesbury. And," she cleared her throat, "and your sister."

He half turned to see her and was struck once more by those eyes. Of the palest blue, they were almost colorless, and yet they seemed to see right into him. He recoiled. The bad feeling returned like a vengeful warrior.

"You're right," he heard himself say. "I've come to ask you for help."

"Help?"

He focused on the tiny crease between her brows because he had the disturbing sensation that if he looked into her eyes anymore she might see too much. "Yes. Help with the business between Lord Hawkesbury and my sister, as you said."

"But how can I possibly be of service?"

"I have need of someone who is capable of finding out information. Blake suggested you because you are associated with Lord Hawkesbury's Players, and they have a tendency to hear and see a great many things when in their patron's presence. Well? What say you?"

***

Alice had been told many times in her twenty-six years that her curiosity would be her downfall. As a child she would sneak around the house listening to the adult conversations, or explore the narrow lanes near her home—the ones she was strictly told not to venture down. Not even a whipping from her father and a near escape from a brothel keeper seeking fresh girls could keep her curiosity and thirst for knowledge in check. Although she kept away from the worst of the lanes after that instance.

Childish curiosity was one thing. Spying on Lord Hawkesbury, a peer of the realm, was entirely another.

"Why not ask one of the players?" she said.

Lord Warhurst gave her a rueful smile, one that sparked a gleam in his green eyes. She'd never seen eyes quite like them, bright one moment and fathomless the next but never revealing too much of what the man was thinking. They reminded her of the emeralds she'd once seen in a grand lady's rings.

"The players were not recommended by my brother," Lord Warhurst said. "You were."

It had been only days since she'd last seen his brother the pirate, Robert Blakewell, and Blake's bride-to-be, Minerva Peabody, who'd become Alice's friend. Min had informed her that much had changed, including Blake ceasing his pursuit of Lord Hawkesbury over the relationship the earl had had with Lilly Blakewell.

It seemed Lord Warhurst was taking up the reins dropped by his brother to save their sister's honor.

Yet it didn't quite make sense. Why all this brotherly fuss over a simple affection? Why the forbidding presence of the brooding Baron Warhurst darkening her tiring house? And why did he need the help of a seamstress?

"My half brother and I don't get along," Lord Warhurst said, crossing his arms over a broad chest. "But I trust his judgment. If he thinks you would make a fair and discreet information gatherer, then I believe him. I also think you have the look about you of someone who would go unnoticed, something which will be of benefit in this endeavor."

The old, familiar pang stabbed her in the ribs. She'd once thought it was jealousy of prettier girls, the sort who turned heads just by walking down the street. But she'd learned after Charles broke her heart that that wasn't the case. Jealousy it might be, but it was the jealousy of a girl who simply wanted to be someone else, someone who *would* be noticed, not for her beauty but for…what?

If she knew the answer she could perhaps make steps toward changing herself, but all she really knew for certain was that she didn't want to be seamstress for Lord Hawkesbury's Players day after day until her death.

She might have been aware of the pang and all it implied, but it still hurt to have her plainness in looks and occupation pointed out so baldly.

"That is hardly a convincing argument," she said, perhaps a little too caustically.

He arched one eyebrow in question.

"Telling me I'm too ordinary to be noticed."

"I didn't say ordinary, nor is that what I meant." He rolled his eyes heavenward. "I simply was stating the fact that people do not always see those whose presence they take for granted." His words were measured, careful.

"Like servants," she said flatly.

"Like seamstresses." He shrugged, as if what he'd said was nothing of importance.

That *she* was nothing of importance.

It was a wonder he had even deigned to speak to someone like her at all, let alone ask for help. Her throat burned as she swallowed back a tide of emotions, ones she thought she'd conquered.

"You must hate it," she said with a lightness she certainly didn't feel.

"What?"

"Asking me for help. A seamstress."

He opened his mouth but shut it again. His stare faltered and he looked away. It was all the answer she needed.

"Which means the task you require me to perform must be important," she went on. A little voice within her warned her not to test this man, not to push him into a corner because he would fight. He was a baron and an imposing figure, standing well above her—and she was no sprite. Yet she couldn't help herself. She wanted to find out as much as she could before she said yes. About the task, and the gentleman.

That she would say yes was a certainty. She needed an intrigue to break up the endless tedium of her days.

"Why do you want Lord Hawkesbury to marry your sister? Does she really love him so much that she would have her brother force him into marriage against his wishes? Or is there another reason? One more…scandalous?"

He lifted his gaze to hers without lifting his head and glared at her beneath long black lashes. The effect was devilish.

So much for backing him into a corner. She hadn't even budged him in the slightest. What she'd done was potentially far worse—awakened a beast with more anger boiling inside him than she could ever know.

"I think," he finally said through a clenched jaw, "that my brother was mistaken. You are of no use to me. Good day." He spun round and shoved the curtain all the way to the side.

"Wait! I can help you."

But he was already halfway across the stage and he didn't look to be stopping. Not the reaction she'd expected. Hot outrage at her impertinence would have been better than this cool dismissal. But at least she now knew her assumption was correct—Lilly Blakewell was carrying Lord Hawkesbury's unborn child.

"I know where Lord Hawkesbury will be tonight," she called after him.

She might as well have flung her words at a wall. He either didn't hear them or didn't care. He simply jumped off the stage and strode toward the arch leading out to Gracechurch Street.

Well. Good riddance. The man was rude. It was a miracle he'd even lowered himself to speak to her.

Nevertheless she watched him go with a sinking heart. He and his family's troubles had been a bump on her otherwise flat week. Now even that distraction was gone.

She sighed and returned to the tiring house, letting the curtain fall back into place. There was no point dwelling on what might have happened if she hadn't opened her mouth. There was still much to be done to prepare for the troupe's transfer to the Rose. Henslowe, the Rose Theatre's owner, had given them permission to perform there on the days Lord Strange's Men weren't using it. The bigger crowds at the dedicated theatre would ensure more money for Lord Hawkesbury's Players and for Alice's father, their tiring house manager. But as his assistant and daughter, she would see none of it. Moving to the Rose would simply be more of the same. Mending costumes, cleaning the tiring house, listening to the actors' complaints and gossip.

She looked down at the clothing bought from Lady Dalrymple. The ensemble of bodice, skirt, and overgown was several years out of fashion, but it was the most exquisite thing Alice had ever worn. The softness of the velvet, the vibrancy of the colors, and the workmanship that had gone into the embroidery were nothing like she'd seen before. She simply had to try it on. Just for a few minutes she wanted to pretend she was someone else, someone important. A duchess or an heiress or even a wealthy merchant in her own right. Anything would be better than this...nothingness. The clothes had beckoned to her like a lover and she couldn't resist. Besides, no one had seen.

No one except Lord Warhurst, and she was not likely to see him again. She doubted he cared enough to tell her father or Roger Style, the company's manager. With another sigh, she removed the hat. She was about to step behind the door used as a screen for privacy when she heard the swish of the curtain opening behind her.

She knew without turning around that Lord Warhurst had returned. She couldn't say how she knew it, she just did. Perhaps it was his presence, so powerful that it surged ahead of him like a flood.

"Why do you want to help me?" he said.

She turned and shrugged. The ill-fitting sleeve slipped off her shoulder. She adjusted it but not before she saw Warhurst's lips purse. In disapproval? Irritation? Or suppressed desire?

"I liked your sister," she said. "And your brother."

His eyebrow forked again. "That may be the case but I doubt it is your sole reason. There must be more for you to risk your livelihood. I'm sure you are aware that Lord Hawkesbury could have you removed from his company if he discovers your involvement in this scheme."

She nodded. "That's why I want something from you in return."

"Money?"

"Not quite." She chewed the inside of her lip, thinking fast. Should she ask him? Would he agree? If she didn't ask, she would never know his answer. And such an opportunity would never arise again, of that she was certain. She *had* to ask.

She lifted her chin and stepped toward him, the better to gauge his reaction. But his only reaction was a lowering of his gaze again to her breasts bursting over the top of the bodice. She cleared her throat but refused to cover herself. Let him look. She wasn't ashamed.

"I cannot take you on as my mistress." He looked up, face flushed, eyes hooded.

"Pardon?"

His flush deepened. "I, er, isn't that what you were asking of me?"

"No! Good lord, what sort of woman do you think I am?"

"I…I'm not entirely sure. To be honest, I've never encountered a woman such as yourself before."

"That is quite obvious."

He bowed. "My humble apologies, Mistress Croft." He blinked rapidly and looked away, pretending to study a Roman shield leaning against the wall.

An awkward silence ensued until she could stand it no longer. "What I do want from you is your patronage, of sorts."

That got his attention. "So you do want money?" He said it without a hint of disapproval, as if he expected it, almost welcomed it.

But what she wanted wasn't quite as simple as an exchange of coins. "I want you to establish me as a seamstress with a shop of my own in a respectable part of the city."

"You want *what*?"

"In essence, you will be my patron, but only until such time that my earnings cover the rent. I have some money set aside to purchase the tools I need. You could also use your influence with certain merchants so that I can buy cloth and other materials at a good price. It would be to your benefit," she said quickly when his mouth dropped open. "The more money that remains in my coffers, the faster I will be able to support myself and you can wash your hands of me. And there is one other thing."

"I don't doubt it," he muttered.

"If you could send some elegant ladies of your acquaintance to my shop, I would be most grateful. You would benefit—"

"Yes, yes, so I see." He shook his head and she thought she heard a low chuckle, but he didn't smile so she couldn't be sure. "First of all, Mistress Croft, you overestimate my influence in elegant circles. As you can see," he stretched out his arms, "I am no gallant."

"True, but your clothes are well made and suited to your…demeanor."

He frowned. "Meaning?"

"They are serious." She thought it wise not to mention she'd seen Puritans wear more cheerful clothing. There wasn't a hint of embellishment in his doublet, even the buttons were covered in the same black material. No slashing, no embroidery, no pinking, and yet the doublet was silk and from what she could see, the tailoring superb. It fit him to perfection, without needing any padding across shoulders or chest. What lay beneath the clothing must also be perfection. The thought made her heart skip.

"I have seen your mother and sister," she forged on, "and they are both women with exceptional fashion sense. If I provide them with some gowns, free of charge of course, to prove my skill then perhaps they could send their friends to me. You could give them the gowns as a gift."

He nodded thoughtfully. "A reasonable plan. And my brother's new bride would require something to wear for her wedding feast. Could you do it?"

"How soon?"

"In a month or two I would imagine."

If she started as soon as possible she should be able to make Min an outfit to rival the queen's. "I should like to make her something special anyway. We have become friends of sorts."

He nodded. "But I'm afraid you mistake my position in this city. I am rarely here and I do not know any merchants. As to renting a shop…" He drew in a breath. "I shall see what I can do."

"I'm sure your brother knows many merchants from his privateering jaunts. Perhaps you could ask him."

He acknowledged this with a curt nod. "You have a solid understanding of business, I see."

"Then we have an agreement?"

"We do, on one condition. That you do not mention this to anyone. We shall rent the shop in your name and in no way will any transactions between us be known. I cannot afford for our connection to be discovered."

"Because you don't wish Lord Hawkesbury to know?"

He hesitated before saying, "Quite."

She chewed her lip again. He wasn't telling her the entire truth. Not that it mattered. The anonymity of her new patron suited her needs too. Her father knew she had some money set aside; she would simply inflate the amount when he asked how she could afford to set out on her own.

"Only my half brother will know," he said, "but if pressed, he'll say he does not."

She was about to ask why when she realized she already

knew the answer. "He wishes to keep Min happy, and to do that he needs to ensure her plays are performed. Upsetting the patron of the company performing them would be a poor move. At least until she is able to sell them to another company."

The green eyes briefly flared and she thought she saw a flicker of surprise in them. Surprise that she could think for herself?

The man grew more pompous by the minute.

"Furthermore," he went on as if she had not spoken, "I think it best that you do not give up your position here with Lord Hawkesbury's Players until our task is complete."

"Agreed. Shall we shake on it?" She held out her hand.

He didn't take it, didn't even acknowledge it with so much as a glance. "You do not wish to know how I want you to gather the relevant information before agreeing?"

"My lord, unless you are asking me to whore for you, I will do whatever is required."

"What makes you think I am not asking you to whore for me?"

She shrugged and lowered her hand. "You seem far too prudish to ask that of any woman. Even a seamstress."

He tilted his head back as if struck. Then, unexpectedly, he smiled. Just a slight lifting of the corners of his mouth at first, then a few twitches until finally a wide grin broke out, as if it had escaped despite his attempts to smother it.

"I can assure you, Mistress Croft," he said, capturing the grin once more and hiding it away, "that I am no prude." He picked up a fine lawn partlet from the top of a pile of clothes stacked on a closed chest. "Nor am I immune to your…charms." His gaze dipped once more to her breasts and this time it was her turn to blush as heat prickled her throat, her face. He closed the space between them until he was so near she could smell him, a pleasing mix of fresh air and man. "So I would appreciate it if you kept those charms covered when next we meet." He tucked the edge of the partlet down the front of her bodice. His long finger grazed her skin, just above the nipple.

She let out a breath and dared not draw in another as it would cause her chest to rise, bringing his finger closer. Closer.

Even though that was exactly what she suddenly, desperately wanted. For this man to touch her. Everywhere. The need throbbed within her like an ache.

But some very deep part of her kept her from drawing the breath that could start something. Or stop it.

Then his finger was gone, leaving the partlet covering the rapid rise and fall of her chest as she sucked in breath upon breath. Their gazes locked and heat flooded her, sliding through her like warm sunshine.

She thought she understood this man from the moment he'd walked in with his conservative clothing and crisp aloofness. Now she knew she did not.

"You said you knew where Lord Hawkesbury would be tonight," he said, voice low and rough.

"I…" She nodded and stepped away, out of reach of his powerful presence. "He's commissioned a performance from the troupe to entertain his betrothed and her family at Hawkesbury Hall."

His brows rose. "The Enderbys?"

She nodded. "I don't usually attend private performances, but I can devise a reason for my presence tonight. I might be able to learn something, if you tell me what it is I need to look for."

He blinked slowly. Then he straightened and put his hands behind his back. "Our task is to find out why Lord Hawkesbury is marrying Patience Enderby when neither he nor the girl wants the marriage."

"He doesn't love her?"

"He says not."

"Nobles marry for reasons other than love all the time."

He gave her a tight smile. "I am well aware of that."

Alice knew Lord Warhurst wasn't married, but was he betrothed to some influential heiress he didn't love? What about his own heart's desire? Did he even have one? A desire, not a heart—although she couldn't be sure he possessed either.

"From what my half brother tells me," Lord Warhurst said, "Hawkesbury is being forced into the union by the girl's father, Lord Enderby." He put a sneer into the name that was so slight she almost missed it. "From the little I know of Hawkesbury, it would take a shifting of the earth for him to agree to something he didn't want to do. He lacks neither money nor power so it must be something else."

"A secret. A very grave one."

"Precisely." He gave a nod, as if impressed that she had grasped the situation. "It is my understanding that the secret Lord Enderby possesses could harm Hawkesbury's loved ones if discovered."

"Who are his loved ones?"

"He has a sister and mother still living."

Alice huffed out a breath. "You have a difficult task."

"Learning the secret will not be easy, I grant you. But with your assistance, I believe we will prevail."

She shook her head. He hadn't quite understood her. "Discovering the secret is only one hurdle."

When she paused he said, "Go on."

"The more difficult problem will be ensuring the secret is no longer a threat to Lord Hawkesbury. You must somehow silence Enderby without letting the secret out." From the grim set of Lord Warhurst's mouth, she knew he was aware of that fact, as he was no doubt aware that Hawkesbury would have already tried purchasing Lord Enderby's silence with something other than a betrothal to his daughter.

"We'll cross that bridge when we discover what Enderby knows," he said.

Alice wasn't so sure ignoring it before they even began was a good idea, but she didn't say so. She was being paid to help discover the secret, not concern herself with events beyond that.

Lord Warhurst raised his hand to silence her. The *clip-clop* of hooves on the cobblestones echoed around the innyard. The rider called for an ostler and their brief exchange was followed by the sound of the horse being led away. The door to the taproom opened and a lively tune strummed on a lute drifted out to the tiring house along with the trickle of laughter and voices.

"I must go," Lord Warhurst said. "It would be best if we weren't seen together. There's a small inn called the Golden Lion near St. Mary le Bow which is out of the way and not likely to be frequented by either Hawkesbury, Enderby, or your players. Do you know it?"

"No, but I'll find it."

"Good. Dine with me at midday there tomorrow." It was an order and Warhurst seemed used to giving them, and having them obeyed.

She nodded because it wasn't in her interests to refuse him. "Until midday then, my lord."

He turned but paused at the curtain. "Thank you, Mistress Croft," he said without fully facing her. His profile was strong with the hard lines of his jaw and straight nose. Alice felt the odd little flutter in the pit of her stomach again and tried very hard not to stare. "I appreciate your assistance," he said. "I will ensure that your safety will not be jeopardized by anything I request of you."

"Your words are noble, Lord Warhurst, but I assure you I am capable of taking care of myself." She wasn't sure why she said it. Perhaps it was a need to assert herself with a man who thought her so far beneath him he was almost too embarrassed to speak to her.

He turned to her fully and his direct, unblinking gaze held hers. She swallowed. "Nevertheless you are now working for me and I take my responsibility to those in my employ very seriously."

"I am not one of your servants," she tossed back.

His nostrils flared but he said nothing. He opened the curtain and walked away.

She let out a long breath and slowly began to remove the costume, beginning with the lawn partlet he'd so deliberately and deliciously tucked into her bodice.

A TEMPTING LIFE is now available.

A MESSAGE FROM THE AUTHOR

I hope you enjoyed reading A SECRET LIFE as much as I enjoyed writing it. As an independent author, getting the word out about my book is vital to its success, so if you liked this book please consider telling your friends and writing a review at the store where you purchased it. If you would like to be contacted when I release a new book, subscribe to my newsletter at http://cjarcher.com/contact-cj/newsletter/. You will only be contacted when I have a new book out.

ALSO BY C.J. ARCHER

SERIES WITH 2 OR MORE BOOKS

After The Rift

Glass and Steele

The Ministry of Curiosities Series

The Emily Chambers Spirit Medium Trilogy

The 1st Freak House Trilogy

The 2nd Freak House Trilogy

The 3rd Freak House Trilogy

The Assassins Guild Series

Lord Hawkesbury's Players Series

Witch Born

SINGLE TITLES NOT IN A SERIES

Courting His Countess

Surrender

Redemption

The Mercenary's Price

ABOUT THE AUTHOR

C.J. Archer has loved history and books for as long as she can remember and feels fortunate that she found a way to combine the two. She spent her early childhood in the dramatic beauty of outback Queensland, Australia, but now lives in suburban Melbourne with her husband, two children and a mischievous black & white cat named Coco.

Subscribe to C.J.'s newsletter through her website to be notified when she releases a new book, as well as get access to exclusive content and subscriber-only giveaways. Her website also contains up to date details on all her books: http://cjarcher.com She loves to hear from readers. You can contact her through email cj@cjarcher.com or follow her on social media to get the latest updates on her books:

facebook.com/CJArcherAuthorPage
twitter.com/cj_archer
instagram.com/authorcjarcher
pinterest.com/cjarcher
bookbub.com/authors/c-j-archer

Made in United States
Troutdale, OR
01/22/2025